Praise for Peter Robinson

'The master of the police procedural'
Mail on Sunday

'Robinson is prolific, but with each book
he manages to ring the changes'
Guardian

'Top-notch police procedure'
Jeffery Deaver

'Near, perhaps even at the top of, the
British crime writers' league'
Times

'The Alan Banks mystery-suspense novels are the best
series on the market. Try one and tell me I'm wrong'
Stephen King

PETER ROBINSON

Many Rivers to Cross

HODDER

First published in Great Britain in 2019 by Hodder & Stoughton
An Hachette UK company

This paperback edition published in 2020

1

A CIP catalogue record for this title is available from the British Library

B format ISBN 978 1 444 78700 9
A format ISBN 978 1 444 78701 6

Typeset in Plantin Light by Hewer Text UK Ltd, Edinburgh
Printed and bound in Great Britain by Clays Ltd, Elcograf S.p.A.

Hodder & Stoughton policy is to use papers that are natural, renewable
and recyclable products and made from wood grown in sustainable
forests. The logging and manufacturing processes are expected to
conform to the environmental regulations of the country of origin.

Hodder & Stoughton Ltd
Carmelite House
50 Victoria Embankment
London EC4Y 0DZ

www.hodder.co.uk

To Sheila

I

Two beautiful women sat talking and sipping chilled white wine in a garden high on a hillside overlooking the Adriatic. Behind them stretched the jagged monochrome mountains of the Dinarides, the peaks so pale as to appear snow-capped. Below, the sea stretched out before them, greenish water in the shallows close to shore, darkening to deep blue further out. The water was dotted with yachts and small islands, and the southern tip of the Istrian Peninsula was visible to the north. At the bottom of the hill lay the village, with its narrow higgledy-piggledy streets and red pantile roofs. A small beach hugged the curve of the bay where the waves broke in white foam against the yellow sand. Instead of a town square, there was a marina surrounded by cafes, where the locals and people who came shopping from the outlying islands moored their small boats.

The youngest of the two women, barely turned thirty-one, went by the name of Zelda, though on her passport she was called Nelia Melnic. Her friend, aged sixty-three, was Jasna Slavić on all her documents, but everyone called her Mati, for mother.

Zelda's lustrous dark hair cascaded over her shoulders and a jagged fringe fell over her forehead, framing her oval face. She had high cheekbones, almond-shaped eyes with a slight Eurasian tilt, black as Whitby jet, full lips and a small nose, slightly crooked where it had clearly been broken. Below her graceful neck was a lissom body, slender arms with a violinist's hands, and the shapely long legs of a catwalk model.

The older woman, Mati, had a different kind of beauty, perhaps better described as elegance, with her short silver hair, pale blue eyes, an expressive, lined face and a strong, wiry body, with the hands of someone who had done far too much manual labour. She had a powerful presence and radiated authority, compassion and intelligence.

Though it was only early May, the weather was already almost too hot for comfort. Fortunately, a light ocean breeze helped to mitigate the heat and humidity. Zelda had a sketch book on the table before her, and as they talked she drew Mati.

Mati poured more wine. 'So, what did you tell your policeman friend about your boss meeting this man he is looking for?' she asked.

Zelda stared out at the water, which rippled like a sheet of the purest blue silk. When she spoke, her voice was unexpectedly deep. 'Nothing,' she answered.

'Why not?'

'I had second thoughts as soon as I walked into the pub and saw him with his friends and colleagues. They were celebrating catching a murderer. I was going to tell him I'd seen this man he's looking for, Keane, meeting with Mr Hawkins, my boss, but I changed my mind.'

'Why?'

'I realised that if I said anything about what I had found out, they would take over. The police.'

'But aren't you police now?'

'No. I'm a civilian. They make that quite clear. I have no police powers. Not that I want any.'

'Surely they're the best people to do the job? Unless you want your own revenge?'

Zelda put down her pencil, offered her pack of Marlboro Gold to Mati, and both women lit cigarettes. Zelda took a drag and watched the swifts swoop and circle over the roof-tops below. The tiles reminded her of Whitby, one of her favourite places in England, home of the famous jet that her partner Raymond had compared her eyes to. 'Yes. Partly,' she admitted. 'I do. But it's not just that. Don't get me wrong, Mati. I like Alan Banks. I believe that he is a good man and an honest cop. But he's still a policeman. It's still the system, isn't it? An institution with its own rules, procedures and codes of conduct. The force.' She paused. 'And I can't say the police have ever done me any great favours over the years.'

Mati tapped some ash off her cigarette and made a face. 'True enough. Me, neither.'

'There was one time, I remember, in Priština, when I managed to break free from my captors for a few moments. I was so naive. I ran up to a uniformed policeman and tried to explain that I'd been abducted and forced into prostitution.'

'What did he do?'

'Do? Nothing. He just scowled at me as if I was something he'd got on the bottom of his shoe and told me to fuck off. I believe "Fuck off, you filthy whore" were his actual words, as far as I could understand. I must confess, my Serbian language skills weren't too good then. The pimps took me back, and I got a beating that put me out of action for two days, which earned me another beating. So, no, I'm not too fond of the police. There's so much corruption. If I passed the information to Alan – that I had seen the man he is looking for meeting secretly with my boss – he would have no choice but to go to *his* bosses with the information. More people would become involved. Government agencies, police forces. That's how they operate. It's hard to believe my boss isn't corrupt himself – and if I can't trust him, how can I trust anyone else in the agency?' She shook her head as she answered her own question. 'I don't think I can. The criminals have infiltrated everywhere. There would be every chance that someone with a strong interest in keeping things the way they are would gain control, or achieve a significant and powerful place in the investigation. Either one of the criminals or an incompetent fool.'

'Do you think they might want you out of the way?'

Zelda scraped her cigarette against the ashtray. 'I'm sure plenty of people would be happy to cut me into small pieces and feed me to the fish. The men I escaped from, the men who first took me and broke me in, the kind of clients I had in Paris towards the end. Many of them have come to prominence in politics or business, even the church, and they don't like loose ends.' She shrugged. 'But that was Paris. Men like that are expected to go with high-class call girls. It's de rigueur, sort of an initiation en route to becoming one of the lads, as the English say. I don't really suppose they'd wish me harm.'

'Still . . .' Mati persisted. 'Someone now in a high position, with something he may regret in his past, some indiscretion, maybe . . . or someone suddenly vulnerable?'

'It's possible. But if an American president can get away with all the things he says and does where women are concerned, I doubt if any of my little peccadillos will give anyone much to fear. No, it's the ones I betrayed who hate me the most. My captors. They lost money because of me.' She paused. 'Anyway, I want to investigate this Phil Keane person myself. I want to find him. After all, he was with Petar Tadić in the photograph I saw, and we all know what pigs Tadić and his brother are. Keane also tried to kill Alan a few years ago.'

Petar Tadić was the brother of Goran, and the two of them had abducted Zelda in the street when she left the orphanage at seventeen, shoved her in a car, punched her in the face and spilled all her worldly possessions across a street in Chişinău.

And that was only the start of a very long journey. The Tadić brothers had made their way up in the organisation since then, she had heard. No longer mere transporters, they had moved into the realm of overseas exploitation and were now close to the top, giving orders rather than taking them, extending their operations from sex trafficking and drugs to money laundering.

'What will you do when you find this Keane person?' Mati asked.

'Try to get him to lead me to the people he works for, then pass on the information to Alan.'

'You would trust the police then?'

'To deal with Keane? Yes. Alan wants him. It's personal. I'm assuming he has evidence he has no desire to hide.'

'And the people Keane works for?'

'A different proposition altogether. I have my own plans for them.'

'Isn't this a dangerous game you're playing?'

'It's not a game,' said Zelda.

'But you could get hurt.'

Zelda gave a harsh laugh. 'It wouldn't be the first time.'

'Killed, even.'

'Well, that would be something new.'

'When will it be over, this mission of yours?'

'I don't know.' She smiled. 'I've got a little list.'

'You and Ko-Ko.'

They laughed, and Mati let it go. That was one of the things Zelda loved about her; like Raymond, she wasn't judgemental. But unlike Raymond, Mati knew exactly where Zelda was coming from. And she knew her Gilbert and Sullivan.

'For this revenge, you would risk everything? The life you have made for yourself with Raymond in Yorkshire? Your freedom?'

'I don't know, Mati. All I know is that I have to try. It may be the only way to stop the nightmares, the flashbacks, the despair, the numbness I feel sometimes.'

'I wouldn't count on it. How far have you got with your search for this man Keane?'

Zelda sighed. 'Nowhere.'

'How long has it been?'

'Four months. The department has only called me in once a month so far this year, for two or three days each time. I've watched Hawkins closely, even followed him after work when I knew I could get away with it.'

'And?'

'Nothing. He either met his wife for drinks, or he went straight to the tube. I didn't follow him there. I recognised his wife from the photo of them he keeps on his bookshelf. I also met her once, very briefly, at his house.' Zelda was a super-recogniser – she never forgot a face – which was one reason why she worked as a consultant helping to build a database for facial recognition of sex traffickers. The other reason was that she had seen a lot of them to remember.

Mati had not been trafficked, Zelda knew, but she carried the history of her country in the lines of her face, lines Zelda was trying to render on paper: the Tito years, the Balkan wars of the 90s, ethnic cleansing, mass murders and the war crimes trials that followed. Mati had been forced to watch as her daughter was gang-raped by soldiers after she had been raped by them herself. She had seen both her husband and her daughter shot and piled into a mass grave along with most of the population of the village where she lived. The only reason her sons had survived was because they had gone to visit her sister in Italy two days earlier. Mati said she had no idea why she had been allowed to survive. Perhaps the soldiers believed it would be more painful for her to live with what she had seen and what had been done to her. And perhaps they were right. Zelda thought there were times Mati wished she hadn't survived.

'So, what are your plans for the future?' Mati asked.

'I don't really know,' said Zelda. 'Things just haven't been the same in the UK since all that Brexit business started.'

'America?'

'Oh, no. Definitely not. Not while that dreadful man is in power. He reminds me of too many of my worst abusers.'

'Where, then?'

'I'll probably go to live in France, if the worst comes to the worst. I have a French passport, after all.'

'Ah, yes. Your mysterious Parisian benefactor.'

Zelda smiled. 'If only you knew.'

'But you would be able to stay if you wanted, wouldn't you? In England? Isn't there a form you can fill in, an application? Couldn't you even apply for citizenship?'

'I suppose so. But I'm not sure I want to stay in a country that doesn't want people like me.'

'Surely not all of them are like that?'

'No. Of course not. Only fifty-two per cent. But apparently that's all it takes. Still, I don't think they can have *all* the foreigners kicked out of the country, no matter what the Leave voters believe. But Brexit has quite destroyed any faith I might have had in England and the English. I remember all those books I used to devour in the orphanage – the Brontës, Jane Austen, Beatrix Potter, John le Carré, Peter O'Donnell, Agatha Christie – and how it was always my dream to live there. But now it's broken. England is broken. And I don't know if they'll ever be able to fix it. At least not in my lifetime. France would hardly be heaven on earth. After all, there's Macron, but . . .'

'And Raymond?'

Zelda smiled. 'Raymond's an artist. He loves the light in France. He'll go with me. And the French love artists.'

'Paris?'

'No. I couldn't. Not after . . . But perhaps we could discover some beautiful, hidden little corner of the countryside that hasn't already been spoiled by foreigners like us. I'm sure I would be able to sneak back in and disappear.'

'Good luck. And in the meantime?'

'We'll stay in Yorkshire. To be honest, we're pretty isolated from the rest of the country up there. We have no close neighbours, and we're a couple of miles from the nearest village. Not that there are any foreigners there. It *is* North Yorkshire, after all. And I'll just carry on with my work, I suppose. Keep an eye on Hawkins. Look for any signs of this Phil Keane in photographs or in the street. Find out what he was doing in London with Petar Tadić.'

'And the policeman?'

'Alan Banks? We are friends. Raymond and I see him and Annie socially, too. They don't press me for information every time we meet.'

'He probably thinks you'll tell him if you find out anything.'

'Perhaps. Though sometimes . . .'

'What?'

'I don't know. Sometimes I think he knows that I'm keeping something back. Just the way he looks at me.'

Mati leaned forward. 'Be careful, Nelia. You should not need me to tell you that, but I do.' It was rare that she called Zelda by her given name.

'What do you think I should do, Mati?'

Mati picked up the bottle and poured them more wine. It was the local grape variety, Malvazija, and very good indeed. Zelda passed the cigarettes again. 'I think you should have another glass of wine, then you should help me settle in the new girl.'

Mati ran a shelter for trafficked girls fortunate enough to have escaped the sex trade into which they had been forced. It was housed on the slope behind them in a rambling old mansion on an acre or two of land. Mati's work was her life these days, and the shelter, a place of healing and safety, was always full. There were even some Yazidi women, and their stories never failed to break Zelda's heart: how their husbands were thrown into pits and shot; how they were forced into marriages with abusive ISIS warriors. Mati's two strapping sons, known affectionately as Ić and Ićić – 'Son' and 'Son Son' – both built like heavyweight fighters and armed to the teeth, took care of security. Once or twice various trafficking gangs had launched attacks to try to take their girls back, but Ić and Ićić had fought them off. In the end, the gangs had stopped bothering. The risk wasn't worth their while; there were plenty more girls for the taking.

Zelda smiled. 'And after that?'

'After that, we'll leave the boys in charge and go down to the village to sample the catch of the day at Martina's. Then perhaps we'll go dancing.'

Zelda picked up her pencil again and added a few more deft strokes before passing the sketch to Mati.

'Do I really look like that?' she said.

'To me you do.'

'I seem very severe . . . very haunted.'

Zelda said nothing.

'And, seriously,' Mati went on, 'I think what you should do is follow your heart, but don't let it rule your head when it senses danger. You have survived much, perhaps so much that you think you can handle anything that comes along, but, believe me, my dear Nelia, you cannot. There's always something else. Something worse.'

Zelda nodded. 'Thank you, Mati. Let's go see to that new girl.'

2

Ghostly white figures moved beyond the runnels of rain that blurred Detective Superintendent Alan Banks's windscreen. As he pulled to a halt on Malden Road, at the western edge of the East Side Estate, one shape detached itself from the rest and stood by his car door.

'Just what we need,' said DI Annie Cabbot, holding a transparent plastic umbrella over her head while trying to manoeuvre it so that Banks could stay dry, too, as he got out of the car. The rain splattered down on the plastic and dripped down his neck. Realising that he would have to lean so close to Annie that their cheeks would be touching, or put his arm around her shoulder and pull her towards him in order to stay dry, he edged away. 'It's OK, Annie,' he said. 'I've been soaked before. What have we got?'

Lightning flashed across the sky, and soon afterwards thunder rolled and cracked to the north. Annie handed Banks a disposable white boiler suit and led him through the taped-off outer cordon into the alleyway that ran between the backyards of Malden Terrace and Malden Close. Banks slipped into the suit and zipped it up. He could feel the rain, warm on his head. At least it wasn't one of those cold winter showers that chilled you to the bone. A spring storm. Much nicer. Heralding a change for the better in the weather. Good for the garden.

'The CSIs have managed to put a makeshift tent up,' Annie said as they approached the square canvas structure within the inner cordon. The tent was artificially lit from inside, despite the fact that it was only late morning. She held open a flap and they went inside. Rain hammered down on the flimsy roof, leaking through and dripping to the ground in spots.

At the centre of it all stood a large wheelie bin of the kind the council supplied for rubbish pickup.

'We've had a look already,' Annie went on, 'and Peter Darby's done with the photos. I thought you'd like to see what we've got in situ.'

Banks put on his thin latex gloves, slowly opened the bin and recoiled from what he saw there: a boy's body with his knees tucked under his chin, curled up, almost like a fire victim. But it wasn't a pugilistic position, and there had been no fire; the boy had been deliberately crammed into the bin.

'The dustbin men found him when they came to empty the bins,' Annie said. 'In with the rubbish. The body's stuck, so the bin wouldn't empty, and one of the men went to see what was wrong. He's still in shock.'

Banks bent forward and peered. The boy was dressed in jeans and a black T-shirt. There were no immediate signs of violence or ill-treatment, but he couldn't actually see very much because of the contorted position the body was in. 'Christ,' he said. 'He can't be more than twelve or thirteen. Just a skinny kid. Any idea who he is?'

Annie shook her head. 'We'll get the house-to-house going as soon as we can get a few more officers here.'

'Which house does the bin belong to?'

'Number six Malden Terrace. Elderly lady, lives on her own. A Mrs Grunwell. She's pretty upset.'

'Hardly surprising,' said Banks. 'Could she tell you anything?'

'Only that she put her bag of rubbish out last night at ten o'clock, as usual, in the bin outside her back gate for the men to pick up this morning, and there was no body there then. As you can see, it was put on top of the rubbish. The dustbin men were running a bit late because of the weather, or it might have been found much earlier.'

'They'll be running even later now. Where are they?'

'In the CSI van. Someone managed to conjure up a pot of tea.'

'What about CCTV? Surely there's some around here?'

Annie shook her head. 'I asked the local PC about that – he was first on the scene – and he told me they've been rendered inoperable.'

Banks smiled. '"Rendered inoperable." That's fine textbook police talk. He meant they've been vandalised?'

'Impression I got.'

'We'd better arrange for a mobile incident unit.' Banks lifted the flap of the tent and glanced around at the estate as the lightning flashed again. 'Sometimes I think it wouldn't be a bad idea to have one permanently stationed here.'

'Now, now,' said Annie. 'And you a loyal *Guardian* reader. Champion of the underprivileged.'

'You don't have to study the crime statistics as closely as I do.'

'Ah, the responsibilities of high office. You could always go back to your nice warm office and scan a few columns of figures while the rest of us do the grunt work in the rain.'

'There's a novel idea,' said Banks, withdrawing back into the tent. 'Remind me to learn how to delegate.'

Shadows moved beyond the canvas walls. Another car door slammed and a middle-aged man in a mac dashed in. Dr Burns nodded his greeting to Banks and Annie and complained about the miserable weather. Banks gestured to the CSIs and turned away as they tipped the bin on its side and began to ease the body out. Finally, the dead boy lay on a plastic sheet on the ground, stiffened into the foetal position by rigor mortis. One of the CSIs pointed to the bin. 'Can we take this for forensic examination?'

Banks glanced into the bin and nodded. 'There might be some trace evidence inside. It's possible he got into the bin by himself, maybe to escape someone, but I very much doubt it. Someone must have brought his body here and dumped him. Most likely by car. And there's very little blood in the bin as far as I can see, which may also indicate he was killed elsewhere.'

Banks bent down and felt in the boy's pockets. He pulled out a small package filled with white powder. He slipped it into an evidence bag and sealed it, then stood up, hearing his knees crack as he did so.

Dr Burns knelt next, and Banks watched him make notations on his clipboard and check the time as his eyes roamed over the body.

When the doctor stood up, he looked grim. 'Four stab wounds as far as I can count,' he said. 'Of course, there may be others I can't see, so when Dr Glendenning gets him on the table he'll be able to tell you more. It's difficult for me to conduct a proper examination given the position and state of the body.'

'It won't be Dr Glendenning,' said Banks. 'The doc's retired. Well, semi-retired. He still likes to stand over Karen whenever he can and make sarcastic comments about her technique.'

'Dr Karen Galway?'

'That's right.' Dr Karen Galway, who had worked for some years as Dr Glendenning's chief assistant, was now an official Home Office pathologist, qualified to carry out post-mortem examinations. She lacked the old doctor's biting humour and irreverent approach, but nobody could fault her work thus far.

Dr Burns nodded. 'Excellent choice. I must say, I'd been thinking Dr Glendenning was getting a bit long in the tooth.'

'Long in the tooth and deep in experience,' said Banks. 'Anyway, what can you tell us so far?'

'Not much,' Dr Burns admitted. 'Those stab wounds are most likely the cause of death. One of them in particular might have nicked or pierced the right ventricle. There's a fair bit of blood, but most of the bleeding would probably have been internal. I doubt it would have taken the poor lad very long to die, if that's any consolation.'

'Not for him,' said Banks. 'How long ago?'

'I can't tell you precisely, but I'd estimate more than twelve hours. You can see full rigor's set in. It was pretty mild last night, and he's young. And he was stuffed in a container. Again, Dr Galway will be able to give you a better idea when she gets him on the table. I'll try to narrow it down a bit with temperature calculations in a minute, but they're not always as accurate as I would wish, either. There are better tests these days, but they need to be done in the lab with the proper equipment.'

Banks nodded. 'The timing makes sense. Twelve hours or so. Mrs Grunwell says she put her rubbish out at ten o'clock last night, and the bin sat there out back in the same row as everyone else's until the dustbin men came a short while ago. It's twenty past eleven now.'

'So, the body would have to have been dumped there after ten?' Dr Burns asked.

'That's right.'

Dr Burns nodded and took out his thermometer. 'There is one other thing . . .'

'That the victim is dark-skinned?'

'Yes. Middle Eastern, I'd say. We don't usually get many people from that part of the world around these parts.'

'True enough,' Banks said. 'I was just thinking about that, myself. It'll make identifying him either easy or bloody impossible. Either way, we'd better brace ourselves. I have a feeling this is going to be a big case.'

Zelda knew that something was wrong the minute she entered the lobby of the unassuming building on Cambridge Circus late that Monday morning. There was usually just one man at the reception desk, and if it was Sam, she would breeze by with little more than a smile and a hello. Today, however, Sam was absent, and the lobby was crowded with strangers, mostly plainclothes police, by the look of them. She was asked for identification and the purpose of her visit twice before she was even allowed to get into the ancient lift. Fortunately, her ID card worked when she put it in the slot, and the lift groaned into life. A woman in a navy-blue suit accompanied her in silence all the way up to the third floor.

When the lift disgorged them, Zelda found yet more unfamiliar faces. It was nearly lunchtime, and she knew that by now the others would have been at work since nine, but everyone had congregated at the far end of the long office, and nobody seemed to be working at all. She didn't even need her pass to open the main door; it was propped open with a wedge. The woman who had been with her nodded brusquely and went back down in the lift.

Two people Zelda didn't recognise sat behind the glass partition of Hawkins's office. The man who sat at Hawkins's desk was grey-haired, red-faced and portly, wearing an expensive pinstripe suit and what Zelda took to be an old school, or regimental, tie. He gestured for her to come in and sit opposite him. A woman, rather severe and buttoned-up, Zelda thought, sat by the side of the desk, at an angle to them both.

'And you are?' the man asked. His accent was every bit as plummy as Zelda had expected, but his voice was high-pitched, producing a strange, squeaky effect. That made it harder for her to take him seriously, and she could tell that he was a man who clearly wanted to be taken seriously. A detective, undoubtedly.

'I think it might be better if you told me who you are first,' Zelda said.

'Oh, dear. Has nobody explained?'

'Not yet.'

'There's been a bit of trouble.' The man fumbled in his inside pocket and brought out an official government identification card. 'I'm Paul Danvers,' he said. 'National Crime Agency.' The photo on the card matched his face.

Zelda nodded and glanced towards the woman, who remained still.

'That's Deborah,' Danvers said. 'Deborah Fletcher. She's with me,' he added with a proprietorial smile. Deborah's stiff, pasted-on expression didn't change. Zelda's overwhelming impression of her was one of thinness – thin face, thin lips, skinny waist and skinny legs. The slash of bright red lipstick didn't help, nor did the navy pencil skirt.

'What is this all about?' Zelda asked.

'I'm afraid we ask the questions, dearie,' said Danvers. 'First of all, may I ask what you're doing here?'

Patronising bastard, she thought. Whatever this is, I'm not going to make it easy for you. 'I work here.'

'In what capacity?'

'I'm sure it's in your file.' Zelda gestured towards the folder on the desk in front of him.

Making a show of it, he opened the file and ran his finger down the list. Finally, he closed it, clasped his hands on the desk and studied Zelda. 'You must be Nelia Melnic,' he said. Deliberately pronouncing her last name with an 'itch', in the Serbian fashion. She thought of correcting him but decided it wasn't worth it. 'And your job?'

'Not in your files?'

'I'm sure it's in there somewhere. But you could save us all a lot of time and trouble if you'd simply answer my questions.'

'I'm a super-recogniser,' Zelda said. 'I remember faces. Every face I've ever seen. In fact, I never forget them.'

'That must be useful.'

'To you, perhaps.' Zelda shrugged. 'To me, it's both a blessing and a curse. Now, what are you doing here? Where is Mr Hawkins?'

Danvers scratched the side of his nose. 'Quite . . . er . . .' He glanced towards Deborah Fletcher.

'Trevor Hawkins is dead,' she said. 'Suspicious circumstances. We're questioning everyone who works here.'

Banks blew gently on the milky brown surface of the tea, watched the ripples and felt the warmth they gave off, then took a sip. It was hot and sweet, and perhaps a bit too weak for Banks's liking, but it came as a treat after the soaking and the grim sight of the boy's body.

Edith Grunwell's living room was an exercise in cleanliness, neatness and economy. Though she had a small cabinet filled with delicate porcelain figurines and a large gilt-framed painting of Fountains Abbey in all its historic and romantic glory over the fireplace, there was nothing excessive about the room, nothing out of place, nothing that jarred with the simplicity of the rose-patterned wallpaper, crocheted antimacassars and beige wall-to-wall carpeting. The armchairs were comfortable, but not so much so as to encourage lingering. Mingled scents of rosemary and thyme came from the potpourri on the windowsill.

Mrs Grunwell herself was thin and birdlike in her movements. The deep-set watery eyes in her wrinkled face looked as if they had seen too much this morning already, and she dabbed at them with a cotton handkerchief. 'I'm sorry,' she said to Banks. 'You must forgive me. I'm not squeamish, I've seen dead bodies, but it was such a shock, something like that happening so close by. The poor boy.'

'You've seen bodies?'

'Don't sound so surprised, young man. I'm eighty-five years old. When you've lived to my age you tend to have seen most things. Especially if you work as a nurse, which I did for many years.' She shook her head. 'I know what people say about the estate, and it has its bad elements, true enough, but it wasn't always like this. The violence. The knives. I must admit, I'm a bit frightened by it all.' She glanced around the room. 'It makes me feel differently about where I live. My home . . . it feels violated.' She gave a little shudder.

'When did you move here?'

'When the council first opened the estate, if that's the right word. July 27th, 1964. They even had a little ceremony, a couple of celebrities cutting the tape. Mike and Bernie Winters, if I remember rightly. Not exactly Morecambe and Wise, but they were very popular in their time. And you can't believe what a paradise it was for a young married couple like George and me. My George, bless his soul, was a farm labourer, and before we came here we lived in a tiny cottage out Relton way. I used to bicycle to and from the Friarage in Northallerton every day, all seasons, even when I was on nights. There wasn't much in the way of household comforts in a farm labourer's cottage. No hot water, an outside toilet, tin tub for a bath, fireplace empty half the time. Even the little paraffin heater we bought didn't help much with the cold. George didn't like to use it. He thought it was too dangerous. But we got by. When we got this place, though, we thought we'd died and gone to heaven. Hot water, indoor toilet and bath, underfloor heating, everything spic and span, in working order. I stood out there in the street, just looking, and cried my eyes out. A miracle. At least . . . that's how it felt then.' She put her hand to her chest. 'Listen to me rambling on. You must think I'm gaga. But my heart's still going like a steam hammer. I always talk too much when I'm nervous or scared.'

'Not at all,' said Banks.

'Of course,' Mrs Grunwell added, 'there's nothing the council would like more than to get rid of me and put me in a home, out of the way somewhere. George is gone and the children all left years ago. Maybe I should let them. But it's still my home, don't you see?'

'I do,' said Banks.

'I'd like to stay here until I can't possibly manage any longer by myself. I feel sorry for these young people not being able to afford a house of their own, but this house has been my home for over fifty years. Still, you didn't come to hear me reminiscing and grumbling, did you?'

Banks, who often found that letting witnesses unburden themselves a bit before questioning helped them relax, merely smiled at her. 'You told DI Cabbot you put out the rubbish at ten o'clock. Is that right?'

'Yes. Like I do every Sunday.'

'And you didn't see or hear anything unusual?'

'No. Nothing. It was very quiet out back. It usually is on a Sunday night, apart from next door's cat now and then. I never have much rubbish. Just one little bag. I've told the council that I hardly need one of those huge bins, but they don't listen. They have their rules, and they don't want one batty old lady marching to the beat of a different drummer.' She grinned, showing crooked, yellow teeth. 'Now, that would give them an excuse to lock me away, wouldn't it?'

The neighbours on Malden Terrace would all be questioned, of course, as would the tenants of the dozen or so houses on the opposite side of the narrow lane, whose front doors were on Malden Close. In fact, officers would canvass the whole of the East Side Estate in the hopes that someone had noticed something and would be willing to share their knowledge with the police, unlikely as that seemed.

Banks had managed to get a decent picture of the victim's face in profile with his mobile, and he showed it to her. 'Do you recognise him at all?' he asked.

Mrs Grunwell studied the image for a long time then shook her head. 'So very young. No, I don't recognise him.'

'Have you seen anyone like him around the estate lately?'

'What? You mean a darkie?'

Banks swallowed. 'Well ... I ... yes, I suppose. A Middle Eastern youth, at any rate.'

'George always called them darkies. Nothing against them, like, so long as they kept themselves to themselves.' She paused. 'But we don't get them around here. Hardly ever. I mean, I think I would have noticed him.'

That was true enough. There was a white belt between industrial West Yorkshire and Teesside. Even the chefs and waiters from the local Indian and Thai restaurants commuted to Eastvale from Leeds and Bradford, or Darlington and Middlesbrough after their shifts. The only truly multicultural area of Eastvale was around the college campus, and even that was probably below the national average. There had never been anything to attract immigrants to rural areas like Swainsdale, not even in the post-war years when the first arrivals from Pakistan and the West Indies started to come into the country, mostly in the north, to work in the cotton and woollen mills of the Pennine valleys between Leeds and Manchester. There were no factories in the Dales, no real service industries to speak of, and farm labour wasn't very open to outsiders. Nor were rural communities. Things were changing these days, of course, but not a great deal, and not very quickly.

'Do you get out and about much?' Banks asked. 'I mean, do you think if he had been local you might have seen him anywhere around the estate, or in town?'

'Don't think that just because I'm eighty-five I can't do my own shopping or enjoy a walk down by the river, young man. I'll have you know I make a point of going out every morning for my newspaper, and as I don't drive, I don't go the supermarket like everyone else. I use the local shops as and when I need them. We have a perfectly good butcher down the road, and a fine greengrocer.'

'I didn't mean to suggest that you're housebound, Mrs Grunwell,' said Banks. 'I just wanted some idea of how well you know the area. Whether you would have noticed if someone like the victim had been hanging around.'

'I'm sure there are plenty of people on the estate I never see. Some don't come out until after dark. But I *do* get out and about. I wouldn't say I notice any more or less than some of the younger people in the neighbourhood.'

'I can't imagine this, but I have to ask,' said Banks. 'Do you know of anyone who might want to do you harm? Anyone who bears you a grudge, who might have wanted to play such a terrible trick on you? Someone who wanted to scare you, or might even have thought it was some kind of sick joke?'

'Good Lord, no.' Mrs Grunwell clutched her handkerchief to her chest. 'I never even thought of that. No. I'm quite sure there's no one like that.'

'Do you get along well with your neighbours?'

'Yes, for the most part. They're very nice. Some of them help me out with little things, now and then. You know, carry my shopping if they see me struggling. Mr Dunne at number fourteen even takes me to the supermarket on occasion. I don't like it, but it would be impolite to say no, wouldn't it?'

'Did you hear anything during the night? A car, or anyone messing about with the bins?'

'We get a few cars going by the end, Malden Road, like, at all hours, so it's nothing unusual. But Sunday's usually very quiet. Come to think of it, I do believe I heard a car quite late last night. And before that it sounded as if someone kicked the bin. Kids do that sometimes, and I thought it was either that or next door's cat, but . . . I don't know.'

'This sound – might it have been the bin lid closing?'

'It might have been.'

'And you heard a car stop before this?'

'No. I heard a car engine turning over. That was after I'd heard the bin sound. Then it made a terrible noise, like when the gears crunch. I'm just assuming it had stopped first, or why would it have made that awful crunching sound starting up? And before you ask, I was quite wide awake. I like to read in bed, and usually I'm asleep after a chapter or so, depending on the book. Last night I was reading Barbara Cartland. I do so like Barbara Cartland. She usually sends me off to sleep in no time.'

'But not last night?'

'No. For some reason, my eyes just wouldn't close. Sleep refused to come. It happens sometimes when you're my age. Old folks don't need as much sleep, they say. Which is just as well, as we can't seem to get it.'

'Can you tell me anything else about this car? Did you hear anyone speak, say anything? Did you hear the car door or boot slam?'

'No. I don't remember anything like that. I was feeling anxious, all tensed up, for some reason. Don't ask me why. I don't believe in premonitions or anything silly like that. There's no reason why I should, except it happens sometimes. If I can't get to sleep I start to feel apprehensive.'

'I know the feeling,' said Banks. 'What time was this?'

'I can't say exactly, but it wouldn't have been that long after I went to bed. Around eleven o'clock, perhaps? Maybe half past at the latest.'

Between eleven and half past. That fit the time span Dr Burns had already indicated, Banks thought. 'And you thought you heard a car engine turning over, then start up noisily, after someone had kicked or opened and closed your bin?'

'Yes,' Mrs Grunwell was twisting the handkerchief between her gnarled fingers. 'How can someone do something like that, Mr Banks? Kill a poor, defenceless young man and put his body in a rubbish bin. I'm frightened. What if they come back? What if it's a drug gang? What if they think I might have seen something?'

'I wouldn't worry about that, Mrs Grunwell. Half the street might have seen or heard something. The gears screeching or the noise from the bin. They can't come back and eliminate everyone.' He realised before he finished that he never should have opened his mouth.

Mrs Grunwell put her hand to her chest. 'Eliminate? Do you think it could come to that?'

'Of course not. And there's no evidence of gang involvement. I can understand why you might be frightened, but really there's nothing to worry about. Perhaps it would make you feel more at ease if there's someone you can call. Your children, perhaps?'

'They flew the coop years ago. One lives in Inverness and the other in Toronto. Couldn't get far enough away. Besides, they're all grown up with families and responsibilities of their own. I'm a great-grandmother, you know. But there's Eunice. Eunice Kelly. She's my best friend. She used to live right next door but now she's in sheltered housing out Saltburn way, by the sea.'

'Do you think she would come and stay with you if you explained the situation? Would it make you feel better to have a friend nearby?'

'Oh, yes. I think so. But I'd rather go and stay with her until you catch whoever did this. She's not got a lot of room, but I'm sure she would clear a little corner for me. I don't need much. And a few days at the seaside would do my nerves the world of good.'

Banks nodded. 'All right,' he said. 'We can handle that. Will you ring her and make the arrangements, and I'll make sure we get a car to drive you to Saltburn. Until then, there'll be a police officer posted by your door.'

'Really? You can do that?'

'Of course I can,' said Banks. Edith Grunwell didn't need to know that they didn't have a budget yet. Hadn't even got the green light for a full investigation. But they would, Banks felt certain. There was no doubt that it was murder, and a nasty one at that. And the victim was so young, not to mention Middle Eastern. Besides, if Area Commander Gervaise didn't approve the budget, then he would bloody-well drive Edith Grunwell to Saltburn himself.

Trevor. Zelda realised she had never known Hawkins's first name until now. 'Dead?' she repeated. 'I can't believe it. How? What happened?'

Danvers arranged a row of coloured paperclips and rubber bands on Hawkins's blotter. The gesture annoyed Zelda, perhaps as much for its prissiness as for its presumption. To her, it was still Hawkins's desk. His paperclips. His rubber bands.

'That's a matter for the coroner to decide,' Danvers said. 'What we're interested in is any information his staff feel might relate to his death.'

'Are you saying he was murdered?'

'Why would you assume that?' Deborah Fletcher butted in from the sidelines.

'Because you said there were suspicious circumstances.'

Deborah shrugged. 'That could mean anything.'

Zelda could see her co-workers, pale and worried, at the far end of the office. It had never been a joyous place to work, and she hadn't really felt that she had got to know any of the others at all well. She hadn't been fully accepted by them, had always been regarded as some kind of freak, an outsider. But now Zelda felt the beginnings of a strange bond with the people behind the glass. She turned to face Deborah Fletcher. 'Perhaps my assumption has something to do with the way you're questioning me,' she said.

'Been questioned in a murder investigation before, have you?' Danvers asked.

Zelda froze. The department knew quite a lot about her and her past, naturally, but she was sure they didn't know everything. Not about Darius, surely. 'That's absurd,' she said. 'I didn't think it was an unreasonable question.'

'Well, seeing as you ask,' Danvers went on, 'no, we don't think Mr Hawkins was murdered. We don't think anything yet. But I'm sure you understand that, given his position, given the work you all do here, questions have to be asked. So I'll repeat my question: do you know anything that might relate to his death?'

'How would I know anything about his death? I've only just heard about it from you and, quite frankly, I'm a bit upset.'

'I'm sorry we were so abrupt.' Danvers gave Deborah a sharp glance. 'It's been a long day already, and not even noon. Is there anything at all you can tell us? Did you never socialise as a group? It would be perfectly natural.'

'No. At least, I never did. There was a sort of department mixer at his house a while ago, but that's all.' Zelda gestured towards the partition. 'I can't speak for them because I am only part-time. Very part-time. I only work here for two or three days each month, usually.'

Danvers raised a bushy grey eyebrow. 'Yes, that's clear from your file. A *civilian* employee. And the rest of your time?'

'Is really nobody's business but mine.'

'Ms Melnic,' said Danvers, 'believe me, in these matters, everything I want to be my business *is* my business.'

'In what matters?'

'I think it would be best if you just answered our questions. We already know, for example, that you're an artist, going by the name of "Zelda", and that you live in North Yorkshire with another artist called Raymond Cabbot, who is more than forty years your senior. You say you were abducted some years ago and forced into the sex trade. We know you met Mr Cabbot in London three years ago, then lived with him in an artists' colony in St Ives for some time before moving north about a year ago.' Danvers smirked and tapped the folder. 'See. It's all in there. At my fingertips.'

How little you really know, thought Zelda. Even so, she felt a surge of anger at the way Danvers laid out his facts as if they were accusations, or evidence of moral lapses on her part, at the very least. 'You *say* you were abducted.' An artist '*going by the name* of Zelda'. Like the artist previously known as Prince, she thought. 'More than *forty years* your senior.' She never thought of Raymond in that way. He was Raymond – bright, solid, brilliant, bubbling over with enthusiasm for life. Raymond. She said nothing. She was certainly not going to fill Danvers in on the details missing from his files. She folded her arms. 'I don't see what any of this has to do with you,' she said.

'Why are you so hostile?' Deborah asked.

'Hostile? How would you feel if you arrived at work to find strangers in your boss's office who tell you he's dead and start interrogating you about your past?'

'I'd feel I was only doing my duty by answering their questions.'

Zelda paused, then said, 'Well, I suppose that is one difference between you and me.'

'Nelia *Melnic*,' Danvers said. Deliberately pronouncing the final 'ic' as 'itch' again. 'You're not British, are you? That's not a British name, is it? And, correct me if I'm wrong, but I think I detect a slight accent.'

'I'm a French citizen. I have a French passport.'

Danvers frowned and turned to his folder again. 'Ah, yes, for "services to the French government".'

Zelda smiled. 'You could call it that.'

'What else? How did you really get French citizenship? They don't give it out with the garlic, you know.'

'The French value their whores, Mr Danvers. Didn't you know that? They offered me the *Légion d'honneur*, too, but I turned it down. I thought that would be going a bit too far.'

Danvers banged his fist on the desk. 'Don't be flippant with me, Ms Melnic. This is a serious business and you're wasting my time.'

'Then don't ask me stupid questions. I applied. They granted it. It did no harm that I had done the police a few favours, that's all.'

'What kind of—'

'Not that kind of favour. I helped them take down some very dangerous men. Same as I try to do here.'

'Are you sure you didn't have some dirt on someone?'

Zelda smiled. 'You'd be surprised how many people I have dirt on, Mr Danvers. That just means that a lot of people are dirty.'

'You're not answering my questions.'

'It's the best answer you'll get from me.'

Zelda had to keep reminding herself that, however much they knew, they didn't know everything. And she certainly wasn't going to tell them any more than she had to. She wasn't even going to tell them about Hawkins meeting Keane. She said nothing.

'Before France,' Danvers said, calming down. 'Is that an Eastern European accent I detect? Romanian, is it?'

Zelda sighed. 'I was born in Moldova, Mr Danvers, as you can no doubt see for yourself from my file, in a town called Dubăsari, in Transnistria, on the river Dniester, not far from the Ukraine border. It's not a part of the world many people know well. And the "c" in Melnic is hard, more of a "k" than a "ch". It's a common enough surname in that part of the world.' Zelda paused, tired of the pointless sparring. 'If you think I know anything, and you want to find out what it is, why don't you tell me what happened and then ask me what I think about it?'

'We don't think you know anything, Ms Melnic. But if it will help to improve your attitude and general level of cooperation, I can tell you that Mr Hawkins died in a fire at his home on Saturday night.'

'A fire?'

'Yes. According to all the evidence, it appears to have been a chip-pan fire.'

Zelda shook her head. 'I don't understand. What is a chip-pan fire?'

'It's just a general term. A chip-pan fire is when someone puts a pan full of oil on the burner to heat up and falls asleep, usually because he's the worse for drink. It catches fire, and Bob's your uncle.'

Zelda had read enough and been around English people enough to consider herself fairly proficient in the quirks and oddities of their language – including 'Bob's your uncle' – but she had never heard the term 'chip-pan fire'. Who on earth would want to make chips when they got drunk? Were fish and chips so important to them? It was yet another English eccentricity she would simply have to accept.

But Hawkins? She hadn't known him well, but one passion of his that was hard to miss was his love of gourmet food and fine wine. She had seen the foodie magazines on his desk from time to time, even heard him discussing reservations at well-reviewed new restaurants over the phone. It would hardly be the epitome of snobbishness to assume that Hawkins had probably never eaten fish and chips in his life, let alone that he had owned a chip pan and cooked them up for himself at home. As for his being drunk, as far as she knew, Hawkins wasn't much of a drinker. Of course, she realised that some drinkers can hide their addiction well, just as a chip-pan fire may not necessarily require the making of chips. She supposed that Hawkins might have had a glass of wine too many and heated up a pan of oil to make tempura, samosas or some such exotic deep-fried treat. It merely seemed unlikely. 'Mrs Hawkins?' she asked.

'Away at her sister's in Bath for the weekend.'

'It must be terrible for her,' Zelda said.

Danvers inclined his head slightly. 'Naturally.'

'Where were you on Saturday night?' Deborah asked.

'As a matter of fact, I was in Croatia. Staying with an old friend. On Saturday night we went down into the village for dinner then out on the town dancing.'

'Dancing?'

'Why not?'

Deborah shook her head. She looked as if she had never danced in her life. 'No reason. And your friend's name and address?'

'I would rather not say.'

'Oh. Why is that?'

Zelda turned to address her remarks to Danvers. 'Her work is secretive and dangerous. The fewer people who know her identity and location the better.'

'Surely you can't think ...? Oh, well, never mind,' said Danvers. 'It's not essential. If you could perhaps produce your flight details and boarding passes, that should suffice for the moment. You understand this is simply for the purposes of elimination?'

'Of course.'

Danvers put down the ballpoint pen he had been clicking for the past few minutes. 'I do hope you realise the serious-ness of the situation, Ms Melnic,' he said. 'You must be aware that, even as a civilian consultant attached to a multi-national policing operation, you are in a unique position, both because of your special skills and, what shall we call it, your personal acquaintance with the area under investigation. Because of what you know.'

Area under investigation, Zelda thought. That was a nice way of putting what she had been through at the hands of people she now worked hard to identify and put away. Talk about English understatement.

'Much of the information you deal with every day is highly secret,' Danvers went on, 'and Mr Hawkins was a high-rank-ing officer of the National Crime Agency, as you know, with strong connections to the security services. You signed the Official Secrets Act. Surely you must be aware of what that means? When something like this happens – whatever the reason – we have a duty to investigate the circumstances. It's also clear that you have lived a somewhat peripatetic and bohemian existence. There are many gaps, many periods during which ... well ... anything could have happened. People change. Loyalties change.'

Zelda nodded. 'Things certainly did happen, to put it mildly. But my loyalties didn't change. I understand what you're saying. I just can't help you, that's all. For a start, I wasn't even in this country most of my life, and for another thing, I've already told you, I'm very part-time here. If you believe that Mr Hawkins was murdered, then I wish you the best of luck with your investigation. If you think that *his* loyalties had changed, then I can't help you with that. He didn't confide in me. As far as I could tell, he was a good man.' Zelda hoped her nose wasn't growing as she spoke, that the itch she felt there was just an itch.

The more she thought about it, the more certain she was that putting a pot of oil on the stove was something that would never have entered Hawkins's mind, even if he had been drinking. And no doubt the ensuing fire would have obliterated any evidence there may have been as to what had really happened.

'Did you ever notice, in the times you were here lately, anything unusual about Mr Hawkins's behaviour?' Danvers asked.

'I can't say that I did.'

'When were you last here?'

'April. A month ago exactly.'

'Did you notice any changes in his behaviour, his routine?'

'No. As far as I could tell, Mr Hawkins was a creature of habit.'

'Did you ever have any disagreements with him?' Deborah asked.

'No. I simply got on with my job. To be honest, it didn't involve working closely with others. Or with Mr Hawkins. Mostly I examined photographs, CCTV and video footage. Sometimes out in the field, but mostly here, at my desk.'

'Did he ever ask you to do anything you found unusual or suspicious?' Deborah asked.

'Like what?'

'Deliver a package or a message, for example.'

'Never.'

'Have you ever seen him with anyone he shouldn't have been with?'

'How would I know who he should or shouldn't be with?'

'You know what I'm talking about. Anyone shady. Anyone you *recognised*, with your skills. From the past, perhaps, or from one of the many photographs you've seen.'

'No,' said Zelda, feeling her nose itch again.

'You said you worked in the field on occasion. I understand you visited airports and train terminals to scan the crowds?' Danvers said.

'Sometimes. If we had information that a person of interest might be coming in, someone from Special Branch or MI5 would come and take me off for the day. But it didn't happen often. My area of expertise is relatively narrow, and very specialised.'

'I think what we're getting at is whether you ever saw Mr Hawkins with any of these people you might have spotted at airports or railway stations?'

'No.'

'And what is your role exactly? How do you work?'

'You already know that.'

'Clarify it for us,' said Deborah.

Zelda swallowed. She never liked this bit. 'Faces,' she replied. 'I told you. I don't forget them.'

'Why should that be of value to this department?'

'You know as well as I do that we're concerned with identifying and, with any luck, eventually catching, anyone involved in the illegal traffic of young women for the purposes of sex.'

'And your own experience as a sex worker would make you an expert on this?' Deborah asked. 'You see, this experience is very unclear in your file. Almost so unclear as to be non-existent.'

Zelda looked at Deborah. She was enjoying this, she thought. Enjoying humiliating her. Or trying to. She sighed.

'I have never been a "sex worker", and I resent your use of the term. "Sex worker" implies I was a willing participant. I wasn't. Not ever. As you said, I have a "personal acquaintance with the area under investigation". That's because it happened to me. It is not something I like to broadcast, but I was abducted at the age of seventeen and spent the next ten years either on my back or on my knees servicing clients. That's when I wasn't being beaten, tortured or raped. And if either of you believe that I might possibly be working on the side of the bastards who did those things to me, then you're more fucking stupid than I think you are.' Zelda noticed Deborah redden and felt a little jolt of pleasure at her reaction to the outburst.

Danvers coughed, put his pen down again and glanced sideways at Deborah. 'Well, I think that's just about all for now. Unless you have any more questions, Deborah?'

Deborah shook her head and scribbled something on her notepad before smoothing her skirt. She avoided looking at Zelda.

Danvers stood up and gave a slightly mocking bow. 'Then we'll trouble you no more, Ms Melnic.'

'What now? What about work? The office?'

'Naturally, a replacement will be found for Mr Hawkins, perhaps on a temporary basis at first. But certainly for the next few days the office will be closed, and the work of the department suspended until we conclude our investigation.'

'So I can go home?'

Danvers frowned. 'We would prefer it if you stayed in London for the time being, Ms Melnic,' he said. 'Just until we've wrapped up our inquiries, you understand. We may need to talk to you again. You can let Deborah know the name and location of your hotel before you leave. And don't forget to give her your mobile number, too.'

And that was it. Danvers resumed his seat and turned his attention back to the file folder. Zelda was dismissed. She wondered if they had been quite so thorough with everyone else, or had her past, her origins and her special role singled her out for suspicion?

'I like your new hairstyle,' Banks said to DI Joanna MacDonald. 'Or does that qualify as a #MeToo remark?'

Joanna smiled and touched her shaggy cap of blonde hair self-consciously. 'Depends,' she said. 'Maybe it's more of a Time's Up sort of thing. Especially as you're not my boss. But thank you, anyway.'

'So what brings you all the way from the bright lights of Northallerton to a sleepy little outpost like Eastvale? Your phone message said it was work-related.'

Joanna raised an eyebrow. 'So what else would it be?'

'I don't know. The pleasure of my company?' Banks liked the contrast between her blonde hair and dark eyebrows, though he knew that it meant highlights. His ex-wife, Sandra, had the same combination, but in her case, it had been a quirk of nature. 'It's just that we don't see you out here very often. Only in those dull meetings back at County HQ.'

'My job's not always dull.'

'The meetings are. Seriously, though, have you never thought of applying for Homicide and Major Crimes? I'm sure you'd be in with a chance. I'd put in a word.'

Joanna laughed, then took a sip of coffee. They were in the Queen's Arms on Eastvale market square that Monday evening. The storms had passed, and the weather was mild, the evening imbued with muted spring sunlight casting shadows over the rain-darkened cobblestones. Cyril, the landlord, had even optimistically risked putting some tables outside after the rain. It was a bit too soon for that, Banks thought, as there could easily be another shower, though one or two smokers clearly begged to disagree. Inside was as dead as usual for a Monday evening. Just the regulars who had been there most of the afternoon propping up the bar and chatting up Cyril's latest barmaid, Louise, a petite Scouse lass with an accent to match. Cyril also had one of his early sixties' playlists going. At the moment, The Shadows were playing 'The Frightened City'.

'As a matter of fact,' Joanna answered, 'the thought actually crossed my mind briefly once, when things seemed a bit too quiet.'

'So why didn't you?'

'Well, you already have three women working under your command: DS Jackman, DC Masterson and DI Cabbot. You also have a female boss, Area Commander Gervaise. I just felt you were sort of trapped between women. I didn't think you were up to handling another. It didn't seem fair to add to your burdens.'

'So you let me off the hook? That's very considerate of you,' said Banks. 'And you're absolutely right. I'm looking for a big, strapping Neanderthal knuckle-dragger to stick by my side when the going gets tough.'

Joanna laughed.

'Now tell me your real reason,' Banks said before taking a long refreshing slug of Timothy Taylor's Landlord.

'Simple, really. You don't need another DI. You've already got Annie Cabbot. You need another DC. Besides, I'm told my prospects of promotion before too long are pretty good exactly where I am.'

'Congratulations. I'm glad for you. Really. And I suppose you're right, we do need a new DC, especially now Doug Wilson's left us.' Banks took a sip of beer. 'So what is it you want to see me about?'

'You're investigating the suspicious death of a young Middle Eastern boy, right?'

'You're pretty quick off the mark,' Banks said.

'Hardly need to be. It was all over the six o'clock news.'

Banks drank some more beer. The Shadows had given way to The Temperance Seven singing 'Pasadena'. Banks had never liked The Temperance Seven. 'Yes,' he said. 'The reporters are already pouring off the London trains. Our media liaison officer Adrian Moss is under siege. But it's only to be expected. Our victim is very young. About twelve or thirteen, we think. And, as you say, Middle Eastern, which is pretty unusual around these parts. Victim of knife crime in a small northern town. Found dead in a wheelie bin in an alley at the back of Malden Terrace, on the East Side Estate, with nothing on him but a small quantity of cocaine in his pocket. Dr Burns said at the scene that the lad was stabbed four times in the chest and abdomen. There are no defensive wounds. It doesn't resemble a fight gone wrong or anything like that. We don't even know the victim's identity yet. We've got a computer-generated likeness, based on a photograph, out all over the place: newspapers, TV, government agencies, asylum seekers' hostels, Islamic groups, immigrant communities and organisations. But we don't even know that he was an immigrant or asylum seeker. Or a Muslim. And perhaps he was born here. Anyway, why are you interested? Can you help us?'

'I don't know. Not with the identification, but maybe with other things.'

'More coffee? Something stronger?'

Joanna held on to her cup. 'No. Nothing for me, thanks. I'm fine. Have you ever heard of a man called Blaydon? Connor Clive Blaydon.'

'Sounds vaguely familiar, but I can't think from where. Just a minute – wasn't he a mate of The Farmer's?'

'The Farmer?'

'George Fanthorpe. "Farmer Fanthorpe." A bit before your time, perhaps. Nasty piece of work. On the surface he was a wealthy country squire – owned and trained racehorses; kept a few sheep, rare-breed pigs and cows; operated a factory that made posh cheese for tourists.'

'And underneath the rustic veneer?'

'Drugs, guns, prostitution, murder.'

'Sounds like him and Blaydon would make perfect bedfellows. Where is your Farmer these days?'

'Inside,' said Banks. 'One of my success stories.'

'Well, on the surface of it, Blaydon's a property developer. A dodgy property developer.'

'Is there any other kind?'

'Yes, well, Mr Blaydon has certainly earned the title. Some of his fixer-uppers make Rachman's look like the Ritz.'

'*Rachman?* I would have thought he was well before your time.' Peter Rachman was a famous slum landlord of 1960s London, mostly the Notting Hill area. His empire consisted of over a hundred mansion blocks, which he subdivided into flats the size of cupboards and filled with recent immigrants, who were unlikely to complain about the living conditions in the days when signs such as NO BLACKS OR IRISH NEED APPLY were stuck in so many rental property windows.

'I did History at uni. Contemporary social history is a hobby of mine. The whole twentieth century, really, but more specifically post-World War Two up to . . . well, the present day, I suppose. Besides, the name came up in my research. That's why they call us Criminal Intelligence, you know.'

Banks smiled. 'I always thought there was another reason altogether. Anyway, this Blaydon is what? A Rachman figure?'

'Sort of. On a larger scale. He started out small but now he's nationwide. North, south, east and west. Worth millions. He buys up old properties – houses, offices, pubs, even hotels and clubs, you name it – does them up on the cheap and sells them for a huge profit, or if location is the main draw, he clears the site and gets a builder to slap up a few cheap prefabs. He's also in the buy-to-rent market. Says he's creating affordable housing, of course, so the council and the government just look the other way. It has also been whispered that one or two members of said councils haven't been shy of taking a bob or two from him. And if they can't be bought they can usually be blackmailed or bullied. Same result for Blaydon, however he gets it. Carte blanche. Loads of money.'

'But that's what property developers and councillors do, isn't it? Flaunt the rules.'

'Cynic.'

'Why would he take such risks committing real crimes when he's already made more than most of us would earn in a life-time from his development business?'

'He's already in the kind of business that attracts the adventurer type. You know, always on the go with some scheme or other, uninterested in the feelings of others, lacks empathy, needs excitement to thrive. Elements of the classic psychopathic personality. I think he may also be motivated by greed, a sense of entitlement and invulnerability, maybe a feeling of being above or beyond the law. And perhaps the risk-taking appeals, too. He's also a gambler, a high roller. Likes to think of himself as a major player. In with the big boys. Who knows? When it comes to the alpha male in full flight . . . well, all bets are off.'

'You've certainly been hitting the psychology textbooks, haven't you?'

'Are you going to take this seriously?'

'I am taking it seriously.'

'Sure.' Joanna glared at him for a moment.

'Tell me why the recent interest in this Blaydon? There must be more to it than dodgy property developments.'

'Very perceptive. If you listen, you might find out. Have you heard about that new development at the bottom of the hill, across Cardigan Drive from the Elmet Estate, on what they used to call the Hollyfield Estate?'

'The Elmet Centre? Yes, I have.' The pre-war Hollyfield Estate had been in decline for years and was finally due for demolition as soon as all its inhabitants had been rehoused. The plan was to use the cleared land, along with an area of the fields to the west, to build more social housing and a new shopping centre and multiplex cinema complex. So far, it was still at the planning stage, but the rehousing had already begun. Slowly.

'That's Blaydon,' said Joanna. 'Along with a couple of local lads known as the Kerrigan brothers.'

'Tommy and Timmy? We're well enough acquainted with them, but we haven't been able to prove anything yet.'

'We know. Anyway, we've been keeping a watching brief on Blaydon, and last night ANPR caught his Merc coming into Eastvale at twenty-five past seven and heading out in a southerly direction at around quarter past eleven.'

'OK. The old lady whose bin we found the body in says she thought she heard someone messing with her bin between eleven and half past, along with a car starting up. Two other neighbours think they heard the same, but we haven't been able to pin down the time yet. I suppose if it were closer to eleven, it might fit with your ANPR timing. But what's a dead boy got to do with a dodgy property developer?'

'Maybe nothing, but bear with me. Nobody saw anything?'

'Of course not. This is the East Side Estate we're talking about. Surely you don't think someone like Blaydon—'

'Shoved in the blade? No. I doubt it very much. Like most people in his position, he keeps the nasty stuff at arm's length, uses his minions. But we don't know who was with him in the car. One thing we *have* discovered is that he surrounds himself with a number of disreputable characters, ex-cons or ex-special forces, even ex-coppers. Tough guys. Mercenaries. Enforcers. And he's lost his driving licence, so he never goes anywhere without Frankie Wallace, his chauffeur. And Wallace is an ex-bruiser, trained in the Glasgow gangs. Surely this Farmer of yours had people to do his dirty work for him?'

Banks thought of Ciaran French and Darren Brody, two of The Farmer's enforcers, who had ultimately contributed towards his downfall. 'Yes. But you don't even know that Blaydon himself was in the car,' he said. 'All automatic number plate recognition can tell us is that a car with his number plate passed the cameras at a certain time.'

'I know that,' said Joanna.

'Then . . .?'

'I didn't say I had a case or anything, did I? It's just that we've been gathering information on Blaydon over at Criminal Intelligence for quite some time now, and while we have no evidence we could use in court, we're convinced that he's involved in a number of criminal activities. Maybe he's up to something in Eastvale?'

'More criminal than property development?'

'As an adjunct. A cover, if you like. We've got him connected with a dodgy accountant and a High Street lawyer suspected of money laundering.'

'What? Here in Eastvale?'

'Don't get your underpants in a knot, Alan. It's all just been flagged. There's no action required as yet. These things take time and careful planning if we're to build a workable case. They're clever, sneaky customers we're dealing with here, not your typical smash and grab merchants.'

'Why weren't Homicide and Major Crimes informed?'

'Like I said, it's a fresh flag. It'll probably be in your next county memo, if you bother to read those. The point is, we've got links, however tenuous, between Blaydon and these two. Not to mention the Kerrigans. It's what we do in Criminal Intelligence.'

'So what are they up to, in addition to planning mega projects?'

'A few things. As you probably know, sterling's pretty low at the moment and the bottom's falling out of the housing market.'

'Tell me about it.'

'Well, it creates an ideal opportunity for foreign buyers. High-end properties, especially. In the millions. Mostly London and the stockbroker belt, of course, but also places like Harrogate, some posher suburbs of Leeds. York. So on.'

'It still doesn't sound illegal.'

'We think some of the buyers are using it as an opportunity for money laundering and that Blaydon is facilitating it for them.'

'The new development, too?'

'Hard to do without some foreign investment.'

'Go on.'

'We've also got pictures of him meeting with various people in various places. A few of the ones we've been able to identify so far are men connected with criminal enterprises, mostly originating in Albania and some of the other Balkan states.'

'What enterprises would these be?'

'Mostly drugs and guns. Possibly sex trafficking.'

Banks thought of Zelda. 'I know someone who might be able to help you with any pictures you haven't identified yet. She knows the sex traffic world inside out, and she's a super-recogniser.'

'I've heard of them. Never forget a face. How terrible to have to carry all that around with you. Everyone you've ever seen.'

'Even the ugly ones,' said Banks. 'The point is, she could help you. She works with the NCA in London on a part-time basis, but she lives up Lyndgarth way.'

'Fine. Fix something up. We'd be glad of the help. Facial recognition software can only get us so far. Anyway, to continue, we're also convinced that Blaydon has access to inside information – not just politicians, but police, too – but we don't know exactly who on the inside is on his payroll.'

'But you know someone is?'

'We're pretty sure. He has an uncanny way of knowing when to lie low.'

'That's why you're here, then, rather than me being over at County HQ?'

'Partly. I wanted to meet somewhere more neutral.'

'Someone at HQ you don't trust?'

'No one specifically. I just thought it made more sense to come over here and talk to you. There was the boy, too. It's your case. I'm not saying these things are connected, but we've no idea yet what Blaydon might have been doing here last night, or who he might have had with him.'

'What did he say?'

'We haven't talked to him yet. I thought maybe you . . .'

'Where does he live?'

'Big old manor house between Harrogate and Ripon. Tuscan-villa style. Fountains, statues, maze, the lot. Handy for the A1, but not so close that the noise disturbs his peace. Surrounded by woods and walls. Tranquil. The business offices are in Leeds, but Blaydon mostly works from home.'

'What's the rest of his history?'

'The short version?'

'That'll do for now.'

'He's sixty-one years old. Started in the property business as a young lad working for an estate agent called Norman Peel, who showed him the ropes. They made a fortune throughout the eighties on Thatcher's right-to-buy scheme, buying up council houses from the tenants who'd been living in them long enough to buy legally, offering an attractive profit margin. Then Blaydon and Peel tarted them up a bit and resold them, sometimes for a massive profit. Including some on your very own East Side Estate, as well as Hollyfield, I understand. After that, they moved on to other kinds of properties and other kinds of money-making.'

'Criminal?'

'Not at first. Not as far as we can make out. Of course, it's often a thin line in his business. Blaydon eventually made enough money to buy a holiday home in Corfu shortly after the millennium, when such places were still affordable.'

'That wasn't long after the Balkan wars,' Banks said. 'What happened next?'

'A few years later, Norman Peel died. Boating accident, apparently. They were business partners by then, and Blaydon took over the reins.'

'Foul play?'

'Oh, definitely suspected. Peel was far too honest and straight to fit in with Blaydon's plans. It happened off Corfu, while Peel was a guest at Blaydon's holiday home, and nobody could prove it was anything other than a tragic accident.'

'So what criminal activities do you think he's involved in these days?'

'Some of it involves the development side. Big time. Company's called Unicorn Investments International. Rather a fanciful sort of name for it, I'd say. He's involved in shopping centres, housing estates like the Elmet Centre project

– you name it. It's a form of insider trading, but he seems to know when to snap up properties pretty cheaply, and suddenly their value is enhanced when a development is announced.'

'One of his developments?'

'Usually. But he sometimes works through others, stays at least at one remove. That's where the Kerrigans come in. As you probably know, they're club owners, not natural property developers, but they're quite happy to front some of Blaydon's more dodgy enterprises for a reasonable return.'

Timmy and Tommy Kerrigan were, on paper at least, owners of the old Bar None nightclub, now renamed The Vaults, just across the market square from where Banks and Joanna were sitting, along with an amusement arcade, also on the square. They were crooks and thugs, suspected of involvement in drug dealing and prostitution, but Banks and his team had never been able to find enough evidence to charge them with anything. Timmy was suspected of an unhealthy interest in teenage girls, whereas Tommy was gay and preferred young boys. Tommy also had a sadistic streak and a nasty temper, ready to explode into violence at a moment's notice. Their temperamental similarity to the Kray twins had been remarked on more than once, to the extent that in some quarters they were referred to as Reggie and Ronnie, though never to their faces.

'Blaydon uses them as middlemen on some deals. Glorified gofers on others. And as you no doubt know, they don't mind getting their hands dirty.'

'What else is Blaydon up to?'

'Drugs, for starters. But he's not a dealer. He doesn't buy or sell them; he merely facilitates their redistribution. People use his properties for sale and storage. But even that's not enough for him.'

'Where does the sex trafficking come in?'

'Again, it's not something he's personally involved in. At least we don't think so. He keeps his distance. But he's connected with pop-up brothels. When you think about it, Blaydon's profession is ideal for that. All those properties standing vacant. Why not make a bit of money out of them? There was a place recently, one of Blaydon's, an empty low-rise apartment building in Scarborough. Seaview Court. Some of the people who lived nearby reported hearing people yelling and seeing blokes hanging around at all hours, used condoms in the street and so on. It wasn't a big deal, so the local constabulary didn't rush to act, and by the time they did get around to checking it out, they'd closed shop and moved on. Like I said, he always manages to stay one step ahead of the law. Needless to say, he denied all knowledge.'

'There's another thing about these pop-up brothels,' Banks said. 'They often rely on trafficked girls, or boys, which means a network of far-reaching and often very nasty connections. As far as the drugs are concerned, Corfu isn't far from Albania, if my geography serves me well. He could have made contacts with criminal gangs over there. I understand that the Albanian Mafia are running most of the cocaine trade over here these days. I don't believe sex trafficking and pop-up brothels are beyond their reach, either.' Banks again thought of Zelda, her history as a trafficked girl and her work in helping put names to the faces of trafficking suspects. She had given him some useful information a while ago about an old adversary – one who got away – called Phil Keane, turning up in London again. But no one had been able to find any trace of him since, and Zelda had had to lie low at work.

'I have to admit,' Joanna said, 'that most of what we've got on Blaydon looks like guilt by association so far. But some of his visitors at home, or people he meets in Leeds city bars and restaurants, office towers, or down in London – ones we've been able to monitor – are very dodgy indeed. He may well be expanding his so-called business interests. There's an Albanian living in London called Leka Gashi we know is involved with the Shqiptare, the Albanian Mafia. And he's in bed with a major drug kingpin, also in London. Taking over, some would say. On the other hand, one thing they say about the Albanian crooks is that they'll try and get their feet under the table by treaties and cooperation. They prefer to make friends first.'

'And then?'

Joanna drew a finger across her throat. 'If that doesn't work, they're known to be extremely violent. The problem is, no one will talk, and none of the police agencies involved can get enough evidence to bring Blaydon in. Like I said, he's always one step ahead. He has men to put frighteners on potential whistle-blowers – or the Albanians do – and people on the inside to steer any dangerous investigations away from him. Occasionally, they'll net a few small fish, but the big ones keep on swimming ahead.'

Banks thought it all over for a few moments, then said, 'OK. So we've got a dead boy on the East Side Estate around the same time as Connor Clive Blaydon's Merc was spotted in the area. Blaydon's a known gangster with some very nasty local and international drugs connections. What are your thoughts? That the dead youth was working for him, or against him? On the take? Something like that?'

Joanna shrugged. 'It's possible. Drugs make sense as far as the victim is concerned. You mentioned earlier that the boy had a small amount of cocaine in his pocket. County lines, maybe? We know they recruit young kids to run drugs, especially crack and heroin, from urban centres to places like Eastvale. And the East Side Estate is just the sort of place they'd set up a trap house to sell from. Maybe the Albanians are taking over the county lines? This murder sounds like the kind of thing they would do if the boy crossed them or held out on them, or stole. Dump the poor kid's body in a rubbish bin. Sends a message.'

'Loud and clear.' Banks knew that county lines were the scourge of small-time local dealers, who were being cut out by the new business model. Instead of meeting your local supplier down at the pub and scoring, you had a young lad sent up from the city and installed in a house, taking orders by a dedicated phone set up for that very purpose – a county line. County lines had fast become the Amazon Prime of drug supply, ousting any number of smaller, independent retailers.

'We've had men canvassing the estate all day,' Banks went on, 'and nobody yet has admitted to ever seeing the lad at all before, never mind on the night he was killed. Of course, we wouldn't be surprised if some of them were lying, but not all. You said earlier that Blaydon had owned property on the East Side Estate, places he bought from right-to-buy tenants back in Thatcher's day. Does he still have any?'

'I'd have to check, but he's probably sold them all by now. He's not in the rental business. It's ironic, isn't it, how most of the homes have ended up being owned by landlords who bought them for about seventy per cent less than their market value and rent them out for more than the council ever did. Talk about a plan backfiring. Anyway, I'd assume that whoever killed the boy probably took his body there by car and dumped it. Right? The killing itself might have happened in one of the surrounding villages, or another part of town.'

'A good assumption,' said Banks. 'We still need to know how long elapsed between the killing and the dumping, and it might not be easy for the pathologist to figure out. We won't know until the post-mortem, at any rate – if then – unless we find out by some other means. But it doesn't help us a lot at the moment to know he might have been killed elsewhere.

We're already extending inquiries out from the estate to the rest of town. Nobody so far recalls seeing any cars around the time he was dumped, only maybe hearing something. We'll keep at it, but it's like getting blood out of a stone.' Banks paused. 'I'm having another pint. Why don't you join me?'

Joanna glanced at her watch. 'Better not. I should get home for dinner. Will you look into it, though? What we've been talking about, a possible connection with your murder? Will you talk to Blaydon?'

'Of course. Is someone waiting for you at home?'

'What's that got to do with anything?'

'Sorry. I didn't—'

'No, no. It's just me. I didn't mean to snap.' Joanna stood up to put on her tailored jacket, suddenly flustered, blushing. 'I . . . I just . . . As a matter of fact, there isn't anyone. It's only me and a Tesco pizza. But I didn't come here to—'

'Then, if you've no objection, I'll skip the extra pint, you skip the pizza, and we'll have a curry just around the corner.'

Joanna studied him through narrowed eyes. He couldn't tell what she was thinking, but he thought she was every bit as attractive and elegant as he had found her when they had first worked together almost seven years ago: tall and slender, a smattering of freckles across her small nose, a generous mouth, watchful green eyes, finishing school posture and stylish dress sense. A Hitchcock blonde, perhaps: Kim Novak in *Vertigo* or Tippi Hedren in *The Birds*.

Finally, Joanna grabbed the back of the chair with both hands and leaned forward. 'Very well,' she said. 'I accept. But we're going Dutch. That clear?'

Banks stood to leave. 'As crystal,' he said. 'A Dutch curry. Fine with me.'

3

When Banks got to his office the following morning, he found a message from Area Commander Gervaise asking him to report to her as soon as possible. He climbed the extra flight of stairs to the top floor and knocked on her door. She called for him to enter, and he wasn't surprised to see Assistant Chief Constable Ron McLaughlin already ensconced in a chair, coffee in hand.

'Alan,' said Gervaise when he had joined them. 'I'm not going to ask you if there are any developments yet because I know there aren't.'

'Not entirely true,' said Banks. 'I had a drink with DI Joanna MacDonald from Criminal Intelligence last night, and she pointed us towards a villain named Connor Clive Blaydon.'

ACC McLaughlin frowned. 'Blaydon?'

'You know him, sir?'

'I wouldn't say that,' said McLaughlin, 'but I know of him. He's some sort of property magnate, as I understand it.'

'Plays golf with the chief constable?'

AC Gervaise raised an admonishing finger. 'Now, now, Alan.'

'The chief constable doesn't play golf,' said McLaughlin, a ghost of a smile on his face. 'She's strictly a squash and bridge woman.'

'Sorry,' said Banks. 'Anyway, he's one of the main players in that new Elmet Centre redevelopment.'

'So what's the murder of a young boy got to do with him?' Gervaise asked.

'That I don't know,' said Banks. He gave McLaughlin a quick glance. 'Maybe nothing. Only DI MacDonald says they've been keeping an eye on Blaydon and discovered he's been meeting with one or two unsavoury characters. One's an Albanian called Leka Gashi, known to be heavily involved in the drugs trade. He's also linked to the Albanian Mafia, the Shqiptare.'

'My, my, Blaydon does get around,' said Gervaise. 'How is this man linked to the murder?'

'We don't know that he is yet, ma'am, but his car was spotted leaving Eastvale last night, just after the time we think the boy's body was dumped. And the boy was carrying a small amount of cocaine.'

'You know this for certain?' said McLaughlin. 'About the car?'

'According to Criminal Intelligence and ANPR surveillance,' said Banks. 'There's nothing specific against Blaydon, except one of his properties was recently used as a pop-up brothel in Scarborough. Unbeknownst to him, or so he says. There could also be this Albanian connection. But it's all speculative right now. We can't even prove Blaydon was in the car that night, but I'll be having a chat with him later today as a matter of course.'

'Tread carefully,' said Gervaise.

'Don't worry,' said Banks, 'I'm not going to go accusing him of anything.'

'Watch out that you don't.' Gervaise put her coffee mug down. 'Golf or not, he's not without influence. Anyway, I wanted to talk to you about handling the East Side case. I suppose you know it's already high profile?'

'Yes,' said Banks. 'I've got a morning meeting planned with my team.'

'I'll organise a press conference for noon,' said Gervaise. 'Make sure you brief me fully before then. I'll be having a meeting with Adrian first.'

Banks nodded. Adrian Moss was a bit of a drip as far as he was concerned, but he did the useful and thankless job of media liaison officer, placing himself as a kind of buffer between the police and the media, translating the needs of one into something acceptable for the other. 'Any chance of more officers?' Banks asked. 'We could do with a lot more help on the house-to-house inquiries, and I need to set up a murder room.'

'I don't want us to be seen to be sparing any expense on this one,' said ACC McLaughlin. 'I know things have been tight recently, and it might seem like a cynical move, releasing more resources for what we know to be a high-profile case, but that's the way these things go.'

'I can't see anyone objecting, sir,' said Banks. 'It *is* the murder of a child, after all.'

McLaughlin nodded and turned to Gervaise. 'Catherine?'

'Plainclothes officers are rather thin on the ground,' said Gervaise, 'but I can let you have civilian staff to man a murder room here at the station. We can also find a few more uniformed officers to help with the door-to-doors and so on. You, DI Cabbot and DC Masterson will be working the case full-time, and I hardly need tell you there'll be no leave until the matter is settled. You can also use our CID resources as you need. Just come and ask. They can also take over general duties day-to-day while you're occupied with this business.'

It was nothing less than Banks expected, though he did feel he could do with another detective on his team. With DS Winsome Jackman away on maternity leave, expecting her first child at any moment, and his second DC, Doug Wilson, having recently left the force, he was lower than he had ever been on staff. The extra uniformed officers would help, of course, but there would still be a lot of work for the three detectives. 'I suppose I can manage with Gerry and Annie for the time being, but I'll want a major trawl for information, especially possible sightings. As of now, we don't know where the lad came from, or how he got here. Someone must have seen him. We doubt he's from around here – nobody on the estate admits to recognising him – and when we found him he had nothing but a small stash of coke in his pocket. No money, no belongings, no identification, no keys. Nothing. That stuff must be somewhere, and someone must have seen him coming and going. Bus station. Taxi ranks. Trains.'

Gervaise nodded. 'We'll get extra uniformed officers and PCSOs out on it today.'

McLaughlin cleared his throat. 'You should also perhaps liaise with drugs squad officers at County HQ, as you require.'

'Thanks, sir,' said Banks, though after his conversation with DI MacDonald the previous evening he wasn't sure which drugs squad detectives he should be trusting.

McLaughlin stood up and straightened his uniform. 'Right. I'd better get back. Catherine. Alan.' He nodded to them, put his cap on and left the office.

'Well . . .' said AC Gervaise, visibly relaxed after her boss's departure. 'That went well. What do you think about the drugs angle?'

'We only found a small amount. Just enough for personal use. As yet, there's no reason to think the boy's murder was drug-related.'

'Come on, Alan. If you take into account that his body was found on the East Side Estate and that DI MacDonald felt it necessary to let you know Connor Clive Blaydon was in the area at the time, I think we can live with the assumption that *something* might have been going on. It has county lines written all over it.' Gervaise stood up. 'I have to go. Don't forget, Alan, brief me after your morning meeting.'

Zelda sat by the window of her hotel room and gazed over the river at the dome of St Paul's Cathedral surrounded by cranes and half-built modern structures that would soon, along with the gherkins, cheese graters, shards and tulips, dominate the entire city skyline. She had had a difficult night, and she was still recovering, feeling tired and numb. It had started, as it usually did, with a nightmare at about three o'clock in the morning, the details of which scurried back into the dark recesses when she woke, leaving only vague impressions of unbearably slow journeys across darkening post-industrial landscapes, through crumbling ruins and over mud as sticky as treacle. There was always someone, or some*thing*, chasing her, or hiding in the shadows, and she could never get far enough ahead to feel safe. She also felt that there *was* nowhere she would feel safe, for the place she was seeking didn't exist, and if it should suddenly be conjured into existence, she wouldn't be able to find it, or she would have to swim so far underwater that she wouldn't have enough breath to get there.

As usual, she woke gasping for air, her heart thudding, and that was when things got worse, when she started remembering the real terrors of her years as a sex-slave: the pain of her first anal rape, a broken nose, a messy abortion in a cheap backstreet clinic in Belgrade, all in excruciating detail, faces included.

So she did what she always did: got up, took two of the tranquillisers her doctor had prescribed and made a cup of chamomile tea. Then she took out her Moleskine notebook and jotted down what she could remember of her dreams. The doctor had told her it would help her come to terms with her experiences, but she didn't think it had done much good so far. Nevertheless, she persevered.

When she had written down as much as she could remember, she put on her headphones. Zelda had three favourite symphonies – Beethoven's 'Pastorale', Tchaikovsky's 'Pathétique' and Dvořák's 'New World' – and she always turned to one of them at such times. She didn't care how corny they were, or how many times she had listened to them. This morning she chose the Dvořák and settled by the window to watch the daylight gently nudge away the darkness as the city came to life in all its quotidian glory, from the first joggers on the embankment to the quickly multiplying hordes of pedestrians heading for work, the rumbling and clattering of commuter trains over Blackfriars Bridge, then the first tourist boats cutting their wakes along the Thames to Greenwich.

And by then the world was beginning to feel bearable again.

That day, the dawn had begun with an unusually rosy glow. Rust-stained tugboats and overloaded barges passed by below her window. The broad dark river fascinated her. It was like a living being, with its swirling oil slicks and currents like ropes of muscle twisting in the wake of the boats. *Sweet Thames.*

Sometimes her head felt almost as stuffed full of random quotes as it was of faces. The words all came from the boxes of books people donated to the orphanage, of course. There weren't only lurid potboilers, detective stories, thrillers and romances, but also hefty Victorian novels and poetry collections, too – Dickens, Thackeray, Trollope, Hardy, Keats, Wordsworth, Spenser – as well as children's books by Enid Blyton, Roald Dahl and Jacqueline Wilson. Zelda had read them all, from cover to cover. Her recollection of words wasn't as good as it was of faces – she certainly didn't have a photographic memory – but it was probably better than average, and she remembered a lot. She was hungry to learn, and those hours spent reading in a foreign language that was becoming more her own every day, were the happiest times of her life. Until the day that life came to an abrupt end.

In those dark hours, as the bad memories ebbed with the growing light, the healing power of the music and the numbing effect of the tranquillisers, she often wondered why she had never been tempted by suicide. But she never had. Once, perhaps, she had come close. In a small and ugly motel near Banja Luka, exhausted and hurting after a particularly long night of rough and filthy long-distance lorry drivers, the idea had reared its head briefly. She had considered whether the belt of the dress that lay draped over the bedside chair would be long enough and strong enough for her to hang herself from the coat hook on the back of the locked door. But she had never got as far as finding out before the door opened again and another man came in.

Thoughts of the past began to dissipate, the music ended and Zelda put her headphones away to make more tea as she contemplated going out for breakfast. Then she began to think about Hawkins and all that had happened since that night Alan and Annie came for dinner just before Christmas. It seemed almost a lifetime ago.

If she was going to stay in London for a few more days, she could do a bit more detective work. She had lain dormant for too long, but news of Hawkins's death galvanised her towards action. Over the past few months, she had thought more than once about reporting what she had seen that evening she had followed him. But to whom? She couldn't be certain that she trusted anyone in the department. It was the same reason she hadn't told Alan. When all was said and done, she had withheld the information for her own reasons. If she had reported on Hawkins meeting Keane, a known criminal, that would have been the end of it one way or another. She would have been cut out of any investigation, if there was one, and she would never find Keane, or Petar and Goran Tadić, the ones she really wanted.

First, she needed a plan. If Hawkins had been meeting Keane to tell him about her interest in the photo of him with Petar Tadić – and what other reason could there be? – it meant that Hawkins was in bed with the enemy, perhaps feeding them information so that some of the most wanted men could evade discovery. Perhaps he had also informed them when Zelda would be on duty at a specific port, station or airport, so they could avoid it. If so, the enemy had turned against him – not unusual in that risky and violent business – and she would like to know why. Had he tried to escape their clutches, tried to break free from them? He should have known the price of that. She also remembered that Banks and Annie had told her that Keane liked fires. He would probably know all about chip pans.

So what could she do? She was marooned in London for a few days, which wasn't an *un*pleasant situation. Normally, she would invite Raymond down for a mini-break, but he was away in America for meetings in advance of an important US exhibition coming up soon. She could do some shopping, go to the Picasso exhibition at the Tate Modern, try to get some last-minute theatre tickets. Shakespeare at The Globe, perhaps? But no. She remembered the last time she'd been there, trapped at the far end of a row, feeling claustrophobic and unable to escape a dreadful production of *A Midsummer Night's Dream*. It had been more like a midsummer night's nightmare.

Anyway, there were plenty of diversions for her in London, but the main thing, she realised, was to work out what she could do about Hawkins and Keane. Danvers and Deborah wouldn't tell her anything, that was for certain, and she didn't really know where to start. She had drawn a blank following

Hawkins on those few occasions over the last months she had been able to do so, but perhaps if she applied herself now, with so much free time on her hands, she might be able to find out more. At least she could make a start by going to have a look at his burned-out house.

Unlike the numerous television depictions of large open-plan offices crowded with scruffy detectives in a fug of cigarette smoke, shirtsleeves rolled up, ties askew, resting the backs of their thighs against desks overflowing with unfinished paper-work, Styrofoam coffee cups in hand and phones constantly ringing, there were only four people present at the Tuesday morning briefing in the boardroom of Eastvale Regional HQ, and all were seated, none smoking.

The room was wood-panelled with ornate ceiling cornices, a chandelier and a large and highly-polished oval table. The accoutrements were all present – the large flat-screen TV set, the ubiquitous whiteboards plastered with photographs of the victim from all angles, indecipherable scrawls and arrows linking one thing to another. And the coffee cups, not Styrofoam but paper. From large gilt-framed oil paintings on the walls, nineteenth-century wool barons with mutton-chop sideboards and roast-beef complexions watched over the proceedings.

Banks gathered up his notes. He had enjoyed his dinner with Joanna MacDonald the previous evening. When she let her guard down even just a little, she was charming and enter-taining company – funny, sharp, intelligent – wise, even. He wondered again, as he often had, why she so rarely allowed herself the lapse, kept herself on such a tight rein. After dinner, he had got home in time for a fairly early night, with very little to drink, and as a result he felt unusually refreshed that morning.

'As of now,' he began, 'we still have nothing much to go on. The boy looks about thirteen years old, he's dark-skinned, maybe of Middle Eastern heritage, but he could have grown up here, for all we know. He's been stabbed four times, and we found a small amount of cocaine in his jeans pocket. Most likely he didn't live locally, or the odds are that we'd have located *someone* who would have seen him around. I know, as you all do, that the East Side Estate in general can be pretty uncommunicative, if not actively against us on occasion, but though there are plenty of drugs circulating, there are few murders there, and it's my sense that the people are in shock. I don't believe everyone we've talked to so far is lying about not knowing the boy.'

'So how did he get there and where did he come from?' asked DC Gerry Masterson.

'That we don't know,' admitted Banks. 'And we need answers. Out of town, most likely, I'd say. There aren't any Middle Eastern families living in Eastvale, as far as I know. It's possible he was a student, I suppose, but I'd say he was too young to be at the college. Again, that can be easily checked. He may have been visiting friends in the area. Something else we'll have to follow up on. Wherever he's from, someone dumped him on our patch and it's our job to find out who. We've got an appeal out with the media, so someone will have to collate the responses, should any come in. The ACC has authorised a working budget, AC Gervaise has okayed over-time and civilian staff to man the murder room, and we have extra uniformed officers pounding the streets.

'Mrs Grunwell, in whose wheelie bin the body was found, says that she put the rubbish out at ten o'clock on Sunday night, as usual, and she heard a car nearby between eleven and eleven-thirty that same night. She also thought she heard someone kick or bump into the bin about the same time. She's eighty-five, but in my estimation, we can take her as a reliable witness on these points. We also got confirmation of the car and the bump from two other houses at that end of the street, so we can probably accept that the body was dumped between eleven o'clock and eleven-thirty on Sunday night. Not so late that there might not have been someone about, but it *was* a Sunday, and things tend to get quiet fairly early then, even on the East Side Estate. What we don't know, in addition to who dumped him, of course, is where he came from or how far he was driven. Gerry, any theories?'

'Well, you wouldn't want to drive very far with a body in your boot, would you, guv? Or in your back seat. I mean, you might get pulled over for speeding or driving through a red light or something. It's risky. There'd also be traces in the car. Blood, for a start, if he was stabbed. You know how hard it is to get rid of those sorts of things completely.'

'You're saying you think he wasn't transported far, then?'

'That would be my guess.'

Banks nodded. 'OK. Sounds reasonable.'

'That may indicate that whoever did it knows the area,' said Annie. 'Its reputation. Knows that we might not be too surprised to find a dead drug user dumped there.'

'Good point.'

'What about CCTV?' Gerry asked.

'There isn't any functioning CCTV on the East Side Estate and not a hell of a lot nearby, either. Right now, it's important for us to keep circulating the computer-generated photo. We've already been sending copies around the media and liaising with local police and representatives from Middle Eastern communities and mosques in Bradford, Dewsbury, Leeds, Huddersfield and other nearby towns and cities. The problem is that we don't know whether he's from Iraq, Jordan, Syria, Lebanon or any of the dozen or more other countries that make up what we call the Middle East. We don't even know if he was a Muslim, though we are making inquiries in mosques. It could be a lengthy process, or we could get lucky.' Banks paused and sipped at his bitter, tepid coffee. 'We also need to know why he was dumped. And perhaps more specifically, why he was dumped in Eastvale.'

'You think it was personal, guv?' Gerry asked. 'Something to do with the owner of the bin?'

'No. As I said, Mrs Grunwell is eighty-five, and I think we can pretty well rule out a vendetta or gang war involving her. No, I think we need to look elsewhere. And why a rubbish bin?'

'Well,' said Annie, 'it might simply have been convenient for someone passing the end of Malden Terrace on the way out of town. I suppose if you had a body in your car and you were after somewhere to dispose of it, a wheelie bin's as good a place as any.'

Banks nodded. 'It would help if we could determine whether it was a warning or a statement,' he went on, 'or simply a matter of arbitrary convenience, as you suggest. Could there be some other reason? It's not as if whoever killed him could hope to conceal the crime for very long by dumping him there.'

'Unless they didn't know which day was bin collection day,' said Annie.

Banks smiled. 'There's always that. We should be glad they're not on strike right now, too.'

'Could it be a hate crime?' Gerry suggested.

'It's a possibility we should keep in mind,' said Banks. 'There's certainly plenty of casual racism. Even Mrs Grunwell referred to "darkies".'

'He could have been dumped as a warning,' Annie suggested.

'Yes. But to whom? And about what? I mean, if his murder and placement in a rubbish bin was a warning of some kind, the person being warned had to be made aware of it, didn't he? That would surely be the point?'

'Can we be absolutely certain that there's no connection with Mrs Grunwell, like Gerry suggested?' Annie asked.

'I very much doubt it,' said Banks. 'You've talked to her. You know what I mean. I doubt that referring to "darkies" necessarily leads to murder.'

'Even so, guv,' Gerry said. 'Maybe she caused some trouble for someone? I mean, old people can be pretty wrong-headed or stubborn sometimes. Cantankerous, even. Maybe somebody wanted to do something and she wouldn't give way? Does she own her house? Did someone want very badly to buy it?'

'Wouldn't it have been easier just to get rid of *her* in that case?' said Banks. 'Surely a fragile old woman is far easier to kill than a fit young lad?'

'Less likely to merit an investigation, too,' Annie added. 'It wouldn't be hard to make it seem like she had an accident.'

'I suppose so,' Gerry said. 'But I'm only speculating on possibilities. If it's a warning, it might just be to say to the old lady "be careful or this could happen to you".'

'I still don't get the connection,' said Banks. 'A Middle Eastern boy and an elderly woman. And what about the coke?'

'Maybe it's not relevant,' Annie said. 'Just a small amount for personal use, like a packet of cigarettes or a hip flask. And perhaps the warning wasn't for Mrs Grunwell specifically, but for someone else on the street. It might have been giving too much away to dump the body in the bin of the person they really wanted to rattle.'

'It's possible,' Banks said. 'In which case, whoever it was meant for will have got the message. We'll re-interview all the people from Malden Close and Terrace, see if we can find a chink in someone's armour. Stefan? Do the CSIs have anything for us yet?'

DS Stefan Nowak, Crime Scene Manager, shook his head and spoke for the first time. 'We've just about finished with the scene. The rain didn't leave us a lot to go on. No footprints, no tyre tracks, nothing like that. Vic Manson worked his magic with the fingerprints on the bin, but they didn't match any on the databases we have access to. The only prints on the cocaine packet are the boy's. The coke's at the lab. We're analysing his clothes. They're pretty generic. The spectrograph might show up something, traces he might have picked up from somewhere.'

'Right,' said Banks. 'Basically, we shouldn't be wasting our time having meetings. We should get out there and get on with the job. There is just one more thing.' Banks had another taste of his coffee, grimaced and went on. 'I had a brief and unscheduled meeting with DI Joanna MacDonald from County HQ yesterday evening,' he said. He noticed Annie roll her eyes. 'As a matter of fact, she got in touch with me when she heard about the body. It seems that Criminal Intelligence have their eyes on a property developer called Connor Clive Blaydon, head of Unicorn Investments International, one of the companies behind the new Elmet Centre development. Lives down Harrogate way. Apparently, his car was picked up by ANPR on the way out of Eastvale around a quarter past eleven on Sunday night. As of yet, we have no reason to link him with the murder except the timing and proximity, but DI MacDonald seems to think he's up to no good wherever he goes, that his interests include drugs and that he might have friends on the inside, so let's keep this to ourselves.

'She also raised the spectre of county lines, as did AC Gervaise earlier this morning. It makes a lot of sense when you consider the age of the victim and the drugs link. We've known that city dealers have been using kids as young as twelve or thirteen to transport and deal drugs for them in small towns and villages all over the country for some time now, though we haven't got hold of anyone to confirm it's happening here yet. Maybe our Mr Blaydon is a middleman in something like that? Maybe he's just starting up? It seems he likes to play with the big boys. He's got some sort of a gangster complex. Gerry, I'd like you to do your thing and put together a dossier on him. DI MacDonald said she'd send over her files this morning. I'll make sure you get them. Have a word with the drugs squad, too. See if any of this rings any bells with them. But be careful what you let slip.'

'Got it, guv,' said Gerry. 'I'm to ask the drugs squad if they know anything about Blaydon dealing drugs without mentioning that I'm asking about Blaydon dealing drugs.'

Banks grinned. 'I'm sure you'll find a way, Gerry.'

'Yes, guv. What else is Blaydon into?'

'Bit of everything, it seems,' said Banks. 'Your typical all-round equal opportunity criminal. Dodgy property deals, pop-up brothels—'

'Pop-up brothels?' said Gerry. 'In Eastvale?'

'Not yet, as far as I know. But stranger things have happened.'

'I can just see your Mrs Grunwell running one of those,' Annie said.

Banks smiled at the thought. 'You may be right at that. There are stranger things than an eighty-five-year-old madam. Perhaps someone can ask her about it when we talk to her again. In the meantime, you've all got your tasks to do.'

Zelda had no idea what she would gain from visiting Hawkins's house – probably nothing – but at least it got her out of the hotel room and gave her something to think about other than her bad dreams and her traumatic past. It was a fine spring day, and hordes of tourists with jackets or sweaters tied around their waists, mixed with the joggers on the wharf, stood with their backs to the river taking selfies with St Paul's in the background. Zelda had chosen jeans, a black T-shirt and a tan kidskin jacket to wear for her outing, with her shoulder bag strapped across her chest and her black hair tied in a ponytail.

Across the Thames, sunlight reflected on the windows of the traffic jammed up on Victoria Embankment. Just past the Oxo Tower, she had to weave her way through a rowdy group of Italian schoolchildren, whose teachers didn't seem to be making much of an attempt to keep them disciplined. At Waterloo Bridge, she climbed the steps between the National Theatre and the BFI and turned left towards Waterloo Underground station, where she took the Northern Line.

Zelda had almost as good a memory for directions as she did for faces. She had only visited Hawkins's house once before, briefly, over a year ago, for a 'department mixer', but the minute she got off the tube at Highgate and made her way up the steps to Archway, she knew instinctively to turn left down the main road, then left again into a residential area of semi-detached houses. Some were painted in light pastel colours, but she remembered that Hawkins's house had kept its basic red-brick facade, with white trim around the bay windows, a porch with two white Doric columns and a post-age-stamp lawn behind a low brick wall and trimmed privet hedges. A short flight of steps led up to the front porch. Today, though, it would have stood out on any street. The windows were all gone and the garden was piled with burned sticks of furniture.

The neighbours were lucky, Zelda thought, when she spotted Hawkins's burned-out house. Though their house appeared to be relatively undamaged, it was also cordoned off, and Zelda imagined the owners had been told to move out until the fire investigators were certain it was safe to return home.

Hawkins's house was still structurally intact – and the only areas that showed fire damage were around the windows and door – but Zelda knew that the inside would be a mess of charred wood, twisted metal, melted plastic, glass and worse. She remembered the kitchen from her one brief visit. It had seemed very modern and high-tech to her, all brushed steel surfaces and professional cookware, which went hand in hand with the idea of Hawkins as a gourmet. She couldn't have said for certain, but she didn't think there had been a chip pan in sight.

What surprised her now was that there was still so much activity around the place. Though the fire engines must have been and gone, a fire inspector's van was parked outside along with two police patrol cars. One uniformed officer stood on guard under the front porch, and as she passed, Zelda noticed a man in a white coverall walking out carrying a cardboard box, which he placed in the boot of an unmarked car. He paused to talk with another uniformed officer, who was sitting in one of the cars, before going back into the house again. Then a woman came out, also wearing a white coverall and carrying a cardboard box. Did they do this at every domestic fire scene? She could see one or two curtains twitching in the nearby houses.

Zelda didn't want to be caught dawdling. They might think she was suspicious if they saw her watching them. She also wondered whether they had CCTV nearby, or someone noting down all passers-by who showed an interest. But it was like a car crash; a person could hardly walk by without stopping for a peek at whatever was going on. So she allowed herself to stand for a few moments. Perhaps she was getting paranoid, or she had read too many spy novels, but she also kept an eye out for signs of anyone following her. She hadn't seen anyone, but that didn't mean no one was there. She was already starting to feel out of her depth in this sleuthing game.

A man came out of one of the houses just in front of her, gave her a quick glance, then crossed the road and went into Hawkins's house. The policeman at the door seemed to know him. It looked to Zelda as if he had probably been questioning the neighbour across the street, and probably not for the first time, as it was nearly three days since the fire. That indicated to her that they might not be quite satisfied with the chip-pan theory.

Zelda started walking down the street and noticed a pub sign about a hundred yards ahead. She checked her watch and saw it was almost one o'clock. Lunchtime. Why not treat herself to a pub lunch and make a few discreet inquiries while she was there?

If Blaydon's mansion wasn't quite as large as Banks had expected, his extensive gardens certainly made up for it. Banks drove through the open wrought-iron gates in a high surrounding wall of dark stone. A gravel drive wound first through woods of ash, hazel, beech and yew trees, which formed a natural tunnel, then through carefully designed and cultivated gardens – a trellised arbour, a wisteria grove or rose garden here, and a gazebo there – leading ultimately past neatly trimmed topiary and imitation Greek and Roman statuary, complete with missing limbs and lichen stains, to a large pond scabbed with water lilies. At its centre stood an elaborate fountain. Water sprayed in all directions from the mouths of cherubim and seraphim with puffy cheeks and curly hair. And was that a maze Banks glimpsed beyond the fountain?

'Bloody hell,' said Banks. 'You'd think he's had Capability Brown in to come up with this lot.'

Though the grounds resembled those of a Tuscan villa, the house itself was bland. It was certainly large, however – three storeys of limestone and brick, complete with bay windows, gables and a low pitched, slate roof. At the front stood an ostentatious porch supported by stone columns.

'Shall we knock or ring the bell?'

'The bell,' said Annie. 'I want to hear what tune it plays.'

The bell didn't play any tune at all; it just made a dull electronic buzz for as long as Banks held the button down. Eventually, a slender middle-aged man in a dark suit and waistcoat opened the door and regarded them with an expression of mixed surprise and distaste. He raised a bushy eyebrow in question.

Banks and Annie pulled out their warrant cards. 'Mr Blaydon?' said Banks.

'Please follow me,' said the man, turning. 'Mr Blaydon is in his study. I'll announce you.'

Banks and Annie exchanged looks, then stood in the large high-ceilinged entrance hall and waited. Banks gazed at the gilt-framed oil paintings hung on the wainscotted walls: a stormy seascape with a listing sailing ship, peasants bent over gathering sheaves at harvest time.

Then the man returned. 'Mr Blaydon will see you now, sir, madam,' he said.

Banks and Annie followed him through a door beside the broad staircase and along a narrow corridor lined with framed pencil drawings, mostly nudes. The butler, or whatever he was, knocked on one of the doors and a voice said, 'Enter.'

The butler opened the door and Banks and Annie entered. A man sat facing them across a large desk, his back to the mullioned windows, which framed a view of the extensive gardens. The desk was scattered with papers, and the rest of the place was similarly untidy. The window was partially open, and Banks could hear birds singing in the garden.

Blaydon stood up, made his way past a couple of piles of paper and shook hands with them both, then went back to his chair. 'Pull up a couple of chairs,' he said, then looked around at the mess and smiled. 'Just dump those files on the floor. I like a bit of disorder. Can't bear everything in its place. It used to be a bone of contention, I can you tell you. Gabriella – the wife as was – she liked everything just so. For the sake of our marriage, we agreed that this room is sacrosanct, though I can't say it did any good in the long run.'

'You've separated?'

'Divorced,' said Blaydon. 'A couple of years back.'

'Kids?'

'One of each. Hang on just a minute.' He pressed a buzzer on his desk and the man who had answered the door reappeared.

'Tea or coffee?' Blaydon asked. 'Or something stronger, perhaps?'

'Coffee would be fine,' said Banks.

Annie nodded in agreement.

'Fine, then,' said Blaydon, and the man went off.

'The butler?' Banks inquired.

'Who? Jeeves? I suppose so. Though I don't think they call themselves that any more. And that's not his real name, of course. Hates it when I call him that. He's Roberts. He helps out around the place. Better than a wife, and much less trouble. Now what can I do for you? You didn't tell me anything over the phone.'

Blaydon looked like a retired academic, thought Banks, who had met a few in his time. The casual lemon sweater over an open-neck white shirt, unruly head of brown, grey-flecked hair, aquiline nose, keen, watchful eyes behind wire-framed spectacles. He wasn't in the least bit imposing; in fact, he seemed perfectly relaxed, as if he might have been sitting there marking a pile of exam papers rather than renting out empty properties to drug dealers or madams of pop-up brothels.

'Were you in Eastvale on Sunday evening?' Banks asked.

'Eastvale? Yes, I was.'

'Why?'

Blaydon leaned back in his chair. It creaked. 'Why? Well, as a matter of fact, I was having dinner with some business colleagues.' He frowned. 'I'm sorry, but what does this have to do with anything?'

'We're investigating an incident,' said Annie. 'We're questioning anyone who might be able to help us.'

'I see. I'm afraid I can't help you at all. I went to the restaurant, dined and left. I saw no incident. What sort of thing are we talking about?'

Banks paused, then said, 'It was a murder.'

'Murder? Good Lord. I think I would have remembered something like that.'

Roberts returned with the coffee, silver carafe on a silver tray, with a matching silver milk jug and sugar bowls. Banks took his black and Annie took milk and one sugar. Blaydon declined. When Roberts had gone, they carried on.

'Which restaurant were you at?' Banks asked.

'Marcel's. Le Coq d'Or. It's on—'

'I know where Le Coq d'Or is,' said Banks. It was tucked away on a narrow side street of twee shops and antiquarian book dealers between Market Street and York Road, at the back of the market square. It was also the most expensive restaurant in Eastvale – in the entire Dales, for that matter – and had been awarded not one, but two Michelin stars. Neither

Banks nor Annie had ever eaten there, and probably never would.

'We often dine there,' Blaydon went on. 'His truffle and—'

'Who were you dining with?' Annie's question stopped Blaydon mid-sentence.

'I told you. Business colleagues.'

'Can you give me their names?'

'I don't want you bothering my friends about such matters. I've told you, none of us saw or heard anything unusual. I'm assuming whatever happened was near Marcel's?'

'Friends?' Annie said. 'I thought you said business colleagues.'

Blaydon gave her a cold stare. 'Business colleagues. Friends. What does it matter? I don't want you bothering them.'

'We promise not to bother them,' Annie said.

'And we'll find out one way or another,' Banks added.

Blaydon sighed and shot them a poisonous glance. 'If you must know, it was the Kerrigan brothers. Thomas and Timothy.'

Banks whistled. 'Tommy and Timmy Kerrigan, eh? Reg and Ronnie. They certainly get around. Fine company you keep.'

'The Kerrigans are respectable businessmen. We do a fair bit of business together.'

'Like the Elmet Centre?'

'That's one project we're involved in, yes.'

'A pretty big one, too. Did you drive to Eastvale?'

'Not personally. No licence, you see. Slight difference of opinion with a breathalyser. I had my chauffeur, Frankie, drive me and wait for me out front. Where did this murder take place?'

'That would be Frankie Wallace?' Banks said.

'Yes.'

'What time did you arrive at the restaurant?' Annie asked.

'Seven-thirty, or thereabouts.'

'And what time did you leave?'

'Late.'

'Around eleven?'

'Around that time, yes.'

'That's rather a long time to spend over your frog's legs and snails, isn't it? Doesn't the restaurant close earlier than that? It was a Sunday night, after all.'

'Marcel is a friend,' said Blaydon. 'He's happy to stay open for his best customers as long as they wish. I mean, it's hardly your Nando's or Pizza Express. And you have it quite wrong about the food he serves. There are no snails—'

'We don't really care about snails, sir,' Banks cut in. 'So you were in Le Coq d'Or having dinner with the Kerrigan brothers, and your driver Frankie Wallace was out front waiting to take you home from half past seven until eleven on Sunday? Right?'

'That is correct.'

'And you didn't leave the restaurant at all during that time?'

'I didn't nip out to murder someone, if that's what you're suggesting. Who was it, by the way? Who was the victim?'

'A young lad,' said Banks. 'We think he might have been mixed up with drugs.'

'It's a terrible thing, these days,' said Blaydon. 'One reads so much about the damage drugs can do. I contribute to a number of rehabilitation centres. Try to do my bit, you know. Give something back.'

'For what?'

'I wasn't born with a silver spoon in my mouth,' said Blaydon. 'I made my way up the hard way. Through sheer hard slog. You're just like all the rest. You slag off entrepreneurs like me, but where would you be without us? Still living in fucking caves, that's where.'

'We already know a bit about how you made your way up in the world,' said Banks. 'But that's not what we're interested in.'

'I'm still trying to work out what you *are* interested in. Is this a fishing expedition of some kind? If so, should I have my solicitor present?'

'What might we be fishing for?' Annie asked.

'Don't ask me.'

Banks took out Peter Darby's photographic rendering of the victim from his briefcase and showed it to Blaydon. 'Ever seen this lad?'

Blaydon squinted at the photo and turned back to Banks. 'No, I can't say as I have. Arab kid, is he?'

'We don't know where he's from.' Banks put the photo away. 'Do you know a man called George Fanthorpe?' he asked.

'Farmer Fanthorpe?'

'Yes,' Blaydon said after a slight hesitation. 'We did business occasionally. But it was some time ago. I heard he was sent to prison.'

'That's right. He'll be away for a while. What sort of business did you do?'

'Nothing criminal, if that's what you're thinking. I had some projects he was interested in investing in. I bought shares in a couple of racehorses he trained. That sort of thing.'

'Pretty pally, were you?'

'I wouldn't say that. It was a business relationship. Maybe the occasional drink. Besides, what does George Fanthorpe have to do with anything?'

'The Farmer had his dirty little fingers in all kinds of pies,' Banks went on. 'I should know. I was the one who put him away. I was just wondering where your interests coincided.'

'I've had about enough of this,' said Blaydon, pushing his chair back from the desk.

Banks sipped some coffee. It was rich and strong. 'Just a few more questions, sir, then we'll get out of your hair.'

Blaydon stayed put. 'Well, hurry up about it, then.' He glanced at his watch. A Rolex, Banks noticed. 'Five more minutes and I'm calling my solicitor.'

'Of course. What do you know about pop-up brothels?'

Blaydon laughed. 'About *what*?'

'Pop-up brothels. I don't see what's so funny.'

'I'm sorry,' said Blaydon. 'I just had this image of opening a book and having a cartoon tenement building pop up with ladies of the night in garter belts and frilly underwear waving from the windows.'

'Own many tenements, do you?' Annie asked.

'Oh, come on. It was a joke. Anyway, what's a pop-up brothel?'

'Exactly what it sounds like,' said Banks. 'It's a brothel that pops up in a vacant house or building for a limited period of time. The people who operate them use online escort agencies and social media to get the word out to those in the know. They can be quite sophisticated.'

'Well, I never. It takes all sorts.'

'I think you'll agree,' Annie said, 'that a man in your business is in a pretty good position to profit from something like that. All those empty properties just sitting there.'

'I hope you're not suggesting that I—'

'Stop playing games,' said Banks. 'Ever heard of a man called Leka Gashi?'

'I can't say as I have.'

'He's a nasty piece of work. An Albanian gangster known to be involved in the drug trade.'

'What makes you think I would know someone like that?'

'It's our business to know these things,' said Banks.

'Have you been watching me?'

'What about that apartment building in Scarborough?'

'What building?'

'Seaview Court, or whatever it was called.'

'Let me get this straight. You're trying to tell me that Seaview Court is a pop-up brothel?'

'Was,' said Banks.

'Do you have any proof of that?'

'You know quite well that we don't. Someone must have tipped you off.'

Blaydon spread his hands. 'As I'm sure you're aware, I don't micromanage every property on my books. There are far too many for that. Are we finished here?'

Banks glanced at Annie and they both stood up. Before they left, Banks leaned forward and rested his palms on Blaydon's desk. 'One thing you might bear in mind,' he said, 'is that pop-up brothels quite often involve girls trafficked from Eastern Europe and elsewhere, mostly against their will. They also bring you into contact with people like Gashi, who can be very dangerous and unpredictable when the chips are down. Their warnings if you step out of line tend to be very swift and very final.'

'You're telling me this, why?'

'I'm telling because you might think you're a very clever man and a big player in their game, but in reality you're not. You're not a match for these people, and you could get yourself very badly hurt, or even killed, if you continue playing at their table. To put it simply, they eat people like you for breakfast.'

Blaydon stood. He wasn't very tall, Banks noticed, and quite slight in build, but he possessed a kind of wired, nervous energy. 'Thank you for your concern, Superintendent,' he said, then bowed towards Annie. 'And DI Cabbot, too, of course. I will certainly bear what you said in mind should I find myself approached by any of the people you mention.'

'You do that, Mr Blaydon,' said Banks. 'And there's no need to bother Jeeves. We'll find our own way out.'

The pub was separated from the houses on both sides by narrow alleys that led through to the next street, and it stood a short distance back from the pavement. There were a few benches and wooden tables with umbrellas out front, for those who wished to enjoy their drinks and have a smoke in the sunlight. By the doors, a blackboard listed the specials of the day. The sagging roof and weathered beams that framed the whitewashed facade showed the pub's age, and colourful hanging baskets and window-boxes gave it a welcoming atmosphere. As it happened, the inside was just as pleasant, with its light pine tables, brass and polished surfaces.

The young barman smiled as Zelda approached the bar and picked up a menu. She asked him for a small glass of Pinot Grigio while she studied it. By the time he delivered her drink, she had decided on the grilled sole and Greek salad. By the way he blushed when he handed her the drink, Zelda could tell he was in love with her already. Well, perhaps not love. She waited at the bar and sipped her wine while he passed her order on to the kitchen. He seemed surprised to see her still standing there when he returned and asked where she wanted to sit. There were plenty of empty tables, and she pointed to one behind her, in his direct view.

'I notice there's been a fire,' she said, gesturing over her shoulder. 'Just up the street there.'

'Yes,' he said. 'Terrible business. Poor fellow died.'

'Did you know him?'

'I wouldn't say I knew him, but he came in here often enough to be called a regular.' He pointed to a small corner table. 'That's where he used to sit. Mr Hawkins. Terrible business.'

'What happened?'

'Nobody knows. Rumour has it there was a chip-pan fire, but . . .' He shook his head slowly. 'Like I said, I didn't know him well, but I can't see it.'

'He didn't like chips?'

The barman laughed. 'It's not that, though I can't say he ever ordered any. No. He just wasn't much of a drinker.'

'How could you tell that?'

'You get to recognise the signs when you do a job like mine. He'd come in now and then, usually after work, I suppose, sip his half pint of Pride and work on his crossword, then he'd be off. Just a bit of quiet time between the office and home. Most serious drinkers would down three or four double whiskies in the time it took him to do that.'

'How do you know he didn't go home and knock back a bottle of whisky?'

'Well, like I said, I don't, really. It's just . . .' He shrugged. 'He didn't seem the type. That's all.' He paused. 'Anyway, why are you interested? Are you a reporter or something?'

'Me? No, nothing like that.'

'Police?'

'Do I look like police?'

'Not like any I've ever seen.' He blushed. 'I mean . . . you know . . . they're usually big burly blokes. I know there are women police, too, but . . .'

Zelda touched his arm briefly and smiled. 'I know what you mean. And thank you.'

'What for?'

'For saying I don't look like a big burly bloke.'

'Oh. Yes. I mean, no. But you haven't answered my question. Why are you interested?'

Zelda didn't really have an answer; she hadn't planned that far. When all else fails, deflect. 'Have the police been around here asking about him?'

His Adam's apple was large and moved as he swallowed. 'Yesterday. Two of them.'

'What did they want to know?'

'Whatever I could tell them. Which wasn't much. It did seem odd.'

'Why?'

'Well, the way they were speaking, as if they didn't think it was an accident.'

'Did they say that?'

'Not in so many words, no. But ...'

'You get to recognise the signs?'

'Well, yes.'

'You're a very perceptive young man.'

Someone called from the kitchen.

'I have to go,' the barman said. 'Please sit down. I'll bring your lunch to your table when it's ready. Another drink?'

Zelda saw that she had almost finished her glass. 'Why not,' she said. 'Thank you.'

She went to sit at the table she had pointed out and took out the photograph of Keane she had copied from the file some time ago. When the barman eventually came over with her food and drink, she slid the picture towards him. 'Actually, this is who I'm looking for,' she said. 'Have you ever seen him?'

The barman studied the photograph. 'That's odd,' he said.

'What is?'

'This bloke. As a matter of fact, I *have* seen him. He was in here. With Mr Hawkins. It's funny because it's the only time I've seen him here with anyone else. I always thought he was a bit of a loner.'

'When was this?'

'Couple of weeks ago. Not much longer. Is it important? You really are police, aren't you? Or something like that.'

Zelda gave him her best enigmatic smile. 'Something like that. I'm afraid I can't tell you,' she said.

'Or you'd have to kill me?'

'Hmm.'

'Well, I don't want to die, thanks very much.'

'Did you tell the police about him?'

'No. Nothing to tell. I never thought twice about it until you showed me the photo just now. And they didn't ask.'

'Is that the only time you've seen him?'

'Yes. Just the once. He's not from around here. Or if he is, he's not much of a pub-goer.'

'Was he by himself or with a woman?'

'By himself.'

'How long did they spend together?'

'Not long. Twenty minutes or so.'

'Who got here first?'

'Mr Hawkins was already here when the other man came in and joined him.'

'Did it seem as if they'd arranged to meet?'

'Now you mention it, yes. It did. At least, when the man came in, he stood for a moment and scanned the room, like you do when you're looking for someone. Then he went over and sat down with Mr Hawkins.'

'How did they seem?'

'What do you mean?'

'Were they arguing or anything?'

'No. Just talking. Like normal.'

'Did they leave together?'

'No. The other bloke left first.'

'How did Mr Hawkins seem then? Was he agitated or anything?'

'No. Just normal. He went back to working on his cross-word.' A group of four people came in, chatting and laughing.

'Oops. Got to go,' the barman said. 'Customers to serve. It's been nice talking to you, Miss . . .?'

'Cathy,' said Zelda. 'You can call me Cathy.'

'Cathy, then. Maybe you'll come back and see us again?'

Zelda smiled. 'Maybe I will.'

When he left she picked at her sole and salad. The fish was cold, but she didn't mind. It had been worth it. She took out her notebook and tried to jot down what she had learned:

1. The police are investigating Hawkins's death further, which could mean that they don't believe it was an accident.
2. Hawkins met with Keane openly in his local two weeks before his death. Perhaps this indicated they felt they had nothing to hide in being seen together? Whatever it meant, they had needed to meet face to face for some reason.
3. Keane drugged Alan Banks and set his house on fire. Hawkins died in a house fire. Is there a connection?
4. Keane is most likely still living in London somewhere.

But how to find him? That was what Zelda didn't know. She didn't even know whether he was using his real name. Didn't even know whether Keane *was* his real name. Perhaps it would be easier to find Petar Tadić first, rather than using Keane to get to him. And after all, it was Tadić she wanted. And his brother. Keane for her was only a means to an end, perhaps one she didn't need.

With Hawkins dead and the department's work suspended, though, the resources of her job were out of reach. On the other hand, she had a freer hand now she didn't have to worry about Hawkins finding out she was asking questions. She wouldn't have been able to come here today, for example, and discover that he had met with Keane again, if she had had to worry about him somehow finding out about it. True, Danvers and Deborah were nosing around, but Zelda didn't think they reported to the enemy. It was one thing to be questioned by the NCA and quite another to be chopped up into little pieces and fed to the fish.

If she could find out where Petar Tadić hung out, then follow him, perhaps he would eventually lead her to his brother Goran. He was the one she wanted most, the one she had bitten, the one who had punched her in the face and had later come to visit her in the breaking house outside Vršac, just over the Serbian border, cracking his knuckles and grinning as he entered her tiny room to wreak his revenge on her helpless body. She wouldn't be so helpless the next time they met. But London was a big city, and she didn't know where to start.

She caught the barman looking at her and gave him another smile. He blushed and pretended to be washing glasses. Zelda polished off the rest of her wine, slung her bag across her shoulder and paid the still-blushing young man before leaving. It had been a long time since she had used her charms to get something she wanted from a man, and she was encouraged to find out that they still worked.

There was one other question she hadn't put down in her notes, perhaps because she was afraid of the answer. But in the interests of thoroughness, she made a mental note to add it to her list:

5. If Hawkins *did* blow the whistle on me last December, why hasn't the gang come after me yet?

Sean and Luke were certain the house was empty, they told the police later, or they wouldn't have gone in there in the first place. Everyone knew the old Hollyfield Estate was on the verge of demolition to make way for new affordable housing and a shopping centre, and that many of its residents had already left for pastures new. Number twenty-six had looked like one of the empty houses left behind.

The backyard was a treasure trove of broken and discarded objects piled high – old bicycle frames and prams, bald tyres, twisted coat hangers, cracked radios, TVs with broken screens, rusty iron bars, empty tins and plastic containers, and even a very heavy old machine that Sean identified as a typewriter. He'd seen one on a TV costume drama not so long ago. While they had sorted through the accumulated rubbish searching for anything worth keeping, Sean had noticed that the back door of the house was slightly ajar. Sometimes they had to break down boards to get into derelict houses, but this one seemed to be inviting them across the threshold. Luke was reluctant to go in at first, but Sean called him a yellow-belly and a scaredy-cat, and that stirred him into action, though he stayed well behind Sean.

The first thing they noticed in the gloom of the ruined kitchen was the smell, which Sean later described as rather like their toilet at home when his dad had just been after a curry from the Taj Mahal. It struck Sean as odd that the sink was still piled high with dirty dishes, but then people left all sorts of rubbish behind them when they moved on to better things. And if you had to move, why bother washing all your dishes first? Sometimes squatters came in and took over, but they were parasites, his dad said. Just in case someone was there, he called out, and got nothing but dead air in return. The place was deserted. Abandoned.

It was when they reached the living room that things got really interesting. And scary. It was hard to see anything clearly at first, as the tattered curtains blocked most of the evening light, but when their eyes had adjusted, the boys were able to make out the back of a chair with wheels in the centre of the room. Sean recognised it as a mobility scooter because his Uncle Ollie used one. He said it was due to his gammy legs, but Sean's mum said it was because he was too fat and lazy to walk anywhere.

Luke hung back and said he thought they should leave, that someone must still live there; surely no one would abandon anything as valuable as a mobility scooter? But Sean said it might be broken, for all they knew, like the stuff in the backyard.

As Luke stayed behind in the kitchen doorway, Sean advanced alone towards the scooter. It wasn't until he got around the side that he saw it was occupied, and his heart lurched in his chest. All he could see was a slumped figure, head to one side, and two fixed eyes, staring at him. Without a word, he ran, Luke only several paces behind him, and they didn't stop until they reached the tree-lined safety of their own street just off Elmet Hill.

4

By the time Homicide and Major Crimes were called to number twenty-six Hollyfield Lane, the main street of the estate on the north-western edge of Eastvale, the sun was low and cast long shadows on the road. The first officers to respond – PCs John Carver and Sally Helms – had followed procedure, securing the scene and calling for paramedics to verify that the victim was, in fact, dead. It was only upon discovering that the deceased appeared to be, on the say-so of the paramedics, the victim of a drug overdose, that DI Annie Cabbot and DC Gerry Masterson ended up there. As yet, the discovery wasn't sufficiently major for them to drag Banks away from his evening out in Gateshead. Annie had enough rank to manage the investigation as senior investigating officer for the time being, and she would report to AC Gervaise as soon as she had gathered a few more facts at the scene. Drug overdoses happened now and then, even in more rural areas like Eastvale, and were rarely cause for a major investigation once the basics had been established.

The sprawling estate of decrepit terrace houses formed a no man's land to the west, beyond the more upmarket detached and semi-detached houses that straggled up tree-lined Elmet Hill and its tributaries towards The Heights, Eastvale's most desirable and expensive enclave. Because the Hollyfield Estate was earmarked for development, many of the buildings were already empty, their windows broken, roofs missing slates, their inhabitants long rehoused elsewhere. Though Hollyfield hadn't earned quite as rough a reputation as the East Side Estate, it had certainly been one of the poorest parts of town in its day, a poverty that was only thrown into relief by its proximity to its more affluent neighbours to the east.

Sean Bancroft and Luke Farrar, the ten-year-old boys who had reported finding the body, were at home with their parents, and someone would talk to them later. First of all, the police needed to examine the scene.

The smell of decay assaulted Annie before she had even got through the front door. Fortunately, the responding officers and attending paramedics had been careful and sensible enough to disturb things as little as possible, and both Annie and Gerry kept their distance as they studied the corpse. The smell didn't come from the dead man, though; he hadn't been dead long enough for that. It came from the house itself – neglect, unwashed dishes, damp walls, rotting food, old socks and blocked drains.

The man appeared to be in his late sixties, though it was often hard to tell with a drug addict. He had long, straggly, unwashed hair, thinning at the temples and on top, and a bushy beard stained yellow around the lips. He was slumped sideways on a mobility scooter wearing baggy corduroy trousers and a threadbare pullover. His left sleeve was rolled up almost to the shoulder, and a needle dangled from a vein at the bend of his elbow. Lucky man, Annie thought. Not so many junkies as ancient as he seemed to be had usable veins left in such an easily accessible part of their bodies. From what she could see of his arm, it was scarred from previous injections, and at one point above his wrist, the skin bulged an angry red, a sign of infection from a dirty needle. The room itself was sparsely furnished, and what there was looked as if it had been salvaged from a scrap heap. The ancient wallpaper was faded and peeling from damp where the walls joined the ceiling. Wet patches dappled the walls, throwing out of kilter the symmetry of the flower pattern.

'Was the overhead light on when you arrived?' Annie asked PC Carver.

'No, ma'am. I turned it on. Had to. I could hardly see a thing.'

'That's OK. I just needed to know. Have you searched the house?'

'Yes, ma'am,' PC Helms said. 'We had a quick shufty around, at any rate. Nothing. It's all much the same as this room. More like a squat than anything else.'

Annie nodded and gestured for Gerry to check the place out, then she turned her attention back to the body. 'Do you know who he is?' she asked PC Helms.

'No, ma'am.'

'OK. There's not a lot more we can do until we get Doc Burns here to check him out. Did the kids say the back door was open?'

'Yes. No signs of a break-in. Neither there nor here at the front.'

Annie squatted and peered more closely at the corpse. She noticed the edge of a worn leather wallet sticking out of his hip pocket. She was already wearing her latex gloves. 'Take note, constables,' she said as she reached forward carefully, grasped the wallet between her index finger and thumb and slowly pulled it from the pocket. 'In case it ever comes up, for any reason, I've removed his wallet from his pocket at the scene.'

PC Carver nodded and made a note in his book.

Annie smiled up at him. 'You never know. Sometimes these little things make all the difference. Let's have a look.' She carried the wallet over to the table by the front window.

Gerry came back from upstairs in time to join the three of them. 'Nothing,' she said. 'Though there's a mattress on the floor in each of the two bedrooms, and it looks as if someone's been sleeping on one of them recently.'

Annie started to rifle through the wallet. It was certainly bare. 'No driving licence,' she said. 'And no debit or credit or loyalty cards, either.'

'Judging by the state of his arm,' said Gerry, 'it's probably a good thing for all of us that he didn't drive. I mean, you know, before he . . .'

'I know what you mean,' said Annie. 'Aha. He's got a senior's bus pass here. Howard Stokes, age 67.'

Annie passed Gerry a scrap of paper she found stuck between two dirty five-pound notes, on which was scrawled something that resembled a mobile phone number. 'Could be his dealer or someone?'

'I'll check it out,' said Gerry. 'Think it was an accident, guv?'

Annie peered at the body again. 'No way of telling,' she said. 'Not yet. Not until the doc gets him on the slab and the experts go over the scene. Who knows, even then? We'll need to find out if he was right-handed, for a start. If he wasn't, we may have another murder to deal with. We also need to know whether his prints are on the syringe, where he might have got the drugs from, and so on. Even if we think we've got all the answers, there'll always be a chance that someone else injected him, wiped the syringe and made sure his fingerprints would be found on it. Vic Manson's good with this sort of thing. Odds are he'll be able to tell us by the angles and impressions whether Stokes would have handled the syringe in that way to get it where it is. I can't see any evidence of it, but there's also a chance he was killed in some other way and it was made to appear like a drug overdose. But who would want to go to that much trouble, I have no idea.'

'Should we call in the super?' Gerry asked.

Annie shook her head. 'No need. Let him have his evening out. I'll talk to the AC in a while and see what she says. You have a chat with Sean and Luke. In the meantime, I'll call for the forensics team. We'll wait here for Dr Burns and the CSIs. We'll get Peter Darby to take some stills and video, too. Then, when the doc's finished, he can get the body wrapped up and transferred to the mortuary at Eastvale General ready for Karen tomorrow morning.'

'She's got the boy from the wheelie bin slated for tomorrow,' said Gerry.

'Right. Forgot.' Annie looked at the late Howard Stokes again. 'Well, he'll just have to wait his turn, won't he? I don't imagine he'll mind all that much.'

After a long telephone conversation with Raymond in New York, who urged her to go and see the Picasso exhibition at the Tate Modern if she had some spare time on her hands, Zelda picked up her book and went out to dine alone. She chose a waterfront restaurant that she had passed on one of her walks around the neighbourhood. The cuisine was French, which was her favourite. The restaurant was noisy inside, and though it was a mild enough evening, it was perhaps a little too cool for some people and she was able to get a table outside, from which she could see the river in all its twilit glory. The tourist boats were still out offering cruises, and tugs and barges plied their trade back and forth, as they had done for centuries.

Still on her Japanese reading jag, she had moved on from Kawabata to Mishima's *Spring Snow*, the first of his *Sea of Fertility* quartet. But every once in a while, she needed a break from serious literature and went back to the books of her youth, sometimes even as far back as Enid Blyton or

A.A. Milne. That afternoon, after her visit to Hawkins's house and the pub, she had found a copy of *Modesty Blaise* in a second-hand bookshop on Charing Cross Road and decided to read through the whole series again. She had read them all years ago, back at the orphanage, but she didn't care. Modesty Blaise was her heroine from her early teenage years, and she knew she could enjoy Modesty's adventures with her right-hand man Willie Garvin all over again. She had already got well into the story in her hotel room. The evening light was still good enough to read by, and she flicked her eyes between the words on the page and the view. Modesty was tied up at knife-point and being forced to phone Willie and lure him into a trap by the time Zelda's food arrived.

Zelda turned to her Sancerre and sea bass, put her book aside and thought over her day. Hawkins's death still troubled her. She hadn't known him well, but that didn't mean she hadn't felt anything at his passing. What a terrible way to go. Of course, she knew more than Danvers did – his meeting with Phil Keane, the man Banks and Annie were after – and that Keane favoured fire as a means of getting rid of people. That didn't mean Hawkins's death had been anything other than an accident, but given the world he and Keane inhabited, in Zelda's opinion they were far more likely to die by violence than anything else.

The main sticking point in her theory was that given the talents Alan had outlined, Keane would have been a docu-ments man, a facilitator of movements across borders, of identity creation and manipulation. Such assets weren't usually asked to kill people. That pleasure fell to others, to specialists whom Zelda had met, men who enjoyed their work and did it as professionally and as bloodily as possible. Still, Keane might have become an obvious choice for some reason – the fires, perhaps – and Hawkins may somehow have fallen afoul of those he worked for. Or it could have been something personal, something between Keane and Hawkins. But the gang wouldn't like that, losing one of their well-placed inform-ants on a whim, so where would it leave Keane? Was he still alive?

But that was all speculation. She needed to find Keane and, if possible, get him to lead her to Goran Tadić. Only then, when she had done what she had to do, could she hand Keane over to Alan and Annie.

She was well aware that she had lost much of her impetus in tracking down Keane after that one sighting had led nowhere. True, she hadn't been in London very often since then, and never for long, but she would be the first to admit that she had felt discouraged. She was no detective. She had no resources to call on to find someone. And for what? True, Keane might lead her to Goran, but there could be other ways of locating him, through contacts she already had. She was in no hurry. She knew that whatever small dent she made, the organisation and its trade in female flesh would go on as ever. This was personal. Of that she was under no illusions.

But Hawkins's death, for whatever the reason, had rekin-dled her interest in the task.

There was really only one other place she might find out something useful, she realised. When she had followed Hawkins that rainy night just before Christmas, when he had met Keane in a Soho restaurant, a woman had come out with them. Keane's girlfriend, or so it had seemed. Zelda had taken photographs and followed the two of them afterwards while they went window-shopping and finally jumped in a taxi on Regent Street. There was a slim chance that the woman and Keane might have been regulars at that restaurant. In which case, perhaps someone who worked there might know some-thing about them. It was a long shot, but then so was this whole business. It would have to wait until tomorrow, anyway. She had had enough of sleuthing for today. She considered checking out the dessert menu, then decided not to bother, drank some more of her Sancerre and went back to *Modesty Blaise*. Modesty would escape. She always did. That was one of the things Zelda so admired about her. The lonely call of a ship's horn sounded from far away, downriver.

It was after nine o'clock and getting dark when Gerry finally arrived at Luke Farrar's house near the top of Elmet Hill. Sean Bancroft was present, too, as were both boys' parents. The boys were sipping hot chocolate and their parents red wine. Mrs Farrar asked Gerry if she would like a glass, but she declined. Much as she would have enjoyed a glass of wine right then, it wouldn't do to accept alcohol from interviewees. Maybe Banks could get away with it, but he was Superintendent and Gerry was a lowly DC. She did, however, accept the cup of tea offered as an alternative. The children seemed no worse the wear for their adventure, and no doubt when the immediate shock wore off, they would end up with an exciting tale to tell at school. Out of the window, the tree branches silhouetted against the night sky swayed and creaked in the breeze that had sprung up. Cars were parked on both sides of the hill, but there was hardly any traffic at that time. Things would be different when the shopping centre was built.

'I won't keep you long,' Gerry said, when she had her mug of tea in one hand and her pen in another, the notebook open on her knee. While she questioned them, she looked primarily at Sean, whom she knew was the elder of the two by several weeks, and who appeared to be the leader. 'Do you often play down on Hollyfield Lane?'

Neither boy said anything at first. They glanced shiftily at one another and eventually Sean said, with a guilty glance towards his father, 'We're not supposed to go down there. But we weren't doing any harm.'

'There are all sorts of dubious characters on the streets,' Sean's father added.

'But you do go, sometimes, right?' Gerry insisted.

Sean nodded. 'Most of the houses are empty now,' he said. 'We thought that one was empty.'

'We like to play in the empty houses,' Luke added.

Sean gave him a withering look.

'That's all right,' Gerry said. 'I was the same when I was a girl.'

Both boys stared at her open-mouthed, as if they couldn't believe that a girl would be brave or adventurous enough to play the way they did.

'Believe me,' Gerry went on, 'you're not in any trouble for going in there.' She glanced at the parents. 'Not from me, at any rate.'

'He won't be going anywhere for a few weeks,' Mr Bancroft said, through clenched teeth.

'Had you seen the man on the mobility scooter before?' Gerry asked.

'Dunno,' said Sean. 'I mean, we didn't get a really good look at him, did we, Luke?'

Luke shook his head. 'We legged it,' he said.

'And it was pretty dark in there.'

'So you don't know if you've ever seen him before?'

'There's a bloke on a mobility scooter with long hair and a beard like his who comes in the park sometimes.'

'What?' said Mr Bancroft. 'In our park?' He glanced at Gerry. 'It's at the bottom of the hill,' he explained. 'Just a small park, like. But our kiddies play there. There's been trouble about people from the old estate hanging around there before. There was a convicted paedophile—'

'A park's a public place, Mr Bancroft,' Gerry said. 'Hard to keep people out. But I get your point.' She turned to Sean again. 'What was he doing when you saw him in the park?'

'Nothing,' said Sean.

'Just sitting there,' Luke added.

'On his scooter?'

'No. On a bench. He'd have it beside him. The scooter. He could walk, but not very much.'

'Did he ever say anything to you or any of the other children?'

'No. He'd usually be reading a book or something.'

'Did you ever see him with anyone else, talking to anyone?'

'No. He was always by himself.'

'Did you hear about that young lad we found on the East Side Estate yesterday?' she asked.

'The boy in the bin?' said Luke, parroting a *Daily Mail* headline.

'That's the one.' Gerry took the computer-generated photograph from her briefcase and showed it to them. 'That's what he looked like. Did you ever see him while you were playing?'

The boys shook their heads. 'He's an Arab,' said Sean. 'Dad says—'

'That'll do,' cut in Mr Bancroft. 'Just answer the lady's questions.'

'Yes, he's an Arab,' said Gerry. 'Though that's a bit of a broad description. Covers a wide area. We don't know what country he came from yet.'

'Is he one of those boat people?' Luke asked. 'Or an asylum seeker?'

'I see you've been keeping an eye on the news.'

'We do it at school,' Sean explained. 'Current affairs. Anyway, we haven't seen him around here. If he did come from the Hollyfield he must be new there.'

'But nobody's new there,' Luke said. 'They've nearly all left.'

'He could be a squatter or something,' Sean argued. 'They take over empty houses, don't they?'

'Not seen him in the park, on the swings or anything?' Gerry asked.

'No,' said Sean, adding for no good reason, 'we always play there with other boys and girls we know, and there's always a grown-up there to keep an eye on us.'

'A good thing, too,' said Gerry. She glanced up at the boys' parents. 'I understand you have a Neighbourhood Watch in the area. Do either of you belong to it?'

Mr and Mrs Farrar said they did. Gerry showed them the photograph, too, and the Bancrofts.

'We've never seen him,' said Mrs Farrar. 'Mind you, we stay on our side of the park. That's our boundary. We don't go over to the Hollyfield Estate. No reason to. To be quite honest, we'll all be glad when it's been flattened to the ground. They say the plans for the new houses are quite nice. Then there'll be the shopping. And the cinema.' Mrs Bancroft smiled at her.

Gerry was running out of questions. Her cosy flat and a large glass of Chardonnay before bed were feeling increasingly attractive. 'When you were in the house, did you touch anything?' she asked the boys.

'No,' said Sean. 'We just walked in the room, like. It was dark and it smelled funny. Then I saw the scooter. It wasn't until I got around the side that I saw the man sitting in it. I saw his hair and his beard first, then his eyes, but that was enough. We ran out of the front door.'

'Was the door open?'

'No. I had to open it.'

'I mean was it locked?'

'Oh. No. It opened when I turned the handle. Why? Do you think someone went in and killed that man? But they could have gone in the back like we did. The back door was unlocked too, and even open a bit.'

Gerry smiled. 'No, we don't think that. It seems like an accidental death. I'm just trying to get all the details straight, that's all.' She set her mug down on the coffee table, put away her notebook and pen and stood up to leave.

'Ooh, look at the time,' said Mrs Bancroft, also standing. 'We'd better be taking Sean home now, too.' She patted her boy's head. 'It's school tomorrow.' Sean scowled and edged away, embarrassed. Gerry winked at him. He blushed.

It was going on for half past eleven when Banks got home from Gateshead, where he had taken his daughter Tracy and her fiancé Mark to The Sage for a Richard Thompson concert: over two hours of mostly powerhouse electric guitar, bass and drums, along with haunting acoustic versions of 'Beeswing', '1952 Vincent Black Lightning' and 'From Galway to Graceland'. RT could certainly tell a long story in few words. There were a lot of songs from the new album, of course, but he had also played some old Fairport Convention numbers, such as 'Tale in Hard Times' and 'Meet on the Ledge', along with 'Wall of Death', which he had first recorded years ago with his ex-wife Linda. Banks's ears were still ringing with the music on the drive home down the A1.

Tracy had been unimpressed in the way only a daughter can be with her father's taste in music. It just wasn't her 'cup of tea' she had said. But Mark had loved every minute of it and talked enthusiastically about the concert all the way back to Tracy's flat, where Banks had dropped them off. Banks already approved of Mark as a prospective husband for Tracy, and this display of good taste cemented his approval. It would be nice if Mark had chosen a more interesting career than accountancy, he thought, but you can't have everything. Besides, he would never be short of work, and he had already introduced an element of stability into Tracy's sometimes erratic life's journey.

Now he was home, Banks felt too wired to go straight to bed, despite the lateness of the hour. He checked his landline phone messages and found only a brief call from Annie about a dead junkie two boys had found in a house on Hollyfield Lane. There was no reason for him to call her back, certainly not at this time of night. He could find out all about it at the meeting tomorrow morning. As there were no other messages, he assumed that the team had got no further with the case of the dead boy since he had briefed AC Gervaise before her lunchtime press conference.

The case had been all over the national news again that evening, mostly because knife crime loomed large in the media these days. Dr Karen Galway would be conducting the PM in the morning, Banks remembered with a sinking feeling, and he would have to attend. Hardly an occasion to look forward to, though he was interested in watching her work and knowing her findings.

He needed music, balm to soothe his soul, but nothing too busy or loud. With streaming services on Idagio and Apple Music, in addition to his own large collection of CDs, now ripped on to his computer, his choices were practically unlimited, which could be a nuisance from time to time. It was surprising how often he could find absolutely nothing he wanted to listen to at any particular moment.

Finally, he plumped for a collection of Takemitsu's guitar music, spare and spacious, just what he needed. He hadn't been drinking at all that evening and didn't feel like opening a bottle of wine so late, so he poured himself a couple of fingers of the Macallan eighteen-year-old, a present from his old boss Superintendent Gristhorpe, which he usually reserved for special occasions. He settled down in his wicker chair in the dim orange-shaded light of the conservatory. He could hear the wind over the music, and several stars shone quite brightly in the clear sky above Tetchley Fell.

It was a sort of special occasion, he told himself, as his mind raced through the spaces between the notes to contemplate his forthcoming birthday with a mixture of awe and sheer terror. True, he was in good shape for a man of his age – especially a man of his tastes and habits. He had stopped smoking years ago, and though he didn't go to a gym or jog, let alone have a personal trainer, he did enjoy long walks in the Dales as often as he could get out there. He would have been the first to admit that he probably drank too much and didn't give a tinker's toss about units and calories, but he also knew when to stop, most of the time. His only real ailments were slightly high blood pressure, which he took care of with pills from the doctor, and a nagging ache in his right hip after the longer walks. Statins had lowered his cholesterol to an acceptable level.

His mental health probably wasn't so great. The 'black dog' of depression had been visiting more frequently and biting more viciously of late. Some days he just didn't want to get out of bed. It wasn't the old teenage laziness coming back, but rather that he didn't want to face the world and felt no interest in the things he usually cared about, even music or work. Sometimes, too, he felt on the verge of tears for no reason at all and suffered from guilt-inducing bouts of self-pity. At work he often felt like Sisyphus pushing that bloody rock up the hill only to have it roll back down again.

He was also alone. There was no one special in his life, as they say, no significant other. He had family, of course –

a distant ex-wife and two grown-up children very much preoccupied with their own lives and concerns: Brian with his band the Blue Lamps, and Tracy, his beloved daughter Tracy, about to get married at last, in her thirties. And he had friends. Not only work colleagues like Annie, Winsome, Gerry, Ken Blackstone and 'Dirty Dick' Burgess, but outsiders, like Linda Palmer, the poet; folk singer Penny Cartwright; Annie's father, the artist Ray Cabbot; along with his partner Zelda, too, now, and psychologist Jenny Fuller. Even Joanna MacDonald. But he had no lover. No companion. No one with whom to share his highs and lows, his successes and failures.

The spaces between the notes seemed to grow longer. Banks sighed and refilled his glass. He wasn't depressed – there was no black dog in sight – but if he went on thinking about his forthcoming birthday he might well end up that way.

He turned his mind to the case, the murdered boy. No money, no identification, nothing but a small wrap of cocaine in his pocket. Had someone emptied his pockets? Or was it the opposite? Had someone *planted* the coke there to misdirect the police? Was the killing nothing to do with drugs, after all? Both Annie and Gerry had suggested other possible reasons at the meeting this morning. The thing was, none of them really grabbed him. He could accept that there might have been another motive, but he could not, at the moment, imagine what it might be.

It had seemed apparent at first that the killer had wanted to delay the discovery of the victim's identity for as long as possible. But perhaps that wasn't the case at all. In Banks's experience, most teenagers didn't carry any identification; they didn't usually have wallets on them. Why did it matter who the boy was? Maybe his killer had simply needed long enough to cover his tracks, escape, fix up an alibi, hide the evidence. Connor Clive Blaydon? Perhaps. But Banks very much doubted he would have carried out the task himself. As Joanna MacDonald had said, men like him used minions for jobs like that. Roberts, the butler? Frankie Wallace, the chauffeur? At least tomorrow he could check Blaydon's alibi at Le Coq d'Or, and perhaps with a bit of luck find out what he was doing in Eastvale on the night the boy died.

Banks sipped his Macallan and let the music flow over him. All of a sudden, he knew what he wanted for his birthday: a guitar. Even if he had to buy one himself, having no one in his life likely to buy him an expensive present. It had been years since he'd played rhythm in a fledgling band called Jimson Weed, who hadn't even managed to survive their first three gigs before splitting up. The lead singer had thought he was a cross between Roger Daltrey and Robert Plant, which also made him God's gift to women.

Banks didn't fool himself that he would ever be able to play the Takemitsu compositions he was listening to now, or any other classical works for guitar, but he could at least learn a few basic chords and belt out the occasional folk song, or strum an old Beatles tune or a bit of Dylan. His cottage was isolated enough that nobody would hear him. Besides, he had heard that learning a musical instrument was a healthy thing to do for the mind, that it helped keep dementia at bay, like learning a foreign language.

The phone started to ring.

Annoyed, Banks glanced at his watch. It was after midnight. Who would be calling at this hour? He didn't recognise the number. Fearing some sort of emergency, he answered as quickly as he could.

'Dad?' came the disembodied voice on the other end.

'Brian? Is that you? Something wrong?'

'No. I'm fine. I'm sorry it's so late, but I thought you'd still be up.'

'Where are you?'

'I'm in Adelaide. It's going on half eight in the morning here. I'm at the hotel.'

'What day is it?'

'Wednesday.'

'Tomorrow, then.'

'It's today here.'

'Smart arse. You know what I mean. Sure you're OK?'

'Never better.'

'Then why the late-night phone call?'

'I've got something to tell you and I didn't want you to find out from the newspapers.'

'You're leaving the band?'

'Something like that. Actually, the band's packing it in. We had a meeting last night and decided. It's been on the cards for a while.'

'But why? You're doing so well.'

'We've been on autopilot for ages, Dad. Just coasting. Pulling in different directions. And it's getting harder to make a living unless you're Ed Sheeran or Beyoncé. The music business has changed so much. It's all streaming now, and the musicians only get a pitiful amount. Even you don't buy records any more.'

'Fair enough. But I would if there were any record shops left.'

'That's what I mean. We're all sick to death of endless touring, just to make ends meet or promote a new single. There seems to be no time left to write songs or have fun any more. It's just constant hard slog, and that's not what any of us want. I mean, I'm not saying we're lazy or anything like that, but I am pushing forty.'

'Mick Jagger and Paul McCartney are over seventy. Even Keith—'

'But that's the point, Dad. I don't want to end up like them. And we don't want to end up breaking apart and hating each other, each blaming the other for the mess we're in. We don't want to end up like the Beatles or Pink Floyd.'

'Or even worse,' Banks said, 'the Gallaghers. So you're going solo?'

'No. I won't say I'll never make a solo album, because I might – I've got enough songs in the works – but no. I'm going into the production side.'

'That's quite a leap.'

'Not really. I haven't been wasting my time with drugs and groupies all these years, you know. I was interested in the studio stuff right from the start, how it all worked, and I've spent time with people who really know what they're doing. I've learned a lot. You might not have noticed, but I produced our last album.'

Banks hadn't noticed. 'Sorry,' he said.

'That's OK. Most people don't notice things like that. Anyway, I'm no George Martin, but I know my way around a studio. I understand the equipment, and I have a good idea of the sort of sound I want from a band. It's hard producing your own music. But with other bands and artists I can see a clearer path. Hear it, more like. It's a real job at last. I thought you'd be pleased.'

Banks laughed. 'I am, I am. But I'm a fan of the band. And you know damn well I've always been proud of you and what you've achieved.'

'I know, Dad. I was teasing. Anyway, I wanted to tell you before you heard it on the news. And don't believe everything you read in the papers.'

'Don't try to teach your grandmother how to suck eggs. I don't believe *anything* I read in the papers. Have you told your mother yet?'

'Next. I thought I'd let you know first.'

Banks felt inordinately proud to hear that he was the first family member Brian had told. 'And Tracy?'

'You or Mum can tell her if either of you is likely to be talking to her soon. Or I can ring her, too, it's—'

'I'll let her know. Don't worry. Not that she doesn't have enough on her mind at the moment, what with the wedding and all that. We went to see Richard Thompson tonight.'

'Fantastic.'

'Tracy didn't think so.'

'She's got no taste. Remember when we were growing up, she used to like the Spice Girls? I'll bet she doesn't even listen to our albums.'

'I'm sure she does. When are you making the announcement?'

'Tomorrow. That's Thursday here. We've got a press conference.'

'In Adelaide?'

'Why not? We've always been big in Australia.'

'No farewell tour?'

'Tonight's our last gig here. We're playing the Thebarton Theatre. The "Thebby", they call it here. It's a great venue. We've got a few dates back home and we'll honour those. I suppose you could call that a farewell tour, though it wasn't planned that way. Maybe you can come and see us in Leeds or Gateshead. But after that . . .'

'Of course I'll come and see you. Then what are your plans? Do you already have a production job to go to?'

'Not yet. But don't worry about me. I've got enough to get by for a while. I'm going to drift around the studios for a month or so. Talk to a few people. See what's available and what'll work best for me.'

'Any idea where?'

'Not yet. Maybe LA. Maybe London. It just depends.'

'Any plans to come home for a while, other than for your final shows?'

'I'll be over for Tracy's wedding next month.'

'Excellent. Come down and stay for a few days. We'll go walking up on Tetchley Fell. Pub lunches in Helmthorpe and Lyndgarth. And maybe in exchange, you can teach me a few guitar licks.'

'You've got a guitar?'

'Not yet. But I've decided I'm buying myself one for my birthday.'

'Good for you, Dad. And happy birthday.'

'Thanks. But I've still got a while left before I get my bus pass.'

Brian laughed. 'OK. Well, I'd be happy to teach you a few chord progressions. And maybe even that odd folk tuning I learned from Martin Carthy.'

'Martin Carthy? When was that?'

'A while back. At your folk singer friend's house. Penny Cartwright.'

'I remember,' said Banks. 'But I didn't know you'd been discussing guitar tunings.'

'Us professionals. What can I say?'

Banks laughed. 'It's a deal,' he said, then paused. 'Are you sure everything's OK?'

'I told you. Never better. We've got the day off tomorrow, after the press conference, and I'm off up to the Barossa Valley with Dennis, our bass player, to do a bit of wine tasting. He's quite the expert. And before you start worrying, it's all right. We've got a driver. I'll bring you a bottle of Peter Lehmann's. I know you like that.'

'Much appreciated. Well, as long as you're sure.'

'It was time for a change, Dad. I'm happy the decision is made.'

'Well, good. Thanks for telling me. And the best of luck. See you soon.'

'Bye. See you soon.'

Banks hung up and felt the emptiness he always experienced after a long-distance phone call. They seemed to magnify the distance rather than shorten it. But he was glad Brian had phoned him with the news. That was a turn-up for the book. There'd be a lot of disappointed fans out there. But Brian seemed genuinely happy with the decision. Relieved. Which made Banks wonder about what big changes might be coming his own way in the near future.

The original guitar works ended, and next came Takemitsu's arrangements of popular western songs, starting with 'Londonderry Air', which was odd to hear after the Japanese style of the other pieces, but no less enjoyable.

'Somewhere Over the Rainbow' came next, and Banks started to feel buoyed by the whisky, Brian's phone call and the music, happy to leave his cares behind for a while. Then 'Summertime' came on, and he knew it would be a while before he dragged himself upstairs to bed. He would have to dig out Billie Holiday's version first.

5

'Good morning, Superintendent.'

'Good morning, Dr Galway. You seem quite chipper this morning.'

'You know what they say. A healthy mind and a healthy body.'

Banks grunted. He still felt tired. It had been a late night. The Takemitsu guitar arrangement of 'Summertime' had indeed led inevitably to Billie Holiday, which led to a drop more Macallan, and so on. He went to bed well after one o'clock, and despite Bruckner's Eighth Symphony, which usually transported him most pleasurably to the Land of Nod – no insult to the composer intended – he hadn't been able to get to sleep for ages thinking about Brian and the Blue Lamps, and the old days he himself had spent as a wannabe rock star with the short-lived Jimson Weed.

'Been for your morning run already, have you?' he asked.

'Uh-huh. Ten-k.'

'No wonder you're so bright-eyed and bushy-tailed. I'm sorry, I didn't mean—'

Dr Galway laughed and said in her melodic Irish accent, 'That's all right. Never apologise, never explain. That only gets you into more trouble. And once you open the linguistic can of worms . . . well . . . what can I say?'

Dr Galway's face sported a healthy glow from the run, and she had most of her slightly greying hair tucked under a cap.

She was an attractive woman, but perhaps better described as handsome rather than pretty or beautiful, Banks thought, pondering on what the differences and distinctions were. She had serious green eyes, in which her intelligence was clear to see, strong features, a rather large nose, thin, tight lips, and a high, domed forehead. Her fingers were long and tapered, her hands smooth and flawless as a young girl's. As far as Banks knew, she was in her mid-forties, married with two daughters approaching university age, and she clearly kept herself in good shape.

She turned to the boy's naked body on the slab, his head supported by a padded block. 'It's odd,' she said, 'but the stab wounds hardly look lethal now, do they? Nothing more than the sort of minor cuts any young lad might get climbing a tree or whatever they do these days.'

'But?'

'Narrow, very sharp, pointed, four-inch, one-edged blade. Maybe a kitchen knife of some sort. Upward thrusts.' She made a gesture in demonstration.

'Four inches isn't very long.'

'It's long enough to kill, believe me.'

'Any other injuries?'

'None. No defence wounds, if that's what you're wondering. I'd say the attack took him by surprise. But look at that.' She pointed to a puckered area on the boy's upper right thigh.

'What is it?' Banks asked.

'Scar tissue. I'll need a closer examination to tell you more.'

'What about time of death? Any idea?'

Dr Galway turned the body over. Gently, Banks thought. 'I've done all the requisite tests, and I can't tell you much more than you know already. Rigor's been and gone, and hypostasis is established in the lower extremities, which agrees with the position in which he was discovered. Death probably occurred sometime between nine and eleven o'clock on Sunday evening.'

'And he'd been in the bin all night?'

'Ten to twelve hours. That's only a rough estimate, mind you.'

'How long had he been dead before he was dumped?'

'Now, that's interesting. I can't give you an exact time, but I can tell you that some time passed between death and the final positioning of the body.'

'Can't you narrow it down a bit?'

Dr Galway smiled. 'Sorry I can't be any more exact than that. Hypostasis starts – that means the blood begins to obey gravity and descend to the body's lowest parts – some twenty minutes to half an hour after the heart has stopped. I can't say how long he survived after the stabbing, but as I have suggested, it wasn't very long. Minutes rather than hours. Anyway, the hypostasis isn't usually visible to the naked eye until around two hours after death. It's also a lot harder to see on darker skin tones. You can tell, however, by the lighter bands – where the body was touching a hard surface, the shoulders, lower back and so on – that the process had started while he was still on his back.'

'How long was he on his back?'

'I can't say for certain. I may get a better idea once I open him up, but right now the best I can do is between one and two hours. You must understand, that does *not* mean I'm concluding that he was on his back for two hours after death.'

'Got it,' said Banks. 'But he was on his back for a short period of time, perhaps being transported?'

'He was on his back for a while. I can't say where or why.'

'OK. We have good reason to believe that he was dumped in the bin between eleven and half past, and you're saying he died maybe two hours before then?' If the boy had been dead for two hours before being dumped in the bin, then he would have died between nine and half past. If he had only been dead one hour, then it had happened between ten and half past. It could make a lot of difference down the line, depending on where the investigation took them.

Dr Galway sighed. 'I said between one and two hours. I don't think it was any longer. I understand your frustration, Superintendent, I really do, but I can only be as exact as science allows me. Shall I continue?'

'Sorry. Any leads on where he's from?'

'I've sent samples to Ms Singh in the lab, so DNA analysis might tell us something. At a guess, though, from experience, I'd say he's probably from Syria, Iraq or Saudi Arabia. Those would be the most obvious choices. But as for how long he's been over here, I can't tell you. There might be some indications from the samples at the lab. Certain chemicals or elements found in the teeth, bones and hair, that sort of thing.'

'What about his age?'

'Again, it's an estimate, but I'd say no younger than twelve and no older than fourteen. He's definitely in early adolescence. There's pubic hair, hints of facial hair, and you can see the testicles have grown already. I'll know better when I've had a good look around inside. Shall I get started?'

'I'll robe up,' said Banks.

'Vicks?'

'For sissies.'

Dr Galway laughed as she applied a little of the vapour rub under her nostrils. 'Call me a sissy then, but you can give me Vicks over a perforated bowel any day.'

'You know it's not good for you to do that?' Banks said. 'Rub it right under your nostrils.'

'I know. Camphor's toxic and shouldn't be swallowed or absorbed.'

'So?'

Dr Galway made a face. 'So bite me.'

'You're the doctor.' Banks put on his gown and cap and took his position far enough away from the slab so Dr Galway and her two assistants had room to manoeuvre. First the doctor carried out a close examination of the body's exterior and spoke her comments to the microphone that hung above the table. There wasn't really anything new. Not that Banks had expected much. The boy had no tattoos or piercings, only the mysterious scar; his pale brown skin was otherwise smooth and unblemished, apart from the stab marks.

'One thing I can tell you before going any further,' said Dr Galway, 'is that there are no signs of sexual activity or abuse, and no recent physical abuse, other than the stab wounds, of course.'

'That's good to know,' said Banks.

When Dr Galway began making the Y incision and removing the boy's inner organs, Banks noticed that she worked slowly and methodically, pausing occasionally to share a thought with her assistants, who looked fresh out of medical school, or to make a comment for the audio record. Dr Glendenning, her predecessor, had been far more cavalier. Brilliant, certainly, but his post-mortems had taken place at a faster pace, a flurry of organs flying here and there – or so it seemed – and, in the early days at least, surrounded by a fug of cigarette smoke. But Dr Glendenning, despite his speed and impatience, had also been thorough.

The organs had to be examined and weighed before being sent for further toxicological analysis to determine the presence of drugs, poisons and malnutrition. Unlikely as it was, there was always a distant chance that the boy had been poisoned before he'd been stabbed.

When she had finished, Dr Galway left her assistants to sew up, removed her surgical gown and gloves, washed and invited

Banks into her office. A family photograph was the only personal item on her tidy desk, and on the wall opposite hung a framed print of Rembrandt's 'The Anatomy Lesson of Dr Nicolaes Tulp'.

She must have seen him staring at the picture because she said, 'Some people think it's a bit gruesome, but I could stare at it for hours. I once went to The Hague for a weekend specially to see the original canvas.' She crossed her legs and leaned back in her chair. 'Anatomy lessons were real social events back in the seventeenth century, you know. Even the general public were allowed in if they paid an entrance fee.'

'Executions were public back then, too,' said Banks.

Dr Galway nodded. 'Yes. I sometimes get the impression there's quite a few people around who wouldn't mind watching them on television these days. But enough of that. What can I tell you from the post-mortem? Well, there'll be a full report in due time, of course, and I don't like preliminary reports, but I'll tell you what I know. Externally, at any rate, the boy's organs were in excellent shape. His aorta and pancreas were punctured by a four-inch knife blade, and the bleeding from the aorta was, I'd say, the immediate cause of death.'

'Dr Burns said at the scene that one of the thrusts might have pierced or punctured his right ventricle.'

Dr Galway shook her head. 'I can see how he might have thought that at the scene,' she said. 'I've seen the photographs, and the body was in a very awkward position to examine. But it was definitely the punctured aorta that caused death.'

'What about that hypostasis you suspected earlier?'

'It is present, to a small degree, exactly where you would expect it to be if he'd been lying on his back.'

'Can you give me a better idea of how long, now that you've opened him up?'

Dr Galway tilted her head. 'You don't give up easily, do you.'

Banks smiled. 'Not in my job description.'

'From what I could see – in my judgement, and based on previous experience – I'd narrow it to an hour, an hour and a half at the most.'

That meant the boy had probably died between half past nine and ten o'clock. Banks would have guessed at a later time simply because it was darker then, but if he had been killed *inside*, the darkness wouldn't matter. 'Thank you, doctor. So whoever killed him had maybe an hour to an hour and a half to get him from wherever he died to the spot where he was found. How long would it have taken for death to occur after his injuries?'

'Hard to say. Almost anything can happen with stab wounds. You'd be surprised how often they're not even fatal. In this case, though, he would probably have survived long enough to feel the life ebbing out of him, poor lad. There was quite a lot of blood, as you saw, and there would have been plenty at the scene, too, but even so, a lot of the bleeding was internal. It often is. The wound closes when the knife is pulled out. Unless you hit a lung, of course, then there's usually bloody spray from the mouth. Whether he could have been saved is a moot point. Personally, I doubt it. A pierced aorta is about as serious a wound as it gets, and even if a good doctor had opened him up immediately, survival would have been doubtful, at best. Whether the intent was to kill or not, I'm afraid that's for the courts to decide. I have no idea what happened, what the killer had in mind. It's rare that anyone knows how to use a knife properly, the way a commando might, for example, or someone skilled in close hand-to-hand combat.' She gestured with a pencil. 'Most people just thrust away and hope for the best. It looks like that's what happened in this case.'

'You mentioned earlier that there are no defensive wounds.'

'That's right. There's no evidence of a fight, as such. I'd guess the poor lad was terrified and backed away from whoever was attacking him.'

'But one of the thrusts struck the aorta.'

'Yes.' Dr Galway paused. 'Apart from the stab wounds, he was in excellent shape. Fit as the proverbial fiddle, though there are indications of malnutrition in the recent past.'

'Malnutrition?'

'Yes. Of course, we'll need close analysis of liver, bones, immune system, amino acids and pancreas, among other things, to determine protein deficiencies and vitamin markers, and to find out just how severe and long-lasting the condition was, but you could see even before I opened him up that he was painfully thin. It's not the cause of death, but it may have played a part, weakened his system. One of the problems with malnutrition is that it's hard to measure, especially if it occurred some time ago and the subject is deceased. It's something a doctor would want to diagnose while the patient is still alive, as it can usually be reversed. The stomach contents showed he'd eaten a burger and chips shortly before death. So at least he was eating recently.'

'What kind of burger?'

'A Big Mac.' Dr Galway laughed. 'Only joking. Autopsy humour. Really, Superintendent. Your guess is as good as mine. I'll get it analysed, if you like. Obviously if certain ingredients are present, that would help us identify its source. I'm afraid we don't have a burger database yet.'

'It might be something worth working on,' Banks joked. 'Pizzas, too. How long before he died did he eat?'

'Not long. The food wasn't digested. Maybe an hour or two.'

That meant Banks could send his team to question all the local burger joints and perhaps find out where the boy had been eating just before he was killed.

'But you can't say how long ago the malnutrition took place?'

'No. Not very recently is my guess right now. Not days. More likely weeks or months ago. Perhaps with the analysis I could give a better estimate. Does it matter?'

'I'm just wondering if he could have arrived in this country recently from somewhere children don't get enough to eat. Maybe by boat or some other means.'

'You mean smuggled in?'

'Yes.'

'I can't possibly answer that. There are children – far too many, in my opinion – living in this country who suffer from malnutrition. I can see where you're going with this, though, and I can see why you're going there, but I'd still advise caution before you come to any conclusions.'

'Of course,' said Banks. 'We'd certainly require corroborating evidence, no matter what your findings. Lacking any evidence of parents or other relatives nearby, I'm just trying to work out where to start searching. If he's a recent immigrant or an asylum seeker, he'll be registered somewhere, and there are checks we can do. If he's illegal, we'll probably be out of luck. It's a start. Any signs of drug abuse? We did find cocaine in his pocket, as you know.'

'None at all. Again, we'll have to wait for a complete analysis of samples to confirm it, but none of the common signs of cocaine use are present.'

'Anything else?'

'There is that scar.'

'What about it?'

Dr Galway paused and glanced at the painting on her wall, as if for inspiration. 'Again, I hesitate to draw conclusions, but it's too broad to have been caused by a knife blade, and it went deep. It also went largely untreated. You just have to look at the scar tissue to see that.'

'So what do you suggest?'

'I have some experience of these types of wounds from my misspent youth, and I'd say it's an old gunshot wound – what you might call a flesh wound, painful but not life-threatening – or perhaps caused by a piece of shrapnel.'

'Where on earth did you get such experience?'

Dr Galway paused before answering, then said, 'Iraq. Courtesy of Mr Blair.'

'Good Lord. How old is it?'

Dr Galway shrugged. 'Hard to say. It's healed. Badly. But it's healed. The tissue is no longer inflamed, and there's no infection. It's a clean scar. Again, perhaps months, maybe a year. He was still growing, so it's hard to know how much it has already been distorted by that process. And malnutrition slows down growth, so that might have had an effect, too.'

'Even so . . . If he suffered from malnutrition, and perhaps bore the effects of a bullet or shrapnel wound, and he came from the Middle East, I think that narrows down our search quite a lot. At least it gives us some idea as to what he was doing here.'

'Escaping a war? Looking for a better life? Don't forget, Superintendent, a fair bit of the Middle East is a war zone at any given time.'

Banks stood up. 'Thanks very much, doctor,' he said. 'You've been a great help.'

Dr Galway smiled. 'It's kind of you to say so. But probably not true. I'll be in touch if I get any further in proving my theories.'

'Please do,' said Banks, and left.

* * *

'Coffee?' said Banks when he bumped into Annie in the corridor back at the station.

Annie held up the folder she was carrying. 'Just let me dump this on my desk. I'm on my way back from the lab. See you downstairs in a couple of minutes?'

Banks idled away the time chatting with the desk officer, who had been fending off reporters for most of the morning. When Annie came down, her jacket slung over her shoulder, they headed out for the Costa on Market Street. One or two members of the press shouted questions, but Banks and Annie ignored them. It was another fine spring morning, and a couple of tourist coaches were disgorging their elderly passengers in the cobbled market square. The Costa wasn't too crowded, and they found a table easily enough. Fortunately, none of the reporters followed them in. Banks inhaled the fresh-ground coffee smell as he stood in the short queue and ordered two lattes.

'How's it going?' he asked after he sat down.

'Fine,' said Annie.

'How's Ray doing?'

'Good, as far as I know. He's over in America at the moment wheeling and dealing.'

'And Zelda?'

'I'm sure she's just fine,' Annie said, a slight chill in her voice. 'I haven't seen her for a while.'

'Did she ever tell you anything more about her search for Phil Keane?'

'No,' said Annie. 'I just assumed it had fizzled out. Why?'

'I don't know. I just got the impression she was holding something back, that's all. She was pretty quiet the last time we were over there for dinner.'

'Can't say as I noticed.' Annie sipped some latte and wiped away the moustache with her napkin. 'Anyway, tell me what you've got from the post-mortem.'

Banks told her, especially about the evidence of previous malnutrition and the scar that Dr Galway thought might have been caused by a bullet or a piece of shrapnel.

Annie whistled through her teeth. 'So the thinking now is that he might have been a migrant?'

'It looks that way. Dr Galway says he was no older than fourteen, maybe even as young as twelve, and we've had no reports of anyone matching his description gone missing, and no hint of worried parents, despite all our appeals. That would seem to indicate that he came over alone and hasn't been processed in any way.'

'Illegal?'

'That would be my guess.'

'But what was he doing up here? I mean, if he came by boat he'd have landed on the south coast, wouldn't he? Kent, Hampshire, somewhere like that. It's a bloody long way up here, and I doubt he had a wallet full of money with him.'

'There's not a lot of people who arrive here by boat, and they've usually come from France. He may have travelled by an overland route, or via Ireland, say. Besides, it's hardly as far from Kent to Yorkshire as it is from Iraq, or wherever he came from, to Kent. Anyway, Dr Galway said he'd probably been stabbed about an hour to an hour and a half before his body was dumped in the bin, so he could have been driven here from as far away as Newcastle or Leeds. Maybe even Manchester, at a pinch.'

'Hardly,' said Annie. 'You'd never get across the bloody M62 that fast, even on a Sunday night.'

Banks smiled. 'Maybe you're right. Anyway, the point is, we know he's not local, and he could have come from anywhere within the radius of about an hour's drive.'

'That includes Blaydon's house.'

'Outside Harrogate?'

'Yes. It's all well and good thinking of them coming up here to find and kill the lad, but what if that wasn't the reason? What if something happened at Blaydon's house that led to his death, and they came up to dump the body?'

'Nice theory, but it doesn't really work with the timing, Annie. As far as we know, they arrived at Le Coq d'Or around seven-thirty and left about eleven. If they had kept the body in the car boot all that time, the hypostasis would have been advanced to the point of being observable to the naked eye. And fixed. It wasn't.'

'Blaydon's driver could have driven off and dumped the body as soon as they arrived at the restaurant.'

'At half past seven? It was still broad daylight then. And what about Mrs Grunwell and the others on the street who heard something around eleven?'

'Maybe they're mistaken? Maybe it was something else they heard? Remember, nobody *saw* anything. Besides, if Blaydon left the restaurant around eleven, he hardly had time to kill the boy and dump him on the East Side Estate before his car was spotted on its way out of town. Especially if the lad had been on his back for an hour or more *before* his body was dumped.'

'We'll check the times with the restaurant. We also really need a push on discovering who the boy was and where he came from.'

Annie spread her hands. 'We're doing all we can. Gerry's been in touch with all the refugee and immigrant agencies in the area, official and unofficial, asylum-seeker hostels and the rest. We have his picture out in the media and we've put out a request for all officers working in high-concentration Middle Eastern areas to put out the word, canvass the mosques and so on. It's a lot of ground to cover. Takes time. I don't see what more we can do. For Christ's sake, *somebody* must be missing him.'

'Maybe not, if he travelled alone,' said Banks. 'Sometimes families send someone on ahead. Maybe he was hoping to contact a relative in the area? An uncle, grandparent, someone like that, who's already settled here.'

'But no one's come forward yet.'

'That's the problem. Maybe they don't watch the news or read the papers. Maybe they don't speak English too well. Maybe they're afraid of the authorities. I can't say I'd blame them. Anyway, keep at it. What's the latest on this other case?'

A mother with two children – one in a pram – took the table next to theirs and smiled apologetically, as if she already knew that her arrival would be interrupting a serious conversation. But the children seemed quiet and well-behaved, the baby sleeping and the toddler working on a colouring book. Their mother spent most of her time staring at the screen of her mobile as she sipped her cappuccino. Banks and Annie lowered their voices, though both of them knew it was unlikely that anyone could overhear. The coffee grinders and espresso machine, along with the constant comings and goings, saw to that.

'Bloke called Howard Stokes,' said Annie. 'I got Gerry on it this morning. Turns out he was a long-term heroin user. Usual pattern of recovery and recidivism. On and off the wagon. Back and forth between heroin and prescription methadone, depending on how much money he had. A few drug-free stretches. A couple of brief jail sentences for drug-related offences when he was younger, but nothing for years. Rehab clinics and so on, but nothing seriously illegal. No known dealing. No complaints against him. No recent arrests. Personal use only. And as far as we know, he didn't resort to muggings or petty theft to feed his habit. Way it seems is he started in the late sixties and never stopped. Strikes me he never heard the bell announcing the end of flower power. From what we could tell at the scene, he didn't pay much attention to his health or personal hygiene.'

'And the cause of death?'

'So far it looks exactly like what it says on the tin: a typical heroin overdose. Either he underestimated the power of the stuff he took, or someone gave him a high enough concentration to kill him. A hot shot. We might find out more after Dr Galway's done the post-mortem. I've also checked with the drugs squad, and there's been a couple of heroin overdose cases recently around the county. It seems there's some unusually powerful stuff about.'

'So it could have been an accident? Just his bad luck, then?'

'Seems that way. Of course, somebody *could* have slipped him a fatal dose. He could even have done it himself. But why? From all I could gather, he seemed a harmless, pathetic old sod.'

'Better dig into his background a bit deeper. A heroin user makes all kinds of dodgy connections, from fellow addicts to dealers and even drug cartels. What about forensics?'

'CSIs haven't had a chance to get to it yet. They're still on the East Side Estate. This is low priority in comparison. I found a mobile number on a slip of paper in his wallet. Gerry tried to run it down this morning, but no luck. It's pay-as-you-go and dead as a dodo.'

'Can we get a list of calls to and from the number?'

'I wouldn't hold your breath.'

'He was found in one of the houses on Hollyfield Lane, right? On the old estate marked for demolition and redevelopment.'

'Yes. Number twenty-six. Rehousing everyone is proving a slow process, especially if it's to be affordable. Stokes was on his pension, for example. Then there's planning, environmental assessments and the rest of the red tape. It seems Stokes was a legitimate tenant, by the way, and not a squatter.'

'If Stokes was on a pension, where did he get the money to feed his heroin habit? You said he hadn't resorted to crime.'

'Dunno,' said Annie, 'but it might be worth following up.'

'You think so?'

'No need to be sarky. There is one other interesting point.'

'Yes?'

'The owner of the property.'

'Blaydon?'

'No. The Kerrigan brothers. On paper, at any rate.'

'Tommy and Timmy? Are they, indeed? So they've branched out from nightclubs and amusement arcades into rental properties.'

Annie smiled. 'I thought you'd find that interesting. They rented it out at a fairly exorbitant rate, too. However, with the new project going ahead, they'll stand to make quite a bundle, especially if they're in cahoots with Blaydon. And Hollyfield abuts Elmet Hill, which is already quite posh and "desirable". There's only that little strip of parkland and Cardigan Drive separating them. As you know, Elmet Hill isn't so far from The Heights, either. Anyway, according to Gerry, there's been a bit of friction between some of the residents up the hill and the people living on Hollyfield. Especially arguments over the park that separates the two. The hill residents sort of see it as their own property. They've even got a Neighbourhood Watch, night patrols and everything. They argued that crime was on the increase. I checked, and it's true. There's been a couple of break-ins recently, and a sexual assault.'

'Hardly surprising,' said Banks, 'the way we've had to cut back on coppers on the beat and patrol cars. I remember that sexual assault. Girl called Lisa Bartlett, right?'

'That's right. Month ago. Gerry investigated it. Sixteen years old. She was on her way home from a dance at the comprehensive. She walked most of the way along Cardigan Drive with a couple of friends, but they peeled off just before The Oak, at the corner there, and she was left to walk the last few yards alone.'

'Remind me. Where exactly was she attacked?'

'She was taking a shortcut through the pub car park and a little stretch of waste ground beyond, leading to Elmet Court, when someone jumped her from behind.'

'I remember now. She didn't see her attacker, did she?'

'No. Couldn't give Gerry any sort of description. The poor kid was terrified.'

'She wasn't raped, though, if I remember right.'

'Nope. That's some consolation. He ripped her blouse, fondled her breasts and grabbed her between the legs before she thinks he must have heard someone coming and ran off.'

'Was anyone coming?'

'No idea. It's possible. She was in the car park behind The Oak, and anyone drinking there from Elmet Hill would probably take the same shortcut on their way home, too. But Lisa didn't see anyone, and no witnesses came forward. She just took her opportunity to break free and run off. She was only about a hundred yards away from her parents' place. Gerry handled it, but I don't think she's got anywhere yet. The case is still open.'

'I can't say I blame the locals for setting up their own security. It might be worth chatting with whoever's in charge. Anything new on Stokes's time of death?'

'Nothing concrete. That'll have to wait until the postmortem. But Doc Burns said it probably happened sometime Sunday, maybe late afternoon, early evening. He couldn't be any more specific than that.'

'Even so,' said Banks. 'We know that the Kerrigans had dinner with Connor Clive Blaydon in Eastvale at Le Coq d'Or on Sunday evening, starting at half past seven.'

'It's a bit of a stretch, though, isn't it, to connect the two events in any way?'

'Maybe. But DI MacDonald says they've got their eye on Blaydon for a number of possible criminal enterprises, including involvement in prostitution and drugs. And we know that Tommy and Timmy are up to their necks in anything criminal that happens in the area, and even if they're not, they make sure they get their cut. Don't you think it's a bit suspicious that the three of them were dining together when this Howard Stokes died in one of the Kerrigans' properties in an area where Blaydon's planning a new development?'

'Well,' said Annie, 'when you put it like that, I suppose it is. And let's not forget, we also think the young lad we found was killed on Sunday evening, too. I'm not saying he's connected with Blaydon or anything, but you said your DI MacDonald did bring up the possibility. And as I said earlier, maybe they were bringing the body up with them to dump it on the East Side Estate. Somewhere you might expect to find a victim of a drug war. When you add it all up, it's one hell of a coincidence. It's just a pity no one actually *saw* the car.'

'Blaydon, the Kerrigans, a dead junkie and a murdered Middle Eastern youth, all in the same night in the same small town? I don't think that can be much of a coincidence.'

'So what next?'

'We keep pushing. When the CSIs finally get around to it, I'd like you to ask them and technical support to make comparisons between the evidence found at Stokes's house with the boy's body. Fingerprints, DNA, fibres, whatever they've got. Just in case. If we're talking county lines, maybe number twenty-six Hollyfield Lane was the trap house, and maybe the boy was the runner. You never know. But first I think I should pay a visit to Le Coq d'Or and see what Marcel has to tell us about Sunday night.'

Annie looked at her watch. 'If I were you, I'd time it for dinner,' she said. 'Who knows, you might get a free bowl of snails.'

The following lunchtime Paul Danvers and Deborah Fletcher turned up at Zelda's hotel. She was about to go shopping, but she couldn't put them off. They insisted on coming up to her room to ask her 'just a few more questions'. She told them the maid was due any moment, and she would meet them in the cafe off the lobby. She didn't want the police poking around in her room, even though she had nothing to hide. They agreed, and she grabbed her shoulder bag and set off for the lifts.

Danvers and Debs, as she had come to think of them, were already sitting outside at a table by the riverside walk, coffees in front of them and buff folders laid out on the table. Ever the gentleman, plump Danvers half-stood and nodded when she arrived. She sat down and ordered a coffee she didn't want.

'How are you today, Ms Melnic?' said Danvers, pronouncing her name correctly this time. 'Feeling better?'

'I'm fine, thank you.'

'Enjoying your time in our capital?'

'I've been here before, you know. I lived here once. Remember?'

'Ah, yes, the pavement artist days. Well, you've left those behind you now, haven't you? Found yourself a famous artist.'

'Can we get on with the questions?'

'By all means.' Danvers took a sip of his coffee, making an unpleasant slurping sound. 'What have you been up to since we last talked?'

'Up to? I don't know what you mean.'

'It's English for "been doing".'

'I know what it means. I also understand its nuances of connotation, that perhaps what someone has been "up to" is not necessarily wholesome, but I still don't know what you're getting at.'

'Let me put it bluntly, Ms Melnic,' said Deborah Fletcher, coming at her from the side. 'Why did you take it into your mind to pay a visit to Mr Hawkins's house yesterday?'

So she had been seen. There was nothing for it but to tell the truth, or part of the truth. 'I was curious, that's all,' she said.

'About what?' Danvers asked. 'To see the damage? Like a motorist slowing down to look at an accident? I can understand that. Do you have a yearning for the macabre, Ms Melnic?'

It had been her comparison exactly: stopping to look at a car crash. 'No more than anyone else. I knew Mr Hawkins. Not well. But I knew him. He was a good boss. Call it a sort of homage, if you will.'

'*Homage.*' Danvers pronounced the word with great relish and a pronounced French accent. 'Yes. Homage. That will do nicely. So it wasn't anything to do with trying to find out if there was anything, shall we say, suspicious, about his demise?'

'You told me there wasn't.'

'Indeed we did.'

'There you are, then.'

'And just exactly *where* are we? You haven't answered Deborah's question yet.'

'I think I have. You told me to stay in London. I had nothing better to do, so I thought I'd like to see the damage.'

'How did you know where Mr Hawkins lived?' Danvers asked.

'I told you. We were all invited to a department mixer there just over a year ago.'

'And you remembered the address?'

'I'm a super-recogniser, Mr Danvers.' Unfortunately, Zelda thought, that meant she could never forget Deborah's sour and unappealing face.

'You also have a good memory for places?'

'So it would seem.'

'Why are you so interested?'

'I told you: I was curious. Wouldn't you be? Your boss dies in a house fire. It's not something that happens every day.' Zelda was beginning to believe that they hadn't seen her go into the pub, and she prayed that she was right. That would be harder to explain, especially if they had found out from the young man behind the bar what questions she had asked him. She remembered no one else entering while she was there, except that noisy group of four towards the end. It could be a cover for an NCA spy. And if Danvers's men had questioned the bartender, he would surely have told them about the photograph she had showed him. She kept her fingers crossed under the table. 'You're taking an undue amount of interest for someone who told me just the other day that there was nothing suspicious about Mr Hawkins's death,' she said.

'Situations change,' said Danvers.

'So now you think there *was* something suspicious? That he was murdered?'

'I'm not at liberty to comment on that. Mr Hawkins headed an important department involved in some very sensitive work, as you well know. We'd be remiss if we didn't cover every angle.'

'Including treating one of his department members as a suspect, because I doubt you're giving the same kind of attention to any of the others. What is it? Is it my background?

Because I'm a woman? Because I'm a foreigner? Because I was forced into prostitution? Because I don't jump every time you tell me to?'

'For God's sake, you don't have to play all the special pleading cards in the deck. As far as we know, nobody else from the office paid a visit to Mr Hawkins's burned-out house.'

'Well, if that's all that's bothering you, I've told you: I was curious. They obviously weren't. I'll be going now. Goodbye.'

'Wait a minute,' Deborah called after her, but Zelda ignored her and carried on walking back to the lifts, then up to her room. She was shaking when she got there and flopped down on the bed to take a few deep breaths. What were they after? Did they suspect Hawkins was bent? Did they suspect her of being involved? Of killing him? They already knew she had been in Croatia at the time of the fire. Were they just fishing? If so, what for?

When she had calmed down, she told herself she had nothing to worry about. Even if the truth came out, she knew that she had nothing to do with Hawkins's death, or his corruption, if that happened to be the case. Fair enough, she was withholding evidence and could get into trouble for that, but she was willing to bet that if she told Danvers who she thought Hawkins was involved with – the Tadićs, Keane – the whole gang would disappear like smoke in the wind. She would rather the authorities didn't find out what she had set herself to do, or she would have to alter her plans drastically. But that was the worst that could happen.

If only she could believe that. In her experience, when the police were involved, the things that happened were often much worse than people could imagine.

Marcel McGuigan was about as French as Marmite on toast and as Irish as Yorkshire pudding, but that he had been blessed with genius by the culinary gods was not in dispute. No less than Gordon Ramsay had said so. And Richard Corrigan. And Michelin, of course. His Eastvale restaurant had opened three years ago to rave reviews, and after the recent awarding of the second star, it had become a destination in itself for many gourmets all over the country. Rumour had it you had to book a month in advance. Rumour also had it that you needed a banker's reference before dining there.

The restaurant was a listed building on a narrow cobbled alley between Market Street and York Road, just behind the market square, an area that boasted a number of bric-a-brac shops, upmarket galleries and antiquarian bookshops. Inside, it was decorated in the old style – dark wood, solid tables and padded chairs, luxuriant wall hangings dotted with a few Impressionist reproductions – rather than some of the more modern, brightly lit, chrome and glass places around these days.

The chef himself, Banks soon found out, was affable and relaxed, not at all the posturing prima donna in a poncy hat that Banks had expected. He wore jeans and an open-neck white shirt and lounged on an easy chair in his office at the back of the restaurant reviewing the evening's menu, black-rimmed glasses perched on the tip of his aquiline nose.

'A detective superintendent,' he said after Banks had introduced himself. 'I've never met one of those before. Do sit down.'

Banks sat in the other armchair and smiled. 'Most people haven't.'

'Nothing to do with the food, I hope?'

'No. Not at all. I've never tasted it myself, but I gather most of those who have agree it's not an arrestable offence.'

Marcel laughed. 'That's good to know. So what can I do for you?'

'It's about one of your customers.'

Marcel raised an eyebrow.

'Connor Clive Blaydon,' said Banks.

'Ah, yes. Mr Blaydon. What about him?'

'He told us he was dining here last Sunday night. Is that true?'

'Yes.'

'And he left around eleven o'clock?'

'I can't vouch for that personally. I wasn't here at that time. Service was over and it had been a long day. But Florence, our maître d' and general factotum, did complain to me the next day that he and his friends had rather overstayed their welcome. She mentioned eleven o'clock. In an establishment such as this, Superintendent, you don't chase your customers out until they want to leave.'

'What time did he arrive?'

'Around half past seven.'

That matched the times on the ANPR. 'So he was here all evening with the Kerrigans?'

'Yes. I know their reputation, but I can't take the moral character of my diners into account. I don't ask for character references.'

'Only bankers' references.'

'Ha. So you've heard that one. Not true, of course. But I'm a firm believer that you get what you pay for. In the case of Le Coq d'Or, it happens to be food of a very high order, and service to match. The Kerrigans like their food, they don't cause any trouble and they're willing to pay the price.'

'I understand that,' said Banks. 'I'm really just trying to find out if Blaydon's alibi stands up.'

'Alibi? What's he supposed to have done?'

'He's not done anything, as far as I know. Just dotting the i's and crossing the t's.'

'Well, they were here all right. The three of them. Went through a fair bit of champagne and claret with their meals. Cognac and Sauternes later, too, I heard. I hope none of them was driving.'

'No. It's not about that. And they weren't. At least Blaydon wasn't. He had his driver waiting out front.'

'Not here, he didn't.'

'What do you mean?'

'Well, you've seen the street for yourself. It's little more than a snicket, hardly the most welcoming surface for motorised vehicles, though you can just about get a Mini down it. He'd never get that Merc of his out at the York Road end. It's narrower there. Besides, if he had parked outside, he would have blocked the entire street, and nobody would stand for that. It's double yellow lines all the way, even for the likes of Mr Blaydon and his driver.'

Blaydon had said his driver was waiting 'out front'. It might have been just a casual turn of phrase, meaning that he was waiting somewhere nearby. Or perhaps Blaydon wanted to give his driver an alibi? Frankie Wallace could have driven anywhere in the area, done anything, while Blaydon tucked into his garlic snails. Even Annie's theory that they had dumped the body early could be possible, if Mrs Grunwell and her neighbours were mistaken in what they said they heard later, or what it meant. And if Dr Galway's assessment of times was not quite accurate.

'Did Blaydon pay by credit card?'

'I'm sure he did. He usually does. But I wasn't here when the party left so I can't say for sure. I can dig it out for you if you like?'

'If you wouldn't mind.'

McGuigan reached for a folder and sorted through the stack of receipts, finally handing one to Banks. It was paid at ten fifty-six. By the time they had all got outside and into the car, it would have been eleven or after. Banks nearly did a double-take when he saw the amount. The tip alone was far more than he had ever spent on dinner for three. He handed the receipt back and asked, 'What time did you go home?'

'Good Lord, don't tell me I'm a suspect, too?'

'Nothing of the sort.'

'I left at about half past nine. They were well into their sweets, and the first bottle of Sauternes, by then.'

'Other diners?'

'The place was fully booked, as usual, but people were beginning to drift away by then. Florence said Mr Blaydon's party was the last to leave.'

'Is Florence here?'

'Not right now. She doesn't start until about five.'

'That's OK,' Banks said. 'I'll have one of my officers talk to her later today or tomorrow.'

'You're being exceptionally thorough for someone who's simply dotting his i's and crossing his t's.'

'Aren't you?' Banks countered. 'Thorough. When you're cooking dinner?'

Marcel laughed. 'I must say, you display a certain degree of ignorance when it comes to a chef's duties,' he said. 'I don't do a great deal of cooking, though I'm quite happy to muck in if someone's sick. I'll even help with the washing up.' He tapped the papers in front of him. 'My job is doing things like overseeing the menus and checking out the quality of ingredients, rather than actually cooking. I'm up well before everyone else, driving around the county sourcing the freshest local meat and produce. I may supervise the preparation of a few sauces this afternoon, but my main job's usually done by the time the diners get here, apart from some last-minute touches. Of course, the prices they pay, they like to see the chef in full regalia, so I usually make a few appearances on the floor – you know, have a chat at each table, make sure everyone's happy, take a bow. But I try not to overdo it. You won't find anyone dropping by the tables here every five minutes to ask if you're enjoying your meal. I also like to hang around the pass and check on what comes out. That's an important part of the job.'

'So you don't cook?'

Marcel shook his head. 'Sorry to disappoint you. At least, not very often. I *can* cook, if that's what you're worried about. I have certificates to prove it, somewhere, and I've worked my way up through the kitchens of many a cafe and restaurant. Have you ever read *Down and Out in Paris and London*?'

'No, I haven't,' said Banks, who had been intending to get around to Orwell for years, ever since reading an essay of his called 'Decline of the English Murder'.

'You should,' said Marcel. 'It's a revelation. Especially the bit about working in the kitchens in Paris.'

'It's on my list.'

Marcel glanced at his watch. 'I don't mean to be rude, but . . .'

'Fine,' said Banks, getting to his feet. 'Sauces to prep. I understand. I'm done, anyway.' He held out his hand. 'Thanks for your time.'

'No problem. I just hope Mr Blaydon *hasn't* done anything criminal. He's a regular customer, and I need the money.'

Banks smiled. 'Oh, I think he's done plenty of things we might describe as criminal, but he's got away with them so far. No reason to think he shouldn't continue to do so.'

Marcel narrowed his eyes. 'I should imagine that his chances are somewhat diminished now, with you on his tail. Still, *c'est la vie*. I can always go back to washing dishes.'

'I hardly think that will be necessary.'

Marcel walked Banks through the empty restaurant to the front door. 'Look, Superintendent,' he said. 'You seem like a fellow who enjoys his creature comforts. Why don't you dine with us here one evening? Bring the wife or a lady friend.'

'Thanks for the invitation, Mr McGuigan,' said Banks, 'but I'd have to mortgage my cottage to do something like that.'

'On the house. My treat. Be my guest. I'll even cook for you. Give me a chance to show off. You'd love it, I guarantee.'

'I'm sure I would,' said Banks, 'but it wouldn't look too good to the chief constable, would it? Fine dining for free.'

'She need never know. As a matter of fact, she's not averse to dining here herself on occasion. She pays her own bill, though.'

'She can afford to.'

Marcel laughed. 'I suppose you've got a point. Shame. But if you change your mind . . .' He handed Banks his card.

'You'll be the first to know. Thanks, Mr McGuigan, and goodbye.'

On several occasions during February and March, Zelda had sat by the same window of the same pub, from which she could watch the restaurant where Hawkins had met Keane and his girlfriend just before Christmas, but to no avail. She had thought they might be regulars and that was why Hawkins had met them there, but she hadn't seen either the woman or Keane since.

While she had watched, she had puzzled over the extent of the woman's involvement. In Zelda's experience, very few women were involved in the criminal enterprise of sex trafficking – there were some, she knew, but not many – so what was her role? She had been with Keane, a forger, and they had gone window-shopping on Oxford Street together afterwards – so if Hawkins had met him to warn him of Zelda's interest, then the woman would most likely have been party to that warning. Or would she? Would it have even meant anything to her? Did they just pass it off as 'business' and say no more about it, or wait to discuss it until she visited the ladies? And if Keane and the woman were still together, might they turn up at that same restaurant again?

This time, Zelda decided to be a little bolder and go into the restaurant rather than watch it through a pub window over the street. After all, neither Keane nor his girl had the slightest idea who she was, unless Hawkins had shown them a photograph of her.

It was a large, bustling, dimly-lit space with a separate bar area, crowded with people fresh from their day's work grabbing a quick drink or two before heading home to face their families. Like most of the English, they seemed to prefer standing outside smoking or crushed together around the bar. The dining area was separated by a small step down, and consisted of a number of tables with white tablecloths and gleaming silver cutlery. It was just as noisy down there as it was at the bar.

Zelda took a table at the back of the dining area, which gave her a panoramic view of the whole restaurant, and settled in with her book. Just another bored businesswoman in town for meetings. She ordered a glass of Chardonnay and a clam linguine, and watched the people come and go.

When her plate and glass were empty, and Willie Garvin had saved Modesty Blaise's bacon, still Zelda had seen nothing of Keane or his girlfriend. She was beginning to think it was a restaurant that Hawkins had chosen because it was near his place of work. But wouldn't he have picked somewhere further away, and perhaps less public, in case he was seen, if the choice of location had been up to him? Maybe so, but perhaps she was overthinking the case. Perhaps Hawkins *hadn't* been meeting Keane to mention his concerns about her interest. After all, nothing had come of it. She was still alive. Perhaps he had never even known that she was especially interested in the photograph of Tadić and Keane. Loath though she was to contemplate it, if Hawkins *had* succeeded in getting Keane paranoid about Zelda's behaviour, and they *were* somehow involved in a criminal conspiracy to do with trafficking, then Keane and Tadić might have thought they needed to do something about her. Something permanent. But they hadn't. And work with Hawkins had gone on as normal, with no further incident, until she had returned from Croatia to discover that he had died in a chippan fire.

The conversations rose and fell. Someone kept emitting a laugh like a witch's cackle, and another a deep foghorn rumble. As usual in crowds, one voice was louder than all the others and had nothing interesting to say. It was still fairly early and the restaurant wasn't too crowded. The later it got the more the throng at the bar thinned out and quietened down, and the more people – mostly couples – came to sit down and eat.

'Would you care to see the dessert menu?' said the waitress.

'No, thanks,' said Zelda. 'But I'll have another glass of wine, if that's all right.'

'No problem. Same again?'

'Yes, please.'

While the waitress took orders from another table, then went off to get the wine, Zelda came to a decision. She took the best photo she had of Keane and his girlfriend from her bag and set it on the table. When the waitress returned with her glass, she said, 'Have you been working here long?'

If the waitress was surprised by Zelda's question, she didn't show it. 'Three years,' she said.

Zelda showed her the photograph. 'Could you please tell me if you recognise either of these people?'

The waitress frowned. Zelda was expecting to be put on the spot, asked why she wanted to know, or some such thing, and she had a weak answer prepared, but it didn't happen. The waitress simply plonked her wine down, then bent slightly to look at the photo.

'They used to come in here,' she said finally. Then, 'Why do you want to know?'

'She's an old friend, and we've lost touch,' Zelda said. 'This was taken a while ago, and she seems to have moved since then. I don't have a forwarding address. I recognised the sign outside, and I was just wondering . . .' Zelda held her breath, fearing the waitress was going to ask her why she had something that looked very much like a surveillance photograph.

She didn't. 'Sorry, but she's not in today,' she said. 'She does come in from time to time. You might catch her if you come back tomorrow. Or I could give her a message to contact you next time she comes in?'

'What time does she usually come in?'

'Around six-ish, maybe once every week or so. She works at Foyles, just around the corner.'

So Zelda had simply had the bad luck to miss her on those times she had sat watching from the pub across the street. 'And her boyfriend?'

'Haven't seen him for ages. I think they must have split up. Would you care to leave a message?'

'No,' said Zelda. 'Thank you very much, but no. I'd rather surprise her.'

'Suit yourself.'

The waitress walked off, casting a puzzled and suspicious backward glance. Zelda felt her heart beating fast. It was partly the thrill of finding the courage to play detective and

partly the sweet smell of success. She had found her. Found
Keane's girlfriend. She had been about to ask the waitress if
she knew the woman's name, but realised that, having passed
herself off as a friend, such a request would hardly seem
necessary. At least she now knew where the woman worked.

Foyles bookshop was huge, but unless the woman worked
in the back all the time, it shouldn't be impossible to track her
down. Zelda checked her watch. It was after eight. The shop
remained open until nine, she knew, but she might have a
better chance if she waited until the following day and took
her time. Instead, she lingered over her wine and her *Modesty
Blaise* until after nine, just in case the woman showed up.
When she hadn't turned up by a quarter past, Zelda set off
back to her hotel, walking all the way in the soft May evening
twilight, down Charing Cross Road and over one of the
Golden Jubilee Bridges, then along the waterfront, smoking a
cigarette as she walked, past the Southbank complex. She
checked behind her once or twice, stopped to look in a shop
window, paused on the bridge to admire the view downriver,
but was aware of nobody following her.

6

The informal meeting took place in Banks's office on Thursday morning. The three Homicide and Major Crimes detectives sat around his low, circular table, with coffee and notepads before them: Banks, DI Annie Cabbot and DC Gerry Masterson. Banks missed Winsome; she was always a welcome voice at meetings such as this, often coming from an unexpected angle or picking out a connection others didn't notice. But her pregnancy had been a difficult one; her blood pressure was too high, and her doctor had insisted she needed complete rest. Her husband, Terry Gilchrist, was only too happy to care for her at home. Still, Banks thought, even if the team was diminished, it was still pretty damn good.

'Anything more on Blaydon?' he asked Gerry.

'DI MacDonald did a thorough job of covering what we've got on him, guv,' said Gerry. 'And so far, he's managed to avoid arrest or even questioning for anything. It's all circumstantial, all guilt by association. And some of the people he associates with are known criminals, like Leka Gashi, who we know has strong connections with the Albanian Mafia. Quite clearly there are deals going on. The drugs squad are aware that the Albanians are taking over the drugs trade, especially in cocaine and heroin. I talked to a DS Norcliffe at County HQ, and he said it's a worrying development. They've forged alliances with the Colombian cartels and pay a pretty low price at wholesale for the stuff, which they bring in through gang-controlled European ports like Rotterdam and Antwerp. And they pass that saving on right down the line. Top quality merchandise, too. They're intent on taking over the county lines, and God help anyone who gets in their way.'

'Is Blaydon a user?' Banks asked.

'Not known to be, but word has it he's not averse to a snort now and then, and he usually keeps a few bowls of happy powder around the place to impress his important friends. Likes to fancy himself a bit of a playboy. More than likely he's working with the Albanians on financial deals behind the scenes, money laundering through his property developments and so forth, sex trafficking through the pop-up brothels. All at several removes. Of course, he'll probably be doing them favours here and there. That's how they work, how they draw people in until they're so deep they can't get out.'

'How's Blaydon's business doing?'

'That's interesting,' said Gerry. 'I'd been wondering myself why someone like him – successful legitimate businessman, multi-millionaire and so on – would get involved in risky criminal enterprises.'

'DI MacDonald said it's probably because he's an adventurer type,' said Banks. 'A gambler by nature. Maybe thinks he's above the law? Perhaps a psychopathic personality? I must say, I thought I could pick up on a few of those traits when Annie and I talked to him. It was a perfect performance. He didn't miss a beat.'

Gerry nodded. 'Yes, I read that bit. The gambling part is certainly true. Apparently, he's a high roller, known to a number of casinos and more than a few bookies. On a bit of a losing streak, too, these days, so word on the street has it. As an aside, he also has a bit of a reputation for holding sex parties at his mansion. There may be a few underage girls and boys present on occasion, and perhaps some trafficked girls.

That could be how he formed his first links with traffickers and the pop-up brothel scene. Like I said, he's a bit of a playboy. Craves attention. Likes to be photographed with celebs. Throws lavish parties for visiting pop stars and dignitaries.'

'Worth bearing in mind,' said Banks.

'But his reasons for criminal activity might even be a bit more mundane than DI MacDonald's speculations would lead one to believe,' Gerry went on. 'Practical rather than deeply psychological.'

'Oh? Do explain.'

'His business. Unicorn Investments International. It's in trouble. I'm sure you know as well as I do that the property business in general has been undergoing a bit of a depression for some time – house prices down, market poor, that sort of thing. Brexit hasn't helped much. Perhaps the only thing it has done is re-energise the trafficking business. They're seeking out new ways, new routes, new documentation, new tricks for dodging inspections. Anyway, if the slump in the housing and property markets are bad news for Blaydon and his ilk, the big downturn in retail is even worse. Retail property values are down. Nobody wants shopping centres any more. They want online mail order. Just look at all the big department stores closing or in trouble lately – House of Fraser, Poundland, HMV, Debenhams, Marks & Spencer. And half the shops in the big shopping centres are empty. That affects retail income streams, and in some cases Unicorn Investments are taking in less in rent than they're paying out in maintenance and general running costs.'

'Blaydon's losing money?'

'Big time.'

'And the proposed Elmet Centre?'

'Not hotly tipped to be a huge success.'

'The Albanians won't like it if they lose their stake.'

'Not much they can do, as we suspect it's all laundered money to start with. But you're right, guv. They'll be after someone to blame before long, and Blaydon's right in the firing line. Still, it hasn't come to that yet, and maybe Blaydon's thinking he can pull his chestnuts out of the fire by being useful to them in other ways. Markets go up and down, and most businesses weather the storms, especially if they don't need to pull out the cash right away. But Unicorn has cash flow problems, and I'm sure Blaydon knows that two things you can always rely on to make money are sex and drugs.'

'So it's financial?'

'Yes, guv,' said Gerry. 'I think so. At least partly. Maybe wholly. I'm not saying Blaydon isn't a shit of the first order, in psychological terms, but in reality, he's also going bust.'

'Excellent work, Gerry.'

'I can't take credit, guv. Most of it's there in DI MacDonald's files. I just tried to put it together as succinctly as I could, in a way that makes sense of recent events.'

'And you succeeded admirably. Anything more on Howard Stokes?'

'I've just come from the mortuary,' said Annie. 'Dr Galway says it's a straightforward heroin overdose. Not a trace of criminal wrongdoing. Vic Manson's fingerprint analysis bears that out. And the prints and the angle of the needle all bear it out. It happens all too frequently. There'll be tox screens and so on, but she's pretty sure it was an o.d.'

'How do we know someone didn't sell him a hot shot?'

'We don't. Dr Galway wouldn't speculate on that. There's just no evidence that anyone did. I mean, if you want to kill a drug addict, an overdose is a pretty foolproof method.' Annie paused. 'There were a couple of interesting points that came up, though.'

'Yes?'

'Dr Galway also discovered during the post-mortem that Stokes was a diabetic. He didn't take very good care of himself, as we know, and there's a good chance he might have lost a foot or a leg before long if he'd carried on the way he was doing.'

'You might also be interested to know,' said Gerry, 'that I checked with the local GPs and dispensing chemists, and Stokes hasn't received any prescriptions for methadone – or anything other than insulin – for at least six months.'

'So he's been getting the real thing from someone?'

'Looks that way, guv.'

'And there's one more thing,' Annie said. 'According to Dr Galway, Stokes had cancer. Pancreatic. One of the worst. It had already spread to the liver and lungs.'

'How long—'

'Not very long at all. She wouldn't say exactly, but I got the impression it was weeks rather than months.'

'So there's even a chance he killed himself?' said Banks.

Annie nodded. 'I'd say so. If you have the means at hand, and you know how bad what's coming is likely to be ... Anyway, I think we can pretty much rule out foul play in Stokes's case.'

'Did the drugs squad have anything to say about Blaydon?' Banks asked.

'Pretty much the same as DI MacDonald told you, guv,' said Gerry. 'They clearly share information with Criminal Intelligence. They suspect that Blaydon is acting as a bagman for the Albanians, especially this bloke Leka Gashi, who's the front man for the northern drugs operations, helping them take over the local county lines and so on. Apparently, Blaydon and Gashi first met up in Sarandë about ten years ago.'

'I've been there,' Banks said. 'Strange place.' He remembered Sarandë. He had been on a Dalmatian Coast and Greek Island cruise with Sandra years ago, and they had docked there to visit some nearby Roman ruins. What he remembered most of all was the approach from the sea – the tall buildings, and how the closer you got, the more you could see that they were empty – that you could, in fact, see right through the holes where the windows and walls should have been. It was hard to work out whether they were unfinished or had been shelled. He also remembered the town square littered with rubbish and the groups of men sitting around roasting a whole pig, then out in the countryside the isolated cottages, like fairy-tale witch houses with strange effigies nailed to the doors to ward off evil spirits. It had been like stepping back in time, at least as far back as a sixties Hammer horror movie. 'OK,' he said. 'Sorry for interrupting. Go on.'

'Remember, Blaydon's got a place on Corfu, and it's just across the water. Even back then, Blaydon was throwing lavish parties on his yacht to impress any celebs and major players passing through, and Gashi was his coke contact. Strictly third division back then, but he's gone up in the world since. There's also a rumour that Gashi helped Blaydon get rid of his partner, Norman Peel. Apparently Peel didn't like the drugs and the Mafia connection, and he was ready to blow the whistle. But Gashi's no longer involved on a day-to-day basis. He doesn't like to get his hands dirty any more. He has a host of minions to do that for him now.'

'Minions like Blaydon?'

'I'd say Blaydon's a bit higher in the hierarchy than that, guv,' said Gerry. 'His value is most likely in areas other than muscle. He's not without political and judicial influence, and if he has people working for him on the inside, especially police officers . . .'

'I see what you mean. The Albanian takeover could upset a few people who've already invested heavily in those routes. Locals.'

'It could,' said Gerry. 'And it has. According to my contact on the drugs squad, we don't exactly have a gang war on our hands, not up here at any rate, but there are a few scuffles on the sidelines, people getting elbowed out of the way, mostly the Leeds dealers. Several hospitalisations, a couple of fatalities.'

'I'll have a word with DCI Blackstone.'

'These days the Albanians can supply a purer product at a cheaper rate,' Gerry went on. 'What's not to like about that?'

'What about our dead boy? Anything on who he might be yet?'

'Not yet, guv,' said Gerry. 'It's starting to look more and more as if he's entered the country illegally, or simply slipped through the cracks. No useful CCTV so far, and only traces of grass and soil and May blossom in the bin and on his clothing.'

'There are no trees or grass on the East Side Estate,' said Banks.

'Oh, come on, guv,' said Gerry. 'It's not as bad as all that. There are a few gardens and a little grass square with swings and roundabouts for the kiddies.'

'And dealers.'

'There's even a tree,' said Annie. 'I'm sure I saw it once.'

Gerry rolled her eyes and went on. 'We do, however, have a couple of sightings that came in from the media appeal. One woman thought she saw the boy on Sunday evening coming out of the McDonald's near the bus station. He was carrying a backpack and wearing a dark zip-up jacket.'

'Dr Galway said that the victim had eaten a burger an hour or two before he died,' Banks said.

Gerry nodded. 'One of the girls there remembers serving him. There weren't a lot of customers around that time. And there was another sighting by the Leaview Estate a bit later.

Neither witness is sure of the timings, and the second one couldn't even be sure it was our boy, but it was either around or just after dark on Sunday. We also managed to track down a bus driver who remembered a Middle Eastern lad getting on in Leeds, at the central bus station there, and getting off in Eastvale. The bus arrived at 9.45 p.m., just as it was getting dark.'

'It's hardly surprising so few people saw him then. Eastvale's pretty dead at that time on a Sunday night. The Leaview Estate?' Banks mused. 'It's not the quickest way from the bus station to Hollyfield Lane, if we're still working on the theory that he was involved in a county line there.'

'It might be for someone who doesn't know Eastvale,' suggested Annie.

'Good point. Did this second witness have anything to add?'

Gerry scanned the witness statement. 'Nothing, sir, except this man also says the lad he saw was carrying a backpack. Wearing it, I suppose.'

'At least the missing items explain why he had nothing but the coke on him. He must have kept his money and stuff in the jacket or the backpack. I wonder what happened to them.'

'Maybe he dropped them off somewhere on the way, guv?' Gerry suggested. 'Somewhere on the Leaview Estate. It was a warm evening, the day before the storm, so maybe he took his jacket off and left it somewhere.'

'If he left it at Leaview, that rather puts our county lines theory to waste, doesn't it,' Banks replied. 'At least as far as Hollyfield Lane is concerned. It's unlikely they'd have two trap houses here in Eastvale. Can we link the boy to Stokes at all?'

'No, guv,' said Gerry. 'Not yet, at any rate. We found no trace of the backpack or jacket at his house. But Stefan's team are still there; if there is a connection, they'll come up with it eventually.'

'You're thinking Howard Stokes was cuckooed, aren't you?' Annie asked.

'It makes sense, doesn't it?' said Banks. 'Isn't that how the county lines operate? Send in a kid to distribute the phone orders out of someone's house. Take over his nest, like a cuckoo. Usually someone who can't do anything about it. Someone disabled, or a vulnerable junkie like Stokes. It explains why he hadn't been getting any methadone scripts and was managing to maintain his habit. They'd pay him in heroin.'

'But why kill him, guv?' Gerry asked. 'I mean, whatever Stokes was, he wasn't a major player. I doubt the boy was, either, even if he was involved. But Stokes did provide them with a safe and solid base to work from.'

'I don't know. Maybe Stokes killed himself because of the cancer? There's a lot we don't know yet. Maybe if the Albanians are taking over . . .'

'A warning?' said Annie. 'Like we thought before?'

'Or a reprisal,' said Banks. 'Let's try knocking on doors along Hollyfield Lane. There must be people still living there.'

'There are, guv,' said Gerry. 'Uniform branch did a door-to-door just after we found Stokes's body. It turned up nothing.'

'You do it again, Gerry. Even if Stokes did die of a genuine drug overdose, it doesn't mean there was no monkey business involved. Show everyone the boy's picture.'

'Right, guv.'

'And up Elmet Hill, too,' said Banks. 'We wouldn't want anyone to think we're favouring the better off. There's plenty of people living up there, and they're not free from suspicion, even though they've got more money. They've got a Neighbourhood Watch, too. It might be worth having a word with some of them. They may have seen or heard something on their wanderings.'

'OK.' Gerry glanced at Annie. 'By the way, guv. DI Cabbot asked me to look into the Lisa Bartlett sexual assault again. As you know, I handled that case, talked to Lisa at the time. She was pretty upset.'

'I can imagine,' said Banks. 'Poor lass. Make her part of your inquiries in the area. Have another chat with her. See if she can remember anything else. Find out if she'd ever seen our boy or knows who Stokes was.'

Gerry made a note on her pad. 'Will do, guv.'

Zelda felt a surge of excitement when she woke up the following morning. She was getting closer; she could feel it. She had slept far better than the previous night and could remember no bad dreams, not even fragments. Her nights were unpredictable, as were the moods of despair and feelings of worthlessness that washed over her like tsunamis out of nowhere and swept all hope away. She had no way of foreseeing them. Or the panic attacks. Sometimes she could guess later that a specific incident had set off the chain reaction – a face in the crowd that seemed too much like one of the men who had abused her, groups of men behaving aggressively, men giving her certain glances or making lewd comments, bedraggled, frightened-looking girls sitting on pavements hugging their knees and keeping their heads down as they begged for loose change. But her panic didn't always require any of those triggers to set it off.

Raymond had learned to leave her alone when such feelings enveloped her, though more and more she found herself going to him for comfort, *wanting* to be held. That had taken a long time. Her psychiatrist, if she had one, would no doubt have noted it as a positive sign, an acceptance of the need for human warmth and help she had spurned for so long after her traumatic experiences. But Raymond never questioned her, never asked for explanations; he simply gave her comfort when she needed it. Maybe that was why she had started to trust him after so long, to love him. She was quite aware that the only two men she had ever loved, apart from her father, whom she could hardly remember, were much older than she was, but she didn't dwell on it. She was happy with Raymond, happy in a way she had never thought she could be again, and as happy as she could ever be, given the nightmares and the shame and the guilt – not for what she had done, but for what she had allowed it to do to her.

That morning she indulged herself in a large latte and a blueberry muffin at the Caffè Nero on the ground floor of the Oxo Tower. Joggers flashed by, and already the tourists were holding up their mobiles for selfies along on the waterfront. Two excited young women, who looked as if they were preparing for a modelling session, sat at the next table and discussed angles and locations with their photographer. With her black hair tied back in a loose chignon, accenting her high cheekbones, and her dark eyes, olive complexion and slender but shapely figure, Zelda herself might have been taken for a model, though her uniform of jeans, white open-neck shirt and kidskin jacket were hardly the apex of *haute couture*. She did notice the photographer glancing at her out of the corner of his eye, as if appraising her, from time to time. It made her feel a little uncomfortable but didn't bring on a tsunami.

Foyles was in full swing when Zelda arrived, a huge, bright book emporium with a wonderful sense of natural light and space. There were the requisite displays of notebooks and gift items by the ground floor cash registers, but beyond stood a wall of recent titles facing out towards the reader. For a few moments, Zelda just stood there, overwhelmed, reading titles but not really taking them in. On her previous visits she had always been either browsing or searching for a specific title, but this time she had no idea where to begin. She had vaguely worked out how she would approach Keane's girlfriend, but not how she would find her in the first place. At least she wasn't working the ground floor tills, so that was a start. These things all seemed so easy in movies, but in real life they were a different matter. She didn't think she looked threatening or dangerous, so she hoped that the people she talked to would trust her and not feel they needed to hide the truth or call the police.

She decided that the best thing to do would be to check out all five floors first, and if there was no sign of her there, she would start showing the photograph around to members of staff. She was nervous about that, as she had no more of an explanation for it now than she had the previous evening in the restaurant. No doubt she would think of something.

And so she began her search, walking each floor, checking the faces of anyone at an information desk, carrying or stacking piles of books, adjusting shelf displays or talking to customers, until she arrived at the gallery and cafe on the fifth floor. The woman serving behind the counter there definitely wasn't the one she was looking for; nor were any of the people sitting at a table enjoying a coffee break.

Zelda started working her way back down again, this time showing the photo to every employee she met. She had no idea how many people worked in Foyles, or how the hierarchy functioned, but one or two people she talked to thought they recognised the woman but just couldn't place her. Some merely seemed suspicious and were unwilling to help her at all.

Finally, Zelda got lucky on the third floor.

'That looks like Ms Butler,' said a young girl on her knees, shelving business self-help books.

Zelda's spirits revived. 'Where can I find her?'

The girl's expression turned guarded. 'Who wants to know?' she asked. 'And where did this photograph come from?'

'I'd just like to talk to her. That's all.'

'I wouldn't want to get her into any trouble.'

'She's not in any trouble. Honest,' said Zelda, dredging up her best smile.

The girl chewed on her lip for a few moments, then said, 'Ms Butler. Faye. She's head of our art department. You should find her on the ground floor.'

Hadn't Banks told her that Keane was involved in the art world when the two of them had crossed swords a few years ago? He had moved on now, if the photograph with Tadić was to be believed, but that didn't mean he had completely left his earlier interests behind.

'Thanks very much,' said Zelda.

The girl nodded and went back to shelving books. Zelda walked down the stairs to the ground floor. She approached a young man rearranging a stack of books on a table centre-piece and asked if Ms Butler was around.

'Faye?' said the young man, glancing around. 'She was here a few moments ago. Must have nipped into the office. Can I help?'

Zelda smiled sweetly. 'No, thank you. I really need to talk to Ms Butler.'

'OK. Won't be a jiffy.'

He disappeared through a STAFF ONLY door and reap-peared a minute or two later with the young blonde woman in Zelda's photograph. It had been difficult to tell her age when Zelda had followed her and Hawkins along Oxford Street just before Christmas, but now Zelda saw her in the flesh, she guessed that Faye Butler was probably about the same age as she was. Faye approached, a puzzled expression on her pixie-ish face, and said, 'Hello. I'm Faye Butler. Ron here says you want to talk to me.'

'Thanks for seeing me,' Zelda said. 'Yes, I'd like to talk to you if you have a few moments to spare.'

'What's it about?' Faye asked, dismissing Ron with a wave of the hand.

'It's about Phil Keane. I understand you go out with him, or used to.'

Faye folded her arms. 'I don't know what you want, or who you are, but I've never heard of any Phil Keane.'

Before Faye could turn and walk away, Zelda held out the photo. 'This *is* you, isn't it?'

Faye paused and examined the photograph. 'Yes,' she said. 'I don't know where you got it, but it's me. Perhaps I'd better call the police?'

Zelda took a deep breath. After the next step, there would be no turning back. 'I am the police,' she said.

'Do you have identification?'

Zelda wasn't sure it would pass muster, but she did have her NCA pass, and it did have the words 'National Crime Agency' printed on it, along with an impressive logo, insignia and her photograph.

'NCA?' said Faye. 'That's the British FBI, isn't it?'

'Some newspapers call us that.'

'It must be important, then. But I still don't know what you're talking about. This man in the picture isn't called Phil Keane. His name is Hugh Foley. And, yes, we used to go out together, but not for a while now.'

It was just after five o'clock when Annie arrived at the wood-panelled facade of Le Coq d'Or. Like Banks, she had never eaten there. The restaurant didn't open until six, so she knocked at the front door and an elegant young woman in a black turtleneck sweater and matching black slacks answered. When Annie introduced herself, the woman said she was Florence and had been expecting someone from the police. She excused herself for a moment, then she returned, carrying a pack of cigarettes, came outside and closed the door behind her. It was a mild evening, and she seemed comfortable enough without a jacket.

'Let's just go down here,' she said, and led Annie a few yards towards York Road, beyond which the limestone castle was visible, high on its hill against a backdrop of blue sky. They stood outside a closed antiquarian bookshop with a window display of beautiful old maps. 'I'm dying for a fag,' Florence went on, 'and Marcel doesn't like me smoking right outside the restaurant, even when it's closed. Says it looks bad. I suppose he's right, really.' She smiled nervously, pulled a Rothmans from her packet and lit it with a green Bic. She took a deep drag and let out the smoke slowly. 'So what did you want to know?'

'About Sunday night.'

'Yes.'

'I understand a man called Connor Clive Blaydon was dining with Tommy and Timmy, the Kerrigan brothers.'

Florence puffed on her cigarette and nodded. 'That's right.'

'Do you remember what time they left?'

'It was just after eleven o'clock. We'd been closed officially for ages, and they were the only ones left, but . . . well . . . what can you do?'

'It does seem rather inconsiderate.'

Florence shrugged. 'A customer's a customer.'

'Big spenders?'

She nodded.

'And generous tippers?'

'Generous enough to make it worthwhile staying late. After all, I've got nowhere to go except my lonely little flat.' She laughed dismissively at herself. 'It's not as if I haven't given Marcel every opportunity, but he's not interested. And his real name's not Marcel, it's Roland.'

Annie laughed. 'Anyone else still there?'

'By then? Only the kitchen staff. They've got a lot of cleaning up to do at the end of a service. Marcel's a real stickler about cleanliness and hygiene. You have to be if you want Michelin stars.'

'When the party left, did you see where they went?'

'They all got into Mr Blaydon's car.'

'It was parked outside?'

'Yes. I opened the restaurant door for them and saw them get into it. A nice black Mercedes. They were all a bit tipsy by then.'

'What about earlier? Was the car outside all evening?'

'Oh, no. They couldn't possibly park there. He had to back out as it was. You can see how the street narrows towards York Road.'

Annie looked in the direction Florence was pointing and saw it was true. It was as Banks had told her.

'So how did he know what time to turn up?'

'Mr Blaydon used his mobile to call the driver when they wanted to leave.'

'And you're sure the car wasn't already waiting outside?'

'Well, I managed to sneak out for a smoke around nine-thirty, just after Marcel had gone home, when the evening's service was officially finished, and it certainly wasn't there then.'

'Was Mr Blaydon in the restaurant all evening, all that time between seven-thirty and eleven?'

'Yes. Wait a minute. He got a call on his mobile and went outside to answer it.'

'What time was this?'

'Around ten.'

'How long was he gone?'

'I don't know. Not long. Five minutes. Ten at the most.'

'And you've no idea who called him?'

'No.'

'How did he react to the call?'

'He didn't, really. He just answered it and went outside.'

'How did he seem? Was he upset? Overjoyed?'

'He didn't react either way. Just like it was some normal business matter or something. I was passing the table, and I heard him tell the others he'd be back in a couple of minutes.'

'What about the Kerrigans? Did either of them leave the restaurant at all?'

'No. They used the toilet once or twice – they had quite a lot to drink – but that's all. The rest of the time they stayed at the table.'

'What was the mood like?'

'Mood?'

'Yes. The dinner. Were they festive, celebrating, business-like, laughing, arguing . . .?'

'Oh, I see. Well, mostly they seemed in pretty good spirits. There were a few toasts – two bottles of Veuve Clicquot. They were certainly quieter earlier in the evening, when there were other diners present. I suppose they let their hair down a bit when they were the only ones left.'

'In what way?'

'You know, raised their voices a bit, that sort of thing.'

'Did you hear what they were talking about?'

Florence almost choked on her cigarette. 'I make it a point not to overhear conversations in the restaurant. Marcel wouldn't approve of my eavesdropping.'

'But surely you can't help it now and then? Even if it's just a word or two.'

Florence flicked ash from her cigarette. 'There's always plenty of other stuff to do.'

A young couple walked by hand in hand and Florence smiled at them.

'Were they just laughing a lot or talking business?' Annie asked.

'Bit of both, really. There was some laughter, especially later, after the sweets and Cognac, but mostly I think they must have been talking business, maybe celebrating a success of some sort.'

'But you don't know what?'

Florence looked around. Annie followed her gaze back towards the restaurant. The street was empty.

'They did raise their voices once, just after the last of the other diners had gone.'

'Who spoke? What did he say? Do you know what it was about?'

'No. But I think I heard one of them . . .' She glanced around her again. 'It was one of those brothers, the creepy one with the milky eye.'

'Tommy Kerrigan?'

'Right. He shouted something about a "fucking Albanian" or something like that.' She dropped her cigarette and stamped it out in the gutter. 'You won't do me for littering, will you?'

Annie shook her head. 'Are you sure that's what he said? About the Albanian?'

Florence shrugged. 'It's what I thought he said. He was definitely angry, though. His brother had to calm him down. You could tell he was ready to hurt someone.'

'Hurt who?'

'Anyone. I've seen him like that before. When he gets like that it doesn't matter. It could easily have been me if I hadn't made myself scarce. They're pigs, those two.'

'Are you sure you didn't hear anything else?'

'There was quite a bit of swearing. And the other brother called me a slut.'

'To your face?'

'No. I was in the kitchen, but I heard him. He said, "Let's tell the slut to bring our bill".'

'Did he give you a hard time when you appeared?'

Florence blushed. 'No, not really. Just the usual. "Come home with me, love, and I'll give you something to smile about." That sort of thing. And he kept calling me "sugar tits".'

All class, Timmy Kerrigan, thought Annie.

'Don't tell Marcel, please,' Florence said, touching Annie's arm. 'It was nothing, really. They're good customers, and he'll think I want him to bar them. He'd never forgive me.'

'Forgive *you*?' Annie said.

'You know what I mean. If it seemed like I was complaining and trying to make something out of it. He wouldn't tolerate behaviour like theirs, but he'd blame me. It was no big deal. It happens.'

'Not so often in a restaurant like Le Coq d'Or, I shouldn't think,' said Annie.

'You'd be surprised. Just because they're posh doesn't mean they're not nasty. Plenty of regulars seem to think they've got "coqs d'or" themselves.' Annie stared at her, mouth open for a couple of seconds, then they both burst out laughing.

When they'd quietened down, Florence said, 'I've got to go now. I still have a few things to do before we open. But there's one more thing that might interest you.'

Annie's mobile started to vibrate but she ignored it for the moment. 'What's that?'

'The creepy one. He looked as if he'd been in a fight. He had a cut over one eye and bruising on his cheek.'

'Ah,' said Annie. 'At least we know there's some justice in the world, then.'

Zelda had expected Keane to have changed his name along with his profession, especially as he was still wanted by the police for the attempted murder of Alan Banks, so she was hardly surprised by what Faye Butler told her. 'Perhaps we could have a private chat somewhere?' she said. 'The cafe? I promise I won't keep you long.'

'All right. You've got me curious now. Fifteen minutes.'

They headed up the stairs to the cafe and found a secluded corner table. Zelda fetched them two coffees and sat down opposite Faye.

'What I'd really like,' Zelda said, 'is to find this man, whatever name he's going under.'

'What's he done?'

'What makes you think he's done anything?'

'Well, the NCA is asking after him, for a start. And if he had a reason to change his name . . . I mean, why would someone do that if they didn't have something to hide?'

'Did you feel he had something to hide when you were with him?'

'He could be very secretive. I never felt I really got to know him. It's like there was always another layer. That was one of the problems, I suppose. I didn't feel I knew the *real* Hugh Foley. If there was one.'

'We don't know that he has done anything yet,' Zelda said. 'We just know that he was friendly with one or two criminals we had under surveillance.' She lay the picture on the table and tapped it. 'What do you remember about this other man in the photo with the two of you?'

'I don't remember anything. I don't even remember his name, if I ever did know it. They went off to a table for a private chat for a few minutes. I was talking to some friends from work at the bar. After that, we left and did some window-shopping. It was near Christmas. Then we went back.'

'Back where?'

'Hugh's hotel.'

'Hotel?'

'Yes. He travelled a lot in his line of work, so when he was here he usually stayed in a hotel. If we wanted to spend time together . . . you know . . . that's where we'd go. I was sharing a flat with two other girls, so it could be a bit awkward going to my place.'

'Do you know where he actually lived?'

Faye frowned. 'Not really. I mean, it never came up. I remember he once told me he was from Portsmouth, but he didn't live there. I think he might have lived on the continent somewhere. At least, that was the impression I got from the places he talked about.'

'The same hotel every time?'

'Yes. He said once you've found a good thing why change it.'

'Must have been expensive.'

Faye shrugged. 'Money never seemed to be a problem with Hugh.'

Zelda realised that she was living in a hotel at the moment, and money wasn't a great problem for her, either, though at least a part of her expenses were covered by the NCA. 'What was it called?'

'I can't remember. It was a small place, one of those boutique hotels with a foreign name. Quite nice, really. A city in Eastern Europe. Budapest? Bucharest? No. Belgrade. That's what it was called. The Belgrade.'

'Whereabouts is it?'

'Fitzrovia.'

Zelda knew the area. She had stayed at a Holiday Inn there once.

Faye blew on her coffee. 'What's this all about? Can't you give me just an inkling?'

She was an attractive woman, and Zelda could see how she would appeal to men. She was taller than Zelda remembered, and she now wore her blonde hair cut short, emphasising her heart-shaped face and big blue eyes. She had a sweet smile, when she chose to flash it. Not too sophisticated, but quick, bright and charming, certainly a good enough companion to show off at a business dinner with the boss. Her figure looked good, too, under the work clothes. Zelda imagined she would scrub up well. The problem was that Zelda couldn't yet decide whether Faye was as crooked as Keane/Foley or merely an innocent bystander. On first impressions, she was inclined towards the latter view, but she was keeping her options open.

'What does he do?' she asked.

'He's in art and antiques, a buyer for a number of swanky galleries. New York. Paris. Milan. Berlin. That sort of thing. He specialises in eastern and southern European artefacts and paintings. The Balkans, Greece, the ex-Soviet republics. Religious icons, that sort of thing. That's why he travels such a lot.'

It was a good cover, Zelda thought. 'Is that how you met?'

'Yes. Here. In the shop. He wanted to order a book on Bulgarian antiquities. It was out of print, and I said I'd do my best to locate a copy for him. Then . . . well, one thing led to another. He was quite charming, and very attractive. I suppose I was flattered. He asked me out for a drink. Then dinner. Then . . . Look, your English is wonderful, but I think I can hear a trace of an accent in the way you talk. Are you from Eastern Europe or somewhere like that?'

'Somewhere like that,' said Zelda.

'Only I met quite a few of them when I was with Hugh. You know, Serbs, Croatians, Bosnians.'

'I'm from Moldova.'

'Where's that?'

'Between Ukraine and Romania. A long way from the Balkans. Far enough, anyway. Did you ever meet a man called Petar Tadić?'

'Petar? From Croatia? Yes. We had drinks with him a few times. He wasn't too bad. Quite gallant, really. Nicer than his brother.'

Zelda felt herself tense up. Petar Tadić had been far from gallant when she had met him. 'His brother Goran?'

Faye hesitated. 'Yes. I think that was his name. He gave me the creeps.'

'What do you mean?'

Faye shrugged. 'You know. He was good-looking enough and all that, but he sort of *leered* at you. Undressed you with his eyes. Made suggestive comments. He'd lean over and whisper behind his hand in Hugh's ear, eyeing me all the while. That sort of thing. Hugh didn't like him, either. I could tell. He just had to do business with him, so he put up with him.'

Zelda nodded. If only that had been all Goran Tadić had done to her: leer and whisper crude comments. 'So when Hugh met the man in the Italian restaurant the evening that photograph was taken, you didn't take part in the discussions?'

'No. I was never involved in any business talks. To be honest, I could hardly imagine anything more boring. Could you? That was one of the things . . .' She let the thought trail off.

'What were you going to say?'

'It doesn't matter.'

'Please tell me.'

Faye studied her for a moment, then said, 'It was one of the bones of contention between us. Hugh's secrecy. And his business. It seemed there was always something going on, always some more important client, buyer or seller to meet, and I was . . . Well, it was always more important than me.'

'You felt you were relegated to second place?'

'Yes. Or third.'

'Did you know who this man he met that night was?'

'No. Hugh just said he was a business contact and he wouldn't be long.'

'Do you have any idea what they talked about?'

'No. It was pretty crowded and noisy. Like I said, I was at the bar chatting. I wasn't interested in Hugh's business meetings. Why are you asking all this? What has he done? He must have done something, or you wouldn't be asking me all these questions.'

'It's more the man he met that we're interested in,' Zelda lied. 'Along with the Tadić brothers.'

'Oh, I see. Well, I'm sorry, but I can't help you there. I know nothing about them. I wouldn't be surprised if that Goran Tadić wasn't up to his neck in something dirty, though. He had that aura about him.'

'Could you tell me anything more about the meeting in the Italian restaurant, from what you saw – your impressions, whatever?'

'What do you mean?'

'Did they appear to be arguing, problem-solving, joking?'

'It was just ordinary, really. Just a discussion.'

'Neither one was angry or particularly animated? No raised voices?'

'No, of course not.'

'Who did most of the talking?'

'Well, whenever I looked over to see if he was finished, Hugh seemed to be talking. I did see the other man try to interrupt once, but Hugh cut him off sharply.'

'As if he was telling him to do something? Lecturing him? Giving him orders?'

'Or giving him a bollocking. Just a mild one.'

So perhaps Hawkins *wasn't* warning Keane about her, after all, Zelda thought. Their meeting could have been about something else entirely, something to do with whatever it was that connected them. 'Did they exchange anything?'

'Like what?'

'Objects, pieces of paper, briefcases, that sort of thing.'

'No, nothing as far as I could tell. You mean like spies? Is he a spy, this man? Is Hugh a spy? Are you?'

'When did you stop seeing Hugh Foley?'

'A couple of months ago.'

'Why? If you don't mind me asking.'

'I can't see as it's any of the police's business, but in addition to what I've already told you, he was a bit of a bastard. I mean, there was already the important business stuff, and the secrecy, and how he was always disappearing; he was really unreliable, not turning up for dates and so on. But in the end it was the fact that he cheated on me that did it. The straw that broke the camel's back, you might say. Or at least *my* back.'

'Who with?'

'There was more than one. I suspected for a while.'

'You caught him red-handed?'

Faye nodded. 'Eventually.' She lowered her voice. 'In flagrante.' Then she put her hand to her mouth and started laughing. 'I'm sorry,' she said. 'But you had to be there. It was in the hotel. I went up once when he wasn't expecting me.'

'And he answered the door?'

'Yes. Opened it a crack. He wouldn't let me in, of course, said he wasn't feeling well, but I could tell what was going on. I even caught a glimpse of her in the mirror.'

Zelda smiled.

'It was no big deal,' Faye went on. 'We weren't serious or anything. It was just a bit of fun. I wasn't heartbroken.'

'Still,' said Zelda. 'A girl doesn't like to be two-timed.'

'Damn right. But I didn't shoot the both of them, or set fire to the bed, if that's what you're thinking.'

Zelda laughed. 'Good. Then I really would have to arrest you.'

Faye seemed uncertain for a moment whether she was joking, then she must have seen the humour in Zelda's expression, because she started laughing again. 'He was a bastard, plain and simple,' she said finally. 'It's not as if he's the only one. There are plenty more where he came from. Sometimes I think all men are bastards.'

'Can't live with them, can't live without them,' Zelda said. 'Have you seen him since?'

'No way. Cross me once, and you don't get another chance.'

'Who was the new girl?'

'No idea. Never saw her before. Or since.'

'Foley hasn't stalked you, harassed you in any way?'

'Lord, no.'

'Tell me about some of these people you met. The Eastern Europeans. Did you and Hugh socialise with them?'

'Yes. Usually at the hotel. They all seemed to hang out there a lot. The others usually had pretty girls on their arms, but the conversation was never up to much. You know the sort of thing.'

'Did you ever hear what they were talking about?'

'Only if we were all chatting together, you know. But some of the girls hardly spoke English.'

'Chatting about what?'

'Small talk, usually. The weather. Brexit. Movies. Football.'

'But not business?'

'Hugh knew it bored me. If they wanted to talk business, they would go off by themselves and do it.'

Zelda was almost convinced that Faye had nothing to do with Keane's secret, evil world. 'You're best out of it,' she said.

'What do you mean?'

'They're dangerous people, Faye. Take my word for it. You got out of their world without any serious emotional damage. You should put Hugh Foley right out of your mind and get on with your life. Are you seeing anyone else yet?'

'As a matter of fact, I am.'

'May I ask who?'

Faye paused. 'Well, it's none of your business, but it's someone here. At work.'

'Nothing to do with Foley and his pals?'

'You must be joking.'

'Good,' said Zelda. 'Excellent.' She stood up and Faye did likewise. 'I'm sorry to intrude on your day. I don't think I'll have to bother you again.'

'It's no bother, really,' said Faye. 'Quite exciting, really, being questioned by the NCA. My affair with a master criminal.'

'I wouldn't put it quite like that,' said Zelda, smiling. 'And it might be best if you weren't to tell anyone about our meeting.'

Faye put her finger to her mouth. 'My lips are sealed.'

At least Banks's office didn't resemble a government waiting room or an administrative annex, he thought. It had comfortable chairs around a low glass table and looked out over the market square, catching a little evening sunshine through its large sash windows, one of which was open a few inches. Banks had no idea what the couple's story was – they had just appeared in reception around six o'clock saying they were the dead boy's aunt and uncle from Huddersfield – but he had a feeling that the offices of foreign authority figures probably had bad memories for them. Even with Annie present, just back from Le Coq d'Or, the room didn't seem overcrowded.

They were in their late thirties, Banks guessed, and definitely of Middle Eastern origin. The uncle wore a brown suit, white shirt and loose tie, and his wife a western-style long dress that covered every inch of her except her head, over which she wore a simple green silk headscarf as a hijab, covering her head and framing her face and frightened brown eyes. She sat erect, knees together, clutching a brown faux-crocodile handbag on her lap. The uncle seemed more relaxed, legs crossed, leaning back in his chair a little. But his eyes also showed nervousness and had dark shadows under them. Banks knew it couldn't have been easy for them to come to the police, and he wondered if that was what had delayed them.

'I am Aimar Hadeed,' said the man, 'and this is my wife Ranim. I apologise, but we do not speak very fine English. Our language is Arabic.'

'We can get a translator if you like?' said Banks. 'It may take a while to set up, but if it makes you more comfortable . . .'

'I think I can manage,' Aimar said. 'It is my wife who does not speak so much.'

Banks smiled at Ranim Hadeed. She gave him a nervous smile in return. 'As you can imagine,' Aimar went on, 'we are both very upset.'

'Understandably,' Banks said. 'Perhaps you can begin by telling me why it took you so long to come here?'

Aimar spread his hands. 'We did not know. We do not read the newspapers. We do not have television. We are not ignorant people. We come from Aleppo, and we are thought to be very Western in many ways, but here we ... we feel lost ... We have a community. People like us, who speak our language. We do not drink. We go out very little.'

'How long have you been here?' Banks asked.

'We came in 2017.'

'And you've lived in Huddersfield all that time?'

'Yes.'

'And how did you find out about ...'

'His name is Samir,' Aimar said. 'Samir Boulad.'

'How did you find out about Samir?'

'A neighbour came yesterday. He told us of the boy who had been murdered in North Yorkshire. He showed us a photograph. It was Samir. And so we came here. Can we see him? Can we see Samir?'

'Yes. Later,' said Banks. 'I would like you to identify him for us. We couldn't find anyone who knew who he was.'

'We did not know he was here.'

'In England?'

Aimar nodded. 'We did not know he had arrived. Such a journey can take a long time.'

'Did you know he was coming?'

'Yes. We knew he had left Aleppo. My sister send us letter, but it takes long to arrive. But we do not know what happens after that. Where is Samir. How he travels. There are many perils.'

'Were you expecting him?'

'We thought he would come to us. Yes.'

'Did he know where you lived?'

'My sister write down address for him, but ... the journey ... many difficulties. Maybe he loses a small piece of paper?'

'And it's a big country,' said Banks.

Aimar smiled sadly. 'Yes.'

'Weren't you worried when he didn't turn up?'

'We worry every day. But we did not know where to look for him or when he would come. You must understand, Mr Banks, that many people make this journey. Many people attempt, but not all arrive. It is always possible he is still in Greece or Italy. Or France. Many people live in camps.'

'So nobody knew where he was living or what he was doing?'

'No. These people who sail boats and drive lorries, they are bad men. They rob and they kill. When you set out, you do not know if you will arrive or if you will drown. Or where you will arrive. How long it takes. It's a dangerous journey. Many rivers to cross. Many seas. There are many routes and many dangers on every one. Border checks, bandits. Samir wanted to come to show he was a true man and to light the way for his mother and father and sisters. To get money for them to come.'

'They couldn't afford to come?'

'They could not all pay, no. These smugglers want much money. And Ranim and I, we could not help. We both work, we clean offices at night, but it is not good job, and not good pay.'

'Samir's family was going to follow?'

'Yes. When Samir could send them money. But sometimes the men with boats, they make you keep paying. Samir very young. Only thirteen. They could make him work many months before they say he has paid them what he owes.'

'Well, he got here,' said Banks.

'But what happened? The paper my friend showed me said someone stabbed him.'

'I'm sorry, Mr Hadeed, but that's true. Yes.'

An expression of pain passed across his face. 'But why? He was only a boy. He never hurt anyone.'

'We don't know why. Until you came here today, we didn't even know his name or his nationality.'

Ranim put her head in her hands and wept. Her husband comforted her. When her tears had subsided, Banks asked if they would like more tea, or coffee. Aimar asked for a glass of water for his wife and Banks fetched it. Annie sat next to Ranim and helped comfort her. Banks was beginning to feel sick and angry. Samir had come all this way, suffered God only knew what trials and tribulations in his rite of passage, only to end up dead in a wheelie bin, without even an identity.

'I won't keep you much longer,' Banks said after handing the glass of water to Ranim. 'Do you know if Samir travelled legally at any stage? Would he have been through the formalities when he arrived here?'

'I do not know. But maybe I think not.'

'It doesn't matter. I mean, we are not from immigration. It's just a matter of checking with authorities to see if we have any record of him entering the country. Was he an asylum seeker?'

'He was scared young boy,' said Aimar. 'I think he maybe just get off boat and run.'

'I want to try and arrange for his parents to come to claim his body. I can't promise you anything, but I will—'

'No!' Aimar shook his head. 'No. You do not understand.'

'What don't I understand?'

'Ali, and my sister Lely. They cannot come here now.'

'Why not?'

Aimar grasped Ranim's hand. She was weeping again. 'Because they are dead,' he went on. 'All dead. Mother. Father. Sisters.'

'My God,' said Banks. 'How?' But even as he asked, he knew it was a silly question.

'Bomb,' said Aimar, and with tears in his eyes and a kind of matter-of-fact finality, he made a flying and diving gesture with his hand, then mimicked the sound of an explosion.

7

DC Gerry Masterson walked down Elmet Hill to talk to Granville Myers, who headed the local Neighbourhood Watch. She had talked to Myers before, while investigating the attack on Lisa Bartlett, and thought it was unlikely that he or any of his team would know anything about the death of Howard Stokes. It had taken place beyond the park, in what might well have been a foreign country. But the visit still had to be made. The residents of the hill area were already complaining about the lack of police presence – hence the Neighbourhood Watch – especially since Lisa's sexual assault a month ago.

Elmet Hill was a strange area. For a start, on printed town maps the main road was always referred to as Elmet Street, but nobody ever called it that. The tree-lined hill that curved like a bow on its way from North Market Street down to Cardigan Drive was known to all as Elmet Hill, and along its path it radiated a number of winding side streets – a Close, a Terrace, a Crescent, a Way, among others – which made up the area locals referred to as simply 'the hill'. It was not to be confused with The Heights, of course, Eastvale's poshest enclave. Gerry had often thought how strange it was to have all three in a row, running downhill from east to west: richest, less rich, poor.

Beyond the small park at the bottom of Elmet Hill ran Cardigan Drive, and over the street stood the decaying and mostly empty streets of the doomed Hollyfield Estate. A popular pub called The Oak stood at the south-eastern corner of Elmet Hill and Cardigan Drive, on the edge of the park, and its beer garden looked out on the trees and the narrow tributary of the River Swain that ran through the park.

The people fortunate enough to live in the pleasant, leafy streets around Elmet Hill were grateful for the short green belt that separated them from Hollyfield, and most people in the neighbourhood were in favour of the new development, although the idea of Elmet Hill being extended through the park at the bottom to form a link with the proposed new shopping centre was a bugbear. Nobody really wanted more traffic running up and down the hill, and nor did they want to lose their park. There were counterproposals, and the local citizens' committee were hopeful they could get some changes made to the present plan.

It was early evening, and Gerry was glad to be out of the squad room. She had just heard about the boy's aunt and uncle identifying their nephew's body. They could now put a name to him: Samir Boulad, from Syria. But they knew nothing else about him yet, except that he had made a long and hard journey away from his family, who had all been killed in a bombing after he left. Just when everyone was starting to think the war was almost over.

Gerry enjoyed the warmth of the sun on her face and her hair as she headed down Elmet Hill, only mildly annoyed that the sunny weather would probably bring out her freckles. Myers lived on one of the many narrow, meandering side streets, Elmet Close, and had said over the telephone that he would be pleased to talk to her again. Though he worked in the sales office of an agricultural supplies company in Helmthorpe, he said he often worked from home these days and would put fifteen minutes or so aside for her visit. So eager did he sound that she rather thought he might have an agenda of his own.

Myers's house was a Georgian semi with a large bay window and a reasonably sized, well-kept front garden, complete with crazy-paving, herbaceous borders, neatly-trimmed lawn and a small patch set aside for herbs. Gerry recognised basil, thyme and rosemary, and could smell their mingled aromas as she passed by. The front door was painted white – recently by the looks of it – with a brass door knocker and four small thick glass panes above the letterbox. There was also a bell, which Gerry pushed, and in no time at all the door was opened by a tall man in navy chinos and a blue and white checked short-sleeve shirt with breast pockets, one of which held a black pen. The white star on its cap protruded pretentiously.

'Come in,' said Granville Myers with a smile. He had a fine head of greying hair and a thin face, with a receding chin that Gerry thought might benefit from a small beard. Once again, she was struck by his resemblance to Nigel Farage. 'We'll sit in the kitchen,' he said, as she followed him inside. 'I've put some coffee on. Will that be all right? I can make tea if you'd prefer. DC Masterson, isn't it?'

'That's right. And coffee's fine, thank you,' said Gerry. The kitchen was a bright, airy room, all clean pine surfaces and gleaming white appliances, with four matching stools around a central island. Myers pointed to one and Gerry sat, resting her feet on the lower bar. The top of the island had a slight over-hang which formed a perfect recess under which her knees fitted snugly. Through the window, she could see the paved patio area in the back garden, with its outdoor grill and white table and chairs, all under the shade of a large striped umbrella and an overhanging willow. Very nice, indeed. The hill wasn't an area of town she knew well at all, and she could see why the locals might like it to remain a well-kept secret. She wondered what the house prices were like. More than she could afford, no doubt; she would be stuck in her one-bedroom flat on the edge of the student area for some time yet, she thought. Still, she had it all to herself, which was more than could be said for many young women away from home for the first time.

When he had poured them both coffee and put out the milk and sugar, Myers sat opposite Gerry and smiled. 'At your service,' he said.

'You may have heard,' she began, 'that there's been a death on Hollyfield Lane.'

'Yes. A drug addict, wasn't he?'

'That's right. A man in his sixties called Howard Stokes. We don't think there's anything suspicious about his death, but we still have to ask a few questions.'

'Overdose, was what I heard.'

'Pardon?'

'A drug overdose. That's what he died of.'

'I can't really comment on that.'

'Most likely self-administered.'

'We don't know that.'

'Oh, come, come, DC Masterson. Remember Lisa Bartlett?'

'Yes, of course, she's—'

'Then you might also remember that Lisa is the daughter of a very good friend of mine, Gus Bartlett, a fellow founding member of the Watch, and she was sexually assaulted hardly a quarter of a mile from here on her way home from Eastvale Comprehensive just a month ago. The poor girl is still traumatised, absolutely traumatised.'

'I investigated the case, as you know,' said Gerry, 'and it's terrible, but you have to—'

'Do you know how long it's been since we've had a regular police presence in this area? An occasional car passing through, let alone an officer walking the beat?'

'Our resources just don't—'

'Then what are you here for? It's not as if your solution rate is that high. I mean, you haven't found out who assaulted poor Lisa yet, have you?'

'Believe me, Mr Myers, it's not for want of trying. She wasn't able to give us a very accurate description of her attacker. But I want you to know we're still working on it.'

'Would *you* be able to give a description? If you were grabbed from behind and . . . and violently sexually assaulted in the dark? Do you really think you would be making notes of your attacker's appearance? I have children, DC Masterson. Including a nine-year-old daughter. Can you imagine how that makes me feel about living here with a monster like that on the loose? Can you?'

'Sir, these occurrences are very rare. Besides, it's not that—'

'Tell that to Gus Bartlett. The poor bloke's at his wits' end. Not to mention his wife, Sally. And Lisa's brother, poor Jason. He's having to try and concentrate on sitting his A-levels with all this going on. My own son's having a hard time of it, too. Jason and Chris are best friends.'

'I'm very sorry for your—'

Myers leaned back and seemed to relax. Now that he had said his piece, his voice took on a softer, more sing-song tone, as if placating a wayward child. 'I'm not blaming you, DC Masterson. I'm sure you're doing your best under the circumstances. No. It's the system. I realise that. A government that would rather spend money on campaigns to keep itself in power than on personal security, education and healthcare. I'm not blaming you personally, but I do think the police could try just a little bit harder.'

'I assure you the Lisa Bartlett case is still being investigated, sir. It's still active.'

'But the death of this drug addict takes precedence. Is that it?'

'Not at all. This is a separate issue.'

'And no doubt you're putting the rest of your resources into investigating the death of that young Arab up on the East Side Estate, eh?'

'His name is Samir Boulad, and he came here from Syria all by himself. And he *was* murdered. There's no doubt about that. Brutally stabbed to death, and we—'

Myers's voice hardened again. 'Are you saying that's worse than what happened to Lisa?'

There was no real answer to that if you were talking to the kind of person who thought an assault on a young white girl was worse than the murder of a Middle Eastern boy, but Lisa Bartlett would heal in time, would go on to live a normal and possibly very productive life; Samir Boulad would not. 'We don't make such comparisons, sir,' Gerry said. 'We have limited resources and we allocate them as best we can. I wish I could send you ten officers to patrol your neighbourhood every night of the week, but I can't.'

Myers ran his hand through his hair. 'I know,' he sighed. 'Believe me, I know. I'm sorry. Put it down to tiredness. I'm out almost every night with the Watch these days. It's tiring me out. All of us. But we can't risk another girl getting assaulted.' He smiled. 'Do you think I really want to give up my evenings to wander these streets until all hours? I'd rather be home with my wife watching TV and having a beer or two.'

'I'm sure you would, sir,' said Gerry. 'But I came to see if you could help us. After all, you *do* patrol the streets around here, even if you don't venture as far as Hollyfield. You know better than we do what's going on in the neighbourhood. How many of you are there?'

'In the Watch? Oh, it varies,' said Myers. 'We don't wear uniforms or anything, you know. We're not some paramilitary militia or vigilante outfit. We just walk the streets, usually in groups of two. My son Chris is also involved on occasion. And Lisa's father and brother. There's my next door neighbour, Bill Parsons; Harry, the landlord of The Oak at the bottom of the hill; the Farrars. Several others. Women as well as men. About twenty in all, but not all active at once, of course. We take turns.'

'Can you give me a list of the members?'

'Of course,' said Myers. 'I'll run off a copy for you before you leave.'

'Thank you, sir. Have you noticed anything unusual in the neighbourhood lately?'

'As you said, we don't patrol Hollyfield,' said Myers, 'and we certainly advise our children not to go there, so I can't really tell you anything about this drug addict. We do know Hollyfield's a haven for addicts and hooligans. They cross the park sometimes. We've had two break-ins lately, as well as the assault, you know, but since we've increased our patrols, things haven't been so bad. We might seem a bit like Dad's Army to you professionals, but we definitely act as a deterrent.'

Gerry wanted to say they hadn't been much of a deterrent on the night Lisa Bartlett was assaulted, but fortunately she was smart enough to realise before opening her mouth that it would be wiser to refrain. 'I know, sir,' she said. 'And we really do appreciate your help.'

'It'll be a red letter day when that whole bloody Hollyfield Estate has been rased to the ground, but until then we have to live next to it.'

'So you haven't noticed any strangers or suspicious characters in the neighbourhood?'

'No. Things have been fairly quiet lately.'

Gerry took the picture of Samir out of her briefcase. Banks had told her to ask about him whenever she talked to anyone in the area, no matter what she was talking to them about. She passed it over to Myers, and he made an expression of distaste as he looked at it.

'The dead boy, I suppose?' he said.

'Yes. Have you ever seen him at all?'

'Around here?'

'Anywhere.'

'No,' said Myers, pushing the photo back over the wooden surface. 'And I think I would have noticed. What would he be doing here? I thought his body was found on the East Side Estate?'

'That's correct,' said Gerry. 'But he wasn't necessarily killed there. And we have no idea what he was doing in Eastvale. That's what we'd like to find out.'

'Do you think he had something to do with the other drug addict's death? Is that what this is about?'

'Other drug addict?'

'This latest one. I'm assuming the boy was on drugs, too, or somehow involved?'

'We have no evidence to suggest that, sir, or reason to think it.' Gerry certainly wasn't going to tell him about the cocaine in Samir's pocket. That piece of information hadn't been released to the media. 'As far as I know, there's no connection between the two. Maybe your son would know something?'

'I can't imagine Chris having anything to do with him, either. I mean, there's the age difference, for a start. Eighteen-year-olds don't usually hang out with younger kids. Besides, Chris is busy with his A-levels at the moment. We're hoping he'll get into Oxford. The teachers have high hopes for him.'

'That's excellent, sir. Where does he go to school?'

'St Botolph's.'

'Ah.' St Botolph's was a minor public school in a moorland hollow a few miles north of Lyndgarth. It had an excellent reputation, and accepted day boys as well as boarders. Gerry knew that schools like St Botolph's also took quite a few foreign students, and for a moment the idea passed through her mind that Samir could have been a pupil there. He was the right age, and he could easily have come from a wealthy Syrian family. But he hadn't, as they had just discovered. 'Do you know anything at all about Howard Stokes, the dead drug addict?' she asked.

'Me? Why would I? All I know is what I've heard on the news.'

Gerry showed him a photograph. 'Have you seen him around?'

'He was that scruffy old bloke on the mobility scooter, wasn't he?'

'That's one way of describing him.'

Myers tapped the photo and nodded. 'I thought so. We had a bit of trouble with him once, hanging around the playground in the park, scaring the kids.'

'What did he do to scare them?'

'It was just his being there. He didn't have to *do* anything. His mere presence scared them. I mean, just look at the photo. Don't you think he's pretty scary?'

'Right, sir.' Gerry gathered her stuff together. 'I'll be off, then,' she said. 'Sorry to trouble you again. And thank you very much for your time.'

'I'll just run off that copy for you. Won't be a sec.'

Myers disappeared upstairs. Gerry heard a humming sound, and he was back in no time waving a sheet of paper.

'Thanks,' she said.

Myers saw her to the door. 'I hope you catch him,' he said. 'Whoever assaulted Lisa. Believe me, I know you have other serious demands on your time, but somehow, when it hits close to home, when it could have been one of your own . . .'

'I understand, sir. And we are doing our best.'

When she had made her escape, Gerry took a deep breath and paused on her way back to Elmet Hill. She should have known what to expect from Myers, even though she had a lot of sympathy with his concerns. The police couldn't patrol as they should, as they used to do. The bobby on the beat was a thing of the past, as the patrol car was quickly becoming, too. The money and the manpower just weren't there. More and more local Neighbourhood Watches like Myers's, and even private security companies, were having to fill the gaps. It was worse in the urban areas, of course, but there was plenty of crime in the counties these days, a lot of it due to drugs. And county lines.

When she got to the corner of the Close and Elmet Hill, instead of turning left back to North Market Street and the police station, she turned right, towards the park and the Hollyfield Estate beyond. One or two people still lived there, and they were more likely to have noticed anything unusual than the denizens of the hill.

Blaydon's driver Frankie Wallace was an ex-middleweight boxer who had never amounted to much more than a second-rate scrapper in the ring. Fortunately for him, he had the brains to retire before he lost the capability to do so. He drifted into low-level criminal activity in the Glasgow gang scene for a while, working as a 'debt collector' for slum landlords and partaking in various other dodgy activities, including illegal gambling and protection rackets. After his second jail term, he came to what little senses he had left and gained honest employment first as a club bouncer, then as chauffeur-cum-bodyguard, first for a wealthy banker in London, then for

Connor Clive Blaydon back up north. He was fifty-one years old and had been working for Blaydon for five years when Banks went to talk to him in his small terrace house just outside the York city centre.

'Evening, Frankie,' said Banks when a sweaty Wallace opened the door in his string vest and rugby trousers. 'Been pounding the crap out of a punch bag?'

Wallace grunted. 'I like to keep fit.'

'Good for you.' Banks couldn't help noticing that Wallace did still look fit, more muscle than fat. His face was a mass of hardened scar tissue which probably didn't even feel incoming punches, and his nose and left ear didn't seem to have recovered from his years in the ring. 'Remember me?'

'I never forget a copper. You're Banks, aren't you? You did me once. Long time ago.'

'That's right. Good to know all those punches you let through your guard haven't done your memory any harm. Can I come in?'

'I suppose you'd better. Excuse the mess.'

The mess wasn't quite as bad as Banks expected for a man of Wallace's intelligence and social skills living alone, though it did smell a bit like a gym at closing time. The living room was untidy but clean, with a massive flat-screen TV dominating one corner. Its obvious focal point, though, was a glass case full of trophies: cups, shields, belts and gloves.

'What is it you're after?' Wallace said when they had sat down.

'A bit of information.'

'I'll no talk about my clients, if that's what you mean. That's privileged, like a doctor or a vicar.'

'I understand you work exclusively for Connor Clive Blaydon these days?'

'Aye.'

'Works you hard, does he?'

'Well, he doesn't drive, himself, so I get plenty of practice, thank you.'

'Where do you drive him?'

'All over the place.'

'Can you be more specific?'

'No. It's between him and me.'

'How does it work?'

'I don't get you.'

'Well, you don't live on the premises. Are you on call?'

'Oh, I see. Aye. He gives me a bell, and I'm there in twenty minutes, tops.'

'Where do you keep the Merc? I didn't see one out on the street.'

'You must be joking. Car like that wouldn't last five minutes around these parts. He keeps it at his place, and I drive over in my wee Toyota when he calls.'

'You'd have to break a few speed limits to get there in twenty minutes from here.'

Wallace just glared at him. 'Speeding now, is it?'

'No. It's the other part of your job I'm interested in.'

'What other part?'

'Messages, errands, muscle, bodyguard stuff.'

'I don't do anything wrong.'

'Not saying you do.'

'So?'

'So what?'

'So what do you want? I haven't got all day.'

'Answer my questions and it'll be over a lot quicker.'

'I am answering your questions, as best I can. You haven't really asked any yet.'

'Fair enough. Do you ever drive Blaydon to London?'

'I told you—'

'Oh, go on, answer me, Frankie. What harm can it do? Just in general. London's a big place.'

Wallace muttered to himself for a moment, then said, 'Aye, of course. The boss does a lot of business there. He's got an office and all that. Nothing secret about it.'

'What do you think of Leka Gashi?'

'Come again.'

'Leka Gashi. The Albanian.'

'Can't say I know anyone by that name.'

But judging by Wallace's darkening expression and the tone of his voice, Banks guessed that was not the case. He filed it away in his mind for future reference. 'Is there something secret about the places Blaydon asks you to drive him?' he asked.

'I didn't say that. It's just his business, that's all. You're putting words in my mouth.'

'OK, Frankie, I'll make it easy. Did you drive Connor Clive Blaydon up to Eastvale last Sunday evening? And now I do want straight answers or I'll take you in.'

'Aye. I drove him. What of it?'

'Where did you drive him?'

'That poncy French restaurant he goes to by the market square. Bloody nightmare driving around there, it is.'

'There's no parking, I understand.'

'That's right.'

'So where did you park?'

'Back of the market square.'

'How long?'

'About half seven to just before eleven, when he rang me to pick him up. Why?'

'Long time to be sitting there by yourself. Don't you get bored? How do you pass the time? Do you read Proust, do *The Times* crossword or something?'

'Give me a break. It's the modern age, Mr Banks.'

'What do you mean?'

'I'm online. With my Galaxy pad. Got Netflix and everything.'

'So you watch movies?'

'Sometimes. Depends. Sometimes I can even get a live game of footie or rugby. Or I watch YouTube. Lots of stuff on there. Fights and all.'

'And on Sunday?'

'*Downton Abbey*. Seen it before, like, but it's worth watching again.' Frankie scratched his armpit. 'I wouldn't half mind giving that Lady Mary a good shag.'

Banks swallowed. 'I'm sure she would appreciate it, Frankie. What about eating?'

Frankie leered. 'That, too.'

'I mean where did you go?'

'Oh. One of those pubs in the market square. I don't remember what it was called.'

'The Bull? The Castle? The Queen's Arms? The Red Lion?'

'One of those.'

'What did you have to eat?'

'Steak and mushroom pie.'

'And to drink?'

'Coca-Cola. I never touch alcohol.'

'Not even when you're not driving?'

'Never. I learned my lessons a long time ago.'

'So apart from taking a meal break in one of the pubs on the market square, you sat in your car all evening?'

'Until Mr Blaydon rang me.'

'And then?'

'Drove back to the restaurant, didn't I? He was just around the corner. Would've been quicker if they'd walked to the car. Bloody pain in the arse getting in and out of that street, but what can I say, that's my job.'

'Was Mr Blaydon alone?'

'No. He was with the Kerrigan brothers, Tommy and Timmy. Right couple of pillocks, those two, you ask me.'

'I wouldn't disagree,' said Banks. 'Did they get in the car with him?'

'Aye. Expected me to drive them home.'

'Where did you drop them off?'

'At their place, just outside town. It was on our way, more or less.'

'Anyone else with you?'

'No.'

'Had you picked the Kerrigans up on your way in?'

'Nah. They'd driven in their own car, but they were too pissed to drive back, silly buggers. Right pair of girls' blouses.'

'Had Mr Blaydon had too much to drink?'

'They were all a bit pissed, if you ask me. But the boss can hold his liquor.'

So much for the privileged nature of the chauffeur-passenger relationship. Banks decided to push it a bit further. 'How did they behave towards one another in the car?'

'What do you mean?'

'Were they chatting, laughing, telling jokes, that sort of thing?'

Wallace wagged a finger at him. 'Don't think I don't know your game. You're not going to get me to tell you anything that was said, if that's what you're after.'

Banks spread his hands. 'But it wouldn't do any harm to tell me the general mood of your passengers, would it?'

Wallace eyed Banks and chewed on his lower lip for a while. Finally, he said, 'Well, if you must know, that Tommy Kerrigan was pissed off about something, but he's always on edge, the creepy little queer.'

'About what?'

'Can't tell because I don't know, and wouldn't if I did.'

'Was he upset with Mr Blaydon?'

'Not specifically.'

'So what was it about?'

'I told you. I don't know. I can tell you one thing, though.'

'What's that?'

'Somebody had given him a thrashing.'

Annie had told Banks that Florence, the maître d' at Le Coq d'Or, had mentioned the cut over Tommy Kerrigan's eye and his bruised cheek. 'Any idea how that happened?' Banks asked.

'No. It wasn't mentioned. Least not while I was around. That's what he was pissed off about, though. Silly wee bugger gets himself into a fight with that temper of his and blames Mr Blaydon.'

'Is that what he was doing, blaming your boss?'

'Well, he was certainly complaining to him.'

'About whom?'

'No idea. Whoever did it.'

Banks sighed. He wasn't going to get much further with Frankie Wallace. 'Is there anything else you can tell me?' he asked.

'I think I've already told you too much,' said Wallace.

'I shouldn't worry about that if I were you. You haven't really told me anything I'd need to follow up with Mr Blaydon.'

Wallace shrugged. 'No skin off my nose. You done now?'

Banks stood up. 'I think so.' He paused at the door, Columbo-style. 'Just one more thing, Frankie. You don't happen to know anything about a bloke called Howard Stokes, do you?'

'Stokes? No, I can't say as I know the name. Why?'

'Found dead on Hollyfield Lane a couple of days ago. Number twenty-six. Drug overdose.'

'Happens a lot these days,' said Wallace. 'Nasty things, drugs. Never touch them, myself.'

'Good for you,' said Banks. 'Only I understand the Kerrigans own the house he was found in, and your boss is heavily involved in the redevelopment plans for the area.'

'Small world.'

'Isn't it just,' said Banks, who had the distinct feeling that Wallace was lying about not knowing who Howard Stokes was as he closed the door and walked back to his car.

The Hotel Belgrade, where Faye Butler had said Keane stayed when he was in town, was easy to find. It occupied part of an elegant five-storey terrace near Fitzroy Square Garden, all white stucco facades behind black iron railings, ornate stonework, steps down to a basement level, heavy blue-panelled doors with frosted glass lunettes. The hotel had no kitchen or restaurant, only a small library bar in the basement, but just next door was a spacious bar and grill, very trendy judging by its popularity and the affluent and carefree demeanour of its clientele. The bar and grill had its own front entrance, as well as a door leading from the hotel's cramped lobby.

Unlike larger hotel lobbies with their crowds and open spaces, The Belgrade wasn't a place where Zelda felt she could hang around unnoticed, reading her book and keeping an eye out. Any unattached attractive woman with no reason for being there would probably be taken for a prostitute and asked to leave. But the bar and grill was perfect. Like the Italian restaurant it was spacious, dim and mostly crowded after work. It was casual enough that a person could sit and enjoy a couple of drinks without being pestered to order food, though their steak frites was excellent, she discovered, and the windows opened on the street outside.

Zelda sat in a corner mulling over the interview with Danvers and Deborah Fletcher again. Danvers had phoned that morning and told her abruptly that she was no longer needed, and she could go home if she wanted. But Raymond had told her he wouldn't be back for perhaps another week, and she didn't feel like being up in Lyndgarth all alone with her mind full of the Tadićs, Keane, Hawkins and bad memories, so she decided to stay on for a while longer and see what she could find out.

Worried that someone might be following her, Zelda had begun taking steps. She had seen enough films to know that stepping on or off a tube train at the last moment often worked, as did entering a shop by one set of doors and leaving by another, or if all else failed, simply jumping in a taxi. Evasive action tipped off your tail, of course, but she didn't care. As she couldn't see who, or how many, were following her – if any were – she didn't know whether she had been successful or not in losing them. But it didn't really matter. At least, not yet.

She always restricted herself to two glasses of wine. She didn't mind getting tipsy in the right company, but if she was going to do what she set out to do, she needed to keep a clear head. There had been a period when she had taken to drink and drugs to help numb her pain. That had worked for a while, but she started to hate the way it made her feel, so she stopped. Doing so hadn't given her much trouble, especially as it was after she had escaped the dark world of forced sex and was starting to carve out an existence as a London pavement artist, a few months before she met Raymond. By the time she met him, she was sober and drug-free, apart from the occasional joint they shared. She only wished cigarettes were as easy to give up, but she had tried and she couldn't. It was especially annoying because she couldn't smoke in her hotel room, or in bars and cafes, places she wanted to sit and relax – like now, in the bar and grill next door to Hotel Belgrade. How wonderful it would be to sip her wine along with the occasional inhalation of cigarette smoke. She had tried those silly vape things, but they had lasted about as long as nicotine gum.

She did her best to be unnoticeable that evening, dressing down in baggy clothes, tying her hair back, going without make-up – even wearing glasses – and it seemed to work. As far as most people were concerned, she was probably just another young office worker on her way home after a hard day's filing or whatever, stopping for a drink or two to help smooth out the tensions of the day, or give her courage to face the husband and kids. The bar staff probably assumed she was a guest at the hotel. At least, nobody had pestered her so far, except a fairly large group asking if she would mind moving to a smaller table so that they could all sit together.

The people at the table next to hers were getting noisier as they reached the third or fourth drink mark. And there was loud music, or at least a thumping bass beat that passed itself off as music. Zelda was starting to feel the onset of a headache.

She had finished her second drink, paid the bill and was about to leave when, all of a sudden, she saw someone whose presence seemed to dampen the sound, charge the atmosphere and make everything feel as if it were at the wrong end of a telescope.

The tall, burly figure walked through the door from the hotel reception. Though he was wearing a crisp white linen suit, bright green shirt and purple tie, and had traded his lank and greasy black hair for closely-cropped salt-and-pepper, there was no doubt in Zelda's mind that she was looking at Goran Tadić, one of the two men who had bundled her into a car when she left the orphanage in Chişinău.

*   *   *

The little park was a real haven, Gerry thought as she passed by the children's playground with its swings, roundabout, slide and monkey bars, and took a winding path down to the side of the narrow beck, where she sat on a bench under the weeping willows. The beck moved swiftly, but it was shallow enough and the water took on the light brown beer colour of its bed. A couple of small wooden bridges, one green and one white, led over to the other side, a swathe of mixed trees and shrubbery, beyond which lay Cardigan Drive and the Hollyfield Estate. A row of stepping stones poked out of the water about halfway between the bridges, and Gerry imagined the children had fun using them. At that time of evening, though, in school term time, there was hardly anyone around. One or two solitary dog-walkers passed her, nodding a hello as they went, but that was about it. It was odd to think that Lisa Bartlett was assaulted so nearby not too long ago. But even the most pleasant of spots can take on a whole new aspect after dark.

Gerry experienced a sense of calm and peace she rarely felt in the town. Even though she could hear distant voices and the traffic on Cardigan Drive, she felt enveloped by nature, enchanted by birdsong and immersed in a green world of willow, ash and holly. She watched tits and finches flitting from branch to branch, saw magpies perched high in the trees and heard the loud cries of the crows as they flung themselves into the sky like harbingers of fast-falling night. The flower beds were a riot of colour. The May blossom had been and gone – coming earlier each year – though a few of the shrivelled blooms still littered the path and grass along with pussy willow and dried catkins.

Gerry had read an article in one of the papers recently about something called 'forest bathing', how it could relax you and remove the stress from your life. You just *immerse* yourself in a forest. The Japanese called it *shinrin-yoku*, and its beneficial effects apparently had something to do with the chemicals trees release into the air. Maybe she would try it. She was all for using her senses to soak up the atmosphere of the woods and leave her cares behind. Maybe the entire Homicide and Major Crimes Unit should come out and try it. She could just imagine Detective Superintendent Banks getting in touch with his inner forest.

She left the bench and tottered across the stepping stones, arms spread like a tightrope walker, and managed to make it to the other side without getting wet. There, she followed the path for another few yards through some dense shrubbery, after which she emerged, rather disappointingly, at Cardigan Drive, which she crossed by the traffic lights to get to Hollyfield Lane. The old estate looked more like a bomb site than a residential area, and pretty soon there would be no trace of it left whatsoever. It had been built on a simple grid pattern, with one main road, Hollyfield Lane, leading west, off which radiated the side streets. The Lane eventually petered out into weeds and wasteland, and beyond that, Gerry could see a lone yellow mechanical digger standing in a field, as if waiting impatiently to get to work.

She passed number twenty-six, the house where Howard Stokes's body had been found. The CSIs clearly hadn't finished there yet, as the place was still cordoned off by police tape and a uniformed constable stood on guard. He recognised Gerry and said hello as she passed.

Gerry started at the far end of Hollyfield Lane, by the waste ground, on the opposite side of the street, and made her way back slowly. Most of the houses were empty, but occasionally she spotted a pair of curtains, and she would knock at the door. No one she talked to admitted to recognising Samir or knowing anything about the man who lived at number twenty-six, except that he was old and scruffy and went about on a mobility scooter. But when she got a bit closer, to number forty-seven, a large woman in her late sixties with frizzy grey hair and a brightly-patterned muumuu dress, who clearly kept her eye on the street, invited her in. The walls of the living room were covered in paintings, most of them original works, as far as Gerry could tell. Watercolours, oils, montages of found objects. It was like a miniature art gallery.

'I was out when one of your lot called the other day,' she said, wedging herself into a well-worn armchair. 'Staying with a friend in Carlisle. They left a note, like, and a contact number, but I haven't got around to ringing it yet. I'll be moving out after the weekend – got some nice sheltered accommodation near the river on the other side of town – so as you can see, I've got quite a bit of sorting out to do. I tell you, that Marie Kondo's got nothing on me. I've already thanked three sacks full of stuff for the joy they've given me and dropped them off at Age Concern. It can be quite heart-breaking sorting through a lifetime's old photo albums and love letters, you know. Quite heartbreaking.'

'I'm sure it can be,' said Gerry, who didn't have any love letters to sort through.

The woman, who introduced herself as Margery Cunningham, leaned forward to pat the chair opposite her. Gerry sat there.

'When you're old, people can't imagine you ever being young,' the woman went on. 'But I had a life. Oh, my, did I have a life. I was quite a beauty in my day, you know.' She pointed to one of the paintings, a watercolour of a nude reclining on a sofa. 'I was a muse. That's me when I was twenty-three,' she said. 'Hardly believe it now, would you?'

'You were certainly very lovely,' said Gerry.

'You're too kind. I was just like you. Only my hair wasn't ginger, of course. But you're a very pretty girl. You'd make a fine artist's model.'

Gerry blushed. 'Thank you.'

'You have the look of those Pre-Raphaelite girls about you. A little sad, a little lost, maybe, but very strong and very beautiful. Sensual. Full of character. I should know. I used to live with an artist.'

Gerry groaned inwardly. She had often thought that if one more person compared her to a Pre-Raphaelite model she would hit them, but she wasn't going to hit Margery Cunningham, of course. Ray Cabbot, Annie's father, was always telling her the same thing, especially when he'd had a few drinks and wanted to paint her in the nude. In all fairness, though, he had produced a wonderful sketch of her, fully clothed, which she had framed and hung on the wall of her tiny flat. Annie usually brought him back to earth, while his girlfriend Zelda would sit there with an enigmatic smile on her face. Gerry didn't get Zelda at all. Naturally, all the men were falling over themselves to be of service to her, even Banks, and Gerry knew something of her troubled history, but she had never been able to communicate with her on the few occasions they had met, finding her distant and unresponsive much of the time.

'I was just wondering if you knew Mr Stokes at number twenty-six,' Gerry said.

'I thought that's who it would be about. I wouldn't say I knew him, but we'd certainly say good morning if we met in the street. He was a gentleman, was Mr Stokes, no matter what they say about him in the papers.'

'What have they said about him?'

'You know. The drugs and all. I never saw him take any drugs, and he never did anyone any harm. And where's the harm, I say, if you choose to spend your days in cloud cuckoo land? Makes a damn sight more sense than spending them in the real world, the way it's going these days, I can tell you. Or spending your life being a nuisance to others, stabbing people and beating people up. He wasn't always on the scooter, you know.'

'How long?'

'A year. Less. It was mostly the diabetes, see. He told me about it once. Gets into your feet, it does. I think he lost a couple of toes. But before, like, when he used to walk around on his own, I never once saw him stumble or stagger. And he always said hello. Like I said, a gentleman.'

It didn't take much to be a gentleman in Margery Cunningham's world, Gerry thought. 'Was he ever suspected of any crimes in the neighbourhood?'

'Believe it or not, we didn't really have much crime, love. Nobody had anything, you see. Not anything worth stealing, at any rate. If thieves wanted good pickings, they'd head off through the park and up the hill.' She laughed, coughed and patted her chest. 'But if you're asking did Mr Stokes cause any trouble around here, then my answer is no. Not that I know of. He didn't have any visitors except when that grandson of his was staying.'

'His grandson?'

'Well, I assume that's who he was. Young lad, anyway. Looked about the right age.'

'Did this grandson visit often?'

'Every week or so. Usually stayed a night or two.'

Gerry brought out her photo of Samir and asked, 'Was this him?'

Margery Cunningham shook her head. 'No, dearie. The boy I saw wasn't dark-skinned. I know who this one is, like, and what happened. Saw his picture in the papers. Terrible. But I've never seen *him* around here.'

Disappointed, Gerry put the photograph away. 'His name was Samir,' she said, though she didn't know why she said it. 'Can you describe this grandson?'

'He was a typical teenager, pleasant enough, but a bit shifty, if you know what I mean. Always seemed as if he was hiding something or up to something. But a lot of kids are like that, aren't they, always looking as if they've had their hand in the piggy bank? Didn't go out much. Rode a bike sometimes. Always wearing a backpack.'

'What colour hair?'

'Fair. And cut short, like they have it these days. I must say I preferred it when I was a young lass and all the lads had long hair.'

She got a faraway look in her eye, and Gerry hurried along to avoid a 'those were the days' digression. 'Tall or short?'

'Medium.'

'Fat or thin?'

'Thin.'

'Clothes?'

'Jeans and T-shirt when it was warm enough. Usually with something written on it. The T-shirt, that is.'

'Can you remember what?'

'No. There were several different ones. Images of the devil or skeletons. That sort of thing.'

'Like heavy metal images?'

'Yes. Like Black Sabbath used to wear.'

'Anything else?'

'Trainers, mostly. White. I don't know what brand. Little ticks on them. They all look the same to me.'

Nike, Gerry noted. 'And when it was cooler?'

'One of those hoodie jackets. The ones that make everyone look like a criminal.'

'What kind of a bicycle did he ride?'

'Now you're asking me. All I can say is, it wasn't like those in that Tour de France that came through here a few years ago. It had straight handlebars, for a start, not those bent ones, like goats' horns.'

'Do you remember what colour it was?'

'Red. Bright red.'

'You're doing really well, Mrs Cunningham. How long ago was he here?'

'Margery, please, love. A while ago. I haven't seen him for two or three weeks now. Maybe longer. Time seems to go by a lot faster these days.'

'Is it unusual for him not to visit for so long?'

'I suppose so. Like I said, he used to come up more often than that.'

'And how long had he been visiting Mr Stokes?'

'Past year or so. Back and forth.'

'Do you know where he went when he wasn't here?'

'No idea, love. We never talked beyond saying good morning. He didn't come and kiss me goodbye. Home to his mum and dad, I suppose, for all I know.'

'Did he have people visiting him?'

'Yes. Odd that, really. When Mr Stokes was there by himself, you'd never see anyone there from one day to the next. But the lad had quite a few visitors. And he was hardly off that mobile phone of his. I've no time for them, myself.'

'What kind of visitors did the boy have?'

'Mostly kids his own age, or older. Some of them seemed a bit seedy. All sorts, really. They never caused any trouble, though. Mostly they didn't stay long.'

'What did Mr Stokes have to say about it?'

'Nothing. Not to me, at any rate.' She paused. 'Oh, dear. How can I say this without sounding judgemental? I mean, I wouldn't want to speak ill of the dead, but . . .'

'Go on, Mrs Cunningham.'

'Margery, please. Well, it's just that Mr Stokes was a bit . . . like he wasn't all there. He was in his own world. I don't know what you'd call it. We used to say retarded, but I don't know what the word is now. But it wasn't his fault.'

'What wasn't?'

'That he hadn't had much education, though he did like to read a lot. He was a bit childlike, if you know what I mean. I think maybe that young lad took advantage of him, having his friends round and all.'

Gerry was getting the distinct impression that this was a textbook county lines operation. But what had happened to the operation? Perhaps the young man in question would be back. Or perhaps he had been replaced by Samir. But Margery Cunningham said she hadn't seen Samir around the neighbourhood, and she had no reason to lie.

'Do you remember the boy's name?' Gerry asked.

'Never knew it.'

'Would you recognise him if you saw him again?'

'I think so.'

'Can you tell me anything more about him?'

'No, love. I'm sorry.' She rubbed her eyes. 'I'm tired,' she said. 'Do you know, I've been here over twenty-five years, but I shan't be sad to leave. It used to be a nice estate, the Hollyfield. Good people. Honest. Decent. For the most part. You got the odd bad 'un. You always do, don't you? But look at it now. Pah. No. Take me to my sheltered flat. That's what I say. I'll live out my days quite happily there. The sooner they knock this bloody place to the ground, the better.'

That was the second time today Gerry had heard that sentiment expressed, she realised as she headed back towards the park.

*　　*　　*

Tadić certainly appeared more presentable than the scruffy, unwashed animal Zelda remembered, as no doubt befit his elevated status in the organisation, but it *was* him. She was certain. Put an ogre in an expensive suit and it was still an ogre. Though she tried to keep a grip on herself, she couldn't help but grab her book and her shoulder bag and rush towards the street exit. As she did so, her bag knocked over the empty wine glass, and it shattered on the floor. His head jerked in her direction. She felt a chill run through her, as if she had inadvertently awoken a sleeping snake or crocodile, some sort of reptilian beast that operated on instinct alone. She kept going, ignoring the nasty looks she got from people she bumped into, until she was out in the street. Once there, she merged with the flow of pedestrians heading towards Marylebone Road and Great Portland Street Underground. She had no idea where she was going, only that her breath was tight in her chest, her heart was pounding dangerously fast and she had to get away from the Hotel Belgrade.

Every now and then she glanced back to see if Tadić was following her, but she didn't see him. Why should he be? It was nothing, she tried to tell herself. A woman gets up and knocks her glass over by accident. People react to the sound, that's all. Besides, the last time he had seen Zelda, she had been just seventeen years old. She looked very different now, and her nose hadn't been broken then. Besides, context is everything. He wouldn't recognise her, and he certainly wouldn't expect to bump into her in a London hotel bar. As far as she knew, they had had no contact after the breaking house in Vršac, and he must have broken in hundreds of girls after her.

Not that he had waited until Vršac to begin the process. They had a twelve- or thirteen-hour drive across Romania first, and Goran Tadić had started as soon as they got on the highway, messing with her clothes, groping her breasts in the back of the car. She had tried to resist but whenever she did, he would hit her again. And though he couldn't take her valuable virginity, it didn't stop him from anally raping her. As the car sped through the wild and mountainous countryside of Transylvania, she could do nothing but lie there face down on the car seat and take it. All she could remember now was the pain, the smell of the dreadful cigar his brother was smoking as he drove and the relentless thumping and surging of the American rap music playing in the car. Finally, she had passed out and only came to a while later, when Goran Tadić was in the driver's seat and his brother Petar in the back with her, ready to take his turn. Again she fought, and again it was to no avail. Even as early as that, she began to learn how they only hurt her more if she fought them, how to find that place outside herself, to watch the actions disinterestedly, as if from a great distance, and to numb all feeling. But she wasn't quite so skilled at the start as she became later. This was before she learned to live with pain, to float inside it. It hurt. She bled. She cried.

She tried to escape through a cafe's toilet window when they stopped for burgers somewhere near Brasov, but Goran was waiting, a cruel smile on his face, and she was punished for that. And so they had their way with her all the way from Chişinău to Vršac. They crossed two international borders, first into Romania and from there into Serbia, and in neither case did the border guards take the slightest interest in these two men and the clearly distraught young girl they had in the car with them. No questions were asked; they were simply waved through. Often, she wondered later whether money had changed hands – it wouldn't have surprised her – but she decided it hadn't. It was just the way things were.

And there he was again, in the flesh, the man who had done all that to her, just walking casually into a trendy London bar in an expensive suit and gaudy shirt, cool as anything, not a care in the world, lord of all he surveyed. She relived that journey through hell as she wandered among the anonymous crowds of the London evening, not knowing where she was going, only that she had to get away, that every good thing she had built for herself since her escape felt as if it was crumbling inside her.

Zelda travelled aimlessly on the tube from line to line, stop to stop. Occasionally, someone would ask her if she was all right, and she would respond with a mechanical nod and a forced smile. What could they do? What did they know, safe in their comfortable middle-class lives with nothing more to worry about than their mortgage payments and the children's exam results? Finally, she found herself at Waterloo and walked back to her hotel.

The rooftop bar was still open, and by then she felt she needed a drink more than she had in a long time. She ordered a large vodka and tonic instead of wine and lifted the glass to her mouth, hand shaking. She must have looked like a serious alcoholic because people stayed away from her. Then she had another drink and sat there staring out at the night skyline, the way she had stared at the dawn skyline in the morning, just a few days ago, when she woke from the bad dreams. Here, from the height of the roof, she had a different view – the Eye; the Houses of Parliament, lit up all gold; Big Ben covered in scaffolding, but always there was the river, its currents like dark sinews twisting, distorting and knotting the reflections of the city lights the way she felt twisted, distorted and knotted inside.

The music was late evening light jazz, and what few conversations there were around her were hushed. It was seduction time, and the young couples were edging closer together, a light touch of thigh to thigh here, an arm casually brushing a breast there. Zelda knew all about it. She had done the seductive sex as well as suffered the violent kind. It was how she had made her living – *their* living – in Paris, and how she had finally made her escape from that world.

After the dreadful car journey across Romania, Zelda remembered being left alone in a filthy room for days – she wasn't sure exactly how many – with her meals delivered, black bread, borscht, gruel . . .

And then, one day, without warning, she was taken into another room, larger, cleaner, with a large bed. After a few minutes a man came in. He was old and fat, and he smelled of fried chicken. He wasn't rough or violent – he was quite gentle, really – but he took what he wanted and left her crying. That was how she lost her virginity. She learned later that it had been auctioned off, and the fat man had won. Apparently, he always won; he was one of the wealthiest businessmen in town, the owner of a chain of fried chicken restaurants.

By the time Zelda got to bed that night, she knew one thing for certain: now that she had seen Goran Tadić again, she had to kill him.

8

The coffee and doughnuts lay spread out on the large oval table in the boardroom on Friday morning. In addition to the core team, also present were DS Stefan Nowak, Crime Scene Manager; Vic Manson, fingerprints expert; and Dr Jasminder 'Jazz' Singh, their toxicology, blood and DNA specialist from the lab. Everyone present seemed tired; Thursday had been a long day.

'You've got some good news for us, I hope, Stefan?' Banks said to DS Nowak.

'Yes,' said Nowak. 'We've been able to link the dead boy, Samir, with the Stokes house on the Hollyfield Estate. Naturally, we can't tell you *when* he was there, but he definitely *was* there.'

'Was he killed there?'

'Unlikely,' said the diminutive Jazz Singh. 'No blood other than Howard Stokes's turned up. And very little of that. If Samir had been killed there, you'd expect ... well, you'd expect to see blood.'

'Unless someone cleaned it up?' Banks suggested.

'Of course. That's where the Luminol came in handy. We were very thorough. Believe me, nobody can do a perfect clean-up.'

'Thanks, Jazz,' said Banks, reaching for a doughnut. 'So what *did* you find?'

'Stefan's team found several hairs with follicles intact on the back of one of the armchairs. They found hairs on the backs of both chairs, actually, but the other ones belonged to Howard Stokes.'

'What about the mattresses?'

'Howard Stokes's hair on one, and someone else's on the other, though it had been turned over, and the mattress itself had been stripped of sheets. It didn't look as if it had been used recently. Not Samir's hair, by the way. Blond and short. There were no follicles, so we couldn't run DNA.'

'It must belong to the boy Margery Cunningham told me about yesterday,' said Gerry. 'The one she thought was Stokes's grandson. The one who came and went. He rode around on a red bicycle and had a lot of visitors.'

'Likely,' said Banks. 'And if there were no traces of Samir on the mattress, the odds are that he didn't spend a night in the house. As he was seen by several people arriving in Eastvale on Sunday evening, we have to assume that he didn't spend very long there at all.' He turned back to Jazz. 'Anything more?'

'That's it, really,' she said. 'The hairs on the chair back contained DNA that matched that of Samir Boulad.'

'And only his?'

'Yes.'

'There's no room for error?'

'One in 1000 million.'

Banks smiled. 'I'll take that as a no. Excellent news, Jazz. And quick work. Thanks a lot. I can't say I know what this all means yet, but it's the best lead we've had so far. It gives us a solid line on inquiries to pursue around Hollyfield. Have another doughnut.'

Jazz grinned and grabbed a raspberry-centred doughnut and poured herself more coffee. 'Obviously Samir's body provided us with an excellent DNA sample,' she said. 'And the match from the hair follicle was also a good source. It made my job a lot easier.'

'So Samir was in the same house as Stokes at some point, and he was there long enough to sit down in the armchair but not to sleep on the mattress. What we don't know is whether they were both in the house at the same time, or *when* this was.'

'I think we can assume they must have been there together at some point,' said Annie. 'After all, it was Stokes's house, and he didn't seem the type to get out and about that much. And it seems likely Samir was there after he was seen in town with his backpack and jacket.'

'Stokes did go and sit in the park and read sometimes,' said Gerry. 'Apparently, he never bothered anyone, but the Elmet Hill crowd didn't approve of his presence there. Granville Myers said he scared the kiddies.'

'Did you talk to the Neighbourhood Watch?'

'Yes, guv. That was the bloke who runs it: Granville Myers. He's in charge along with Lisa Bartlett's dad, Gus.'

'Anything?'

'Claims to know nothing about what goes on in the park or on the Hollyfield Estate. He seemed a bit defensive when it came to his son, Chris, so I did a bit of rooting around. Seems Chris Myers is in his final year as a day student at St Botolph's, sitting his A-levels at the moment, along with Lisa Bartlett's brother Jason. Chris has his own car to drive himself to school and back each day. Usually gives Jason a lift. He's bright. Expected to take a place at Oxford. Anyway, I seemed to remember he was involved in something a while ago, so I just checked back through the old incident reports and discovered that last year Chris Myers got caught – along with several of his fellow pupils – at a noisy student party near Eastvale College, where drugs were present, mostly ecstasy and marijuana. They all got off lightly, a slap on the wrist, and for what it's worth, Myers had no drugs in his possession. Apparently, the quantities were small and they were doing no harm.'

'Interesting,' said Banks. 'Youthful high jinks, most likely, but let's keep young Chris and Jason in mind as regards the drug connection. They might know a bit more about what went on in number twenty-six Hollyfield Lane than their parents can tell us.'

'Right, guv,' said Gerry.

'Let's move on. There are still no sightings of Samir in Eastvale before the Sunday he was killed, right, which – assuming he would have stayed the night if he'd come before – goes along with not finding traces of him on the mattress and pillow in the spare room. So what do we make of all this?'

'That Stokes was cuckooed?' Gerry suggested. 'And that Samir just arrived at Hollyfield Lane on Sunday evening, for the first time, to sell drugs. That something went wrong.'

'A replacement cuckoo, then?' said Banks.

'I think so,' Gerry said. 'The other boy had been gone about two or three weeks, according to Margery Cunningham. Though she did say her sense of time might be a bit off. It was a while, anyway. It probably took them that long to get every-thing organised and set up again.'

'OK,' said Banks. 'So it was all change in the county line. Someone took it over.'

'The Albanians?' suggested Annie. 'Along with Blaydon and the Kerrigans?'

'Possibly. But was it a hostile takeover, or what? What happened to the other boy, the fair-haired one?'

'Well,' Annie replied, 'both Howard Stokes and Samir are dead. Even if Stokes did die of a genuine heroin overdose, it still all points towards a drug war on some level. And I'd say that it is pretty hostile.'

'So whoever got displaced might have been taking revenge by murdering Samir?'

'Maybe,' said Annie.

'And it could even have been the fair-haired lad who did it?'

'Again,' said Annie, 'I don't think that's beyond the bounds of possibility. Either him or his controller down in Leeds probably came up and did it. Remember, we have a bus driver who saw Samir get off a bus from Leeds, and they would have been in a position to know where he was going.'

'Where does Blaydon fit in?' Banks asked.

'Blaydon doesn't live in Leeds,' said Annie, 'and he has a respectable veneer. I still can't really see him running a county line drug operation.'

'Me, neither,' said Banks. 'But I *can* see him being somehow involved, doing a favour for someone who did, someone he wants to impress, who may be in overall charge of a number of county lines.'

'The Albanians again?'

'Very likely. Leka Gashi and his pals. And Blaydon was either trying to ingratiate himself, or he owed them one. We already know he has a history with Gashi going back to Corfu ten years ago, and their possible collusion in the murder of Blaydon's business partner at the time, Norman Peel. I think we'd better have another chat with Mr Blaydon soon.' Banks glanced over at Vic Manson, who seemed as if he had something to add. 'Vic, you found Samir's fingerprints in the house, didn't you?'

Manson nodded. 'Others, too. It's kept us busy for quite a while. Stokes, naturally, and several unidentified sets.'

'Any matches so far?'

'A couple. I put them through IDENT1. One, so far, is a match with prints from the break-in at The Crown and Anchor last month, and another set are a match for a lad on file we arrested for dealing E around the college towards the end of last year.'

'Which would seem to point towards the Stokes house being used as a county lines distribution centre,' Banks said. 'Good work, Vic. You, too, Jazz.'

'There's more,' Vic Manson said.

Banks raised an eyebrow. 'Go on.'

'We still don't know who did The Crown and Anchor break-in, and the prints don't help us with that, but the lad who was arrested for dealing got a suspended sentence, and he's still in the Eastvale area. Name of Cleary. Tyler Cleary.'

'Got an address?'

'Can't say for sure if he's still there.'

'It's a start. Gerry?'

'I'll find him and talk to him, guv.'

'There's something else that might interest you,' Manson said.

'Yes?'

'I remember when we went in through the back, the evening the two lads found Howard Stokes . . .'

'Right,' said Banks.

'Well, DC Masterson mentioned something about a boy who'd been seen hanging around the house before, and that he rode a red bicycle.'

'That's right,' Gerry said. 'That's what Margery Cunningham told me, at any rate. The fair-haired lad rode around on a red bicycle. Most likely delivering drugs, filling the orders.'

'Well, there's a pile of rubbish in the backyard,' Manson said, 'and if I remember rightly, one of the items half-buried in it is a red bicycle frame. It's a long shot. It might not be the one, but . . .'

'Christ,' said Annie. 'I went in through the front the other night, and I had no reason to search the backyard. Sorry.'

'Don't worry,' said Banks. 'Well spotted, Vic.'

Manson grinned. 'It's over in the lab right now. There's a chance we'll be able to get some dabs. Blondie might be in the system.'

'Absolutely. And Gerry, maybe you can keep digging around Elmet Hill and Hollyfield, now that we know Samir was in the Stokes house for sure, however briefly.'

'Right, guv,' said Gerry.

Banks stood up. 'One more thing. Annie, will you put someone on tracking all the CCTV available around the hill and Hollyfield areas for last Sunday evening? Get them on it ASAP, and gently remind them there's overtime in the budget. I doubt there'll be much of value, but now we know where to look and what to look for, we might find something interesting.'

When Zelda woke early the following morning, she had a splitting headache, and the bright sun shining through her hotel window didn't help at all. She had forgotten to close the curtains. With an effort, she pushed herself out of bed and closed them. She found some paracetamol in her bag and swallowed three with a glass of water. Then she lay down again. She couldn't go back to sleep, she knew that; she could only hope that the headache would fade and that she would stop feeling sorry for herself. If she was going to get any further in her endeavour, she was going to have to focus. Her reaction last night had been instinctive, she knew; the memories that rushed back on her seeing Goran Tadić had been a visceral tsunami. And so she had run. She hadn't been able to help herself. Accept it. Failure. That was nothing new to her. But get over it. Get a grip.

What would Modesty Blaise have done? she asked herself. Modesty Blaise wouldn't have let herself get into that situation to start with. And if she had, Willie would have come to the rescue. But Zelda didn't have a Willie Garvin. She had a feeling there weren't any Willie Garvins in the real world.

So she lay there as the paracetamol slowly took effect and did nothing for the rest of that day but lounge around in bed, watch television, drink a lot of water and order room service.

By seven o'clock she was feeling human again and ventured down to the hotel dining room for her evening meal. As she toyed with her stuffed chicken breast and sipped her mineral water, she began to think about a plan. She realised that she had wanted to find Keane because he could lead her to the Tadić brothers, whom she wanted to kill. One more than the other: Goran. Perhaps the loss of his brother would be suffering enough for Petar.

But she had no plan.

She took out her Moleskine and worked through the details. Writing it all down was a risk, but it was how she worked best; besides, she had no intention of letting anyone else read it, and she knew quite well that if she did go through with it, nobody would ever be found, and there would be no investigation.

1. Do I have the right to take a human life?
Of course not. Nobody does. But I have done it before, that is true. I killed Darius, but I was fighting for survival, for escape. It doesn't matter that I felt no remorse – I was too traumatised by my experiences at their hands for any feelings other than relief – it was still self-defence. And he was the one who started out armed. Darius ruined many lives, including mine, and the Tadić brothers have perhaps ruined many more. But does that justify me playing avenging angel

and killing them? I don't know the answer and may never know; it's an argument I can have with myself for ever, and I'm certainly not going to ask anyone else for a judgement.

2. Can I carry it out?
I don't know. Do I have the courage, the skill and the brains to go through with it? Goran Tadić is a formidable opponent, strong and ruthless. I'm weaker, and I'm alone. Whatever method I use, I will have to employ more stealth than strength. And if I don't want to get caught, which I most certainly don't, I'll also need a good escape plan and a method that will leave no evidence linking me to the body. It's a tall order, and I'm not sure I can carry it out.

3. How would I do it?
What method should I use? I have no access to poisons and know nothing about them. I might be able to get my hands on a gun through some old contacts down here, but a gun would be noisy and there would be too much forensic evidence. I don't know how to use one, anyway, and would probably end up shooting myself in the foot! It would be nice if I could make it appear like an accident – push him under a tube train, for example, or a bus – but that would be difficult to orchestrate. He probably doesn't use the tube, anyway. Besides, that would have to be done in public, and someone might see me. Knife crimes are common and kitchen knives are certainly easy enough to buy without arousing any suspicions. Maybe that's the way to go. But first I will have to render him unconscious. My tranquillisers are probably not strong enough. It would take too many of them, and their presence would be hard to disguise. But I still have some of the flunitrazepam my French doctor prescribed before it was taken off the market there. That's

powerful stuff. It will work faster, too. Twenty to thirty minutes. I certainly don't want to be in a hotel room with Goran Tadić for too long, waiting for him to fall asleep. Flunitrazepam is also soluble in water and alcohol, which is perfect.

4. Is there anyone I can get to help me?
NO.

When Zelda thought of the task ahead in those terms, she felt ready to give up. She ordered a coffee. The alternative would be to admit defeat and go to Alan and tell him where she had located Goran Tadić, who would almost certainly lead him to Keane. Let the police deal with the lot of them. But it still came down to trust. She might trust Alan, but he was one small cog in a large machine, and she didn't trust that machine one bit. All it took was one man, a whisper in the right ear, and you wouldn't see Petar and Goran for dust. Or Keane. And even if there wasn't an informer in the ranks, which she very much doubted, then the evidence against them – if any was found – would be lost or destroyed, or a jury would be nobbled. Somehow or other, the course of justice would be perverted, and they would walk away scot-free.

So she had to regain her resolve, harden herself. There was only her, and she had to get close to Goran Tadić and do it herself.

Which led to one more important question:

5. *Will he recognise me?*

Because if he knew who she was and didn't let on, she would be walking into a deathtrap.

*   *   *

In addition to various rental properties around town, the Kerrigan brothers also owned a nightclub and a video arcade on opposite sides of the market square. They had their offices in the club, which used to be known as the Bar None until they took it over and refurbished and rebranded it as The Vaults. It was an unimaginative name, perhaps, but they had brought in flashy new lighting and cocktails with cheeky names, like 'Sex on the Beach' and 'Between the Sheets', and sold mostly imported bottled beer. They also employed a local DJ keen to make a name for himself on the national scene, and the kids flocked in. There wasn't much else to do in Eastvale after ten o'clock, especially if you were too pissed to drive to Newcastle, Leeds or Manchester, where there were better clubs.

The Vaults was located under the shops across the cobbled square from the Queen's Arms and the police station. Banks walked down the steps at ten o'clock that Friday night, when the place was just opening, flashed his warrant card at the bouncer and headed past the long bar with its array of coloured bottles and glasses, across the dance floor with its disco ball and revolving lights, to the offices at the back. He gave a shudder as he remembered the last time he had been there, when it was still called the Bar None, to a crime scene involving his then chief constable's daughter, Emily Riddle, found dead from a batch of poisoned cocaine in the ladies' toilet.

Fortunately, the music wasn't too loud so early in the night, and the DJ hadn't begun his fierce sampling routines, where a snatch of an old Elvis song might appear under the robotic rhythm and synth sounds of an electro dance number.

Once through the door, he could hardly hear the noise of the club at all. He knocked on the door marked PRIVATE and entered to find Timmy Kerrigan alone at his desk.

Kerrigan stood up. 'Mr Banks. An unexpected pleasure. Please, sit down. Take a load off.' He moved an office chair for

Banks to sit on. Banks sat. 'You should have told me you were coming.'

'What would you have done, Timmy? Organised a brass band?'

Timmy Kerrigan just laughed. It came out as a giggle, the way most of his laughs did.

'No Tommy tonight?' Banks asked.

Kerrigan sat down again and swivelled his chair to face Banks. 'He's got other business, down in the big city. We're not Siamese twins, you know. Not joined at the hip, or anywhere else, for that matter.'

'You'll have to do, then.'

'Charmed, I'm sure.' Timmy Kerrigan was the size of a rugby prop forward, but gone to fat. Short golden curls topped a plump round face with a disarmingly youthful peaches and cream complexion. His blue eyes were heavy-lidded and guarded. He must have been in his fifties, but he looked as if he had never had to shave. He was wearing his trademark navy pinstripe suit with the handkerchief poking out of the top pocket and a psychedelic waistcoat, quite dizzying, its buttons straining tight against his stomach.

His younger brother, Tommy, Banks remembered, was very different – long, thin, lugubrious, one milky eye from a badly thrown dart or an accident with a knitting needle, depending on whose version you believed, cropped dark hair and a gaunt, pockmarked face. They always made Banks think of Laurel and Hardy, though the resemblance was merely a matter of size and shape.

Though they looked to be a comic duo, and it was very tempting to laugh at them, you did so at some risk. They were smart businessmen, local celebrities in their way, and had bought up quite a bit of Eastvale over the years. They weren't without political clout on the town council or in the planning offices. No wonder they had proved useful to Connor Clive Blaydon in his Elmet Centre development. If you wanted to develop anything around Eastvale, you could do a lot worse than have the Kerrigans on your side.

But behind the respectable facade, Banks knew, lay corruption, bribery, blackmail, intimidation. And it didn't end there. Though there was no hard evidence, the Kerrigans were also suspected of having their hand in drugs and prostitution, and that, Banks thought, was where the strongest connection with Blaydon came in. And perhaps also the link with Gashi.

Kerrigan got to his feet again. 'Pardon my manners. You just took me by surprise. Would you like a drink? Drop of single malt, perhaps?'

Banks saw the bottle of Scapa on the cocktail cabinet. 'Don't mind if I do,' he said.

Kerrigan poured them both a healthy measure and sat down again. Banks took a sip and sighed. 'Lovely stuff,' he said. 'I'll get to the point. I'm sure you've heard about the murder we had here a few days ago.'

'That young lad found in the bin? Terrible business. I sometimes wonder what this town is coming to.'

'And the suspicious death of Howard Stokes.'

'Come again. I haven't heard about that one.'

'It wasn't as big a headline. Old junkie. Died of an overdose.'

Kerrigan shrugged. 'Must happen all the time.'

'Thing is, he died in one of your houses.'

'He did? Which one?'

'Hollyfield Lane. Number twenty-six.'

'But that whole area's condemned. It's been scheduled for redevelopment.'

'Yes, I know,' said Banks. 'But I'm sure you know too that there are still one or two people hanging on there, waiting for rehousing.'

'Well, that's terrible,' said Kerrigan. 'But I don't see what it's got to do with me? I'm not the bloody rent collector. Not any more. Anyone who's left isn't paying a penny. That's the deal. Surely you can't hold me responsible for the actions of my tenants?'

'Not at all,' said Banks. 'I simply wondered if you knew about it.'

'Well, no, I didn't.'

Banks fished photos of Samir and Stokes from his briefcase and held them out to Kerrigan. 'Recognise either of these faces?'

Kerrigan studied the photos one at a time and passed them back. 'No, sorry.'

It was hard to tell with habitual liars like Kerrigan, but Banks got a feeling he wasn't lying this time. 'You were dining at Le Coq d'Or on Sunday evening with Connor Clive Blaydon, weren't you?'

'Yes. We had some business to discuss.'

'The Elmet Centre?'

'As a matter of fact, yes. That was our main area of interest. But I don't see what that has to do with anything.'

'Who is the Albanian?'

'Who?'

'The Albanian. I understand your brother referred to an Albanian at some point during the evening.'

Kerrigan frowned. His skin looked like pink plastic. 'I didn't hear anything like that.'

'He had some bruising on his face. A cut.'

'Oh, that. Minor disagreement at a business meeting. That's Tommy all over. You might remember, he's a bit of a hothead.'

'An Elmet Centre meeting?'

'I don't recollect the exact circumstances. You'd have to ask him.'

'And he's out of town.'

'Yes.'

'Was it the Albanian he disagreed with? Gashi.'

'It may have been an Albanian who thumped him. I don't know. I wasn't there. Tommy's a bit of a racist. I try to talk to him, but you know what it's like with some people. Attitudes like that, they're entrenched. We argue all the time. He's a Leaver, and I'm a Remainer. How's that for a divided household?'

Banks sipped some whisky. 'It must give rise to some pretty lively arguments.'

'You don't say.'

'Anyway, we think this boy Samir might have been connected with drugs, and as we know Mr Blaydon is connected with an Albanian drug lord called Leka Gashi, we wondered if you might have run into this fellow, too?'

'Gashi? No. You mentioned him earlier. But then, I can't say I know any Albanians. Or anything about drugs. As far as I know, Connor's a property developer. Simple as that.'

'Nothing's quite as simple as that, Timmy. The Albanians are moving into the drugs trade here in a big way, taking over local supplies, county lines, the lot. They've got direct links to the Colombian cartels and the 'Ndrangheta, the Calabrian Mafia.'

'I must say, you sound as if you know your stuff, Mr Banks. I can tell you've done your homework. Then, that's your job. But this is all way outside my area of expertise.'

'Which is?'

'Why, club management, of course. And the video arcade business.'

'And Tommy?'

'The same. He also handles most of the rental properties.'

'So he's the one I should talk to about Howard Stokes?'

'I honestly don't think he would be able to tell you anything more than I can. As I said, we don't keep tabs on our tenants. They've got the houses rent-free until they find alternative accommodation. I can't say fairer than that.'

'When do they have to be out?'

'We don't actually have a fixed starting date yet. Just waiting for the final details to fall into place. The sooner the better, though.'

'About that video arcade – we've had one or two tips that some of the kids from Eastvale Comprehensive are buying drugs there.'

'If that's the case,' said Kerrigan, 'it's being done behind my back. I'll certainly have a word with my staff about the issue, though.'

'Good. Appreciate it. How's business?'

'What business? Where?'

Banks looked around. 'Here,' he said. 'The arcade. The properties. You know, in general.'

'It's difficult times we live in, Mr Banks. So much uncertainty. And uncertainty's bad for stability, which is what we'd prefer in our markets. But you go with the flow, swings and roundabouts, slings and arrows. It all works out in the wash. We can ride out the storm. I'm optimistic.'

Banks tried to think when he had last heard a metaphor as mixed as that last speech, but he couldn't. 'Glad to hear it,' he said. 'Just a couple more questions, then I'll leave you to your evening. I understand Mr Blaydon received a phone call on his mobile in the restaurant at about ten o'clock last Sunday evening. Am I right?'

'I believe so. Yes. Though I can't say I made a note of the time.'

'Can you tell me who it was from?'

Kerrigan made a steeple of his chubby fingers. 'I'm afraid I've no idea. He simply answered the phone, listened for a moment and then excused himself.'

'How long was he gone?'

'Not long. Five minutes, perhaps.'

'How did he seem? Did the phone call upset him, make him happy, unhappy, what?'

'Neutral, really. He just said he had a small business matter to take care of, and he'd be back in a few minutes. We were finishing our sweets at the time.'

'I understand Chef McGuigan does an excellent job there.'

'We're lucky to have such an establishment in town, Mr Banks. You really should try it.'

'Not on a poor policeman's salary.'

Kerrigan paused and licked his lips. 'I'm sure something can be arranged.'

'Are you offering me a bribe, Timmy?'

'Heaven forbid! Nothing of the sort. Merely a favour for a friend. I'm afraid that when it comes to the good things in life, I'm a champagne socialist. I think we should all be able to enjoy them, not just an elite few. Don't you agree?'

'Would that I could indulge myself,' said Banks. He put his empty glass down on the desk and stood. 'Well, it's been a pleasure.'

'All mine, Mr Banks. All mine.'

Kerrigan stood up and they shook hands. His was pudgy and clammy. The dance floor on the way out was a lot noisier and more crowded than it had been when Banks first came in, and he had to thread his way through the bobbing, gesticulating crowd of dancers. The DJ was hopping about playing with two turntables against the electrobeat, speeding them up, rotating them backwards, slowing them down. Banks was relieved when he got outside into the relative quiet of the market square. It was after dark, and a few couples and groups of young people were drifting over from the pubs towards The Vaults. Banks eyed the Queen's Arms, still lit up and relatively busy, but he had already had one drink that evening, and he decided he would be better off heading home and enjoying a drop of Macallan in his conservatory, perhaps with some Marianne Faithful to go with it.

If Zelda had really wanted to date a racing car driver who talked about nothing but himself and his cars, she soon found that it would be very easy to do so. The hard part was getting away from him. He was handsome enough, and he knew it. He also thought he was macho and exciting, and perhaps he was, but that didn't interest Zelda. All she really wanted to know now was that she still had her appeal, and so she was making a trial run in her hotel's rooftop bar after dinner that night. It had taken the man less time than it took the barman to pour her a glass of white wine to settle next to her and start a conversation. It had taken her slightly longer to get rid of him, but he got the message eventually and wandered off to survey the other pickings.

For some reason, the whole set-up reminded her of her time in Paris. In luxury, many might say. She had a spacious apartment not too far from the Champs-Élysées, where she did her 'entertaining'. She didn't even have to seek men; they were sent to her. Many were considerate and tender, even cultivated and interesting, unlike those she had known in the cheap brothels and sex clubs of Eastern Europe.

But she was still a whore. And she was still a prisoner.

She had no family, so they couldn't force her into working for them with threats to hurt loved ones. Nor did she owe them money. But Darius made it perfectly clear that if she cheated him or ran out on him, he would find her – he had the means to do so – and would personally supervise her dismemberment. While she was still alive. She was also accompanied by two 'bodyguards' when she went shopping, or whenever she took a meal break in the local brasserie. Whatever money she made – and she had no idea how much it was – went to the organisation. Darius had bought her at a 'sale' in Sarajevo: an auction, where she and the other 'lots' had been forced to parade in a kind of sick catwalk, first scantily clad, then naked, while prospective buyers lined up to feel the firmness of their breasts and the tightness of their vaginas. In certain cases, a free trial might be approved, though she was fortunate in avoiding that. She soon discovered that Darius was repelled by women and would no sooner touch one of the girls than he would a rabid dog. Though she was never sure, she was fairly certain that he preferred men.

She was lucky, people told her. Darius was no backstreet brothel-keeper. He had a stable of high-class call girls in Paris, and they got the crème de la crème of clientele. Government ministers. Visiting Hollywood celebrities. Leaders of industry. It was there that Zelda had learned to use her natural charms rather than simply lie back and open her legs. Some of the men were quite sophisticated and appreciated conversation and little sensual touches, like a massage. Not all wanted sex. Sometimes she felt like a geisha.

But she was still a whore. And she was still a prisoner.

Darius wore bespoke suits, drank the best champagne and had the best drugs – that was where Zelda picked up her coke habit. It helped get her through the day, and the downers at night helped her forget where and what she was.

Then came Emile, a very important client, she was told. A government minister tipped for even higher office. After two visits, during which he never laid a finger on her, Emile told her he was in love with her. She didn't know what love was outside of the books she had read, so she didn't really know if she felt the same way. But she said she did. It made him happy. And if he was happy, Darius was happy. And if Darius was happy, he wouldn't beat her so often. For despite his fancy suits, champagne, drugs and cologne, he was a brute underneath, just like those brutes that had abducted her.

Emile started plotting her escape. He would leave his wife and they would live together in Paris, he said, and when he had time off, he had a beautiful villa in Provence where they could stay. It would be idyllic, a wonderful life. He couldn't bear it that she had to see other men; he wanted her all to himself. She couldn't imagine what that might be like, but he was kind and she enjoyed his company. As time went on, she began to trust him and love him in her way. So together, they formed a plan. Emile was an important figure in a department of the French government, and he said he could help her get a passport if she helped him bring down Darius. She said she would. What were a few months more if they meant freedom? But she remembered Darius's threat, and she knew that he meant it. The only way she could ever be entirely free of him was to kill him.

'Is this seat taken?'

Zelda snapped back out of her memories. 'Sorry?'

'This seat – is it taken?'

Zelda waved her hand. 'Oh. No. Not at all.'

'I'm surprised to hear that.'

Zelda turned to face the stranger, an American by the sound of him. 'Why would that be?' she asked.

'A beautiful woman like you.'

Oh, Christ, thought Zelda, here we go again. 'I'm sorry to disappoint you,' she said.

'Can I buy you a drink?'

'Sure,' she said. 'Every little bit helps. I just got some bad news from my doctor, and I could do with a pick-me-up, as well as someone to talk to. You can commiserate with me.'

'White wine?' He edged closer. 'Nothing too serious, I hope?' A note of caution crept into his voice.

Zelda spoke between sniffles. 'He says the penicillin should get rid of it, but in the meantime it hurts like hell every time I have to take a piss.'

'Oh, Jesus,' he said, got up and hurried off.

When he was far enough away, Zelda knocked back the remainder of her drink, smiled to herself, then stood up, straightened her shoulders and headed back to her room. Trial run successful, she decided. Tomorrow, she hoped, it would be time for the real thing.

9

Lisa Bartlett's house was on Elmet Court, a residential street branching off about halfway down Elmet Hill and winding its way south. Though smaller than the Myers's house on Elmet Close, the houses there were Georgian-style semis with bay windows and tiny lawns enclosed by privet hedges. Most had driveways and garages, so there were very few vehicles parked in the narrow street.

Gerry had known Lisa only in the wake of her sexual assault, so she had no idea what she had been like before. Now, several weeks later, she still appeared very much affected by her experience – eyes dull, hair lacklustre, generally fidgety, anxious and unable to look people in the eye. That Saturday morning, she sat slumped on the sofa, legs curled under her, wearing ice-blue jeans and a big woolly sweater whose sleeves covered her hands. Her mother sat beside her, stiff and straight, hands clasped on her lap. Mrs Bartlett was an attractive woman of about forty, Gerry guessed, though the strain of family upheaval was starting to show in tension lines around her eyes and mouth. Though it was a warm day, the electric fire blazed away and Gerry felt herself stifling.

'Lisa hasn't been out by herself since the incident,' Mrs Bartlett said. 'We've had to talk to the school and put off her GCSEs until next year. Even poor Jason's having a difficult time concentrating on his A-levels. Can I get you a cup of tea or anything?'

Gerry sensed that Mrs Bartlett was reluctant to leave her daughter's side, though she still felt the need to be hospitable. 'No, thanks,' she said. 'Nothing for me.'

'I can't imagine what you want to ask her. We've been over it all time and time again.'

'It's not specifically about Lisa's case,' said Gerry. 'Though that still remains my main concern. We were just wondering if what happened to your daughter might be related to other events around the neighbourhood in the past month or so.'

Mrs Bartlett frowned. 'Other events? What on earth can you mean?'

'I'm sure you're aware of the two suspicious deaths we've had in Eastvale recently?'

'Yes, but one was a drug overdose, and the other was that poor Arab boy. A stabbing, I understand? While it's not something we're used to having around here, I gather it's not exactly unknown. I can't see what any of it has to do with our Lisa.'

'Do you know anything about either of these deaths, Lisa?' Gerry asked.

Lisa just shook her head.

'Howard Stokes lived on Hollyfield Lane, across Cardigan Drive, just beyond the park. He used to go around in a mobility scooter. He was in his sixties, with long hair and a beard. Did you ever see him?'

'I don't understand why you're asking Lisa all these questions,' Mrs Bartlett interrupted. 'This man can hardly have had anything to do with what happened, can he? I mean, if he was on a *mobility scooter*.'

'Of course not,' said Gerry. 'We very much doubt that he was capable of a physical assault. But Mr Stokes mixed with some rather unsavoury characters, had some dodgy visitors to his house on Hollyfield Lane. I just wondered if Lisa had seen him around the area. More specifically, seen him *with* anyone.'

'No,' said Lisa. 'I mean, I saw him in the park sometimes, if it was a nice day. He'd just sit on a bench there reading a book. I mean, he wasn't weird or talking to himself or anything. He never bothered anyone.'

Gerry nodded. 'Did you ever notice anyone coming in or out of his house?'

'No. I don't know which house was his. I was never near that estate. I mean, it's across the park. You can see it over the trees from up the hill, but not from here.'

'You never walked through the estate?'

'I never needed to. I'd come back from school on Cardigan Drive and then cut up through the pub car park.' She gave a little shudder and wrapped her arms around herself.

Gerry remembered that Lisa Bartlett went to Eastvale Comprehensive, while her brother Jason was a day boy at St Botolph's. 'Like you did on the night it . . . of the attack?' she asked.

'Yes.' Lisa looked at her mother. 'But I haven't been there since.'

'It's OK, Lisa. Had you walked through there after dark before?'

'Oh, yes. I used to do it all the time. I never worried about it. Nothing ever happened there before, not until . . .'

Mrs Bartlett grasped her daughter's wool-covered hand in her own. Lisa snatched it back. Gerry became aware of the loud ticking of the mantelpiece clock, its works exposed under a glass dome. She took out her photo of Samir. 'Did you ever see this boy around the neighbourhood? Anywhere?'

'Is he the one . . . you know . . .'

'That's him,' said Gerry. 'He was called Samir. He came here all the way from Syria, by himself.'

'Where were his mum and dad?'

'They stayed behind. The family couldn't all afford to go. They were killed in a bomb attack a few weeks ago. He never knew.'

'I suppose he was lucky in a way, then,' said Lisa.

Gerry frowned. 'Lucky? He was stabbed to death.'

'I mean he died before he knew his whole family had been killed by a bomb.'

'I suppose so,' Gerry agreed. 'When you look at it that way. Did you ever see him at all?'

'No. I think I would remember. We don't get many Syrians around here.'

'I don't follow,' said Mrs Bartlett. 'If this is the boy you found in a wheelie bin on the East Side Estate, what could he possibly have been doing near here?'

Gerry took a breath and went on. 'We think he may have been killed elsewhere, then dumped on the East Side Estate.'

'And you think . . . the same . . .?'

'No,' said Gerry. 'I'm not saying we think it was the same person who attacked Lisa who killed Samir. They're very different crimes. There are just too many coincidences, that's all.' She looked at Lisa again. 'The man on the mobility scooter, the one you saw in the park sometimes. His name was Howard Stokes and he died around the same time as Samir. At least we think he did.'

'So you think the two are connected?' Mrs Bartlett asked.

'We know they are,' said Gerry. 'We just don't know how or why.'

'And Lisa?'

'We're talking to a lot of people in this area, people who might have noticed something. Lisa was a victim of crime in the same neighbourhood where we think two people later died. It would be a pretty sloppy detective who didn't follow up on that.'

'I suppose so,' said Mrs Bartlett. 'But I still don't see how Lisa can help you.'

The door opened, and a gangly teenage boy, whom Gerry assumed to be Jason Bartlett, came in.

His mother immediately jumped to her feet. 'Jason. How's the revision going?'

Jason shrugged. 'OK, I guess.' He smiled at Lisa and touched her chin. 'How you doing, little sister?'

'Gerroff, Jason,' Lisa complained, moving away from her brother's touch.

'Now, children . . .' said Mrs Bartlett.

Jason flopped down in the free armchair. 'What's going on?' he asked.

'I'm glad you're here,' said Gerry. 'You might remember me from before, when—'

'I remember you,' said Jason. 'Have you lot caught him yet?'

'No, we haven't,' Gerry admitted. 'Not yet.'

'So what's it all about, then?'

'Jason, mind your manners.'

'It's all right, Mrs Bartlett.' Gerry showed Jason the photograph of Samir.

'Is that him?' he asked. 'You think he's the one who did it?' He passed the photo back. 'He hardly looks old enough.'

'Idiot,' said Lisa. 'He's not the one.'

'I wouldn't be surprised if it was a darkie, mind you,' said Jason.

'Jason!' Mrs Bartlett reddened. 'What have I told you? I won't have talk like that in my house.'

'It's *our* house, Mum. And I was only expressing an opinion. Can't I do that?'

'Based on what?' Gerry asked. 'Your opinion.'

Jason looked flustered and glanced at his sister. 'I thought that's what you said, Lisa. That it was a coloured chap.'

'I said no such thing! You're just trying to put words in my mouth.'

'Lisa,' said Gerry, 'do you have any reason to think your attacker was non-white?'

'No. I . . . It was him. Jason. He got me thinking it might have been. He says it's usually people like that who . . . you know. He got me all confused. But I didn't really see his hand. I couldn't tell the colour he was. It was too dark.'

'Lisa, are you saying you did see your attacker's hand, but that you just couldn't see it clearly? You never told me that before.'

'I . . . I think I did. I just . . . I was too upset and confused.'

'And Jason convinced you that your attacker might have been black?'

'But it was dark,' said Lisa. 'How would I have been able to tell?'

'Would it surprise you to know that most sexual predators are white?' Gerry said. She turned to Jason. 'Did you give your sister any reason to think her attacker may have been black?'

'I might have suggested it,' said Jason, slouching deeper in the chair. 'So what?'

'But you've no evidence?'

'How could I have? If you lot can't find out who did it, how do you expect me to?'

'Jason, that's enough,' said his mother. 'I won't have you being rude to a guest in our own home.'

'It's all right, Mrs Bartlett,' said Gerry. 'It's a version of the butler or the passing tramp. Nobody likes to think it could be someone just like them who's committed such a crime. Jason's just angry and frustrated, isn't that right?'

Jason looked at her with sulky aggression. 'If you say so.'

'Did you ever see that boy Samir around here?' she asked him. 'No.'

'Any other boys around Hollyfield Lane?'

'Sometimes. From Cardigan Drive, like. They'd be coming out of that house where that bloke who died lived.'

'Howard Stokes? You saw people coming from his house?'

'Sometimes. Shifty-looking lot.'

'How did you know it was his house?'

'Saw him coming and going a couple of times. I mean, maybe he was just visiting like the others, but he did hang out in the park. I just assumed . . .'

'What about a fair-haired lad, medium height, sometimes rode a red bicycle?'

'That's pretty vague. Nobody stands out. Lots of people ride red bicycles.'

'Fair enough. Did you see any activity there last Sunday?'

'No. But I wasn't around then. I was playing rugby over in Helmthorpe.'

'Did you ever go to number twenty-six Hollyfield Lane, Jason?'

'What do you think I am? Everyone knows if you spend too much time over on the old estate you're bound to catch something.'

'Did you know the house was used for the sale of drugs?'

Jason turned away. 'Doesn't surprise me.'

'Ever tried drugs?' Gerry knew she was pushing it, with the mother there, but Jason's immediate reaction was enough to tell her that he had, and that he was lying if he said he hadn't.

'I think we've had about enough for now, don't you?' Mrs Bartlett said to Gerry. 'Jason needs to concentrate on his revision, and Lisa needs time to get well again.' She tapped Lisa's knee. Lisa flinched.

'That's all right, Mrs Bartlett,' said Gerry. 'I think I've just about finished here for the time being. Sorry if I've upset anyone.'

'It's not that,' said Mrs Bartlett. 'But . . . well, we're all a bit over-sensitive at the moment, aren't we?'

If Zelda was going to carry out her decision of the previous evening, she realised, she needed to make some preparations before heading to the Hotel Belgrade again.

She still didn't know whether Tadić had spotted her last night when she knocked over her empty glass in her hurry to escape. True, she had felt his attention suddenly shift towards her, but that was probably just instinct on his part, a natural reaction to any unexpected sound or movement. He couldn't have caught more than a glimpse of her from behind as she made her way through the crowd. He probably wouldn't even remember. When it came down to it, she couldn't even be certain that he would still be at the Hotel Belgrade, or if he would come to the bar for a drink. But Faye had said they hung out there, and they were creatures of habit. The place was some sort of centre of operations for the loosely-knit criminal gang. The odds were, Zelda thought, that if Goran Tadić was still staying there, he would show up before too long.

Besides, she had appeared very different then from the way she planned on looking tonight. Her clothes had been baggy enough to make her seem frumpy, especially with the cheap glasses she had worn, and her hair had been a mess. Tonight she was going to be elegant, sexy and enchanting, and to that end, she spent a while in the hotel's spa, visited a nearby hairdresser, then went shopping and bought a new dress. She already had a nice tan from the trip to Croatia.

The dress was important. It was essential that it didn't look obvious, tarty, or anything like a hooker. Yes, she needed to be sexy and alluring, but in a subtle way. Nothing was to be overdone. It wasn't that she thought Goran Tadić was a particularly subtle human being – he wasn't – but that she didn't want to draw too much attention to herself. Subtle but sexy. Casual elegance. The way she planned it, she wouldn't be out of place at the hotel bar. If she got the appearance right, everything else would fall into place.

She found what she was after in Little Black Dress, a shop where she'd had success before. It wasn't black, but oxblood, knee-length, bare-shouldered, halter-top style. She also bought new underwear, black and lacy. Finally, she bought a jade pendant on a silver chain to go with the new look, and strappy white sandals, with the heels just high enough to accentuate the curve of her calves. She decided to go bare-legged and spent some time in the bath shaving her legs. Her last port of call was John Lewis, where she bought a set of sturdy kitchen knives.

When she was finally ready, she studied herself in the mirror for anything that seemed overdone. She looked like a woman on her way to meet a date, perhaps for a night at the theatre or a meal at a good restaurant, which was exactly the way she wanted to appear.

'I don't do that stuff any more,' said Tyler Cleary, when Gerry tracked him down to the college pub that evening. The music was loud, and the bar was crowded, but she managed to usher him to a reasonably discreet corner for a chat.

'That's good, Tyler,' she said. 'This should be very quick then.'

'What is it you want to know? I want to get back to my mates.'

'You used to go to a house on Hollyfield Lane to score drugs, right?'

Tyler stared at her. He was a rather slack-jawed spotty youth with a shock of unruly dark hair falling over his eyes. 'You expect me to admit to that? You must be mad.'

'Tyler,' Gerry said. 'We know you did. We *know* you were there. It's a drug house. We found your fingerprints all over the place.'

Tyler picked up his pint and slopped a little over his jeans before he got it to his mouth and swallowed some. 'I don't have to say anything.'

'No, you don't,' said Gerry. 'But it would be best if you did.'

'Why's that?'

'Because if you don't, I'll take you into the station and have a search party down to turn over your flat.'

'You wouldn't.'

Gerry stared him out. 'Try me.'

'OK,' said Tyler. 'Suppose I did talk to you. Are you offering me immunity?'

'I'm not offering you anything. I will say, though, that I'm not interested in your drug use.'

'That's all in the past.'

'Whatever. Not interested.'

'OK. But how do I know you're not recording this? Show me your mobile.'

'Screw you,' said Gerry, getting up and taking Tyler by the arm. 'If you think I'm going to show you my mobile or let you search me, you've got another think coming. Come on, we're off to the station. And don't forget your sentence is only suspended, not permanently cancelled.'

Tyler struggled, but Gerry's grip was firm. He bumped into the table and spilled more beer. 'Hey, wait, wait a minute!' he said. 'There's no need for violence. It's cool. OK. What do you want to know?'

'That's better,' said Gerry.

They sat down. Tyler rubbed his arm. 'It's poison, that stuff,' he said. 'Drugs.'

'I already know that,' said Gerry. 'I just want to know how it worked.'

'How what worked?'

Had this boy actually been admitted to Eastvale College? Gerry wondered. If he had been, there were serious problems with the admission requirements. Talk about unconditional acceptance. You didn't even need a brain to get into this place, it seemed.

'The set-up. The drug operation on Hollyfield Lane.'

'I don't do it any more.'

Gerry sighed. 'Tyler. You're beginning to sound like a stuck record. I'm not after you for drugs, believe me. If I were, you'd be in a cell already. All I want is information. Pure and simple. Of course, if you don't—'

Tyler put his hand up, palm out. 'No, no. It's all right. I'll talk to you. It's just that you can't be too careful, that's all. Go on, ask away.'

'Thank you,' Gerry muttered under her breath, and out loud, 'How did it operate?'

'You just phoned this mobile number, like, and put in your order.'

Gerry showed him the number she had copied from the scrap of paper Annie had found in Howard Stokes's wallet. 'This number?'

Tyler frowned in concentration. 'I'm not sure. But it looks about right.'

Gerry put the number away. 'How did you first find out what number to phone?'

'A mate told me.'

'How did he know?'

Tyler shrugged. 'Dunno. Internet, I think. Facebook, something like that.'

'How many people knew it?'

'No idea.'

'So what did you do next, after you phoned in your order?'

'You waited until Greg came up with the stuff.'

'Up from where?'

'Leeds, I think.'

'Who was this Greg?'

'Dunno. I just knew him as Greg.'

'Go on.'

'There was this old bloke there as well, but he was always on the nod. I think it was his house.'

'Howard Stokes.'

'I didn't know his name.'

'How did you know when the drugs had arrived?'

'Easy. It was all done over the mobile. One line. That's why they called it county lines.'

'I know that,' said Gerry, quickly losing patience. 'So, as far as you were concerned, you just phoned in your order, then went to pick it up when the delivery came, right? And you made all the arrangements through the one phone number.'

'That's right.'

'What happened? How did it end?'

'Greg just stopped coming.'

'How long ago?'

'About a month ago. I had an order in, but he never turned up with it. Pissed a lot of people off, I can tell you.'

'Did you meet any of the other customers?'

'Not that I remember. It wasn't like a doctor's waiting room, you know.'

'But you just said a lot of people were angry.'

'Figure of speech. I was, so I assumed others must have been in the same boat.'

'Did you go to Hollyfield Lane after Greg stopped showing up?'

'Once. I just wanted to know what was happening, like, if they'd made alternative plans. I mean, I wasn't addicted or anything, but you know . . . I was used to it.'

'And who did you see?'

'Just the old bloke in the wheelchair who lived there.'

'And what did he tell you?'

'That there'd been some trouble, and the line was down, but it would be up and running again soon as they sorted out some personnel and supply problems.'

'So what did you do?'

'In the end I found another bloke in Leyburn.'

'What are you taking?'

'*Was.* I told you, I'm off it now. Just a little coke.'

'That's highly addictive. Are you sure you've kicked it?'

'I was never addicted. Just a snort now and then doesn't do any harm.'

Gerry didn't believe for a moment that Tyler had kicked the habit. He was too twitchy, even now. She wasn't going to take him in, but she would pass on information about a source of cocaine in Leyburn to the drugs squad, if they didn't already know about it.

'Was Greg the only one you ever met selling the stuff at Hollyfield?'

'Yeah.'

Gerry took out the photo of Samir and showed it to him. 'Ever seen this lad?'

Tyler examined the photo. 'Isn't that the kid who got killed last week? Put in a wheelie bin?'

'That's right.'

'Never seen him.' Tyler passed the photo back. Gerry thought he was telling the truth.

'We think he was Greg's replacement,' she said. 'Or all set to be. Are you sure you didn't take any deliveries from him over the past month or so, since Greg packed it in?'

'No. I told you, I found someone else. In Leyburn. Then *I* packed it in. Besides, I'd remember if I had met him.'

'And you never went back to Hollyfield?'

'No. Why would I?'

'OK,' said Gerry. 'So you're saying the old man told you things would be up and running again soon, but they weren't?'

'Right.'

'What about the line? The phone number?'

'Dead, wasn't it?'

'And you didn't get a new one from your mate?'

'No. Nothing. They just, like, abandoned us all. Just like that.' He drank some more beer. Gerry finished her slimline tonic and closed her notebook. She hadn't learned a lot, but it hadn't been an entirely wasted visit. At least she thought she had managed to add a bit more evidence to the mounting pile that showed Samir *hadn't* turned up in Eastvale until the day he was killed. Or if he had, he had been lying very low. And she knew his predecessor's first name was Greg. But she still didn't feel any closer to knowing who had killed him.

IO

On Saturday night, Zelda waited until nine o'clock before she entered the bar and grill at the Hotel Belgrade. As luck would have it, there was a vacant seat at the bar between two couples, both far too interested in their respective partners to pay her any attention. She was also pleased to note that her style of dress was not at all out of place. The dressed-down crowd might be sitting at the tables, but up there at the bar, most of the men and women were dressed for an evening out. She looked just like a woman waiting for her date.

When the barman asked her what she wanted, Zelda ordered a vodka and tonic. The only thing she really missed was smoking. She wished she could light up while she was sitting there with her drink. Not only was she feeling a nicotine craving, but her nerves needed calming. The barman placed a bowl of mixed nuts and nibbles in front of her, but that wasn't quite the same. She tried one piece; it tasted like salty cardboard.

There was a flat-screen television behind the bar, and Zelda half-watched *The Voice* with the sound off. It was better that way. She could hardly sit and read her book at the bar tonight. She was too nervous to concentrate, anyway. She kept glancing at her watch. The knife was in her handbag, and she felt so conscious of it she was certain the whole place knew about it, that everyone knew what she was planning to do. What if he didn't come? What if he didn't pay her any attention? Was she attractive enough?

Then, around the same time he came in the previous evening, she saw the familiar figure reflected in the mirror behind
the bar and held her breath. He paused in the entrance from
the hotel lobby, straightened his tie and surveyed the bar. She
couldn't be certain, but she thought his eyes may have lingered
on her a fraction longer than on anyone else. She hoped it
wasn't because he recognised her.

There was no room at the bar, and she could hardly move
somewhere else. Besides, it would be too obvious. If he was
interested, he would find a way to her. It shouldn't be too hard
to attract him, as she was the only unaccompanied female at
the bar. Their eyes locked in the mirror, and Zelda thought
she noticed a glimmer of interest.

She noticed him studying her back as he walked towards the
bar in a direct line, perhaps making sure she was alone. She
made a point of looking at her watch and drumming her fingers
on the bar, appearing vaguely annoyed. She held her breath as
he stood slightly behind her and the couple beside her, leaning
forward between them to catch the bartender's attention. He
caught her eyes in the mirror again and gave a little smile. As
he leaned, she felt his arm brush against her bare shoulder,
nudging her just enough to jar the drink in her hand.

'Sorry,' he said. 'It is very crowded here tonight, yes?'

Zelda remembered the voice, though the accent had
smoothed out, become more Americanised, over the years.
She felt her throat constrict. She somehow managed to smile
and nod.

'Please, let me buy you a drink,' he went on.

'It's not necessary.'

'But I insist.'

'Well, in that case . . .'

He was wearing the same white suit as he had last night,
though this time with a purple shirt and yellow tie. She guessed

he had been in his late twenties when he and his brother abducted her just over thirteen years ago, so he had now probably just turned forty. He seemed to be on familiar terms with the barman, who didn't even need to ask him what he wanted but served him a large measure of whisky along with another vodka and tonic for her. The whiff of peat from his glass told her it was an Islay single malt.

For a while he stood there beside her drinking and chatting easily with the barman. It didn't take him long to get through his first whisky. Then the couple to Zelda's right left. Tadić took the seat next to hers with the slow, easy motion of a confident man and signalled for another drink. He glanced towards her, raised an eyebrow in question and nodded towards her glass. Zelda shook her head. 'No, thanks,' she said. 'I'm still working on this one.'

'Are you waiting for somebody?'

'Is it so obvious?'

'You were looking at your watch.'

'Yep,' she said. 'He's late.'

'Have another drink with me while you wait. Go on. One more won't do any harm.'

'OK,' she said, pushing her glass forward. 'Thanks. You're not from around here, are you?' She was hoping he wouldn't catch on to her accent. Most people didn't.

'No,' he said. 'Zadar. Croatia. Goran is my name.' He held his hand out to shake.

Zelda shook it. Her little hand was lost in his, and she could feel the strength in his grip. She was five foot six, and he must be at least six inches taller. She began to have grave doubts about the success of her mission. There was no way she could put the pills in his glass here in the crowded bar, she had already realised. They would have to wait until he got her up to his room, which she predicted from the look in his slightly hooded eyes wouldn't be very long. Not one for extended conversation, Goran Tadić.

'Cathy,' she said. 'Lovely country, Croatia.'

'You go there?'

'Once. Just the tourist spots – Split, Dubrovnik. But I remember Zadar. Isn't that where the sea plays music? I was on a cruise with my husband.'

He seemed thrilled that she knew Zadar. 'Yes, is sea organ. Beautiful music.' Then his face took on a disappointed expression. 'You are married?'

'Divorced. I should have said ex-husband.'

'And this man you wait for? Boyfriend?'

'Nobody important.'

'You stay here at this hotel?'

'No.'

'You live here? London?'

'Yes.'

'It is a fine city.'

'You like it here?'

'Oh, yes. Many beautiful women.'

She smiled shyly and looked down. 'You're a real charmer.'

'But you are the most beautiful. This man is not coming. He must be very foolish.'

'Very rude, I'd say.'

He clinked glasses. 'Bottoms up. Is that what you say here?'

Zelda laughed. 'Some people do.'

'It is so difficult here to know what is right. English language so difficult. Very easy to make mistake, say wrong thing.'

'Your English is very good.'

'You think so?'

'Sure.'

His arm brushed lightly against hers, and she had to remind herself not to flinch. Her stomach was in knots already. The drink helped, but she would have to be careful. She didn't want to end up drunk and being taken advantage of. On closer inspection, he wasn't bad-looking, in a macho sort of way. The salt-and-pepper hair and five-day stubble suited him and gave him an aura of maturity and authority he hadn't possessed back then. His clothes sense could perhaps have been a bit more subtle. The suit was Hugo Boss, but the shirt and tie were definitely over the top. Still, he looked as if he had gone up in the world, and he probably didn't make long drives to abduct young girls from orphanages in Moldova any more. Not that any of this made a scrap of difference to Zelda. His slightly hooded cobalt blue eyes seemed restless, and when they fixed on her, she felt as if she were being undressed, just as Faye Butler had said.

She also noticed a crescent-shaped scar high on his right cheek and wondered if it had been there on the night he and his brother abducted her. She couldn't remember it, but then she hadn't had anything on her mind other than fighting him off and escaping. She reached out and touched it gently. 'Have you always had that?'

He put his hand to his cheek self-consciously. 'Accident. When I was very young.' He downed his whisky and ordered another with a snap of his fingers. He glanced at her glass, which was still half-full, and she shook her head. He was on his third large whisky already, certainly giving her a start by drinking so much so fast, she thought. It ought to speed up the action and effects of the flunitrazepam. On the other hand, maybe he was one of those people with a constitution that could stand just about anything. She would soon find out.

'Is getting more busy here,' he said as someone leaned over him and shouted out a drinks order.

'Yes. I must say, I'm dying for a cigarette.'

His expression brightened. 'You smoke?'

'Yes. I know, I know, it's a terrible habit and—'

'No. No.' He pointed at his chest. 'Me. I smoke, too. So difficult these days.'

'We could go outside,' Zelda said tentatively.

'I have room here,' he said. 'We can smoke there.'

'But aren't all the rooms non-smoking now?'

He just smiled. 'Bah.'

'Well . . . all right,' she said. 'Shall we leave our drinks here, for when we come back? I'm sure the barman will—'

'We take them. Drink and smoke good together. Right? I have more whisky in room.'

Zelda smiled. 'Right.' She grabbed her bag and followed him out, drink in her other hand. As far as she could tell, nobody paid attention to them leaving. Both bar and grill were noisy and crowded now, and the lights were dim.

It was mid-evening, and Banks was listening to Nico's *The End* and thinking about Samir when he heard his doorbell ring. He wasn't expecting anyone, so he moved cautiously to the front door and looked through the sitting room window. There was an unfamiliar car out front. He hadn't heard it pull up because he'd been in the conservatory at the back of the house. It was hard to make out exactly who was standing there, just from his profile in the twilight, but Banks had an inkling that turned out to be right when he opened the door and saw Detective Chief Superintendent Richard 'Dirty Dick' Burgess on his doorstep, large as life.

'Banksy,' Burgess said, stretching out his hand.

Banks shook. He had given up trying to get Burgess to stop calling him Banksy. The harder he tried, the more the bastard did it. 'What the hell do you want at this time of night?' he asked.

'Well, that's a fine northern welcome,' Burgess said, stepping into the room. 'I thought you lot were supposed to be friendly. It's all right. Don't worry. I'm not after a home, or even a bed for the night. Got a young lady here, have you?'

'There's nobody here but me.'

'Sad, Banksy, sad. And I used to envy you your good luck in that department. Especially that lovely young Italian bint you had a few years ago. Well, the two of us can have a nice uninterrupted drink and natter about old times, can't we?'

Banks led the way through to the conservatory, where he had been watching the rose and lilac traces of sunset in the sky through the dip in the hills between Tetchley Fell and the Pennines.

'Lovely,' said Burgess, rubbing his hands together. 'Nice view. I don't believe I've been in the inner sanctum before.'

Banks realised that was true. In all the years they had known each other, neither had been in the other's home.

'What's this music?' Burgess asked.

'Nico,' Banks told him.

'Hmm. If the dead could sing . . . Give me a shake if I fall asleep. Anything to drink?'

Banks used his remote to turn off the music halfway through 'Secret Side', one of his favourites. Annoyed as he was at the interruption, he had to admit that Burgess had a point; there was something definitely otherworldly about Nico's songs and voice. 'What do you fancy?'

'Got any lager?'

'I might have a can or two of Stella left.'

'Stella? Aren't we posh? OK. That'll do fine, I suppose.'

Banks went into the kitchen and got a tin out of the fridge and a glass from the cupboard above. He also picked up the bottle of Negroamaro he had just opened. He would probably need another glass of that, maybe two. One often did with Burgess.

'To what do I owe this pleasure,' he said after handing Burgess the tin and glass and refilling his own. He noticed that

Burgess had taken his favourite chair, the one with the best view, so took the one at a right angle to it.

'I suppose you know I've been working quite closely with the NCA lately?' Burgess said.

'I'd heard,' said Banks. 'How's that going?' Burgess seemed healthy, he thought. He'd lost a bit of weight around the middle, and the bags under his cynical grey eyes had grown smaller. He still had that seen-it-all, world-weary look, which had perhaps escalated to a seen-even-more and still-world-weary look. Banks had been feeling more world-weary himself for the past couple of years. It was getting to be that kind of world. Wearying. He didn't know whether it showed in his eyes, or in the bags underneath them. No one had told him that it did.

'Well . . .' Burgess went on. 'It means a lot of drug cases, a lot of gang stuff, organised crime. That world's changing fast; the new boss isn't the same as the old boss. He's just as likely to slip a knife between your ribs as he is to give you a Christmas bonus. Anyway, that's not what I've come to see you about.'

'What is it, then?'

'Do you know a woman called Nelia Melnic?'

'Can't say as I do.'

'She's some sort of local artist. Goes under the name of Zelda.'

Banks paused, his drink halfway to his mouth. 'Zelda? Yes. Of course. That's Ray's partner.'

Burgess nodded. 'Only her name came up, and when I found she was living in North Yorkshire with an artist called Raymond Cabbot, my antenna immediately started twitching. Isn't your DI called Annie Cabbot? Your old squeeze.'

'That's right.'

'So who's Ray, then? Her brother?'

'It's her father,' said Banks. 'He moved up here from Cornwall last year.'

'Her father! Bloody hell. Have you seen her? Nelia? He must—'

'Be old enough to be her father, yes. Grandfather, maybe. I know.'

Burgess shook his head slowly. 'What a bloody waste.'

'Oh, I wouldn't say that.' Banks paused to drink some wine. 'Think about it. You're easily old enough to be her father, too, when it comes right down to it. Anyway, what does the NCA want with Zelda? As far as I know she works for them as a consultant.'

'Super-recogniser. Yes, I know.'

'Then . . .?'

'I also know a little bit about her background, what a hard time she's had of it. Though I must say, from the photo, that she—'

'Yes,' said Banks. 'She's a looker all right. Stunner, you might say. But why are you interested? Apart from the obvious.'

'You do me a disservice, Banksy. This isn't about her looks. I was just making a passing comment, that's all. No matter what you might think of me, I'm not insensitive. When I think about what she must have suffered over the years it makes me want to throttle someone.'

'So what's wrong? Has something happened to Zelda?'

'No. No. Nothing like that.'

'So the point of your visit is . . .? Not that I'm not happy to see you, of course.'

'Naturally. My point? Does it make *her* want to throttle someone? Not literally, you understand. Or maybe it is literal. I don't know.'

'She goes down to London every now and then and spends a few days studying photos and videos of suspected sex traffickers and their contacts and gives what information she can to the NCA for their database. That's all I know about her job. I asked for her help when she said she saw a photo of Phil Keane in London with a Croatian trafficker she recognised. She never told me his name. Classified, I suppose.'

'Probably Petar Tadić,' said Burgess. 'He's a real piece of work. Operating over here now far too often for our liking, and someone we've been very interested in lately. Is Keane the bloke who set fire to your house?'

'Yes.'

Burgess whistled through his teeth then gulped some lager. Banks watched his face. He seemed to be mulling over something that had just occurred to him. 'What happened?' Burgess asked finally.

'Nothing,' said Banks. 'She drew a blank. That was just before Christmas.'

'What you've just told me puts a new complexion on things,' Burgess said. 'I need a moment to reshuffle.'

Banks worked on his wine and listened to the silence stretch.

Finally Burgess spoke. 'OK,' he said. 'This goes no further, understood?'

'Understood,' said Banks.

Tadić didn't make a move in the lift, for which Zelda was grateful. The hotel room was small and seemed to be dominated by the bed, but that was London hotels for you. At least it was tidy. Zelda was willing to bet he hadn't been there since the maid service earlier in the day. As soon as they got in, he hung the DO NOT DISTURB sign on the door, switched on one dim corner lamp, put his drink down on the desk and said, 'I must use toilet.'

He went in and she soon heard the splashing of his powerful stream. Hands shaking, she took the three two-milligram capsules of flunitrazepam from her handbag and dropped them into his whisky, then used the wooden stirrer she had brought from the bar to stir it up. Next, she lit a cigarette with shaking hands and went to stand by the window. It looked out on the square below. The streetlights had just come on and it was quiet at that time of the evening. Twilight. She inhaled the acrid smoke deep into her lungs before exhaling it in a long plume. The irony of using the date rape drug on the man who had raped her wasn't lost on her. She wasn't sure whether she had given him enough or too much, but Tadić was a big man and six milligrams ought to be enough. Christ, she hoped it worked. The alternative didn't bear thinking about. She was pretty sure that he didn't know who she was. And being arrogant and stupid in equal parts, he was so certain of his own attractiveness that he wouldn't think for a moment he was being set up. Especially by a woman. If he did know, he was a far better actor than she had given him credit for.

As it turned out, solubility didn't really matter. As soon as Tadić came out of the bathroom he tossed back the rest of the drink in one and drained the glass. Without even looking at any dregs there might be, he picked up a half-full bottle of Glenmorangie from the little nook where the tea and coffee makings were kept and filled it up again. Zelda let out the breath she had been holding.

'You want?' he said, offering her the whisky.

Zelda turned her nose up. 'I don't like whisky,' she said.

He opened the minibar and took out a miniature vodka. 'Good? Yes?'

Zelda nodded and he poured for her. She stubbed out her cigarette in a saucer, added tonic water to the vodka and smiled. She had no intention of drinking any more.

Tadić bent over a cupboard under the drinks area and Zelda saw he was entering his code for the safe. When he had got it open, he brought out a plastic bag of white powder, a small mirror and a razor blade, and grinned at her. 'You like?'

Christ, the last thing she needed him to do was start snorting coke. That would probably nullify the flunitrazepam completely, or at least delay its onset. She didn't want a coked-up Tadić on her hands. 'I like,' she said and moved as sexily as she could. 'But maybe later? When we are tired?'

Tadić shrugged, then lounged on the bed, propped up against the pillows, and patted the place beside him. There was really nowhere else for Zelda to go except a hard-backed office chair at the desk under the window, so she sat and leaned back beside him. The pills were supposed to take between twenty minutes and half an hour to start working, and Zelda didn't think that would be fast enough, the way time seemed to be dribbling slowly away right now. It was a lot of time to keep Tadić occupied, and she very much doubted that conversation would do the trick. She picked up a remote control and switched on the television, hoping it would distract him.

He turned it off. The next thing he did was light a cigar. That would give her a bit of time, she thought, as the smoke spiralled, caught in her throat and took her back to the nightmare car journey across Romania. There was no ashtray, but he brought over the saucer from the tea and coffee tray.

'Do you have any music?' Zelda asked.

'Music?' He switched on the bedside radio, which was tuned to a station that was playing old standards by Frank Sinatra, Sarah Vaughan, Tony Bennett and the like.

'What you do?' Tadić asked, puffing on his cigar, drink in hand.

'Advertising,' Zelda said.

'Ah. Is good job, yes?'

'Not bad. You?'

'Importing goods.'

That was one way of putting it, Zelda thought. She glanced sideways, hoping for signs that the drug was taking effect. He hadn't shown any yet, but it was early days. She felt as if her heart was going to burst through her chest if it beat any harder or faster, and her muscles were stiff with tension. She was also feeling nauseated by the cigar. If he didn't collapse soon, she thought she would just have to make a break for it. Abort the mission. She calculated the distance to the door. She thought she could make it. He slipped off his tie and opened a couple of buttons on his shirt so that Zelda could see the thick gold chain around his neck, and his salt-and-pepper chest hair.

She lit another cigarette, a further delaying tactic. Tadić, cigar in mouth, got up and refilled his glass. Luckily, he seemed to have forgotten about hers, which was still full. How long had it been?

Zelda noticed that his movements were beginning to seem a little uncoordinated. Perhaps it was just the booze, but it was a good sign. He put his glass down on the bedside table after one large gulp. His hand brushed her bare shoulder and arm. She felt herself shiver, but not with pleasure. He clearly misinterpreted the signal because he took her cigarette from her hand, put it out in the saucer, then leaned over to kiss her. The next thing she knew, his rubbery lips were squirming on hers, tasting of cigar smoke, his hand squeezing her breast so hard it hurt. He took her hand and placed it between his legs, so that she could feel his erection. She thought she was going to be sick and disengaged herself as quickly and gently as she could. 'Whoa. Easy, boy,' she said. 'There's no hurry, is there?'

'What you want? You don't want coke. You don't want fuck. What you want?'

'What I really need,' said Zelda, 'is to go to the toilet.'

'I come with you. I like to watch.'

'No.'

Tadić grinned and lay back on the pillows, one hand casually stroking her breast. She thought she could see traces of confusion in his eyes; they were losing their sharpness and focus, as if becoming aware of something wrong. She got up and went to the toilet, closed the door then put the seat and the top down and sat. How long would it take? How long could she get away with? She could hear the muffled sound of the radio – a song she knew from her childhood in the orphanage, Frank Sinatra singing 'High Hopes' – but nothing else. The smell of cigar smoke had got everywhere and was making her feel even more ill than her nerves were.

Finally, she thought she couldn't get away with staying in the toilet any longer, so she opened the door slowly and peered out. Tadić was as she had left him, slumped on the bed, only now his shirt was undone all the way. His trouser belt was loose, his zipper down, his eyes closed; his drink balanced on his chest, which rose and fell slowly. But he must have heard her come out, for he stirred as she edged towards the bed, and his hooded eyes half-opened.

'Take your clothes off,' he said, slurring his words. 'Strip for me. Strip for Goran.'

'What?'

'Undress for me. Now. Please.'

He gave his head a shake, as if to clear the cobwebs, and let it fall back against the pillows with a dull thud. He almost missed the bedside table with his glass as he put it down to wave his hand at her. 'Go,' he said. 'Strip.'

The drugs were working, Zelda thought, with a surge of relief. His coordination was going. The waving hand might have belonged to someone else. She couldn't tell what he said next, as his voice was so muffled. He tried to get up again but couldn't seem to manage it. But his eyes were still open and he was still looking at her. Time. She needed more time. Slowly she moved to the bottom of the bed, sliding her sandals off. She reached around and unfastened the tie at the back of her neck, letting the halter neck fall slowly over her throat to her breasts. He smiled and made a deep grunting sound, but his eyes remained fixed on her and she thought she could see him nod.

She slid the dress all the way down and stepped out of it. He tried to sit up but couldn't make it. Just when she thought she didn't need to go any further and was thinking of reaching for her bag, he barked another command for her to keep stripping. Frank Sinatra was singing 'Try a Little Tenderness', which was hardly suitable striptease music, but she did her best. Zelda swayed in time with the music, reached behind her back, unclipped her bra and let it fall to the floor beside her dress.

She felt so exposed and vulnerable that she was close to tears, and she thought she wouldn't be able to go on, but her memories gave her strength. He tried to push himself up from the bed with his arms behind him; he managed to get to a sitting position, but his upper body seemed to be wavering and a sweat had broken out on his forehead. He was making a groaning sound deep in his throat. Zelda hooked her thumbs in the top of her panties, gritted her teeth and slid them down over her thighs. If this was the price she had to pay, so be it.

When she had finished and stood there naked in front of the bed, the music still playing, Tadić gasped, fell back and gave a long sigh, then went silent. Zelda stood stock-still for a few moments, watching, listening, but he made no movement. His eyes were closed. Carefully she moved closer to listen to his breathing. It was slow and shallow, but he was still breathing. She lifted an arm and let it fall. It thudded back on the bedcover.

Zelda took the knife from her handbag and sat astride his chest. With both hands, she lifted the blade high in the air and . . . she froze. She couldn't do it, couldn't kill a sleeping man. Not even a monster like Goran Tadić. She let her hands fall and clutched the knife to her stomach. Come on, you fool, she chastised herself. This may be your only chance. Don't forget what this man did to you, did to all those others and will do to others to come. The world will be a better place without him. *Kill him.* The images rushed through her mind, the pain of his rough thrusts, the scratching of his beard against her shoulder, the sickly cigar smoke and soundtrack of pounding rap music.

Again she raised the knife high, but again she couldn't plunge it. For a moment, it was as if she was looking down on the scene from above, seeing this half-crazed naked woman holding a knife, and the man unconscious beneath her. She watched herself lower the blade, hold it against his throat, and she willed herself to push. She couldn't. The blade pricked his skin. Blood welled up. She held it over his heart and tried there. Still nothing. Once more, she raised the knife.

He opened his eyes.

He reached for her, grasped her breasts.

Then she was inside the half-crazed woman again. She *was* the half-crazed woman.

She brought down the blade as hard as she could.

The knife struck him full in the throat. Zelda pulled it out. Blood sprayed on her thighs and belly. His hands went to his throat, and his breath started coming in sharp bubbling rasps. Zelda raised the blade again, and hardly watching where it went, plunged it down into his left eye. He gave one last twitch, almost tossing her from her perch on his chest, and that was it. She felt the blade go all the way through and stick in the inside of the back of his skull. She wiggled it loose, and as she pulled it free, his eyeball slipped out and dangled over his bloody cheek. She didn't need to feel his pulse to know that he was dead. There were no more gurgling sounds, no more movement.

Zelda collapsed with a sob on the other side of the bed, crying, shaking from head to toe. She didn't know how long she lay there before stirring, making her way back to the bathroom, vomiting down the toilet and running the shower. She stood under it as long as she could and as hot as she could bear it, then dried herself off. She washed the knife in the sink, watching the diluted blood trickle down the plughole. Christ, she had done it. She had killed Goran Tadić. Now, after the release, the numbness set in. She felt nothing when she walked back into the bedroom and saw his bloody corpse on the bed, but she knew the reaction would come later.

Zelda dressed quickly and gathered her things together, making sure she didn't leave anything behind. As one final measure, she took a towel from the bathroom and wiped off every surface she thought she might have touched. She didn't think anyone would be checking for fingerprints or DNA, but it seemed the sensible thing to do, the thing people always did in the movies. The thing Modesty Blaise would do.

There was no way Tadić's people were going to allow any sort of official police investigation into what had happened to him. They would probably find his body first. Then they would cut it into pieces, get rid of it and clean up the room. Nobody would ever find it or know what happened. Before Zelda left, she took one more look at him lying dead on the bed, the matted bloody hair on his chest, the eyeball hanging out. Christ, how she hated him. Now he wouldn't be able to harm anyone ever again.

She checked the corridor, saw there was no one about, left the DO NOT DISTURB sign in place, then took the lift down and walked out through the front door without looking back. Around the corner, she hailed a taxi and took it straight back to her hotel. There would be no more trains tonight, but she would be on the first one tomorrow morning, back up to Yorkshire to wait for Raymond, to resume her life again and try to put all this madness behind her.

'Nelia Melnic worked for a man called Trevor Hawkins. Old style NCA, if you can imagine the organisation being old enough to have such a thing. He ran a department out of Cambridge Circus dealing with sex-trafficking in all its ugliness. But you probably know that already. Last weekend, Trevor Hawkins was killed in a house fire. Investigators say it was a chip-pan fire, though no one figured Hawkins for a chip eater, unless they were triple-fried in goose fat. Anyway, the body was too badly burned to reveal any signs of drugs, and there were no indications of physical violence on the bits that remained. There's no forensic evidence of criminal activity, but the investigating team knows that fires can easily be made to look like accidents. That said, there are no signs of a break-in, and nobody saw anyone visiting the house that evening. Not that that means anything. Most of them were either out or watching telly behind closed curtains. His immediate neighbours were away. His wife was visiting her parents in Bath for the weekend. No one even noticed the fire until it was too late.'

'So you think—'

'I don't think anything, Banksy. I haven't finished yet. We were concerned about outside interference. And quite rightly. It's an international matter. But you've just given me a bit of information I didn't have; the NCA doesn't have. That Nelia Melnic saw a photograph of Keane with a Croatian trafficker. No doubt Hawkins saw it, too. And then Hawkins dies in a mysterious fire. What would you think?'

'I wouldn't jump to conclusions,' said Banks. 'I'm sure that Hawkins and Zelda saw pictures of lots of traffickers in the course of their work. But I agree it might be more than a mere coincidence. Zelda didn't tell me his name, but she did say that he's evil and he likes to hurt the girls.'

'Would she have identified Keane for them, too?'

'Probably not. She didn't know who he was until Annie showed her the photograph of Keane we have. It was the other man she recognised.'

'Tadić? That makes sense. The NCA team are very interested in him now he seems to be spending a lot of his time over here organising transport and destinations for the trafficked girls. But the point is that this Zelda woman walked by Hawkins's burned-out house earlier this week. One of our men was photographing everyone who passed by, just in case.'

'I suppose she was curious,' said Banks. 'He was her boss, after all.'

'That's exactly what she said. But would you go to the trouble of taking the tube to walk past your boss's house if it burned down?'

'Surely you can't think Zelda had anything to do with the fire?'

'We know she didn't start it. She was in Croatia at the time. We've checked with the airlines. We've no idea where she went, but she rented a car from Franjo Tudman Airport in Zagreb. And we don't believe she hired someone to do it in her place. In fact, we have no reason to believe that she had anything to do with Hawkins's death at all. But she did walk past his house. We were wondering why, what it is she's after. And after what you've told me, we now have in Keane a man who likes fires, and kills. So you tell me.'

Banks shook his head. 'I have no idea. I haven't seen Zelda in a while, and Ray's away in America. You want me to talk to her?'

'If you would. She's in London, but she's been informed she can head home as soon as she likes. We need to keep this low-key, Banksy, and the impression I get from the investigating team is that she doesn't much like cops, even though she works for them. The chief investigators, Paul Danvers and Deborah Fletcher, have interviewed her twice now, and they said she was quite bolshy on both occasions. Mind you, Danvers walks around like he's got a stick up his arse, and as for poor Debs, well, frigid stick insect would be a compliment. But I thought this Zelda might respond better to a casual chat with a friend, rather than a police interview.'

'I'm a cop, too, you know.'

'I know. But you're also a friend of hers. And I know your liberal sympathies, your soft centre. You're exactly the right kind of sucker for a story like hers. See if you can find out what she knows that we don't, and what she's up to.'

'If you think I'm going to try to trap her into—'

'I'm not expecting you to do anything of the kind, Banksy. I know you and your sense of loyalty all too well. It's admirable, if a tad inconvenient at times. Be as up front with her as you like. It doesn't matter. As I said, she's not a suspect. We just want to know why she's so interested, and if she knows or suspects anything about Hawkins she's not telling us. If you want to bring down Keane, my friend, whether it's for personal revenge or whatever, you could do a lot worse than have the NCA owing you a favour.' He held up his empty tin and waved it back and forth. Banks went into the kitchen to get another for him and refilled his own glass at the same time.

'What do you know about this Petar Tadić character?' he asked Burgess when he came back.

'Not a lot,' said Burgess. 'He's got a brother called Goran. Croatians. They both started out in the transportation side of the sex trafficking business quite a few years ago, based in

Serbia but working all over the eastern Balkans – Romania, Moldova, even Ukraine and Belarus. Wherever the beautiful, vulnerable young girls were. And the ones they couldn't persuade to travel overseas with fake offers of modelling careers and secretarial college, they simply snatched off the street. But they've worked their way up to the exploitation level now. They work more with the end-users. That's why they're spending so much time over here.'

'Pimps?'

'Sort of. Certainly no better than. But not directly. They're more like pimps to the pimps. They supply the needs of pimps. They don't stand at the brothel door and take the money. They do the strong-arm stuff as well, if it's called for. In fact, they're quite brutal. They flatten the competition if they have to, and they don't spare the rod with the girls, either, if they step out of line. Literally.'

'Drugs?'

Burgess shook his head. 'Only insofar as they need to supply the girls from time to time to keep them subdued, and to give themselves the occasional snort, of course, or fuel a sex party. A little happy powder now and then. But not operationally, no. They might consort with dealers and suppliers, mind you. It's a mixed-up world they're in, and where you find one crime, you're as likely as not to find a dozen more. Most of the drugs are down to the Albanian Mafia, these days, and the Calabrians, the 'Ndrangheta. And you cross them only at your peril.'

Tadić sounded like the sort of supplier Connor Clive Blaydon might be working with on his pop-up brothels, Banks thought. Neither of them exactly down on the shop floor, but pulling the strings from a distance – Blaydon as someone who had access to the properties for use and Tadić with access to the girls and drugs. And of course, Tadić might also be rubbing shoulders with the Albanians, especially Leka Gashi. 'Do you think Zelda's in any danger?' he asked.

Burgess thought for a moment, then said, 'Depends. I'm assuming she's not stupid enough to go stirring up a hornets' nest, so there's no real reason why she should be. On the other hand, if she's got some sort of crazy plan in mind, who knows . . .? But she, more than anyone, ought to know how dangerous these people are, what they're capable of. I don't imagine she's been running around asking questions about Keane, has she?'

'Not that I know of,' said Banks. 'And I certainly advised her not to. Like I said, it came to nothing. Why do you think this Hawkins chap was killed, if indeed he was?'

'Danvers believes he was, and that it was because he functioned as the traffickers' man on the inside. These high-powered criminal enterprises don't get very far without insiders, and they create corruption on as wide a scale as they can. One or two upper-echelon traffickers have managed to avoid capture this past year or two, and the most obvious explanation seems that they were warned in advance. Danvers thinks Hawkins was on their payroll and something went wrong. Mind you, he's got no evidence to back this up. Hence his interest in the girl.'

'And you?'

'I'm not entirely convinced. Hawkins may simply have got too close to Tadić or his organisation for their comfort.'

'And they sent Keane to kill him?'

'Why not?'

'Because Keane's a forger, not a hit man. Surely they've got people they can use for jobs like Hawkins's?'

'Of course. But Keane likes to set fires. Maybe they wanted a bit of variety? Maybe Keane wanted the job? Maybe it was his way of proving something to them? After all, he set fire to a narrowboat and to your house up here in Eastvale. It's clearly a hobby of his.'

'Maybe,' said Banks.

'And a fire has the advantage of pretty much destroying any evidence there might have been – paper trails, that sort of thing.'

'It's possible.'

'We have the photograph of Tadić with Keane, and maybe we also have Hawkins either on Tadić's tail or on his payroll, depending on which theory you believe. Either way, he could have become a liability. So they set the fireman on him. Maybe Tadić's usual killer was on another job, out of the country, in jail, whatever, and he used the best means he could find to hand.'

'Where do you think Zelda fits in with all this?'

'I don't know,' said Burgess. 'Given her history, you have to assume she might have come across Tadić at some point or other. How long has she been out of the game?'

'She wasn't in the game,' snapped Banks.

'Sorry. That's not what I meant. Wrong choice of words. Don't be so sensitive. She's been over here about four years, right?'

'I think so,' said Banks. 'Ray met her about three years ago in London, and she went to live with him first in Cornwall, then up here. I'm not sure how long she'd been in London before they met. She had been working as a pavement artist down there and was apparently a bit of a ragamuffin back then, so maybe not so long.'

'Let's say she's been free four years, then,' said Burgess. 'The Tadić brothers have certainly been in the business much longer than that. Where's she from?'

'Moldova.'

'That's part of the area the Tadićs operated in. Their paths could have crossed. Maybe when she saw the picture of Petar

Tadić with Keane she told Hawkins you were interested in Keane for reasons of your own. I don't know. That may have set him on a dangerous path. But look on the bright side. She's got you to protect her. Her knight in shining armour.'

'Come on,' said Banks. 'I'm being serious here. I like the woman. And I like that she and Ray make each other happy. If you're going to take the piss out of me, fair enough, but try to be serious when it comes to her safety.'

'I don't know what you expect me to do. Put her under protection? You know as well as I do that we don't have the resources to provide guard duty.'

Banks ran his hand over his hair. 'I know,' he said. 'I only hope you're wrong about all this.'

'Take hope, then. I often am.' Burgess downed the rest of his lager and glanced at his watch. 'Sorry, I have to love you and leave you,' he said, groaning as he got to his feet. 'I've got an early morning meeting in Newcastle and a room waiting for me at the Mal.'

When Zelda got back to her hotel, she knew there was no hope of sleep. She undressed, showered again, hot and long, then fell back on the bed trembling, eyes wide open.

Why did Tadić have to open his eyes? If he had just fallen unconscious, as he was supposed to do, she wouldn't have gone through with it. It had been different with Darius; she had been fighting for her freedom, for her life, and he had been the last thing standing in her way. But this time was different. This time it had been premeditated, cold-blooded murder.

She was a long way from Modesty Blaise now.

Zelda got up, took a vodka from the minibar, downed it in one then poured herself another, which she set down on the bedside table. She picked up the TV remote and turned it on.

There was a talk show on with an idiotic host and even more idiotic guests trying to sell their latest movies or shows. But she needed background noise; in the silence she would go mad.

She went over the scene in her mind, the craziness of it all. Even now, so soon after, when she tried to picture herself sitting at the hotel bar waiting for Goran Tadić to come in and pick her up, she could hardly believe what she had done. Or the journey up to his room, the nearness of him in the lift; the cigar smoke on his breath, choking her, bringing back memories of that terrible car journey; his musky deodorant fighting a losing battle against sweat and testosterone; the hurried doctoring of the drink, his greedy slurping it down; then the almost interminable wait, the striptease, 'Try a Little Tenderness.' After that came the moment that cut the person she was now off from the person she had been until then. The murder. Brutal, bloody. And perhaps the worst thing of all was that, despite her fear, her hesitations and her protestations to herself, in some deep, dark part of her soul, she had enjoyed it.

She reached for the second vodka and sipped it, feeling it burn all the way down. Had she done everything that needed to be done? She went over her actions again – the clean-up, wiping off her prints, the blood, showering. She knew there was no way she could rid the room or his body of every trace of her, that if a police forensic team went over it, they would find something to point to her. But she also knew it would probably never come to that.

Then she realised with a shock that she had forgotten to do one thing. Get rid of the knife. She had cleaned it, but it was still in her bag. And the rest of the set was still in the drawer. She could keep them all, of course, take them home and use them, in plain view like Poe's 'The Purloined Letter', but it would be more sensible to get rid of them all.

She jumped up off the bed, dressed quickly in jeans and a cashmere jumper, tied her damp hair at the back of her neck, then took out the knife from her handbag and placed it back with the others in the box the set had come in. As an after-thought, she ripped the cellophane off the cardboard box, so the water would get in and make sure it sank under the weight of the knives. Not that it mattered. Even if they floated out to sea, no one would be able to trace them to her. But best be careful.

It was a mild evening and there were plenty of people strolling along the riverside. Couples holding hands on their way home from restaurants or pubs, parents with grumbling children returning from a long, tiring day of sightseeing. Pleasure boats went by, lit up for the night-time champagne cruises, all the romance of the Thames.

There was nowhere Zelda could be completely free of passers-by, so she chose a dark spot far enough away from any restaurant or bar – and, as far as she could tell, CCTV – and crossed the stretch of grass that separated the path from the wall. There was no one else standing near her, and the path was now a good ten or twelve feet behind. She leaned her elbows on the wall as if contemplating the view. The tide was well in and the water just below her swirled black and oily. Some of the windows in the office buildings across the river were still lit up, and she could see the occasional silhouettes of late workers walking about in the offices. But they were too far away to see what she was doing.

When there were no boats passing in front of her and no one behind, she slipped the box of knives out of her bag and dropped it over the side. It made a satisfying plop, and she felt a sense of relief, seeing it go down, as if by getting rid of the weapon she had shed some of the burden of the crime.

Just then, she heard a voice behind. 'Is everything all right?'

She turned sharply, hand on her heart and saw a young man in jogging gear standing on the grass in front of her.

'Only you were looking a bit lost,' he said, sounding less sure of himself now he could see her at least partially in the city darkness.

'I'm fine,' Zelda said, dredging up a polite smile.

'It's just . . . you know, sometimes people . . . I don't mean to be . . .'

'Honest. I'm fine,' Zelda reassured him. 'I wasn't thinking of jumping. I was just enjoying the peace and the view.'

'Oh. I'm sorry I interrupted you, then, if everything's OK.'

'It's fine, really. I'm going now, anyway.'

The young man studied her for a moment, as if to make sure she was telling the truth, then he nodded and set off jogging along the path again. Her heart still pounding, Zelda made her way back to her hotel room.

Banks stood at the front door watching the car churn up gravel as it headed down the drive. When the sound of the motor faded, there was silence except for Gratly Beck. It was a warm evening – perhaps the warmest of the year so far – and Banks realised it had been a long time since he had sat by the terraced falls and enjoyed a nightcap al fresco. It was already dark, a clear night, with stars glittering in the sky, so he went back for his wine, then climbed the wall and sat on the grassy bank of Gratly Beck by the terraced waterfalls, looking down on the lights of Helmthorpe in the valley bottom.

Talk of Keane had brought back memories of the night it happened. Much of it was blurred, as he had been drugged, but he remembered the sensation of being unable to move a muscle while also being aware that the flames were rising all around him. He remembered 'Death and the Maiden' playing on the stereo and thinking it was the last music he was ever going to hear. He had thought it was all over, then he felt himself being manhandled, and the next thing he knew he was lying on the gravel drive with Annie and Winsome bending over him.

He came back to the present at the sound of a night bird in one of the trees that lined the banks of the beck further down the slope, towards Helmthorpe. He thought of what Burgess had told him and wondered whether Zelda – and therefore Ray – really was in danger. Nobody in the trafficking organisation would know she was doing the job for the NCA, or where she lived, unless there was an informer working there. And if that informer had been Hawkins, he could easily have tipped off Tadić that Zelda was working there, with her special knowledge and skills. But if he had done that, why hadn't something happened already? Couldn't they find her? Was it more to their advantage to have her doing that job? The devil you know . . .

Burgess wanted to know how much Zelda knew, or suspected, and perhaps when Banks knew that, he would be better able to gauge any danger to her. Burgess was right, though; neither he nor Ray could protect her full-time, and they couldn't expect the police to do it. He could only hope that she was not in danger. If she was, it was probably his fault for bringing Phil Keane to her attention in the first place. But that photograph of Keane with Tadić, if that was who it was, hadn't led to anything. Surely Hawkins would have had nothing to report about her, even if he had been working for the traffickers. Zelda wasn't the only one in her office, the only threat to them, and Tadić's gang could hardly murder them all. The thought calmed him down a little, but even then, he couldn't get rid of that nagging worry at the back of his mind. He would call her tomorrow, find out when she was coming home.

As he finished his wine, Banks found his thoughts turning to Samir. He was still feeling depressed from his meeting with the boy's uncle and aunt on Thursday. Samir had come on ahead to 'light the way' and make money to send his family so they might follow him, but somehow or other he had lost the address of his aunt and uncle and had probably – so Banks thought – ended up drifting into, or being forced into, working for a county lines drug dealer. Perhaps he was earning good money, or perhaps, like so many trafficked refugees, he was working off a debt which only grew bigger day by day. For Samir, in a way, had been stolen from his normal life, just as surely as Zelda had been stolen from hers. They had both made long journeys and encountered many obstacles. And the damned thing was that Samir's parents had been killed in an explosion after he had left Syria, and he had had no idea that they were dead. He had been working to make money that could never bring him what he wanted. His family. And now he was dead, too.

Banks drained his glass, climbed back over the drystone wall and crossed his gravel drive to the cottage. Perhaps just a touch more Negroamaro and some Dylan before bed. The Nico moment had passed. He had been listening to the fragments and outtakes of *Blood on the Tracks* recently, and for some reason that had given him the desire to listen to its predecessor, the underrated *Planet Waves*, for the first time in a few years.

II

Banks listened to Carolyn Sampson singing Bach's 'Mein Herze schwimmt im Blut' as he drove to Blaydon's house. A Bach cantata seemed appropriate for Sunday morning. The traffic was light, and soon he was driving once again through the wrought-iron gates and along the winding drive under an arch of trees to Blaydon's estate, focused on the job at hand.

There were several cars parked at various angles on the gravel apron in front of the house, and someone had put a bowler hat on the head of one of the stone cherubs. When Banks turned off his engine and got out of the car, he could hear music coming from inside the house. Not a thumping, pounding beat, but something a bit more middle of the road. It took him a few moments to realise it was Fleetwood Mac's 'Rhiannon'.

He rang the doorbell, expecting Roberts the butler to answer, but Blaydon himself opened the door. He was wearing an orange terry cloth robe and had a white towel draped around his neck.

'Banks,' he said. 'What a surprise! You've caught me quite unexpectedly. But then I suppose that's your intention, isn't it? Anyway, do come in. There's a bit of a party still going on, I think, but it shouldn't interrupt our business. Whatever that may be.'

Banks followed him across the cavernous hallway. 'Party?' he said. 'It's almost noon on Sunday.'

'Is it? I believe we started on Saturday afternoon, but you know how hard it is to get rid of guests sometimes. One can't simply ask them to leave. Anyway, don't be such a stick-in-the-mud. Is there ever a bad time for a party?'

On their way to Blaydon's office, a teenage girl in a pair of stiletto heels, and nothing else, walked past them. She looked a bit lost, so Blaydon pointed and said, 'The pool's that way, Steffi, love.'

She wobbled off. 'Granddaughter?' said Banks.

Blaydon laughed. 'Niece, I think. But not mine, thank God.'

'Have you ever come across a Croatian called Tadić?' Banks asked as they entered the office, which was in much the same state as it had been the last time he visited. 'Petar Tadić?'

'I can't say as I have. What business is he in?'

Banks nodded towards the departing girl's behind. 'Supplying young girls like her.'

The corner of Blaydon's mouth twitched in a semblance of a smile. 'Then I'd have to say no. Honestly, I have no idea where she came from. I suppose I must have invited her.'

'Unless she came with one of your guests.'

'There's always that.'

They settled down in the office, and Banks studied Blaydon. He seemed fairly fresh and youthful, considering he'd been throwing a party since the previous afternoon. Perhaps he had slept, or perhaps it was down to the white powder Banks guessed was around somewhere. But he wasn't interested in that. If he wanted, he could call in the drugs squad and get a search warrant, but that wasn't his intention, either. 'There've been some developments since we last talked,' he said. 'I wanted to sound you out on a few things.'

'Oh? Such as?'

'For a start, we've identified the dead boy as Samir Boulad, a migrant from Syria. We've also been able to link him with a house on Hollyfield Lane, where we found the body of an old junkie called Howard Stokes. The house is owned by Tommy and Timmy Kerrigan.'

'Fascinating,' said Blaydon. 'But what's that—'

'We think the boy was working as a cuckoo in Stokes's house, selling drugs in the Eastvale area.'

'I'm sorry, you've lost me. A "cuckoo"? Is that slang for something?'

'You've heard of county lines?'

'Read about them in the papers. Whatever will these blokes come up with next?'

'We also know that Leka Gashi is most likely involved, taking over a number of county lines based in Leeds and supplying the outlying rural areas, including Eastvale. Remember him? Last time I talked to you, you said you'd never heard of him. But you've been seen with him, and we also happen to have found out that the two of you have known one another for about ten years, through your home on Corfu. He lived just over the bay, in Sarandë.'

'I know a lot of people in that area,' said Blaydon. 'Nothing wrong with that. I've been a resident there on and off for almost twenty years.'

'But Gashi is Albanian Mafia, and we think you've been helping him set up his operations locally.'

'Me? Seriously?'

Banks nodded. 'Seriously. A favour here, a favour there.'

'But why would I need to resort to criminal activity when I'm making a bloody fortune legally?'

'I'd say, for a start, you rather fancy yourself in with the big bad boys, but perhaps even more important than that, your business isn't doing too well these days. You're not making a fortune. The property development business in general is in a depression. Shopping centres are closing down, and there's a slump in the housing market. All of which means you have a lot of real estate and a lot of debts, but no obvious way of improving your profits or your cash flow in the immediate future. Things could only get worse, of course, the political situation being what it is.'

'Interesting economic analysis,' said Blaydon. 'Completely wrong, but interesting.'

'So your business is doing fine?'

'I've diversified enough to compensate for a bumpy ride in the property markets,' he said. 'And the Elmet Centre *will* be built, and it will be a great success. Multiplex cinema, restaurants, high-end stores and boutiques, the lot. It's what Eastvale has been wanting for a long time. Not only that, it'll be a destination for people from more depressed areas further north – Darlington, Middlesbrough, Stockton, Chester-le-Street. Because you know as well as I do that no matter how depressed an urban area is, most of the people still have a car and a steady supply of booze, fags and fish and chips. And they like to have fun.'

'That's a pretty cynical view of the north-east,' said Banks.

'But true, nonetheless.'

'When you were at Le Coq d'Or on the Sunday evening Samir was murdered, you received a call on your mobile at about ten o'clock. Who was it from?'

'I don't remember any phone call.'

'Think back. You went outside to take it.'

'Oh, yes,' said Blaydon. 'Now I remember. That would have been Oliver. My son.'

'What did Oliver have to say?'

'I honestly don't remember. It wasn't anything important, anyway. Just some minor business matter. Why?'

'And for that you needed to go outside?'

'Don't you know it's rude to talk on the phone at the dinner table?'

'What's your business with the Kerrigans?'

'It's none of yours, but as you already know, they own a fair bit of the Hollyfield Estate, and that's going to be an essential part of the new Elmet Centre and housing complex. We have interests in common. It makes sense to work together.'

'What about The Vaults?'

'Hardly my scene. Some demented DJ and a night of trance or drill music? And, by the way, I've got a bone to pick with you.'

'Me?'

'Yes. What have you been saying to Frankie?'

'Nothing much. We interviewed him briefly, after we talked to you last time. That's all. Why?'

'Poisoned him against me, more like. He's quit on me.'

'Quit?'

'Yes. I'm going to have to find another driver now. It's a bloody inconvenience.'

'I'd apologise if I thought I were responsible,' said Banks. 'What reason did he give?'

'He didn't. Just said it was time to retire. Simple as that. I wouldn't mind but he's only about fifty. Got a good few years left in him yet.'

'Early retirement? Maybe that's all it was about?'

'Maybe.' But he didn't sound as if he believed it.

Banks stood up. 'How about showing me around the palace now I'm here?'

'What, now?'

'No time like the present. Who knows if, or when, I'll be back again?'

Blaydon gazed at Banks, seeming to consider his words for a moment. Banks wondered whether he was trying to remember if there was any evidence of drugs or drug use. Finally, he said, 'OK. Why not? Follow me.'

Banks followed. Apart from one of the bedrooms being used by a threesome in the throes of sexual passion, nothing interesting appeared to be going on in the rest of the house. But the place was definitely palatial. Blaydon could, if he wanted, accommodate a whole centre-full of asylum seekers and still have room to spare. It seemed amazing to Banks that one man had this all to himself. He sometimes felt that his own cottage was too big for him, and he should move to a flat if he wasn't planning on getting married or living with someone, which he wasn't. But this was true excess. No doubt, along with Roberts and Frankie, there were other servants to keep the place clean, and perhaps even to cook for Blaydon and his guests. A Michelin star chef, perhaps? McGuigan himself? Banks doubted it.

Finally, they came to the pool at the back. Not exactly Olympic-size, but not far off, complete with two-level diving board. It was all indoors, under glass or thick Perspex, which gave it the appearance of an outdoor pool, and on a day like today, with blue skies and sunshine, it looked perfect, rippling like a pool in a Hockney painting.

Banks had seen one or two people drifting about the house on his tour, but there were more here, mostly in loungers dozing or reading, and a number of well-endowed women in bikinis, or bikini bottoms, at any rate. Banks checked surreptitiously, but he didn't see any bowls full of cocaine. Fleetwood Mac played on quietly from hidden speakers. The naked girl sat on the edge of the pool swirling her stilettos in the water. A man swam leisurely lengths. Another naked woman stood by the edge of the pool swaying to the music, oblivious to everyone else. At the far end, near the diving board, two thickset men wearing dark suits and sunglasses sat up to attention when Banks entered the pool area. Blaydon gave them some sort of a sign, and they relaxed back into their loungers.

'Minders?' Banks asked.

'You can never be too careful.'

'Where's Jeeves today?'

'I gave Roberts the weekend off. He's not much of a party animal.'

The pool was clearly the end of the guided tour. 'How about the grounds, too?' Banks asked.

'Another time. I've got business to attend to.' Blaydon started heading back towards the front door, and Banks followed.

'Some nice cars out front,' Banks remarked. 'Jag, Rolls, Merc, a Beemer.'

'I know some wealthy people. It happens in my line of business.'

'Drugs, prostitutes?'

'Very fucking droll, Banks. And now perhaps if you've got what you came for, you can get off my property and leave us in peace?'

'My pleasure,' said Banks, smiling and doffing his non-existent cap in the doorway. It was all show, as he happened to see that one of the suits and sunglasses was watching them from across the hall. Surely it could do no harm to lead them to think Blaydon was friendly with the police? And the suit only saw Banks smile as he tapped Blaydon gently on the shoulder and said goodbye. He couldn't see Blaydon frown and flinch, as Banks did.

Before Banks could leave the property, his mobile went off. Thinking it might be Zelda replying to the messages he had left that morning on her landline and mobile, he pulled over on the gravel drive and answered. But it was Annie calling from the station. Everyone was working today, it seemed.

'Yes?' he answered. 'Anything new?'

'Where are you?'

Banks explained about his visit to Blaydon.

'OK,' she said. 'A couple of PCs have been viewing CCTV footage for the last two days, and I think they've finally come up with something.'

'What is it?'

'The Hollyfield area. You were right in that there's not very much available, but it seems The Oak has installed CCTV recently, since the assault just outside their car park a month ago.'

'Lisa Bartlett?'

'That's right.'

'And . . .'

'There's a car. A black Mercedes S Series.' She read out the number plate. 'It's Blaydon's. The one Frankie Wallace was driving on the night Samir was killed.'

'What time?'

'Five past ten.'

'In The Oak's car park, on the Sunday of the murder?'

'Yes.'

'That's just across the road from Hollyfield Lane.'

'So what are we going to do about it?'

'I'm not so far away from Frankie Wallace's house right now. Want to meet there?'

'Give me half an hour.'

'Will do,' said Banks, and set off under the arch of trees.

It was light well before six o'clock. Zelda showered again, dried her hair, dressed and packed what few things she had.

The taxi seemed to float through almost empty backstreets and main thoroughfares to King's Cross. There were very few commuters or business travellers around, but the place was buzzing with groups of tourists enticed out by the fine weather.

Zelda used her credit card to buy a first-class ticket on the next train that stopped at York. Northallerton was closer, but that was too much to hope for on a Sunday morning without a change. She didn't have long to wait. The 8.48 would get her there by 11.04.

The first-class carriage wasn't very full, even though week-end upgrades weren't terribly expensive, and she had managed to get an unreserved single forward-facing seat. Soon they were passing the Emirates Stadium, then on past Alexandra Palace and through the London suburbs into open country-side. The attendant came around with weak coffee and took breakfast orders. Zelda wasn't hungry, but she realised she hadn't eaten since lunchtime the previous day, so she ordered some eggs and a croissant and sat back to try and relax.

It was a journey she usually enjoyed, splitting her time between reading and gazing out of the window. And it was another beautiful day. But Zelda felt cut off from it all, as if the world outside were merely projected on a screen. There was no way she could concentrate on her book.

The events of the previous evening at the Hotel Belgrade were still fresh in her mind, and whenever she shut her eyes, she saw Goran Tadić opening his, then the knife flash down and the mess that followed. Her breath would get stuck in her throat, and she would start to panic, certain that anyone who saw her would know what she was reliving.

They passed Peterborough, Newark, Grantham, Doncaster. Zelda thought and thought about what she had done and whether she would ever have to pay the price. She was certain that Goran's gang would make sure any evidence of his murder was swept under the carpet, and that there would be no police involvement. But what then? Would they just let it go or carry out their own investigation? And if that led to her, would they carry out their own form of vengeance? She shiv-ered. It didn't bear thinking about.

But what if his pals didn't find him first? What if a hotel worker had become suspicious of the DO NOT DISTURB sign for some reason and opened the room and called the police? If the police got to the scene before Petar Tadić, Keane and the others could dispose of Goran's body, they would start to ask questions. Would the trail lead to her? She had cleaned up, but had she done it well enough? Would they find the waitress from the restaurant and Faye Butler? The young jogger who had approached her as she was dumping the knife in the river? Would they be able to find the knife? Would the water have washed away all her fingerprints and any remaining traces of Tadić's blood?

Even if there was no forensic evidence, they could probably trace her movements. Someone would remember the attractive woman in the hotel bar, would remember that she had let the victim pick her up and take her to his room. Forensic officers would go over the room carefully. They would find traces of her. A hair here, a fingerprint there. DNA. The staff at the hotel reception desk must have seen them walking towards the lifts. Maybe someone had even seen her hurrying out alone after the murder. The concierge? The taxi driver? They would tell their stories. Describe her in detail. And what about the security cameras? An identikit image would be published in all the papers and shown on television.

By the time the train stopped in York, paranoia had Zelda in its grip, and she was convinced that the police would be waiting for her. But they weren't. The large station seemed fairly busy, and she was lucky to find a taxi idling out front. The Lyndgarth cottage was a good fare for the cabbie – close to forty pounds plus tip. Zelda settled in the back and tried to breathe normally. They could be waiting for her at the cottage, of course. She checked the Sky and BBC news bulletins on her mobile. There was nothing reported about a body being discovered at a London hotel. And Zelda was sure that if it hadn't been discovered yet, that was because the others had got to it and made it disappear. She started to relax as the taxi drove around Eastvale and into the moorland near Lyndgarth. Soon she was at her door fumbling for money in her purse. The driver seemed happy with the fiver she added to the fare, and he even waited until she had got her door open before driving off. That certainly didn't always happen these days.

The interior was as she had left it – which was tidy, for the most part, with the dishes washed and put away, the sink cleaned, living room dusted and electrical items unplugged. She plugged them all in again and boiled the kettle for tea. Luckily, it was a warm day, and she didn't need to turn on the heating. The Internet router was still working fine, she saw, and once again checked the news sites. Again, there was nothing.

She had realised in the taxi that she'd had her mobile set on airplane mode since before her visit to the Hotel Belgrade, and when she had turned it off to check the news, she had noticed there was a telephone message from Alan Banks. In the cottage, the message light was flashing on the landline in the kitchen, too. Just for a moment, she panicked. Alan again? What if he was on to her? He was a policeman, after all. But she dismissed the idea as absurd. That wasn't how they operated.

The message on the landline was from Alan. He was asking her to get in touch with him as soon as she got back. He sounded serious, and for a moment she wondered again if he could possibly have found out anything about what she had been doing, but soon decided that he couldn't. Well, she was back now, she thought, so she reached out for the landline and dialled his number.

Banks had to wait only about five minutes a few yards down the road from Frankie Wallace's house before Annie pulled up behind him in her grey Nissan. There were no grounds or landscaped gardens here, not even a postage-stamp lawn between the pavement and the front door.

Frankie let them in grudgingly, and they sat in the living room opposite the large flat-screen TV, in the shadow of the old boxing trophies. A suitcase lay open on one of the chairs, half-filled with shirts and underwear. Frankie bent over and started rearranging them.

'Going somewhere, Frankie?' Banks asked.

'Aye. I'm going back home to Scotland,' Frankie said. 'Glasgow. Living's cheaper up there.'

'Why now?'

'I'm retiring. Had enough.'

'Surely you're too young to retire?' Annie said.

'I've got a nice little nest egg that should see me through, pet.' He paused and looked around the room. 'And this place should bring me a bit more when I finally sell it. No more yes, sir; no, sir; three bags fucking full, sir.'

'So what's brought this on?' Banks asked.

Frankie paused in his packing, moved the suitcase on to the floor and sat down. 'I've taken a few punches in my time,' he said, 'and I had the sense to get out of that game before I got knocked into the middle of somewhere I could never get back from. But that was child's play compared with this lot.'

'Which lot?'

'The fucking Albanians and all the rest of those fuckers.'

'Leka Gashi?'

'Aye. He's their boss. Nasty fucking piece of work, and I've met a few in my time.'

'What about them?'

'They make me nervous, that's what. They're always hanging around the house, and I don't like the way they've been looking at me lately. One of them thumped Tommy Kerrigan just for looking at him the wrong way. I've felt like thumping the wee pillock more than once in the time I've known him, but this bloke did it. Just like that.'

'You must have known they were violent types right from the start, Frankie.'

'It's not just that. They've got no moral compass, Mr Banks. That's what's wrong with them. Not all of them, I should imagine. I'm not a racist, and I'm sure there are plenty of decent, honest Albanians around. But not the ones that my old boss has taken to hanging around with. I've done a few things I've been ashamed of over the years, but . . .' He shook his head. 'Pool parties with drugs and underage girls, boys, trans, you name it. Bestial acts. Casual brutality. They've got no shame. They're a corrupt and vice-ridden lot, and I've had enough of them.'

'I never knew you were such a moralist, Frankie.'

'Aye, well, ye can't always judge a book.'

'They're Mafia,' said Annie. 'What more do you need to know?'

'Aye . . . well . . . you haven't seen what I've seen.'

'And Mr Blaydon?'

'Getting pulled in deeper and deeper by the minute. They're corrupting him. But I'll no turn rat, if that's what you're thinking. He's been good to me over the years, and it's only since he's taken up with this lot that things have started to change for the worse. They tell him to jump and he asks how high.'

'Have they got something on him?'

Frankie gave a harsh laugh. 'Aye. Money. Put it this way: they've invested heavily in him and his projects, and not with the kind of money you can easily pull out, even if it hadn't already gone bye-byes.'

'Laundered money?'

'I'll no say. That's not my place. I don't understand it, truth be told, and I don't want to. All I know is they've got him by the short and the curlies, and he does his best to put a brave face on it.'

'You're not sticking around to help him?' Annie asked.

'Bah. He won't listen to reason. D'ya think I haven't tried? Last time I was up there, I left in fear of my life, the way those goons he keeps by his side looked at me. No. I've had enough. I'm away.' He returned to rearranging the suitcase.

'Have you witnessed them do something specific, Frankie? Have you seen them kill someone?'

'I'll no turn rat.'

'I understand you have no interest in turning informer,' Banks said, 'but do you think you could maybe help us out with just one little thing?'

Frankie sighed. 'Depends. What might that be?'

'Could you tell us what really happened that Sunday evening you drove your boss into Eastvale for dinner at Le Coq d'Or? We know you ate at The Red Lion on the market square earlier, but we also know the Merc was parked in the car park at The Oak around ten o'clock. You weren't in there drinking. What happened during that time?'

'I've told you.'

'The truth, Frankie. We can take you in, keep you for twenty-four hours, then release you. Let the world know how helpful you've been, helping the police with their inquiries. Or you can tell us what we want to know right now and set off for Glasgow before it gets dark. Your choice.'

'Bastard.' Frankie sat in silence for so long that Banks thought he had clammed up. Then he rubbed his lumpy nose and said, 'Aye, I suppose I can tell you. As far as I know, no laws were broken. It was all perfectly simple.' He eyed Banks with a glint of humour. 'You know, you had me wondering what you were on about last time we talked. You've been barking up the wrong tree, laddie.'

Banks was about to tell him that he would be the judge of that, but stopped himself when he realised that such a criticism might discourage Frankie from saying anything more. 'In that case, then . . .' he said. 'Do explain. Put me right.'

'It's all as I told you. I drove Mr Blaydon to the restaurant, couldn't park right outside because the street's so fucking narrow and parked at the back of the market square, like I said.'

'This was what time?'

'Just as I said before. About half past seven.'

'Go on.'

Frankie lit a cigarette. It was unfiltered, Banks noticed. 'I watched *Downton Abbey* on Netflix, went for a bite to eat at one of those pubs on the market square.'

'The Red Lion,' said Annie. 'We checked.'

'Aye, well, you can tell them they need to put a bit more meat and less gristle in their steak and mushroom pies.'

Annie smiled. 'I'll do that.'

'Anyway, a bit later I gets a call from the boss, like.'

'Blaydon? Can you remember what time?' Banks asked.

'Not exactly. It was after dark. Maybe ten o'clock or thereabouts.'

That fit with the time Blaydon got the phone call in Le Coq d'Or, Banks noted. 'OK. What was it all about?'

'The boss told me he'd got a call from Gashi in London telling him there'd been a bit of bother at a house on Hollyfield Lane. As we were nearby, the boss told me to drop by there and pick up a young lad and his belongings, then drive back to the restaurant to pick him and the Kerrigans up and head for an address in Leeds. Well, I'm just the driver. I do what I'm told.'

'What address in Leeds?'

'I don't know. It never came to that.'

'What happened?'

'I drove over and parked in the pub car park then walked across to the house, number twenty-six Hollyfield Lane.

I went round the back, down the alley, so I was less likely to be seen. It was a pretty rundown area of town, but I knew that already on account of I'd driven Mr Blaydon there before on that Elmet Centre business.'

'You knew that particular house?'

'No. Just the general area.'

'If there was nothing illegal going on, why didn't you just park on the street and approach from the front?'

'Because I didn't know what I was getting myself into, all right? I was being careful, is all. It's my training kicking in. And because . . .'

'Yes?'

'Because life was getting unpredictable with the boss, all right? I didn't know what was waiting around the corner.'

'You were worried it might be a trap of some kind set up by Gashi?'

'It crossed my mind.'

'OK,' said Banks. 'Carry on.'

'Thank you. When I went in the house—'

'Was the back door open?'

'Yes. The back door was open. When I went in the house and walked through to the front, I saw the front door open and a young lad dash out into the street. I couldn't really see much of him, like, just his silhouette. It was dark, and there were no lights on in the room. I called out that I'd come to pick him up and take him home, but he legged it. Must've been scared, I suppose.'

'Do you have any idea why you were supposed to take him home?'

'No. At least, not until I saw what was in the room.'

'Howard Stokes's body?'

'I knew it was a body, but I'd never heard of Howard Stokes, not until I saw his name in the papers later. Anyway, I ran out into the street – like I said, it was dark by then, and most of the street lamps there are busted – and I was just in time to see him running off into the distance. Well, I wasn't going to try and chase him, was I?'

'Which way was he going?'

'Come again.'

'What direction did he run off in?'

'Oh. He turned right out the front door and legged it up the street.'

Towards Cardigan Drive, Banks thought, the park, and Elmet Hill beyond. 'So what did you do?'

'Wasn't much I could do, was there? I might not be past it yet, but I've never been much of a sprinter. Besides, if he didn't want a ride back to the city, I wasn't going to bloody force him.'

'What about his things?' Annie asked.

'Mr Blaydon had told me to bring him *and* his stuff back with me. There was a backpack and a dark jacket beside it, so I took them with me and went back out.'

'Did Mr Blaydon specifically ask you to make sure you got the lad's backpack?' Banks asked.

'Yes.'

'Do you know what was in it?'

'No. And I didn't want to.'

Drugs, Banks knew. Frankie probably knew, too, but there was no percentage in his admitting it. The delivery. So Samir had arrived in Eastvale with instructions to go to Stokes's house, the trap house, spend a day or two distributing the wares and delivering orders, working the line, then return to Leeds. But what happened when he got there? Or before he got there? Had Samir killed Stokes? No. Dr Galway had been certain that Stokes had died of a drug overdose, and it was unlikely that Samir knew how to administer a hot shot and make it look like an accident. Besides, why should he kill anyone? So he had arrived at the house, found Stokes dead and panicked. He had called the county lines number and asked what he should do. Then what?

'Did you find a phone among his stuff?'

'I think there was one zipped up in the jacket pocket. It felt heavy and bulky like a mobile, anyway.'

'But you didn't examine it?'

'No. I just carried the stuff back to the Merc, bunged it in the boot and drove back to the market square.'

The CCTV had lost the Merc after it had left The Oak's car park, so Banks had no way of knowing whether Wallace had made any other stops on his way. He doubted it, though, as the timing worked out. Besides, Mrs Grunwell had said she heard a crunching of gears as the car set off, and the Merc's gears were smooth as silk. 'What about later, when you picked up Blaydon and the Kerrigans?'

'It wasn't much later. Ten or fifteen minutes. Naturally, Mr Blaydon wanted to know where the boy was, but he wasn't going to ask in front of those two numpties. After I'd dropped them off, he asked me, and I told him.'

'How did he react?'

'He was a bit pissed off, but not that much. Seemed glad I'd got the backpack, most of all.'

'I'm not surprised,' said Annie. 'The Albanians would no doubt want their drugs back.'

Frankie grunted. 'I don't know nothing about that.'

'What happened to the backpack?' Banks asked.

'I don't know. I never saw it again. Mr Blaydon took it and the jacket with him when I got him home.'

Banks figured that Blaydon got the phone call in Le Coq d'Or from Gashi, who may have answered the dedicated county line call from Samir, or had the message passed on to him by one of his minions. As Gashi was far away in London, he asked Blaydon to go fetch the boy and his drugs and get them back to Leeds. It didn't matter that Blaydon was already in Eastvale. Gashi had no reason to know that; it was a mere coincidence, and a convenience. He would have expected Blaydon to drive up to Eastvale from Harrogate, anyway. It was a lot closer than London, and that was probably exactly the kind of favour Gashi asked for to get Blaydon even more deeply enmeshed in his games. As far as Samir was concerned . . . well, he'd freaked out and run away, and Gashi and Blaydon would both no doubt have imagined that he would make his way back to Leeds eventually, that he just got scared and bolted. Even if he never made it back, it didn't matter to them; he was hardly likely to talk, and he was expendable. There were plenty more where he came from. Most important, they'd got their drugs back. All they had to do was lie low until the fuss died down and then start up again somewhere else. No doubt by that time, however, Gashi would have started to have doubts about Blaydon, and just how much use he was to them, especially now the Elmet deal was going sour and the Hollyfield house was no longer available.'

'What time did you see Samir running out of the house?'

'Samir?'

'The Middle Eastern boy who was killed.'

'That was him? I'd no idea. I couldn't see the colour of his skin. He was fast, I'll say that for him.'

'What time?'

'A bit after ten. Ten past, maybe.'

'And you got back to the market square when?'

'Maybe half an hour later. Bit more. Mr Blaydon doesn't like me smoking in the car, so I had a couple of cigarettes in The Oak car park, then drove around a bit.'

'Why?'

'I like driving. It relaxes me. And to be honest, I was a bit disturbed.'

'By what you'd seen?'

'By everything that had happened.'

'Did you have any idea what was really going on that night?' Banks asked.

'No,' said Frankie. 'I was just doing my job. I didn't know, and I didn't want to know.'

Banks couldn't tell whether he was lying, but it didn't matter. Whatever part Frankie had played, it was a minor one. 'Tell me, Frankie,' he said. 'Are you sure you didn't run after the lad and catch him? Then one thing led to another?'

'There you go, see,' Frankie spat. 'Typical copper talk. Tell you what I know and that's the thanks I get.'

'Maybe you're just telling me as much as you want me to know. Or as much as Blaydon wants me to know.'

'Well, you can think what you like, but you'll not get any more from me, and you'll not prove anything is other than what I've told you, either.'

'And the boy?'

'No idea. Never saw him again.'

'The last you saw of him?'

'I told you. Running up the street, vanishing into the night.'

Into the *park*, Banks thought.

After leaving Frankie Wallace to his packing, Banks got home to Newhope Cottage early enough to cook himself a reasonably healthy meal of salmon, rice and asparagus – mostly in the microwave – and do a spot of tidying up around the place before Zelda came. She had replied to the message he had left and suggested she would drop by later in the evening.

Banks went around the cottage putting CDs and DVDs back in their cases and on the shelves, washing yesterday's dishes, giving the wood floor and carpets a quick run around with the vacuum cleaner, dumping the contents of the laundry basket into the washing machine and generally getting in touch with his domestic side. When he looked out of the conservatory on to his small back garden and saw the bindweed and the mint growing wild, he knew he would have to find a weekend afternoon to spend out there. He wasn't much of a gardener – even basic maintenance was a chore – and he usually hoped poor weather would provide him with an excuse for staying indoors, or for venturing out for a long walk around Tetchley Fell – for good walking weather and fine gardening weather were not the same thing at all in his book.

Before leaving York, Banks and Annie had struggled with whether to arrest Frankie, and decided in the end against it. Let him run off back to Glasgow. He was clearly scared – and if a hard man like Frankie Wallace was scared, then there was something to be scared of. They could lock him up, even if only for a short period of custody, but what would be the point? They would have to let him go eventually, as they had no case against him, no evidence. Best to let him go. He had always been at best a minor villain, hired muscle, and he had certainly had no reason to kill Samir.

And the timing didn't work. According to Dr Galway, hypostasis indicated that Samir had been dead on his back for between an hour and an hour and a half, and the witnesses on Malden Terrace had heard the car close to half-past eleven. By then, Blaydon's Merc had already been spotted by ANPR well on its way out of town. Besides, Banks believed his story and was starting to have a few new ideas about that whole business.

Even if they found evidence later that Frankie had been involved, it wouldn't be too difficult to track him down in Glasgow, or wherever he went. Banks had asked the local forces to keep a discreet eye on him, and his car number plate had been flagged for ANPR recognition. Wherever Frankie Wallace went, he wouldn't be completely out of their sight until this was all over. In addition, Banks had already arranged to send out a CSI team from York CID to carry out some blood tests on Blaydon's Merc and have a good poke around his mansion and grounds. Just in case.

It was getting dark. The sun was setting west of Tetchley Fell outside the conservatory windows, and the sky between the hills was streaked with vermillion, purple and grey. Satisfied the place was as spic and span as he could get it without hired help, he checked Apple Music on his mobile – set up for him by his son Brian on his last visit – and streamed a Sally Beamish viola concerto. Then he poured himself a glass of Nero d'Avola and settled down to read Ben Macintyre's *The Spy and the Traitor* and wait.

It was about half past nine when Zelda pulled up in her little Clio runabout and rang his doorbell. Banks put his book aside and went through to answer the door. She followed him along the hall and into the kitchen.

'Sorry I'm so late,' she said. 'You know what it's like when you get back from being away for a while.'

'No problem,' said Banks. 'Drink?'

'What are you having?'

'Red wine.'

'That'll be fine, please.'

Banks poured her a glass and invited her to follow him into the conservatory. She had visited before, with Ray, and seemed quite comfortable, taking the same wicker chair she had sat on the last time she was there.

She looked a little drawn, Banks thought, as if she hadn't been sleeping very well. She wore hardly any make-up, so it was easy to see the dark shadows under her eyes contrasting the paleness of her skin. She was still beautiful, with classic bone structure, perfectly proportioned features and eyes a man could lose himself in. Tonight she wore her hair in a long ponytail and had dressed in jeans and a red knitted polo-neck jumper. She never wore much perfume, but a fresh and pleasant scent of orange and bergamot drifted over from her general direction.

They clinked glasses and drank.

'Nice,' said Zelda. 'What is it?'

Banks told her about the Sicilian Nero d'Avola he had enjoyed on a short break in Taormina earlier that year and the case he had ordered to be delivered from a wine merchant there. 'You can't get it here. Not this particular winery, anyway. Like most countries, they keep their best wines for themselves and only export the rest.'

'It's very good,' said Zelda.

'Yes. Have you eaten?'

'I'm fine, thank you. What's the music?'

'Sally Beamish,' said Banks. 'I'll turn it off if you like.'

'No. Leave it on. It's good. You always play *interesting* music.'

Banks settled down in his chair. It was dark outside now. The stars were out, and the table lamp reflected its orange glow in the glass. They chatted for a while about Zelda's time in London, how much she loved the city and how sad she was about the whole Brexit mess.

'Sometimes I think it's not Europe people want to leave but England itself,' said Banks. 'Life here can be quite depressing, but it's no good blaming the EU for that. Change needs to happen here first.' He shrugged. 'But I'm not a politician. I don't have a seat to keep, or a need for power.'

'I think you get plenty of power in your job, don't you?'

'I suppose so. The power of arrest and so forth. I've seen coppers abuse it, the same way politicians abuse theirs.'

'And perhaps conditions are bad in the cities, but it is beautiful here, isn't it?'

Banks nodded. 'I'm very lucky, and I know it.'

'Me, too.'

'Why sound so sad? There's nothing wrong, is there?'

Zelda shook her head and tried to smile. 'No, it's not . . . I mean, I get scared when I come to love something so much. Afraid I will lose it. Life has always been like that.'

'I think we all have a bit of that in us. Imposter syndrome. A sense of not deserving what we have. Or survivor's guilt.'

Zelda shot him a direct glance. 'I don't feel guilty about surviving,' she said.

'I know. I didn't mean that. I meant . . .'

Her tone softened. 'It's all right, Alan. I think I know what you meant. Forgive me. It's just my job that makes me this way. The faces bring back so many bad memories. But many girls are far, far worse off than me.'

'Yes.' Banks stood and topped up their drinks. He would need to open another bottle soon. 'If you want to smoke,' he said, 'it's OK. I'm sure I can find an ashtray somewhere.' Though Banks had stopped smoking many years ago, he felt that if he invited someone into his house whom he knew was a smoker, then he should permit that person to smoke. As it turned out, most didn't; very few of his friends smoked, anyway.

Zelda shook her head. 'No, it's fine,' she said. 'I'm trying to smoke less than five cigarettes a day, and I've already reached my limit today. But thank you.'

'So what do you want to see me about?' he asked.

'I thought it was you who wanted to see me?'

Banks laughed. 'Well, it's true I would like to talk to you. Nelia.'

She raised a perfect eyebrow. Banks wondered if she had had it microbladed since he had last seen her. 'So you know my name,' she said.

'Nelia Melnic,' Banks said. 'It's a fine name. Why change it?'

'It was the name they gave me in the orphanage,' Zelda said with a shrug. 'A Romanian name. I thought it was time for a new one. Do you think it gives you power over someone if you know their real name, like in magic?'

'No,' said Banks. 'It just came up, that's all.'

'I can't imagine how. Anyway, I found out my real name, before the orphanage. I told you before that my parents were Russian, or "Russian-speaking", as they say in the old republics.'

'Will you tell me?'

'Why?'

'I'm just curious, that's all.'

Zelda seemed a little embarrassed by his request. Her skin flushed, and she seemed to become suddenly shy. 'I don't know.'

'It's not about power or anything,' said Banks. 'I would just like to know.'

There was a long silence, and for a while Banks thought she wasn't going to tell him, then she said softly, 'Ekaterina Mikhailovna Polinskaya.' Then she put her hand over her mouth and gave a soft laugh. 'Quite a mouthful, isn't it?'

'It sounds like someone out of a Russian novel,' Banks said.

'So now you know everything. I am putty in your hands.'

It was Banks's turn to laugh. 'So what do I call you now?'

'I remember that my father used to call me Katja. But I think we would be best to stick with Zelda, don't you?'

'I like Katja, but Zelda's OK with me, if you prefer it. After F. Scott Fitzgerald's wife?'

'*Tender is the Night* is one of my favourite books,' Zelda said, 'but no. It's *The Legend of Zelda*. A Nintendo game I used to play in Paris when I was bored, between clients. Not that that happened often enough.'

'I don't know much about video games.'

'You haven't missed anything.'

'And I must confess that I haven't read *Tender is the Night*, either. There are so many books I should read. Including those big Russian novels.'

Zelda laughed. 'You'd never get past the names.' She leaned forward a little and pushed a long strand of free hair behind her ear. 'It is good to be here, Alan. I think I needed cheering up.'

'Glad to be of assistance.' Banks paused. 'I understand it's been a difficult week for you? You haven't told me everything.'

Zelda seemed immediately wary again. 'Oh? What do you mean, "everything"?'

'Well, when you told me about London earlier, you didn't say you'd gone there from Croatia, or that when you arrived, the first thing you heard was that your boss had died in a house fire.'

'Oh.' She seemed relieved. 'Yes. It's true.'

'And I asked myself if you, like me when I heard about it, would make the connection and wonder if it could have anything to do with our old friend Phil Keane?'

'It did cross my mind. You told me he liked to start fires. But why would you think this Keane knew my boss, Mr Hawkins?'

'Your boss would have seen the photographs, surely? It's not such a long stretch from there, especially if Keane is involved with known traffickers.'

'Of course. But why would you think Keane would harm Mr Hawkins?'

'Are you still looking for Keane, Zelda?'

'I never stopped. Just nothing happened for so long. There have been no more photographs of him. I'm sorry.'

'And then?'

'The fire.'

'Whitescape' was playing now, all long, drawn-out chords, flurries of sound and crashing percussion behind. 'Why did you walk by the house?'

Zelda looked down into her wine glass. 'I don't know,' she said. 'I just wanted to see for myself. It was terrible. A ruin. They said it was an accident.'

'But you think differently?'

'How do you know about all this? My name? The fire?'

'A friend. Another policeman.'

'And he wants what?'

'Nothing. He knows the detectives who talked to you.'

'Danvers and the one he called Deborah?'

'That's right.'

'They think I killed Mr Hawkins?'

'No. But they think there's something you're not telling them. You think there's something odd about it all, don't you?'

'I didn't tell them about Keane.'

'I'm afraid I let that slip to my friend.'

'It doesn't matter. Anyway, I don't think Mr Hawkins was the kind of man to get drunk and then put a chip pan full of oil on his burner, if that's what you mean.'

'So you suspect that someone helped him do it?'

'I think it is possible, yes. But I'm not investigating the case. Perhaps you are. Is that why you're asking me all these questions?'

'No. I told you. A friend of mine dropped by and told me about it. He found out about your connection with Ray, and he knows Annie through me. He put two and two together. He works with the NCA. I don't think they're entirely happy with the chip-pan theory either.'

'So they asked you to question me to see if I know anything I'm not telling them?'

'Sort of. But it's nothing as sinister as that. He just asked if I'd have a chat with you about it, see if you knew anything more. Nobody thinks you had anything to do with it, Zelda. Besides, they know you were in Croatia at the time.'

'That's true.'

'With an old friend?'

Zelda nodded.

'It's OK,' said Banks. 'I'm not asking you for an alibi. I trust you. I don't think you had anything to do with what happened.'

'I don't like being interrogated. You're supposed to be my friend.'

'I'm not interrogating you, and I like to think I am your friend. Friends need to be honest with one another.' Banks went into the kitchen, opened his last bottle of Nero d'Avola and changed the music with his mobile, choosing an album called *Blues Dialogues*, a series of blues-themed violin pieces played by Rachel Barton Pine. When he got back, carrying the bottle with him, Zelda was sitting exactly as he had left her, a slightly petulant expression on her face. She accepted a refill, then Banks filled his own glass and sat down. 'I'm sorry,' Zelda said. 'There is just so much on my mind. So much I want to forget. I get upset when there are too many questions.'

'Just understand this, Zelda. I'm not out to get you or trip you up. I'm on your side. I'm also in the midst of a very nasty and very depressing case at the moment, involving the murder of a thirteen-year-old Syrian migrant who was stuffed in a wheelie bin on the East Side Estate.'

Zelda looked sadly at him. 'Yes,' she said. 'I read about that. It sounds terrible.'

'It is. And it's throwing up all kinds of connections.'

'Not Phil Keane?'

'Not yet, no. But it wouldn't surprise me. We think the boy was involved in a county line drug operation that fell afoul of an Albanian gangster called Leka Gashi. Ever heard of him?'

Zelda shook her head. 'No,' she said. 'But you need to be careful. I do know something about the Albanians from experience.'

'You were there?'

'Briefly. Tirana. I don't want to talk about it.'

'You don't have to. Gashi and his cohorts are taking over a number of local drug operations and managing to dispose of the competition as they do so. Another name that came up was Tadić. Petar Tadić. A Croatian. Does that name mean anything to you?'

But Banks hardly needed to ask. Zelda seemed to freeze, turn rigid, as she said through a clamped jaw, 'No.'

'Zelda. I know you know who he is. He's the other man in that photograph with Keane, isn't he?'

Zelda paused for a while, then nodded.

'Why didn't you tell me? It might have helped.'

'Because he was of no interest to you. You wanted to know about Keane. I told you Tadić was a bad man who liked to hurt girls.'

'Did he hurt you?'

'Yes.' Her voice was barely more than a whisper.

'Is that who you were visiting in Croatia?'

'No. Of course not. He is someone I would stay away from. I was visiting a friend. Tadić is not a friend.'

'Who, then?'

'A woman. She runs a hostel for girls who have escaped. And that's all I will tell you. She values her privacy more than anything.'

'All right,' said Banks. 'I understand Tadić had risen in the organisation.'

'That's no surprise. Men like him always do.'

'And Keane is involved in whatever's going on? In what happened to you.'

'No. I didn't know Keane. I have never met him. He must be new. He wasn't around when I . . . all those years ago.'

'Can you help me any more? Help me find Keane through Tadic?'

Zelda shook her head.

Banks felt that she was still holding something back, but he knew better than to pursue it any further tonight. Her defences were fragile. No matter how tough her hard life had made her, there was a vulnerability and sensitivity about her that, Banks thought, once broken, once trespassed upon, would leave her defenceless. Instead, he smiled at her. 'OK, interrogation over. Shall we finish the bottle?'

Zelda cocked an eye at him. 'Are you trying to get me drunk?'

'Zelda, if three glasses of wine are enough to get you drunk, you're not the woman I thought you were.'

Zelda laughed, a loud but strangely musical sound, and held out her glass. '*Za Lyubov*,' she said when it was full, and tossed a good part of it back in one.

'What does that mean?'

'It's a Russian toast.'

'I thought that was *na zdarovye*?'

'That's what everyone thinks. They're wrong.'

'*Za Lyubov*, then,' said Banks. 'When is Ray coming back?'

'I'm not sure,' said Zelda. 'Soon, I hope. A few days.'

'You miss him?'

'Of course. Not his music, though.'

'No Edgar Broughton Band or Quintessence tonight, don't worry.'

Zelda laughed. 'He is like a little boy. But his paintings . . .' She sighed.

'And your work?'

'Bah. Nothing. Trinkets. Pleasant wall hangings to be sold at country fêtes like on *Midsomer Murders*. You watch that?'

'Afraid not,' said Banks. 'I'm a George Gently fan, myself.'

So they talked for a while about television, music, painting, movies and books. Zelda, it turned out, had not only read all of the big Russian novels Banks aspired to – *in Russian* – but she had also read most of the big European novels, too, from *Pamela* to *Ulysses*. When he told her he didn't know where she got the time, she said she had read most of them at the orphanage, in her teens, and it was true she had little time for reading after her abduction, and scant access to books. Banks felt bad for bringing up the subject when he saw the deep sadness in her eyes.

It was late, and Banks was about to suggest calling a taxi, considering how much they had drunk, when Zelda suddenly said, 'Can I stay here tonight, Alan? I don't want to go back to the empty cottage alone. I know it's silly, but I just want to know that there's someone nearby. Can I stay? I can sleep on the sofa. I promise I won't be any trouble.'

Banks swallowed. Here he was, sitting across from one of the most beautiful women he had ever met in his life, and she was asking if she could stay the night. 'Of course you can,' he said. 'But you don't have to sleep on the sofa. The spare room's made up.'

'Are you sure? I feel like I've pressured you.'

Banks smiled. 'It's yours whenever you need it.'

She stood up and bent to put her arms around him. 'Thank you,' she said, kissing his cheek. 'God bless you, Alan Banks.' Then she spoke a few words in Russian he didn't understand and stood up again.

'Do you want to go up right now?' Banks said.

Zelda nodded. 'If it is not too rude. I'm tired. It's been a very long week.'

'OK.'

Banks got up and led the way back down the hall to the staircase. 'I don't think I've got a spare toothbrush,' he said.

'But you can check in the bathroom. There might be one in the cupboard.'

'No problem,' said Zelda.

Banks opened the door to the spare bedroom, where Tracy or Brian slept when they visited. It was small, with only a single bed, but there was a nice view of the woods, and on a warm night like this, Zelda could open the window a few inches and enjoy some fresh air and hear the dawn chorus in the morning.

'It's perfect,' said Zelda. 'Thank you.'

'I'll be just next door. You know, if you need . . .' Banks backed away, turned and went back downstairs, embarrassed. He heard the bathroom door open and close as he went.

Once back in the conservatory, he found his heart was beating so fast he wasn't sure whether he should have another glass of wine. But he poured himself one anyway. He changed the *Blues Dialogues* for Véronique Gens singing Chausson's 'Poème de l'amour et de la mer' and turned the volume down so as not to disturb Zelda. He heard the toilet flush, water running in the sink, then the bathroom door creaked open and closed again. Every sound seemed magnified by her presence, the strange and unsettling presence of a beautiful woman in the cottage. Finally, he heard the door to the spare room shut, and then only silence from upstairs. He would give her a while to settle down and fall asleep before he went up to his own room.

As he sat and listened to Véronique Gens's warm and sensual vocals, his heart slowed down, but the rest of his body didn't. Desire tingled in every vein and muscle. If only that kiss on the cheek had missed and hit his lips . . . It didn't bear thinking about, but how could he *not* think about it? Our thoughts are not crimes; our desires are not felonies. But why do they feel as if they are? It is only in acting upon them that the fault lies, he told himself, no matter what William Blake said about sooner murdering a baby in its cradle than nursing an unacted desire.

But he still felt guilty for hoping, for that one brief moment when Zelda asked to stay, that she had meant she wanted to stay and sleep with him. The guilt wasn't so much because of Ray, but more because of Zelda's past, the way she had been constantly mistreated, used and abused by men. Was he no better than them? If some pimp came up to him right now and said he could sleep with her for a hundred or two hundred pounds, would he pay it? Zelda was younger than his own daughter Tracy, yet still he lusted after her. Just how *good* was he when it came right down to it? He felt both relieved and disappointed that it wasn't *him* she wanted, merely the proximity of another human being. Relieved because he wouldn't have to deal with the consequences of sleeping with Zelda, and disappointed because, well, because it was Zelda, and the damn thing was that he didn't only lust after her, he *liked* her.

Banks drank the last of the wine and tried to comfort himself with the thought that his virtue was most unlikely to be put to the test: there wasn't a hope in hell that things with Zelda would go any further. His feelings would remain unrequited. They would remain friends because that was what she needed most, even though what he needed most was not so much another friend as a lover. It was small comfort, but it was the best he would get for the moment.

12

When Banks came downstairs on Monday morning, Zelda was already up, sitting in the conservatory with a cup of coffee, reading the *Guardian*. She looked up and smiled when Banks walked in. 'Good morning. I hope I didn't wake you.'

'Not at all,' said Banks.

'I made coffee. But what do you eat for breakfast? I couldn't find anything.'

'Ah,' said Banks. 'Right. I'm not much of a breakfast person, really. A cup of coffee, then hit the road, that's me.'

'But breakfast is the most important meal of the day.'

'So they say. Whoever they are. I've never quite been able to believe it, myself. I think there's some bread left, though. And I've got marmalade.'

Zelda made a face. 'The bread is mouldy.'

'Oh, sorry. Well, I'll happily take you out for breakfast. They do a pretty decent full English down on Helmthorpe High Street.'

'The coronary special?'

'Some people call it that.'

Zelda stood up. 'I suppose I should go home. I just wanted to make sure I thanked you for . . . you know, for everything.'

'It's nothing. Are you sure you're OK to go, Zelda? I have to go to work – it's going to be a busy day, today – but you're welcome to stay here as long as you want.'

'No. I can go. It's fine. I feel much better now. Thank you.'

'There's nothing wrong?'

'Nothing.'

'If you need anything . . . I mean, the spare room's always here for you.'

'I'll be all right. It was just my first night back, that's all. Nerves. I don't think I've ever been by myself up there before, and sometimes my memories are not good to be alone with. But Raymond will be back soon.'

Banks followed Zelda towards the front door, where she picked up her jacket from the hook. 'Thank you once again, Alan,' she said. 'See you soon?'

'Absolutely.'

And Banks stood there feeling like an idiot, waving to her little Clio as it disappeared down his drive. She knew; he was sure she knew what he had been thinking. It must be obvious just from looking at him. It must happen to her all the time. What a bloody fool he was. He had lain awake most of the night, conscious that she was sleeping only feet away, imagining her body, its outline under the thin sheet. She must think he is like all the men she has ever met, all the perverts and abusers. Once, she had cried out during the night, he was certain. He had almost gone to her to ask what was wrong and offer comfort – he would have been happy just to lie beside her and hold her – but realised what a mistake it would have been to enter her bedroom in the middle of the night.

Anyway, Zelda was gone now, and it was time to get a grip. Banks went back to his coffee and stood at his conservatory windows enjoying the early morning light dappling the hillsides, the blue tits flitting from branch to branch in his garden, a robin poking about on the lawn for an early worm. There were things to be set in motion today, including a search of the park at the bottom of Elmet Street, and people to talk to. He was starting to feel very much as if he was coming to the end of this investigation. He couldn't say that he knew who had killed Samir, or why, but he did feel that he was finally on the right track.

On his way down the A1 to Leeds later that day, Banks listened to Jeremy Irons reading T.S. Eliot's *Four Quartets*. He wouldn't have professed to understand it, though there were moments of surprising clarity, but he responded to the music of the language, and Irons performed it beautifully. He was supposed to get together with his poet friend Linda Palmer to discuss it over a long leisurely Sunday lunch together next week, and she would no doubt, as usual, enlighten him.

That morning in the station had produced one interesting lead. Vic Manson had managed to pull several sets of fingerprints from the red bicycle frame abandoned in Howard Stokes's backyard, and one belonged to a boy called Greg Janson, who turned up on IDENT1. Janson had been arrested two weeks ago in a round-up of suspected drug users in a Leeds squat, so his address was on record. He hadn't been charged with any crime yet, but his fingerprints and DNA were still on the database, and could be kept there for up to six months. Tyler Cleary had mentioned to Gerry that his contact on Hollyfield Lane was called Greg, so this was most likely the fair-haired boy Margery Cunningham had told Gerry about. If he was, then he should know something about the county lines operation in Eastvale. It also made perfect sense that the other end of the line, where the drugs came from, was Leeds.

DCI Ken Blackstone had said he would be happy to meet Banks at Greg's place of work, a garage on the ring road near the Horsforth exit. Janson worked the four until midnight shift, so Banks timed his arrival for five. They had arranged to meet in the Asda car park behind the garage, and Banks figured the quickest way to get there was to turn off the A1 at

Wetherby and join the ring road near the golf club, then head west through Moortown and Weetwood.

He switched off *Four Quartets* as he negotiated the numerous ring road roundabouts and the Leeds rush-hour traffic. He had just got to the start of 'East Coker', with its famous opening about the end being in the beginning. It seemed a good place to stop.

He found the car park at the big roundabout without much trouble and immediately saw Ken Blackstone leaning against his silver Focus enjoying the mild May weather. Banks angled his Porsche into the next spot.

'Looking a bit shabby, isn't it?' Blackstone said by way of greeting.

'All it needs is a good wash and brush up,' Banks replied. 'Besides, there's no such thing as a shabby Porsche. It's just got character, that's all.'

Blackstone laughed and held out his hand. 'Good to see you again, Alan.'

Banks shook it. 'You, too.'

Blackstone nodded towards the garage. 'Shall we?'

'Lead the way.'

They walked between parked cars and across the busy Asda lot, then arrived at the garage. 'Greg works in the shop,' said Blackstone, pointing past the pumps to the door. Banks made his way past the magazine rack and down an aisle flanked by crisps and sweet snack foods and walked to the counter. There were two young lads working there, both wearing jackets that bore the name of the brand of petrol they were selling. One had a name tag that read 'GREG'. Both were busy.

Banks and Blackstone waited until Janson had finished with his customer then introduced themselves. Greg didn't react much; he seemed neither interested nor worried to find two police detectives asking if they could talk to him.

'I'll just ask the boss if it's all right to take an early break,' he said, then opened a door behind him and made his request. He must have received an affirmative answer because he came back, ducked under the counter at the far end, where the newspapers were, and accompanied them outside. 'Mind if we go over there?' he said, pointing to a wall by the back of the Asda lot. 'Only there's no smoking near the garage, and I'm dying for a fag.'

Banks smiled and nodded. He remembered the feeling, though it came back to him only rarely these days. As far as he knew, Ken Blackstone had never smoked, but he seemed happy enough to go along with Greg's request. Blackstone was coming to resemble Philip Larkin more and more every time Banks saw him. Or Eric Morecambe. He wasn't sure which.

They reached the wall, and Greg sat down and lit up. He was of medium height, skinny and fair-haired, which matched the description they had. 'What is it you want?' he said. 'I've been a good boy lately.'

'I'm sure you have,' said Banks. 'But we want to talk to you about Eastvale. Hollyfield Lane.'

Greg blew out smoke and nodded slowly. 'That's all behind me now,' he said. 'I know you lot have a hard time believing anyone can turn his life around, but that's what I've done. I've got a decent job, a nice little flat and a girlfriend, and things are going really well for me.'

'I'm glad to hear it,' said Banks. 'And, believe it or not, I'm not here to judge you or in any way ruin what you've got going. I'm not interested in what drugs you did or didn't take or sell. Do you admit you were a cuckoo in Eastvale?'

'Be a fool to deny it, wouldn't I, as it's probably on record? That was obviously what the police were interested in when they arrested us, but I wasn't carrying enough to get done for dealing.'

'There's definitely a crackdown on county lines,' Banks said. 'Who was the gangmaster?'

Greg drew deeply on his cigarette. After he'd blown out the smoke, he said, just as Frankie Wallace had said the previous day, 'I'm not a snitch. Even if it mattered.'

'It doesn't?'

'He's dead, so I'd say not.'

'Then I can't see any reason why you shouldn't tell us. Can you?'

Greg thought for a while, then said. 'OK. It's Lenny G. Like I said, it doesn't matter. He's dead. That's why I got out myself.'

'What happened?'

'I don't know all the ins and outs. I was low-level. A cuckoo, as you say, with an old junkie called Howard on Hollyfield Lane, up in Eastvale.'

'Howard Stokes?'

'Yeah. You know him? Nice bloke. Real gentle soul, old sixties type, but fucked up, you know, up there.' He pointed to his head. 'Years of sticking that fucking poison in his veins.'

'Howard's dead,' said Banks.

Greg's eyes went wide. 'Is he? Fuck. How?'

'Overdose.'

Greg sucked on his cigarette again. 'Had to happen eventually, man.'

'So how did you operate?'

'I picked up the stuff, carried it there, usually on the bus, hung out in that filthy old condemned house he lived in for a few days and sold what I'd got to whoever had ordered it, along with maybe some new customers, friends of friends. I got to know people. Regulars, like. A good crowd. But I got pulled.'

'Pulled?'

'Yeah. The timing couldn't have been better, really. It was all a bit chaotic. There was a changeover at the top. Lenny G used to be the big man, top of the tree. Then all of a sudden, he wasn't. And the next thing I knew, he was dead.'

'Excuse me, but was Lenny G Leonard Grainger?' Blackstone asked.

'I believe that was his full name, yeah,' said Greg. 'But we all called him Lenny G.'

'Found floating face down in the Leeds-Liverpool Canal out Rodley way,' said Blackstone to Banks. 'He'd been gutted.'

'Ouch,' said Banks. 'How long ago?'

'Three weeks.'

Greg seemed to turn pale. 'I didn't know that,' he said. 'Just . . . you know . . . that he was dead. *Gutted.* Fucking hell.'

Blackstone nodded. 'It was nasty. So what happened? We've still got it down as an unsolved murder.'

'Your guess is as good as mine,' said Greg. 'I wasn't here at the time it happened. I was up in Eastvale. My last visit, as it turned out, though I didn't know that at the time. The county line just went dead. When I got back to the city and went round to the centre back in Seacroft, there were two blokes I didn't know, and they wanted the money I'd collected on the shipment. Foreign accents. In the end I just gave them it and bunked off. Never went back. I was wanting out, anyway. My girlfriend didn't approve of the line of work, and I have to say, the foreign blokes scared me a bit. And the place was empty. It looked like they were moving somewhere else to run their operations. Then word got out that Lenny was dead. But not how. Lenny wasn't so bad. He paid well. He'd had a tough life.'

'Tough death, too, by the sound of it,' said Banks. 'So what did you do next?'

'Got busted, then released pending charges. It was my chance to get away, break free from the life, and I haven't looked back.'

'So who took over? You mentioned strangers with foreign accents.'

'Word has it there's this Albanian cunt in charge, interested in going county, and the blokes I saw were part of his crew. I don't know the big guy's name, but I think he stood in the background all the time I was there. In the shadows. Only saw him that once, all smiles, expensive suit, but you could tell, you know, that he was a vicious cold bastard underneath it all. He wasn't a big bloke, not threatening in that way at all. But he had a cruel mouth. And nasty eyes. Really nasty eyes.'

'Leka Gashi,' said Blackstone. 'We worked that out, but we've no evidence. Of course, he was out of the country at the time the crime was committed. He doesn't usually do these jobs himself, though I've heard he's not averse to administering a bit of punishment when the occasion merits it.'

Banks turned back to Greg. 'How long were you operating up in Eastvale?'

'On and off for about a year.'

'How many lines was Lenny G running?'

'About six. All roughly the same distance as Eastvale. Different directions, like. Furthest was out on the coast. Runswick Bay.'

'That's a tiny place,' said Banks.

Greg shrugged. 'What can I say? There are markets for that shit everywhere. And I know you won't believe me when I say it, but I never actually touched the stuff myself. A few joints, maybe, booze, yeah, but never the hard stuff. Heroin. Crack. Never.'

'I can't see as you've any reason to lie to me,' Banks said. 'When we've finished, my colleague here might like to talk a few things over with you. Is that OK?'

Greg lit a second cigarette. 'I've already told you pretty much all I know, man. And I don't want any of this coming back on me. From what I've heard, those Albanians can be really fucking nasty when the mood takes them.'

'But they don't know you. You only met them once. You never actually worked for them.'

'Even so. They don't like loose ends. Would *you* take the risk? Besides, I don't really know anything. Basically we were just glorified mules. We took the stuff up to the trap house, passed it on to the users and collected the money. They used us kids because we were least likely to be stopped or picked up. The younger the better. And believe me, Lenny G absolutely knew if you came back with one penny less than you ought to do.'

Banks took the photo of Samir Boulad from its envelope and passed it to Greg. 'Do you know this lad?'

'Little Sammy? Sure,' said Greg, handing it back.

'Was he one of the sellers?'

Greg nodded. 'Poor sod. I read about what happened. The bastards. Poor little Sammy. He was only, like, twelve or thirteen. He was the youngest of the lot of us. Looked like butter wouldn't melt in his mouth.'

'How did you meet him?'

'He just turned up one day. A bunch of us used to hang out in this little park in the city centre after dark, you know, share a few tins of cider, smoke a few spliffs, have a laugh. Most of the kids had left home, and some of us were living in a council house on an estate up Gipton way. It was supposed to belong to Kit's dad, like, but he was in the nick, and his mother had done a runner, so we stayed there. Nobody seemed to mind. We invited Sammy back. He'd got nowhere to stay. He'd been sleeping rough. He was a nice kid. Quiet. A bit sad. Christ, you should have seen him eat, though, if you put some food in front of him. Like a fucking vacuum cleaner.' Greg smiled at the memory.

'He'd left his family behind in Syria. Did he speak any English?'

'Yeah. Pretty well. Lenny G really took to him, groomed him real nice, bought him Nike trainers, taught him the ropes. Sammy, he didn't really know what it was all about. I mean, he knew it was drugs, and he knew it was a bit dodgy, but Lenny paid well and Sammy was, like, desperate for money to send to his family so they could come over. That was like his goal in life, his only reason for doing what he did. He loved that family. And it was easy work. All he had to do was go to the trap house, hand out the orders and bring back the money. He'd got away from some gang in Birmingham or somewhere who'd helped smuggle him in to the country and wanted him to work off his debt. Like, for ever. Slave labour. They even wanted him to let blokes fuck him up the arse. But Sammy did a bunk.'

'Did he say what this gang in Birmingham was called? Any names?'

'Nah. Never mentioned no names. I don't think he knew.'

'Didn't he know about his parents?'

'What about them?'

Banks paused. 'They're dead. The whole family. Killed by a bomb the last weeks of the war in Aleppo.'

'Oh, fuck.' Greg shook his head. 'He didn't know. At least not when I left. The bastards didn't tell him, if they knew. They kept him working the line thinking he'd one day have enough to help his parents, and all the time they were fucking dead.'

'Looks that way,' said Banks. 'Which line did he work?'

'Malton.'

'Did he ever mention an uncle and aunt in this country?'

'Yeah, but he said he'd lost their address. Lost all the photos of his family, too, poor kid. One of the boats he was in sank, like, and they had to get rescued by some Italians. That was when they still let people in. The paper disintegrated. All he knew was they lived somewhere up north.'

'Big place,' said Banks.

'Yeah.' Greg paused. 'It was really sad, man.'

'What was? There's something else?'

'Samir could speak English pretty good, but he couldn't read it very well. I guess he was used to Arabic, or whatever they speak in Syria, but our letters were mostly meaningless shapes to him. I asked him more than once if he remembered what it said on the paper, the address, even just the town, but he couldn't reproduce it for me. He'd no idea. Poor sod. He used to write letters home, but he'd no return address. My girlfriend let Samir use her address – the flat in Yeadon – but nothing came for him. He was really gutted. Every day he expected a letter from home, but nothing came. Now we know why.'

Banks swallowed. 'Nearly done now, Greg,' he said.

Greg nodded, pulled on the cigarette then trod it out. 'Yeah. I'll have to get back in soon, or the boss'll go spare. He's all right, but . . .'

'Have you any idea what happened to Samir after you left the gang?'

'Not really. He was still there when I left, and I heard most of them stayed with the Albanians. Why not? I mean, nothing changed but the personnel at the top and the place they operated out of. Maybe he even paid more than Lenny G. Easier for him not to have to start right from scratch again when he already had a crew that knew the routine.'

'And Samir was still living in the council house with the others when you left?'

'Yeah. They was all set to move somewhere else, though. Kit's dad was due to come out of jail.'

'Do you know where they moved to, or where the new centre for the lines is?'

'No, man. That was after I'd gone. Didn't know, didn't want to know. I didn't look back. I can't tell you anything more.'

'When did this all happen?'

'It all started about a month ago.'

'And Samir was still working the Malton line when you left?'

'Yeah.'

'Any idea when they might have moved him over to Eastvale?'

'No. But it takes time to make the changes and redo the set-up. You need the lines, the trap houses, the cuckoos. I mean, most of it was already there, in place, but whenever someone new comes in they like to do it their own way, don't they? And I might not have been the only one who split. I'd say at least two or three weeks to get everything reorganised and back in smooth running order. Maybe a month.'

'Can you direct us towards anyone who's still working out there?'

'No. I told you, I don't know how the Albanians have reorganised it all. I don't know nothing about them. I don't stay in touch. And I won't shop my old mates.'

Banks wasn't certain that he believed Greg knew nothing, but he didn't think he was likely to get much more out of him. The kid was clearly scared and desperate to hold on to the fragile new life he had made for himself. 'It seems as if Samir got your old gig, Greg. We're pretty sure he was working the Eastvale line out of Howard Stokes's house when he was killed – or he was about to take it on, at any rate.'

'What'd they do to him?'

'Stabbed,' said Banks.

'Poor sod. But I thought you said Howard was dead?'

'We're not quite sure of the sequence of events, but we believe they both died around the same time. A week ago Sunday.'

'The Albanians?'

'Maybe. But why?' Banks asked.

Greg shrugged. 'Dunno. Maybe Sammy was skimming, though I'd have thought he'd know better than that after being trained by Lenny G.'

'Did Samir take drugs?'

'He did a little coke. I think it was mostly a matter of being like one of the big boys, you know, to fit in, be one of the lads. I mean, I don't think he had a serious habit or anything.'

'Might he have stolen from the new boss?'

'Samir? I don't think so. Maybe he threatened to tell or something? Or they did it as a warning, or to teach someone else a lesson? I don't know. I've got to go now.'

They watched him walk across the Asda lot and go back into the garage. 'I'll talk to him later,' Blackstone said. 'I don't think he's going anywhere.' Then he glanced at his watch and looked at Banks. 'How convenient. Time for an early dinner.'

Zelda hadn't slept very well the previous night, either, but it had nothing to do with Banks's proximity. She liked Alan well enough, but not *in that way*. If truth be told, she never thought of men *in that way* at all. Even Raymond, though she had gone to his bed of her own free will. She had been living alone in a caravan at the artists' colony he had invited her to join for three months before she went to him for the first time. She didn't know why. He was old, but he wasn't fat, and he didn't smell of fried chicken, sweat and cheap cigars. He smelled of paint and turpentine. That first night, she slid between the sheets beside him, and he put his arm around her and held her to him. She fell asleep with her head resting on his shoulder and, for the first time in weeks, she had no nightmares. She would have been happy just to lie down with him and talk and cuddle for ever, but, later, things took their natural course. Now she felt lucky that even though they were together *in that way*, Raymond was gentle and undemanding in his lovemaking, and it was far from the be-all and end-all of what kept them together. With Raymond, that was probably down to age; with Zelda it was experience.

The memories, the associations, were simply too disturbing. When your body becomes a plaything for monsters, you come to hate it. A lot of the girls she had met self-harmed. The masters didn't like that. Their punishments were severe but never left marks. Some girls even succeeded in committing suicide, and there was nothing the masters could do about that except take it out on the ones still left alive.

Without thinking too deeply about it, Zelda knew that *in that way* could never work for her with anyone else but Raymond. Not after all she had been through. It might have worked with Emile, but he was dead. She knew she was damaged, that a part of what she was – her womanhood – had been taken from her. And two of the men who had taken it were now dead at her hand. But she could live with that. She knew that other women's lives were different, but she could live with what she was, and what she had done. And living had to be enough. People sometimes asked if she felt she could ever be the same after her experiences, but she always replied that there was nothing for her to be the same as; they had taken everything from her before she even got it herself.

But had her life come to be dominated by revenge, by the need to kill? Where would it end? Any real list would be very long indeed, and she had to ask herself if that was the existence she wanted. Or jail, where she would inevitably end up. She was lucky not to have been caught so far. Alan was no fool. The cops were no fools. They had their methods, and they would uncover her, not cover up, the way they had done with Darius. In killing Darius, she had done the authorities a favour, had done to him exactly what they wanted done. Darius had a lot of dirt on a lot of famous and powerful people. Household names. Government ministers. With Emile's help, Zelda had done their dirty work for them, had even uncovered his store of blackmail material for them, and they had rewarded her with a passport and her freedom. They couldn't state that publicly, though, so she had had to leave France. She lost Emile for ever, too.

There had been no mention of a body found in a London hotel in the morning paper she had scanned at Banks's cottage, as there surely would have been if Goran Tadić had been left there after her visit. Back at home, she scoured the Internet news sites and still found nothing. By mid-afternoon, she became certain that what she had thought would happen had happened. They had got there first, before any hotel employees, and they had removed his body, destroyed all traces of his murder. If there was to be any investigation, any retribution, it would belong to them, not to the police.

Now it made sense for her to stop. Let Petar Tadić live to suffer the loss of his brother.

But there was one more, if only she could find him.

In the early years of her enslavement, Zelda had been too distraught to think very clearly about anything, but later she had begun to wonder just how the Tadićs had known to wait for her near the orphanage on the day she left. Then, once or twice, in the brothels, she was certain she saw girls who had been with her in the orphanage. On one occasion, she had the opportunity to ask if this was true, and it turned out to be so.

It wasn't a great leap of logic from there to realise that someone inside the orphanage was providing the information –
either selling it or being blackmailed into giving it – and the
most logical choice was the orphanage director: Vasile
Lupescu. The problem was, she didn't know where he was.
Her sources told her that he had retired and no longer lived
in Chişinău, but nobody so far knew where he had moved to.
So he was still out there. He would be quite old by now, she
realised, perhaps dead, but she would like to find out for
certain.

Zelda would have to lie low for a while. She would have no
opportunity to discover whether Hawkins had been killed, or
the fire had been an accident. Even when the department
started operating again, she would have to keep her head
down. She would have liked to finish what she had started and
help Alan find the man who had tried to kill him, but it was
getting too dangerous.

Even Vasile Lupescu would have to wait for a while.

Banks and Blackstone settled into their comfortable seats at
an exotically decorated Thai restaurant in the city centre.
There were painted Buddhas and deep maroon panelled
walls, each panel marked out in ornate gold trim. The smells
of herbs and spices – coriander, star anise, cumin and lime –
were mouth-watering, and the food, when it came, was just as
good, from the spring rolls to the pad thai, fried rice and green
chicken curry they shared. The only drawback was that the
restaurant sold only bottled beer, so they settled for cold
Singha.

'Do you think you can track down someone from the county
lines at this end and get them to talk?' Banks asked.

'I don't know,' said Blackstone. 'We've got a couple of drugs
squad officers working undercover. They might be able to

come up with something useful, but they won't want to risk blowing their cover. What do you want to know?'

'Most of all, we'd like to know when Samir started working in Eastvale. We have no sightings of him there before the day he was killed, and then two witnesses saw him arriving from a Leeds bus carrying a backpack.'

'That would be the drugs,' said Blackstone. 'Any sign of it later?'

'No. It disappeared, along with his jacket. We know that Connor Clive Blaydon's chauffeur took them from the trap house on Hollyfield Lane the night Samir and Stokes died. Gashi had phoned Blaydon earlier and asked for a favour. I just have a feeling the timing is important, but there are still too many gaps in what we know.'

'Blaydon? So he's involved in this?'

'He's connected with the Albanians. Gashi in particular. They've known each other for years, and they're involved in a property development Blaydon is managing.'

'You can bet whatever money they invest will be dirty.'

'Too true,' said Banks. He washed down a mouthful of pad thai with his Singha. 'Any loose gossip your men might pick up would be useful,' he said. 'Something like this happens, people talk. They can't help themselves. Maybe they think they're being careful, but that's not always the case.'

'Right,' said Blackstone. 'I'll see what I can do. Pass the roti.'

Banks passed him the roti basket and Blackstone tore off a strip and spooned up some green chicken curry with it.

Banks worked on his Singha. It would have to do him for the evening, because he planned on driving back to Eastvale. 'What do you know about the county line operations here?' he asked.

'Just what I read in the papers,' Blackstone joked. 'No, seriously, it's becoming a real problem. It's not only here, but all over the country. Some are big operators, like Gashi with his Albanian Mafia and Colombian connections, but there are plenty of smaller entrepreneurs, too.'

'What was this Lenny G like?'

'Medium. He didn't have anywhere near the clout and product Gashi's got, more like a small-town operation by comparison. But he managed to supply heroin and crack cocaine to quite a few towns and villages that could have done without it. Now they've got the same drug problems as we have here in the city. And Gashi's adding coke to the mix, too, as well as crack. High quality coke direct from the Colombian cartels.'

'Yes, we know about that,' said Banks. 'What about spice and fentanyl?'

'On their way, no doubt.' Blackstone sighed. 'But it's the access to high quality coke that's the real problem at the moment.'

'What do you think happened with Lenny G?'

'I think he was unwilling to give up his empire, little as it was. The Albanians are happy to work with people, as long as they have the upper hand and get most of the profits. But if you don't want to play along . . .' He drew his finger across his throat.

'Do you think Gashi would have gone as far as killing one of his runners?'

'He might have. Not personally, but he might have had it done if he had good reason. To keep the others in line, say, or as a punishment for some transgression. People like Gashi don't worry about consequences. It would mean nothing to him. They don't hesitate. If they want to do something, they do it. What about Blaydon?'

'Again, he's a possibility, but not personally. He has minions, too. Have you seen him here?'

'Not me specifically,' said Blackstone, 'but I've heard he pays visits. He has an office down by the quays.'

'And Gashi?'

'He doesn't live here, either. Another frequent visitor. He lives in Mayfair, when he's not back in Albania. Blaydon has a lot of connections, and you wouldn't take any of them home to meet your mother. He likes to be seen hobnobbing with personalities, too – you know, TV presenters, footballers, the occasional pop star or politician. Word has it he supplies them with coke and imported girls and everyone has a good time.'

'Except the girls. Yes, I've seen the dregs of one of his pool parties.'

Blackstone nodded. 'Except the girls. But to be honest, he's never caused us much trouble, not so as we'd be after him, anyway.'

'He's slippery,' said Banks. 'But he's got something to do with this county lines business, and he's got so many empty properties I'm sure he feels it would be almost a crime *not* to use them as pop-up brothels or trap houses.'

'I see you're learning the lingo.'

Banks smiled. 'Got it from the *Sunday Times*. I don't think they really talk like that. Anyway, I hear Blaydon's business is in trouble.'

'It's a bad time for property developers, that's true. That why he's edging closer to crime?'

'I think so,' said Banks. 'That and because he likes the idea of being thought a bit of a pirate. There are plenty of people who still think supplying people with what they want – i.e. drugs and sex – is a heroic venture. By the way, have you heard anything about our favourite madam Mia Carney lately?'

Mia was a woman they had encountered the last time Banks had worked with Blackstone in Leeds. She had been running a sort of 'escort service' fixing up poor university students with wealthy sugar daddies and had the misfortune of running into some unsavoury characters. Banks had saved her life, and as a consequence felt proprietorial. Besides, he liked her.

'As a matter of fact, I have,' said Blackstone. 'I think you know she got a suspended sentence. It seems she took her brush with death and prison seriously and moved out of the escort business altogether.'

'So what's she doing?'

'Working for the student housing association.'

Banks looked at Blackstone open-mouthed, then they both started laughing.

13

The following morning dawned every bit as mild and clear as the previous one, and this time Banks was alone in his cottage. He didn't bother with breakfast but poured a travel mug of coffee to go and set off for Eastvale. His sleep had been fitful but far more refreshing than the night before. He had spoken briefly with Zelda on the phone the previous evening when he had got back from Leeds. She had telephoned him to thank him for his hospitality and company, and let him know that she had had a good time and not to worry, she would be OK now.

When Banks got to the station, he discovered that Annie and Gerry were down at the park at the bottom of Elmet Hill – or the top of Hollyfield Lane, depending on your perspective. When he phoned Annie's mobile, she told him the CSIs thought they had found something interesting. Banks set off immediately.

The little park was marked off by lines of police tape for the second day of searching. Perhaps it should have been done before, Banks worried, but the evidence linking Samir to the Stokes house, and Frankie's statement that the boy had run *towards* the park, were what had clinched the matter.

Uniformed officers stood guard at regular intervals to keep away curious onlookers and, more to the point, aggressive journalists. The case was still attracting a lot of publicity, especially since the revelation of Samir's identity and the possible county lines connection. The media came armed with cameras and mobile phones, which doubled as cameras and voice recorders. One man stood with a bulky television camera hefted on his shoulder. Adrian Moss, the media liaison officer, moved among them, chatting with those he knew here and there, while at the same time making sure no one overstepped the mark. Even Banks had to agree that Moss had earned his salary this month.

Banks signed the clipboard and slipped under the tape, joining Annie and Gerry by the side of the beck, next to the children's playground. Over the narrow strip of fast-moving water, the woods and bushes were full of CSIs and police officers in disposable white boiler suits, carefully grid-searching every inch of the ground.

'What have they got?' Banks asked Annie.

'Don't know yet,' she said. 'They're being very thorough.'

A few minutes later, one of the searchers marched out of the undergrowth with a scruffy young man in jeans and a white shirt, bent almost double as the officer twisted his arm up his back. 'Found something nasty in the woods, sir,' he said, letting go.

The young man swore and rubbed his arm. 'Fucking police brutality,' he said and turned to Banks. 'You saw that.'

'Saw what?' said Banks.

'You're all the fucking same.'

Banks held out his hand. 'Phone, Donnie,' he said.

'What?'

'Mobile. Come on. Hand it over. You don't want to end up down the nick, do you?'

'Interfering with the freedom of the press now, are you?'

Banks took a step towards him, and Donnie Vickers, intrepid reporter for the *Eastvale Gazette*, handed over his mobile phone. It was the kind that didn't require a password to access the camera and photograph functions, which was all Banks was really interested in. He deleted a couple of blurry snaps of men in white searching through the bushes and handed it back. 'Let's have a level playing field, Donnie, there's a good lad,' he said, pointing to the others behind the tape. 'Now off you go and join your mates.'

Donnie ambled off, still rubbing his arm, grumbling and scowling over his shoulder. Adrian Moss took him by the arm when he got to the police tape, and Banks turned back to Annie and Gerry.

'I can't imagine they've found anything much,' Annie said. 'Remember that bloody deluge the morning after the killing, when we found the body?'

'I remember,' said Banks. 'But the weather's been good since then. Dry, too. Who knows, if Samir was killed around here, with all the shelter the trees and bushes provide, we may still find traces. We can't assume that he knew where he was going when he ran off this way. Look at it from his point of view: he's stuck in a gloomy old house on an empty estate with a dead body. He's probably seen more than enough of them in his time, but that doesn't necessarily make the situation any easier. Perhaps it sets off memories he's managed to suppress for a while? Whatever the reason, when the back door opens and big Frankie comes lumbering through, it's a breaking point for Samir, and he takes off. Remember, he's never seen Frankie before, doesn't know who he is. And, maybe, just maybe, he ends up here.'

'Then what?' Annie asked.

'That's what we don't know yet. But I hope whatever it is they've found might make it a bit clearer.'

'Sir? I think they're ready for us now,' Gerry said.

Banks turned immediately towards the woods and saw one of the white-suited searchers gesturing for them to enter the

woods. 'Be careful,' she said, 'there's some thorny undergrowth around here.'

And indeed there was. Banks found himself scratched on
several occasions as he made his way into the shrubbery, and
judging from the curses behind him, so did Annie and Gerry.
Finally, they came across Stefan Nowak standing in a clear-
ing. It was cool in the shelter of the trees.

Without preamble, Nowak pointed at the ground. 'You can
see the ground has been flattened here and there.'

Banks saw that Nowak was right. Without the CSM's trained
eye, though, the disturbance to the ground would have been
easy to overlook.

'Unfortunately, there's no telling *when* this occurred,'
Nowak went on, 'but you can also see that this area has been
reasonably well sheltered.'

They looked up. Banks saw that above them stretched a
perfect canopy formed by the overhanging branches and light
green leaves of the trees.

'It doesn't mean nothing got through, of course,' Nowak
went on, 'but it would certainly have kept out a good portion
of that shower.'

'Annie said you'd found something,' Banks said.

'Yes.' Nowak walked over to the shrubbery at the base of an
ash tree and used a stick to lift up the hanging fronds and
branches. 'Look here.'

Banks's knees cracked as he crouched. At first it was too dark
to make out anything much at all, but then he saw that some of
the lower leaves were dotted, or smeared, with a dark substance.

'I think it's blood,' Nowak said. 'Anyway, we're taking
samples, and Jazz should be able to determine pretty quickly
if it's human and, with a bit of luck, whose. Don't get your
hopes up yet; it could be animal blood. A bird killed by a cat
or something.'

Banks stood up slowly. He found that if he got to his feet too suddenly these days he became dizzy. His doctor said it was due to a drop in blood pressure, most likely because of the medication he was taking, but if he had any other symptoms, such as fainting, chest pain, headaches or heart palpitations, he should come back immediately. He didn't have any. Not yet.

'Good work, Stefan,' Banks said. 'Anything else?'

'Quite a lot, actually, but we don't know how much use most of it is.'

'Anything you *think* I may be interested in?'

Nowak pointed to a nearby tree. The long grass at its base was flattened in one spot. 'Near that tree there, we found these.' He held out a plastic bag containing what looked at first like two cigarette ends, but on further perusal turned out to be roaches.

'So someone's been using the park as a spot to smoke up,' Banks said. 'That's hardly surprising with the decent weather we've been having lately.'

'Again, we don't know if this is from before or after the murder, but it was under the foliage there, and there's a good chance there might still be DNA.' He then brought out another package. 'With this we've got an even better chance, though. Chewing gum.'

Banks looked at the grey lump. He knew that chewing gum was a great place to find saliva samples, even after some time out in the open. Of course, there was no saying whether it had come from the same person, or people, who had smoked the joints, let alone whether it had anything to do with Samir's death. But it was progress. And Adrian Moss would view it as something new to keep from the media, so they would at least get the feeling that things were happening in the case, albeit behind their backs. They would already be curious about all the activity in the little park that morning.

Nowak drifted back to his team as they prepared to approach yet more sections of the search grid. Banks turned to Annie and Gerry and looked at his watch. 'Time for a meeting,' he said. 'How about an early lunch? The Oak's not more than a hundred yards over there, and I hear they do a lovely giant Yorkshire pudding stuffed with roast beef. Sorry, Annie.'

Banks watched Annie picking miserably at her vegan burger, made from tofu, beetroot and God only knew what else. At least the juices that dripped from it resembled real blood.

'Beats me why you lot have to go to great lengths to make pale imitations of meat products, blood and all, when you're trying to avoid the stuff,' said Banks.

'I'm not a vegan,' Annie said. 'They're not *my* lot. So don't pick on me!'

Gerry laughed, cut off a lump of Yorkshire pudding and dipped it in her gravy. 'Look at Gerry,' Banks said. 'There's someone who actually seems to enjoy her food.'

Annie pushed her burger aside. 'Put me right off my lunch now, you bastards.'

'I'm sure not eating anything at all is probably even better for you.'

Annie grunted.

Banks knocked back some Dalesview bitter and returned to his meal. They were sitting in the beer garden of The Oak, surrounded by the woods at the corner of Elmet Hill and Cardigan Drive. In one direction, through the branches and pale green leaves, they could see the dark slate roofs of the old Hollyfield Estate, and in the other, the elegant, tree-lined slope of Elmet Hill.

'I'm beginning to think that maybe we've been looking at this case all wrong,' Banks started.

'In what way?' Annie asked.

'We've been assuming all along that it had to do with Blaydon and county lines, and Gashi taking over.'

'And it doesn't?' Gerry said.

'I'm not so sure.'

'Well, they're certainly a part of it,' Annie countered. 'We know from what Greg Janson told you that Samir worked the Malton county line for Lenny G, and it's probably safe to assume he was on his first Eastvale run for Gashi. We also know that Blaydon is connected with the Albanians through the Elmet Centre redevelopment, as well as possibly through drugs and girls, as well as personal history. Samir was seen walking from Eastvale bus station with a backpack the night he was killed, he had been inside Howard Stokes's house, and Howard Stokes was being cuckooed, a vulnerable drug addict persuaded to let them use his house – rent-free from the Kerrigans – as a distribution centre in exchange for heroin. I don't see what the problem is, using those facts as our starting point.'

'That's all they are, though,' said Banks. 'A starting point. And they don't lead anywhere.'

'What does?'

'Have you ever really wondered *why* anyone might have killed Samir? Gashi or his mob, for example? Or Blaydon? Or Frankie? What motive they might have?'

'We've been over all that,' Annie said. 'Because he stole some coke or threatened to talk, and they wanted to use him as an example.'

'Or because he wanted out?' Gerry suggested. 'And he knew too much?'

'But what could he possibly know?' Banks said. 'Yes, he delivered and sold drugs for the Albanians. Maybe he stole a little – though Greg Janson doesn't think so – but not enough to bring about his murder. Maybe he knew Gashi's name. But so do we. It's no secret. What good does that do us? And Gashi knows that, too. It doesn't matter to him. Besides, the Albanians don't just stab people, they gut them. Remember Lenny G? No, I can't really see Samir being a threat to the county line. Remember, he also needed the gig to make money to bring his family over from Syria. The family he didn't know were all dead.'

'And maybe pay off the Birmingham gang who helped smuggle him in, too,' Annie added.

'OK,' said Banks. 'We don't know much about them, it's true. Is that another possible direction to look? His smugglers?'

'Well, I'd ask the same question that you just asked,' Annie said. 'And that's why?'

'Same answer. He knew too much? He ran away from them? He owed them a lot of money and refused to pay? These people have long memories and a long reach, you know.'

'But killing him would hardly get them their money back, would it?' said Gerry. 'And how would they find him?'

'I don't know how. But these organisations rely on terror, Gerry,' Banks said. 'You know that. They don't only rely on the threat of retribution, they rely on the reality of actually carrying it out. Painfully. Sometimes you just have to write off a debt to make a point – and remember, that's what we thought the murder might be about right from the first. Boy in a wheelie bin. Example. Warning. It's just a matter of to whom and about what.'

'So you think it's this smuggling gang based in Birmingham?' said Annie.

'I'm saying it's a possibility. That's all. Maybe they traced him and tracked him down.'

'I suppose it's just possible,' Annie agreed. 'At a pinch.'

'But you don't like it as a working theory?'

'Not really, no. It sounds both too pat and far-fetched at the same time.'

'I agree,' said Banks.

'Then . . .?'

Banks pushed his plate aside. Already a couple of fat blue-bottles seemed interested in the congealing mess. 'I'm just casting around in the dark, Annie, trying to construct alternative scenarios. And I do have one I'm leaning very much towards, though we'll need a lot more spadework first, and a bit of luck with the forensics.'

'What's that?'

Banks rested back in his chair, careful not to overdo the tilt on the soft grass. 'We've been working on the assumption that Samir was killed because of his connection with county lines, with drugs, or, as I suggested just now, with people smugglers.'

'So what's wrong with that?' Annie asked.

'Nothing. But it hasn't got us anywhere, has it?'

'I don't know about that, guv,' Gerry said. 'It's thrown up Blaydon, the Kerrigans, Frankie Wallace, all sorts of villains.'

'But we don't have any evidence against any of them.'

'We know from what Frankie told us that Blaydon was definitely involved,' said Annie.

'Maybe. At least we know he told us that he got a call from Blaydon asking him to bring Samir out of Hollyfield that night.'

'That shows that Blaydon was somehow involved, doesn't it?'

'Yes. But we've suspected that all along, haven't we, proof or not? Ever since my meeting with Joanna MacDonald, anyway.' The waitress came and collected their plates and empty glasses. 'Coffee, anyone?' Banks asked. They all said yes and Banks went to the bar to order them. As he waited for service, he mulled over the ideas he'd been having as he drove to Eastvale and hung around in the park that morning, and the more he thought, the more he realised there might be something in them. But he – the entire team – would have to reboot and tread carefully.

The bartender said the waitress would deliver their coffees, and when Banks got back to the table he found Annie and Gerry deep in discussion about the traces of blood Stefan Nowak's team had found in the park.

'Let's hope it's useful,' Banks said. 'But in the meantime?'

'You said you had a new theory,' Gerry said. 'Want to share it?'

'It's not really new. I've just been concentrating a bit more on the actual physical facts we have to work with, rather than the vague relationships, the criminal organisations, the drugs and so on.'

'And what conclusions have you come to?' Annie asked.

'That all we know so far – if we believe Frankie Wallace, which I do – is that Samir was frightened in the house, and when Frankie came in, he bolted. He bolted in the direction of that park over there, and his body ended up in a wheelie bin on the East Side Estate about an hour later. What happened during that hour? We don't know. What do we think might have happened? The CSIs found blood traces in the park, possibly human, possibly Samir's. Jazz will be analysing them. I think there's a very good chance the blood *is* Samir's, which means it was more than likely he was killed in the park he ran towards after Frankie entered the house. Well, if Frankie didn't run after him, find him and kill him, then who did? Who else from the drug operation was in the neighbourhood at the time? Blaydon? Gashi? The Kerrigans?'

Gerry looked puzzled. 'Nobody, guv. Not as far as we know. Not in the park.'

'And is there any reason to think that there might have been someone else there we missed?'

'Not really,' Annie said. 'I mean, why would there be? How could anyone *know* Samir would run there?'

'Exactly,' said Banks.

'I still don't see what you're getting at, guv,' said Gerry. 'Are you suggesting that someone else from Blaydon's or Gashi's organisation just happened to be loitering in the park at the right time and took the opportunity to kill Samir for some reason?'

'Not at all,' said Banks. 'I'm saying the opposite, that it would be most unlikely. My point is that maybe what happened to Samir had nothing whatsoever to do with Blaydon, Gashi and whatever it was they were up to. Nothing to do with the Kerrigans and the Elmet Centre redevelopment. Nothing to do with any of it. That we've let ourselves be comprehensively sidetracked.'

'By whom?'

'Not by anyone but ourselves,' Banks answered. 'We think we've been working on a crime with clear motivation and opportunity – drugs, organised crime – but what if the whole thing was completely unplanned and unexpected? What if Samir was just in the wrong place at the wrong time? What if the crime had nothing to do with the other stuff, but every-thing to do with the park?'

'And you're assuming he was killed in the park?' said Annie.

'Yes. As I said, I don't think there's much doubt that the blood Stefan's team has found is his, do you? We'll have to wait for analysis, of course, but I'd bet next month's salary on it.'

'And?'

'Well, who do you think might have been likely to be in the park when Samir ran there? I think it might not be a bad idea to go and have another word with Mr Neighbourhood Watch, don't you?'

Granville Myers led Banks and Annie through the bright kitchen to the paved patio area in the garden at the back, where four white fold-up chairs were arranged around a circular table with a brightly striped umbrella, under the shade of an overhanging willow.

The weather was warm enough for Banks to remove his jacket and hang it over the back of the chair. He noticed an outdoor grill in the corner by the door, which reminded him that he had been planning on buying one for a couple of years now but hadn't got around to it. He thought he could probably master the basics of grilling a burger or steak; it would be something quick and easy he could make after a long day at work, leaving only a minimum of washing up. Spring seemed to have morphed into summer so much more quickly than usual this year, and he realised his mind was still stuck in winter. Time to get a move on and catch up with the seasons.

'I can't imagine what it is you want to talk to me about,' Myers said. 'I told the other young lady everything I know. Which is nothing.' In front of him on the table were a half-finished glass of orange juice and an open paperback copy of the latest Lee Child.

'Just a few minor details, if that's all right with you?' Banks said.

'I don't suppose I have much choice.'

'There's always a choice, sir,' Annie said. 'And it's always best to make the right one.'

Myers scowled at her. 'Thank you for that gem of wisdom. What is it you want to know?'

Banks gave Annie a slightly annoyed glance, hoping to indicate that she was getting Myers's back up too much too soon.

True, he seemed a puffed-up, self-important pillock, and he did look a lot like Nigel Farage, but there were ways of treating such people in an interview. Still, Annie had been angry and sarcastic a lot lately. Banks wondered if it had anything to do with Ray and Zelda. Best leave that for the moment, he decided.

'It's about Sunday night,' he said. 'The night of the murder.'

'But I went over that with—'

'Yes, I know you told DC Masterson all you knew, but sometimes we find it's useful to go over old ground with fresh eyes, so to speak. As you may know, we've been working in the park at the bottom of Elmet Hill for the past couple of days.'

'A neighbour told me,' Myers said. 'I can't imagine why.'

'I was wondering if you knew that the place was a hangout for marijuana smokers, casual sexual liaisons and other such things?'

'What? The park? That's ridiculous. It's not anyone from around here, I can assure you.'

'Who else, then?'

'Hollyfield.'

'Come on, there's hardly anyone left there, Mr Myers. No, I think your days of blaming every local evil on the Hollyfield Estate are just about over, especially now that Howard Stokes is dead.'

'What are you suggesting? That's the old man who was found dead over there of a heroin overdose, isn't it?'

'Yes. Howard Stokes. He lived on Hollyfield Lane for many years. Lived a perfectly normal life.'

'You can't tell me that's a normal life. A drug addict. Not unless you're a bloody *Guardian* reader and you think everything most decent folk view as abnormal is normal, and vice versa.'

'As it happens, I do read the *Guardian*, Mr Myers, but that's by the by. A *Mail* man, yourself, are you?'

'*Telegraph*,' Myers grunted.

'Admirable. The thinking man's *Mail*. Anyway, what concerns me now is the extent of the after-hours activity in the park and what you, as head of the local Neighbourhood Watch, might be able to tell me about it.'

'I told you, I know nothing about it. You surely don't think I've been down there smoking marijuana, do you?'

Banks laughed. 'I very much doubt it. But it strikes me that you might have known what the park was being used for, and you and your colleagues might have made the occasional sweep of the area, just to discourage it. Your son, Chris, for example, was reprimanded for drugs just last year.'

'Nothing came of that,' said Myers. 'Chris was completely exonerated. He had no drugs in his possession whatsoever.'

'No, but he was in a place where drugs were being consumed.'

'No charges were brought. You've no right to bring that up. Chris has no criminal record. All mention of what happened should be expunged from your records.'

Banks thanked his lucky stars for the old incident sheets and glanced at Annie. 'Let's move on, then,' he said. 'You *are* in charge of the Neighbourhood Watch, so it can hardly be unusual to assume that you have some idea of what's going on in the neighbourhood, can it? I'm simply asking for the benefit of your expertise. Doesn't that seem reasonable?'

'On the surface of it, naturally it does,' Myers blustered. 'But in reality, I'm sure you know as well I do that our brief stops at Cardigan Drive. We don't police Hollyfield.'

'Nobody does,' said Banks.

'Well, you know what they say. Physician, heal thyself.'

Banks sighed. 'If only it were that easy. We don't have the resources. That's why we rely on people like you to help us.

People who have some sense of pride in their neighbourhoods, people who value the safety and security of their families and neighbours. We know we're falling way short.'

Myers seemed to puff himself up. 'Well . . . er . . . as you put it like that, yes, we are certainly aware of the constrictions the police work under, and we're more than happy to help. After all, it means we're helping ourselves, doesn't it?'

'It does,' said Banks. 'Glad you see it that way.'

'But it doesn't alter the fact that I'm still afraid I don't know anything. We never did patrol Hollyfield, and these days there seems even less point, as there's hardly anyone left living there.'

'But did you or any of your fellow watchers patrol the *park* that Sunday night? Did you see Samir suddenly appear there, and in the confusion of the moment, stab him?'

'That's absurd!' said Myers. 'Now you're accusing *me* of murder.' He got up. 'I want my solicitor. Immediately.'

'Calm down, Mr Myers,' said Banks. 'Keep your hair on. I'm merely asking you a question: did you or any of your colleagues kill Samir Boulad?'

Myers eased himself back into his chair. 'Then the answer's obvious. No. But I suppose that's what you'd expect me to say, whether I'm guilty or innocent. And I can assure you that I'm innocent.'

Banks shrugged. 'I've known plenty of murderers who like to confess.'

'I am *not* a murderer. And for your information, there was no one patrolling the park that night.'

'Are you certain about that?'

'Of course I am.'

At that moment a tall, athletic boy with golden curls flopping over his pasty face came through the back gate; he stopped dead when he saw his father sitting with two strangers. Myers looked as if this new presence was the last thing he wanted.

'Uh, sorry,' said the boy, making to sidle past them and go into the kitchen.

Banks stood up. 'You must be Christopher Myers?'

Chris shifted uncomfortably from foot to foot. 'Uh, yeah, that's right.'

Banks introduced himself and Annie. 'Why don't you join us for a minute?' he said. 'There's a free chair.'

'Er, I think I'd better . . . you know . . .'

'Please, sit down,' said Banks, a steelier edge to his voice. 'This won't take long.'

Chris eased himself on to the chair, which was far too small for him. He stretched his long legs out to one side.

'We were just talking about the park,' Banks went on. 'You might have noticed some activity down there today?'

'Yeah. I wondered what was going on.'

'We've got new information,' said Banks. 'We've got the CSIs and forensic officers going through the place with fine-tooth combs.'

'Oh, right.'

'Ever been down there, Christopher?'

'Chris. Everyone calls me Chris. The park? Well, sure. I mean, I grew up here. We used to go and play on the swings and stuff.'

'I mean more recently.'

'I've passed through it, you know, but it's not somewhere I'd hang out.'

'Why's that?'

Chris shrugged. 'Dunno. Just isn't, that's all.'

'Do you pass through it on your way to number twenty-six Hollyfield Lane to buy your drugs?'

'My what?'

'Don't listen to him, son,' said Myers.

'Are you sure you don't sneak down to the park for the occasional spliff?'

'Mr Banks!' It was Granville Myers again, half-standing. 'That's a bit much, isn't it? First you accuse me, and now you accuse my son.'

'I wasn't aware I was accusing him of anything except smoking an occasional joint,' said Banks. 'That's illegal, but we tend to overlook it most of the time.'

'You're insinuating that Chris was in the park on Sunday. That he killed this Arab boy.'

Chris looked confused. 'What's going on, Dad?' he asked. 'Who's accusing who of what?'

'Were you?' Banks asked. 'In the park when Samir was killed?'

'Of course not,' Chris said.

'No harm in asking,' said Banks. 'Anyway, we've come up with a lot of interesting new trace evidence from the park, so we'll know the truth soon enough.'

'Evidence of what?' Chris asked.

'I'm afraid I can't say at the moment. Just that it puts a whole new complexion on things, and it may well send the investigation spinning off in a whole different direction.'

'Well, that's great,' said Chris, but he didn't sound as if he meant it. He was twitchy now, eager to leave his chair. 'I've got an exam tomorrow morning. I'd better . . . you know . . .'

'Right. Sorry to have kept you,' said Banks.

Chris got up and walked towards the kitchen door. 'Good luck,' Banks called after him.

Chris half-turned. 'What with?'

'The exam.'

'Oh, yeah. Right. Thanks.' And he hurried inside.

'Seems a bit on edge,' Banks said. 'A bit twitchy.'

Myers scowled. 'Hardly bloody surprising, is it, the way you treated him just now. As if he doesn't have enough on his plate already with these exams to worry about. You're jeopardising the boy's future with these wild accusations. Do you realise that, Superintendent? In fact, I'm going to—'

'I suppose it prepares them for later life,' said Banks.

'What?'

'Exams. The stress.'

Myers seemed confused. 'Is there ... I mean, I've had enough of this. I need to go and see if Chris needs anything. If you . . .'

Banks glanced at Annie, and they both stood up. 'No, that's fine, Mr Myers. We're finished for the moment. We know where to find you if we need to talk to you or Chris again. It's a great little spot you've got here. Easy to settle in for the afternoon, I should imagine.'

'If you're finished, then.'

'Right. We're off. Don't get up. You stay here. We'll see ourselves out.'

'Believe me, it's no trouble,' said Myers.

Chris Myers was nowhere in sight. His father stuck with Banks and Annie all the way to the front door and seemed to close it behind them with a great deal of relief.

14

The following morning, Banks left Annie to dig up as much background as she could on the Elmet Hill Neighbourhood Watch and its members and took Gerry with him to St Botolph's. While it seemed unlikely that a member of a Neighbourhood Watch group would murder an interloper, it wasn't entirely impossible, Banks thought; especially if tensions were running high in the area, as they perhaps were after the burglaries and the sexual assault on Lisa Bartlett. Any members of the Watch Annie discovered to have criminal records would certainly be brought in for questioning.

Banks took the road north-west out of Eastvale, skirting the top of Elmet Hill, and turned off at the second exit of the big roundabout at the edge of town, which led deeper into the dale, to Lyndgarth and beyond. It was a B-road, which meant the surface wasn't always smooth, and in places it was so narrow that there was a need for passing places. Luckily, they encountered little traffic coming from the other direction. Trees lined the road in a variety of gnarly shapes and sizes. As he drove, Banks played a selection of Vivaldi arias sung by Cecilia Bartoli, and Gerry seemed happy to sit back in silence and enjoy the music flowing over her.

Banks had been asked so many times why he didn't have lower ranking members of his team drive him around, and he always answered that he preferred to drive himself. It was partly a control issue – he didn't fully trust anyone else – and partly because the Porsche inherited from his brother had come to fit him like an old glove, despite the various insurance forms and waivers he had to sign before being allowed to use his own car at work rather than some wreck from the police garage. This way, if he got involved in a police chase and smashed it up, the county wouldn't be liable.

Several miles beyond Lyndgarth they crested a rise and came out from the obscuring shade of roadside trees to see St Botolph's spread out in a natural trough of land like some fairy-tale castle held in the palm of a giant's hand. The school was a rambling Victorian construction, though on a relatively small scale, built in 1866 of local limestone, complete with turrets and gables. The grounds were extensive, scattered with numerous buildings, both original and more modern additions, including dormitories, stables, storage areas and a chapel with lancet stained-glass windows. There were also the inevitable green swathes of playing fields with rugby posts, and smaller pitches, clearly intended for cricket, along with tennis courts. All in all, it was quite a sight, and Banks stopped in a lay-by for a few moments to let Gerry take it all in.

'Not seen it before?' he asked.

'No, guv. It's like something out of *Brideshead Revisited*. You know, on the TV, when Charles Ryder first sees Brideshead.'

'I didn't know you were a fan.'

'I'm working my way through great box sets. It was on the list.'

'That was filmed at Castle Howard, you know.'

'I know. I've always wanted to visit, but it's prohibitively expensive.'

'Well, St Botolph's isn't quite as magnificent, but it's free. Unless you want to be a pupil there, of course.'

'No, thanks. I've had my fill of posh schools.'

'Of course. I remember. Merchant Taylors', wasn't it?'

'That's right.'

'And you still a lowly DC.'

Gerry laughed. 'That's all right, guv. I've still got my sights on the chief constable's job.'

Banks gave a mock shudder. 'I couldn't imagine anything worse.' He drove out of the lay-by and wound his way down the road to the school, surrounded by open fields and moorland on both sides, all under a great blue dome of sky scattered with fluffy white clouds. As they floated over, the clouds cast shadows, which seemed to chase one another across the landscape.

Banks parked outside the main building. 'The head said he'd meet us in his office,' he said. 'It's on the second floor.'

It was exam time, so there weren't the usual number of pupils dashing about the high-ceilinged corridors, or up and down the broad marble staircase. One or two young boys paused to stare at them and whisper as they passed. Probably, Banks thought, having highly erotic thoughts about Gerry, with her coltish figure and flowing red hair. Their footsteps echoed as they walked up to the second floor, where they found someone who looked like a teacher to direct them to the head's office. Once there, they knocked and entered a reception area where a young woman with a stuffy formal manner asked them to be seated and wait, that Mr Bowen would be with them soon.

It didn't take long before they were summoned to go in. Though it had happened before in the course of his investigations, Banks had never been quite able to separate these official visits to the headmaster's office from those he had been required to make as a pupil at his local grammar school, after passing the 13+ examination and finding himself transferred from the secondary modern and all his friends. He still felt that same sense of trepidation, the quickening heartbeat, even an anticipatory tingling around the buttocks at the thought of the caning to come. Of course, schools didn't do such barbaric things any more, but the memory remained – the music teacher with his slipper called 'Johan Sebastian'; the divinity teacher who always said, 'This is going to hurt me more than it hurts you' before every thrashing; the art teacher who took a run like a fast bowler before letting rip. Bastards all. And no doubt dead bastards by now.

But Roger Bowen was hardly so frightening. He was young, for a start, and quite handsome, with a fine head of thick brown hair and not a trace of grey. Banks put him in his late thirties at most. He also had an affable manner and a sporty air about him – more cricketer, perhaps, than rugby player – and a strong handshake, neither too firm nor too limp and clammy. He wore a white shirt and what looked like an old school tie, but there were no gowns or mortarboards in sight. The mullioned sash window was open several inches, letting in a light breeze, a whiff of scented spring air, the thwack of leather on willow and the shouts from those pupils lucky enough to be practising out in the nets instead of writing A-levels. Bowen bade them sit and sent for tea, then leaned back in his chair with his hands linked behind his head.

'So what can I do for you?' he asked. 'You were suitably non-committal on the telephone.'

'Occupational habit,' said Banks.

'Well, I know I haven't committed any crimes, so unless things are going to take a positively Kafkaesque turn, I will assume that you want to see me about some aspect of the school. A pupil, perhaps?'

'I'll come straight to the point, Mr Bowen. It's about Christopher Myers. He is a pupil here, right?'

'Yes. Yes, of course he is. But I'm puzzled. What could Chris possibly have done that merits police involvement?'

'It would be best if I didn't talk about that just for the moment.'

'You're fishing?'

'We call it looking for evidence.'

'Ah. Semantics.'

'Mr Myers is helping us with our enquiries,' said Gerry.

Bowen laughed, and even Banks managed a smile. 'Got it in one, DC Masterson,' he said.

'Well, in that case,' Bowen went on, 'I'm still not sure how I can help you, but ask away.'

'Has Myers ever been in trouble?'

'No more than any other boy his age. The usual adolescent pranks.'

'Smoking behind the cycle sheds?'

'I'm afraid our cycle sheds don't offer that much cover. Besides, you'd be surprised how many young people just don't seem to smoke these days.'

'Not cigarettes, at any rate.'

'We don't tolerate drugs here, Superintendent.'

'According to our information, Myers was issued with a stern warning last year after being discovered at a party where drugs and alcohol were present. He was seventeen at the time.'

'That did get back to me, and I certainly had words with him, as I'm certain his father did. I repeat, though, we don't tolerate drugs here at St Botolph's, and there have been no issues along those lines involving Chris Myers.'

'Anybody else?'

'That would be between myself and their parents.'

'Me and his or her parents,' said Banks.

'I beg your pardon?'

'Don't mind me. Semantics again. I'm just old-fashioned. I even use the subjunctive on occasion.'

Bowen smiled. 'A regular Philip Marlowe.'

'One of my heroes. OK, so Myers hasn't been involved in drugs here. Is there anything else we should know? Does he get into fights, for example?'

Bowen frowned. 'Not that I know of. I'm not saying we don't have any fights here. Of course, it happens. Boys will be boys and all that. But not Myers.'

'Any trouble with weapons? Knives, especially.'

'With Myers?'

'Anyone.'

'No. Naturally, they're not allowed on school premises, and I'm happy to report that we've had no incidents, and I have never had to confiscate one. None of the other masters have, either, as far as I know.'

'Would they tell you?'

'Anything like that would have to be reported.'

'To the police, too?'

'Definitely. If we thought crime was involved. Possessing a dangerous weapon would be very high on our list of report-able offences.'

'Glad to hear it.'

'Is there anything else?'

Banks glanced at Gerry. 'We're trying to get a general sense of what Chris Myers is like,' she said. 'What kind of boy he is. We were thinking this would be a good place to start.'

Bowen's tone changed when he spoke to Gerry, much as his facial expression did when he looked at her. Definitely something there, thought Banks.

'On the whole I'd say he's pretty normal,' Bowen said.

'Good at sports?'

'Reasonably. He's not much of a rugby player, but then, neither was I. If I had to pick *his* sport, I'd opt for tennis. Not Wimbledon quality, mind you, but definitely passable.'

'And academically?'

'He's bright. Could apply himself more, but that's hard when you're eighteen and your hormones are raging. Terrible time in life to be doing exams, I'd have thought.'

Gerry laughed. 'At least there are no girls here to distract him.'

'Yes,' said Bowen. 'I thought that was rather a pity when I first came, but I suppose I've got used to it by now. I'm still not sure it's entirely healthy, but I doubt it does any lasting harm. After all, Myers is a day boy, so what he gets up to when he goes home is out of our control. No doubt there are parties and girls.'

'Does he have a girlfriend?' Banks asked.

'I have no idea about his private life,' said Bowen. 'I should imagine he's much like any other young lad in that respect.'

'Is he gay?'

'Not to my knowledge. But you'd really have to ask him that question.'

'Is he headed for Oxford?' Gerry asked, picking up the questioning again.

'It depends. He has an offer, but it's contingent on his getting three A⋆s. He'll have to buck his ideas up a bit for that result, and he doesn't have much time left.'

'So all in all, you'd say Chris Myers was a well-balanced boy, pretty typical for his age, maybe brighter than most, and with a promising future ahead of him?'

'That would just about cover it,' said Bowen.

'You sound a little hesitant there,' said Banks. 'After all, you've just given the lad a glowing reference.'

'Actually, those were your words.'

'But you agreed,' Banks said.

'Up to a point. I mean, nobody's perfect. Chris can be disobedient. He sometimes talks back to teachers, plays truant on occasion and, well, there was that drugs incident, even if it did take place out of school.'

'What about bullying?' Banks asked.

'It happens. I won't deny it. But we try and nip it in the bud if we can.'

'Myers?'

Bowen shook his head. 'No. Chris is neither a bully nor the victim of bullying.'

'What about dishonesty? Plagiarism, cheating in exams, that sort of thing. What do you think of him morally?'

'That's a lot of questions,' said Bowen. 'As far as I know, he's neither a cheat nor a plagiarist. My staff and I are quite aware that students can purchase essays over the Internet, for example, so we're always on the lookout for anything that seems inauthentic. But I think you would be aware of it yourself, if you were a teacher. It's usually not difficult to tell if the work a student presents isn't his own. Chris has a perfectly fluent, though somewhat pedestrian, writing style. His spelling is usually correct – though that may well be due to a good spell-check programme – and he is not without original ideas. I'm not making out he's a genius or anything, but he has a good mind when he decides to use it.' Bowen smiled to himself. 'You might say that laziness is one of his less admirable attributes. But he usually gets the work done and does it well. Otherwise, there would be no possibility of his taking a place at Oxford.' He put his hands palms down on the desk and half stood. 'And there,' he announced, 'I have to leave things. I have a class in fifteen minutes, and it wouldn't do for the head to be late.'

Banks and Gerry stood and thanked him for his time. At the door, Gerry paused. 'I got the impression when you endorsed the superintendent's summary of Christopher's character, that you weren't entirely comfortable with it. Was there something he omitted? Something he got wrong?'

'You're very perceptive, DC Masterson,' Bowen said, then to Banks, 'You'd better watch her. She'll go far.'

'Oh, I know,' said Banks. 'Private school education. Cambridge. Chief constable next stop. I have no doubts.'

Bowen looked at Gerry again and raised an eyebrow. 'Indeed. I'm even more impressed.'

Gerry blushed and struggled for composure. 'Is there anything to it?' she asked. 'Did we miss something?'

Bowen sat down again, rather heavily this time. 'I'm probably speaking out of turn here,' he said, 'though I'm fully aware there's no binding confidentiality agreement between teachers and students. It's not so much Chris who worries me, as much as the company he keeps.'

'Anyone in particular?' asked Banks.

'Jason Bartlett. They're very close friends. Chris gives him a lift to and from school, as Jason doesn't own a car, and the public transport situation is horrendous. And Jason, of course, is nowhere near as bright as Christopher.'

'What's the problem?' Banks asked.

'Nothing specific. Just that I think Jason is becoming a bad influence. I know the boy has had problems at home. His sister . . . Terrible business. And that has really affected his exam prospects. There's another slightly worrying aspect to his development, too. You know we have a school magazine? No? Well, we do. Not so long ago Jason Bartlett submitted an article for publication. It was rejected, and I was urged to read a copy by the editor. To put it in a nutshell, it was a scurrilous, racist diatribe. Against foreigners in general, but mostly against the more visible groups. Claiming they're no better than animals and are all sexual predators. Giving examples like Rochdale and Rotherham. You may or may not know it, but we have a rather large percentage of foreign students here at St Botolph's, and such an article would have been most offensive or upsetting had they seen it.'

'I see,' said Banks. 'Have there been any incidents involving Bartlett and his views? Has he been involved in any propagation of hate literature, for example?'

'Not that I know of,' said Bowen. 'And I think I would know.'

'Any specific targets? Names?'

'No. The article was the first I knew of it, and it was general in scope. You could see the influence of certain far-right views. English Defence League, UKIP, Yaxley-Lennon, that sort of thing. Second-hand ideas. Not something we encourage around here, as you might imagine. It was also unexpected. According to his form master and other teachers, he's very quiet in class.'

'Has Myers ever echoed any of these ideas?'

'No. Not as far as I know. Not in public, at any rate.'

'Can I see a copy of the article?'

'You can take it with you,' said Bowen, going over to his filing cabinet and rummaging around until he found what he was looking for. He handed it to Banks.

Banks nodded. 'Thank you, Mr Bowen. You've been most helpful. We'll let you get to your class now.'

On the way back to the car, Gerry said, 'You didn't have to tell him that, guv. About me going to a private school. And Cambridge.'

'You shouldn't be afraid to blow your own trumpet, Gerry. After all, it'll be your main occupation should you ever rise to the heady rank of chief constable. Besides, I think you made an impression there. Much longer and I guarantee the good headmaster would have asked for your telephone number.'

Gerry didn't do or say anything, but Banks could tell she wanted to nudge him hard with her elbow.

*　　*　　*

The whole Bartlett family was sitting around the television watching *Emmerdale* when Banks arrived that evening after teatime, having spent most of the afternoon reading over the article Jason had written and talking with various contacts about some of the racist ideas he had expressed. The family was clearly annoyed at being interrupted, but Gus turned the volume down and seemed resigned to answering a few questions.

'Mostly it's Jason I'd like to talk to,' said Banks.

'What have I done?' said Jason. 'I haven't done anything wrong.'

'Nobody's saying you have,' said Banks. 'I just want a word, that's all.'

'We're all staying,' said Gus.

Banks nodded. 'Very well. Suit yourselves.' So they all settled back in their chairs and waited. *Emmerdale* went on with the sound turned down.

Jason looked both furtive and distracted. 'I've got an exam tomorrow afternoon,' he said. 'So please hurry up. I've got revision to do.'

'What is it?' Banks asked.

'Media Studies.'

'Ah. Watching television.'

'Shows how much you know.'

'Jason!' said his mother. 'Manners.'

'Well, he was making fun of me.'

'It was a joke,' said Banks. 'Obviously in poor taste. I'm sorry.'

Jason said nothing.

Banks turned to Gus Bartlett. 'I understand you work with Granville Myers on the Neighbourhood Watch?' he said.

'That's right.'

'I was wondering if any of you out there noticed anything odd on the Sunday night before last, when the Syrian boy,

Samir, was killed. Do you have written records, reports and so on?'

'We do,' said Bartlett. 'But Sally Villiers keeps those. She's a secretary at the town hall, for the council, like, and she's skilled at that sort of thing.'

'Do you submit incident reports?' Banks smiled. 'If it's anything like us, you'd have to write even the slightest detail up in triplicate.'

Bartlett laughed. 'No. It's not that bureaucratic. But we do keep records. Incident reports, as you say. I mean, a good deal of our job is intelligence. Not so much catching criminals in the act as keeping an eye on neighbourhood trends, suspicious strangers hanging about, that sort of thing.'

'Do you photograph them?'

'Sometimes. Some of our members do, yes.'

'Get a lot of strangers?'

'Not many. No.'

'What about recently? Before the Sunday in question. Just from memory.'

'None I can think of, no.'

'And that evening?'

'I'd have to check, but I don't think there was anyone from the Watch out that night. Sundays are usually pretty quiet.'

'Burglars' night off?'

Bartlett laughed. 'I see what you mean. But it's true. We've rarely had any kind of incident on a Sunday evening.'

'So nobody was out on patrol that night?'

'No.'

'Are you sure you weren't in the park with Granville Myers?'

'I . . . no. As I said, we didn't go out Sunday night.'

'Ever had any incidents down in the park?'

'That's not really part of our territory.'

'It seems like the ideal place for people up to no good to hang out. Hey, Jason?'

'Why look at me?'

'You know. Lads get up to all sorts. I did, myself. Smoking. Maybe sharing a bottle of whisky. You know the sort of thing.'

'No.'

'So, Mr Bartlett, you never had any trouble down there?'

'As I said, we don't patrol the park, specifically, but if anyone had seen or heard anything, I'd certainly know about it.'

'Lisa? I know the memory might be painful for you, but do you know anything about what goes on in the park?'

Lisa shook her head. 'I was on the shortcut through the car park at The Oak to the hill. I didn't walk through the park. I never do. It's too scary after dark.'

'Why?'

She hugged herself as if she were cold. 'No reason. It's just a scary park, that's all.'

'But if nothing ever happened there . . .?'

'I wouldn't walk through there alone. That's all.'

'OK.' Banks leaned forward and looked at Jason. 'We think that Samir, the Syrian boy, ran from Hollyfield Lane up to the park on the night he was killed, but we don't have any reports of him going anywhere else after that. It's a bit of a puzzle. Can you help us?'

Jason just shrugged and averted his eyes. His father said, 'But he must have gone to the East Side Estate. Isn't that where his body was found?'

'Yes,' said Banks. 'But that doesn't mean he was killed there. Besides, it's quite a long walk from here.'

'I don't understand.'

'It's a matter of timing. Do you have a car, Jason?'

'No.'

'That's right. Mr Bowen told us. But Chris Myers does, doesn't he? Your best mate. He gives you a lift to school and back.'

'So what? And why have you been talking to Bowen about me? What's he got to say?'

'We'll get to that later,' said Banks. 'In the meantime, we think Samir's body was dumped on the East Side Estate. Most likely by car.'

'Now, wait a minute,' said Gus Bartlett. 'You're not accusing our Jason of this murder, are you?'

Banks glanced from one to the other. 'I'm not quite sure yet,' he said. 'We're still waiting on the lab results of traces we found in the park. At the scene. I have a suspicion it might be one or the other of the boys, though. Unless you also smoke marijuana.'

'That's ridiculous,' said Gus Bartlett.

'Not at all. Obviously, the killer wanted us to think Samir had been killed on the East Side Estate, that it was just the kind of place where a boy like him might have lived and died. The thing is, nobody's ever seen him there. Nobody knew him.' He turned to Jason again. 'He was thirteen,' he said. 'He left his family in Syria because they could only afford to pay the smugglers for one passage. The idea was that when he got here, he would find an aunt and uncle, get work and send money home. But it didn't happen like that. God only knows what privations he suffered on the journey – kids like him go through everything, from rape to robbery – but he made it, having walked over a good part of the continent. It took him months. He found a group of smugglers who got him into this country, but by then he'd lost his relatives' address, and he had no money left. They kept him a virtual prisoner in Birmingham, in slavery, working off his debt. He got away and fell in with a bad crowd in Leeds, got involved in selling drugs. He was no angel. But he was only thirteen and a long way from home. He was still saving money to get his family over. And guess what? His family were all dead. Killed in a bomb attack not long after Samir left. And the irony was that he never knew. He never knew he was selling drugs for nothing.'

'That's a very sad tale,' said Gus Bartlett, 'but I don't see what it has to do with us.'

Banks looked directly at Jason. 'Does that really make Samir "no better than an animal", Jason?' he asked.

Jason reddened and turned away. Everyone else seemed nonplussed by the question. Clearly, Jason had not apprised his parents of his racist views.

Banks stood up. 'Ask your son,' he said to Gus Bartlett. 'He knows what I'm talking about.'

He noticed that Lisa was crying.

'It *is* a sad story, isn't it, Lisa?' he said. 'Anyway, I must be off. We've had a lot of developments down at the park today. I don't know if you've seen our forensic officers at work, but pretty soon we'll have a DNA profile of the killer, then all we have to do is match it up with one of our suspects.' He looked at Jason again, but the boy's eyes were still averted.

'Well, I wish you luck, Superintendent,' said Gus Bartlett, 'but I assure you it's got nothing to do with us.'

'I do hope not,' said Banks. 'And thank you. We'll need all the luck we can get. Bye, then. Bye, Lisa. Mrs Bartlett. Bye, Jason.'

But Jason didn't look up or mumble a goodbye in return. He seemed lost in his own world.

When Banks got back to Newhope Cottage after talking to the Bartletts that evening, he found a note from the courier company to the effect that there was a package too large for his letterbox waiting for him round the back. Curious, he walked around to the wooden chest he had been having packages left in for years and found that whatever was in it was so big it wouldn't shut properly.

He carried the large, well-wrapped box into the front room and started to remove the wrapping. It seemed to take for ever, and he had to fetch a box-cutter from the kitchen drawer, but he knew what it was before he managed to cut off the last strip of cardboard and saw the envelope taped to the case. He opened it up and pulled out the card, which read:

HAPPY BIRTHDAY AND
HAPPY STRUMMING, DAD!
LOVE,
BRIAN

A *guitar*. But not just any guitar. When he opened up the case, he saw it was a Martin D-28, just about the best acoustic guitar on the market. He took it out and held it in his hands. Then he strummed it and found, naturally, that it was out of tune. That would be the first job.

There was a care package of extras with it, and Banks found spare strings, plectrums, a cleaning cloth and an electronic gizmo you attached to the neck, which told you the note of each string as you tuned it. He found something else, too: a copy of Bert Weedon's *Play in a Day*, the legendary manual used by Eric Clapton, George Harrison, Pete Townshend and John Lennon, among others. Not that Banks imagined he would ever be able to play as well as any of them, but at least he would get the same start.

He had tears in his eyes as he stroked the smooth wood and rested it on his knee. He had been quite resigned to buying his own guitar – and it certainly wouldn't have been a Martin

– but this was a wonderful gesture from his son, and it almost overwhelmed him. It wasn't even his birthday for another two weeks, but that didn't matter. No doubt Brian wanted to get it to him *before* he bought an inferior model for himself.

The guitar put the Hollyfield case quite out of his mind as he tried to work out how to use the gizmo to tune it. He remembered that strings were supposed to be EADGBE, which was a good start, and soon found that if he tightened or loosened each string in turn, the electronic tuner showed him what note he was playing.

He had managed to tune the first three strings when his phone rang. He cursed, but when he saw it was Gerry, he put the guitar aside. He had been expecting her to ring. 'Yes, Gerry? How did it go?' he asked.

'Just as you expected, guv.'

'Excellent.'

'You were right. It wasn't long after you left that Jason Bartlett came out of the house, made a quick call on his mobile and then met up with Chris Myers at the end of his street.'

'So it's the kids, not the parents. Well, well. Where did they go? The park's still taped off and under guard, isn't it?'

'Yes. They went to The Oak, sat in the beer garden, had quite a long natter.'

'Any sign of Lisa or the parents? Granville Myers?'

'None. Just Chris and Jason. I couldn't hear what was going on – I didn't dare get too close for fear they'd notice me – but they seemed to be arguing on the way down there. It looked as if Jason was panicking and Chris was trying to calm him down. There was a bit of arm-waving, and at one point they stopped while Chris held Jason by the shoulders, gave him a good shake and seemed to be trying to make a point. But I couldn't get any closer, guv. They know who I am. They'd have spotted me.'

'That's OK. I think we'd better make our move first thing in the morning, though, don't you?' said Banks. 'Give them both a chance to spend a sleepless night with their consciences, if they have any, then bring them both in. With any luck, we should have some lab results from Jazz by then. Even if we don't, I can't risk either of them making a run for it. Or give them time to clean up the car any more than they probably have done already. Let's put an officer on watching the Myers garage, just in case. We'll want their computers and mobiles, too. There should at least be evidence of Jason's racist activities in his Internet browser usage. I think we've got enough to get the boys talking if we employ a bit of creativity here and there, push them to the edge. One of them is bound to crack. We'll need to arrange for duty solicitors to be available if we don't want any delays, too. OK?'

'Right you are, guv,' said Gerry. 'I'll get right on it.'

'And Gerry?'

'Guv?'

'Good work. Soon as you've got things arranged, get a good night's sleep. You'll need it.'

15

Naturally, both Jason's and Chris's parents made a big fuss when the police came by the following morning to take their sons in for interviews under caution, search their rooms, and impound their computers and Chris's car for forensic analysis. Both sets of parents trailed down to the station behind their boys and demanded to be present at any interviews. As both suspects were over eighteen, their requests were denied. Jason was placed in interview room one, and Chris in room three, both with their duty solicitors. The outraged parents went back outside the building and threw themselves into slagging off the police to the assembled media crowd, who loved every minute of it.

While Chris and Jason waited in the sterile and stuffy interview rooms, listening to their lawyers brief them, the team went to Banks's office, where they drank strong coffee, planned strategy and simply let time pass. At one point, Banks sent Gerry over to the lab to find out the status of the tests. It was too soon, but Jazz had determined so far that the blood was human; the DNA test had been underway for a while. There was a good chance she would be ready later in the morning. Banks wasn't too concerned, as he knew it would work just as well as a threat. Under PACE, they could hold the boys for twenty-four hours, anyway, by which time Jazz would certainly have finished her tests. If Chris or Jason had stabbed Samir, then they would *know* already that his blood was in the park, and perhaps also that their DNA was on the roaches or chewing gum found there, too. Still, a positive result before or during the interviews would certainly help. And a murder weapon.

'Let's take Jason first,' Banks said. 'Annie, you come with me. Gerry, stay on top of the lab.'

If Gerry was upset at being excluded from the interviews, she didn't show it. Banks and Annie marched to interview room one, dismissed the constable standing guard over Jason and sat down. In contrast to Chris Myers's golden curls, Jason had straight dark hair over his ears and down to his collar. He was also a little overweight. Not obese, exactly, but not as slender and athletic as his friend. He looked as if he would be the last one to be picked for the rugger team at school games.

And Jason was nervous. He had clearly been biting his knuckles and fingernails, though he tried to stop when Banks and Annie entered. It wasn't long before he was chewing on them again. Sitting beside him was Harriet Lucas, a duty solicitor Banks had worked with before on a number of occasions; he had always found her fair and unflappable.

'I don't know what all this is about,' Jason said, 'but I've got an important exam this afternoon.'

'We'll inform your school if we need to keep you beyond the exam's starting time.'

'But . . . that's hours yet. You can't . . .' He turned towards Ms Lucas, who simply shook her head once.

'The exams can wait,' said Banks. 'There'll always be another opportunity. It takes as long as it takes, Jason. If you cooperate, we'll be done in no time.' But you won't be heading out to sit any exams, he thought.

Then Annie started up the recording machines and cautioned Jason. When Ms Lucas had explained the caution to him, and he had said that he understood, they began.

'You know why we're here, Jason,' said Banks. 'Wouldn't it be easier and quicker if you just told us what happened that Sunday night in the park?'

'What Sunday night? I don't know what you're talking about.'

'A week ago last Sunday, when you and Chris Myers were down in the little park at the bottom of Elmet Hill smoking marijuana.'

'We weren't there. And you can't prove anything.'

'Oh, yes, we can. We turned up quite a lot of evidence there yesterday, and the scientists have been working overtime on it.' He glanced at his watch. 'We're expecting the results any moment. We told them to bring what they found straight here to us.'

'I don't believe you. Even if you did find stuff, you can't know when it was put there, or who by.'

'If we find Samir's blood, we'll know that it wasn't put there after that Sunday night, because that's when he was murdered.'

'A bit melodramatic, Superintendent,' Ms Lucas interjected.

'That doesn't mean anything,' said Jason.

'What about if we find your DNA in the saliva on those roaches, or the chewing gum?'

'I don't chew gum. What roaches?'

'Didn't you know? We found two roaches in the woods there, close to where we found the blood. We think you were there smoking up when Samir turned up and you killed him. You forgot to take them with you when you left the scene. Sloppy, Jason.'

Jason said nothing. Banks thought he could hear the wheels turning.

'We know Chris was involved with drugs because he was caught at a drug party last year,' he went on. 'You're his best mate. It's no great stretch to say you were involved, too, even if you weren't at that particular party.'

Ms Lucas whispered in Jason's ear, and he said, 'No comment.'

'How long have you been carrying a knife, Jason?'

'I don't carry a knife.'

'But you were carrying one on the night we're talking about, weren't you? Why? Were you nervous about being in the park, about being out so near Hollyfield after your sister had been attacked? She said she was scared to walk through there by herself.'

'That's stupid.'

'Mr Bartlett says he wasn't carrying a knife,' said Ms Lucas. 'I think we should leave it and move on unless you can prove differently.'

'Fine. But is it really so stupid, Jason? Ask yourself. I don't think so. What do you think of people from the Middle East? What do you think of Muslims?'

'What? I don't think anything about them.'

'I think you do. I've read your essay. You talk about "migrant hordes streaming over the sea and through the ports" and "open floodgates poisoning our society, our culture". You say that if it's allowed to go on, we "won't be able to live by our own laws in our own country any more and there won't be any jobs left for honest, decent white people". You call them "no better than animals" and accuse them of "raping our women". You say we need to leave Europe and close our borders. Did you write that, Jason?'

'So what if I did? It's true. A person's entitled to his opinions, isn't he? It's still a free country. At least it was last time I looked.'

'Don't you realise that even if we end free movement throughout the Union, it won't mean getting rid of migrants, of *all* the migrants, especially the Pakistanis and blacks that seem to bother you so much? They're not from Europe, Jason. Samir wasn't from Europe.'

'I know that. They're all the same, though, when you get right down to it. They're all foreigners. They're different from us. They're contaminating our culture, our breeding, our way of life.'

'We've got your computer, Jason. We're well aware of the sick websites you've been visiting, the kind of hate literature you've been reading. Is that what spurred you on to kill Samir?'

'I didn't kill anyone.'

'Was it Chris, then? Did he do it? We know it happened when you were both in the park that night and Samir ran there from Hollyfield Lane.'

'How can you know that? You weren't there. You're just bluffing, trying to trick me into confessing to something I didn't do.'

'If you tell us now, Jason, things will go better for you. If you help us.'

Jason folded his arms. 'We didn't do anything.'

'Where's the knife, Jason? What did you do with it?'

'I told you. I don't know what you're talking about.'

'Superintendent, I thought we'd left the knife behind us?' said Ms Lucas.

'They didn't do that,' said Banks. 'They took it with them.'

'Cheap shot. You know what I mean. Stick to the script.'

'Why did you do it?' Banks asked Jason. 'Surely it wasn't because he saw you taking drugs? Surely you didn't think he'd tell? And so what if he did? Was it because he was Middle Eastern? One of *them*? The migrant hordes. He was just a child, Jason. He was only thirteen.'

Jason just shook his head.

Banks let the silence stretch for a while, then handed over to Annie. 'Did you know Samir before that night in the park?' she asked.

'No,' said Jason. 'I mean no, I didn't know him at all. Ever. Stop trying to trick me. And there wasn't no night in the park.'

'Is that where you got your drugs? The house on Hollyfield Lane? Did you know it was a trap house for the county line?'

'You're way off beam. I don't know what you're talking about.'

'Don't you? Am I? Did something go wrong? Did Samir short-change you? Did he sell you a bad product?'

'I never bought nothing off of him.'

'You're a bright boy, Jason. Look at you, you go to a posh private school. Your sister doesn't. Lisa only goes to Eastvale Comprehensive. That's how she got assaulted, walking home from there after a dance. Did you think it was Samir who did that to her? Or someone *like* him? Maybe if she went to a private school, like you, it would never have happened. How does that make you feel? Does it trouble you?'

'It's not my fault. I hate that fucking school, all right? I never asked to go there.'

'So what happened?'

'My dad. Mum and Dad. They wanted me to go, become a doctor or a lawyer or something. Go to fucking Oxford or Cambridge or somewhere. I never wanted it. They could only pay for one of us to go.'

'And you were their best bet?'

Jason just glared at her.

'Interesting as all this is, DI Cabbot,' said Ms Lucas, 'I can't really see the point in this line of questioning. Can we move on to the matter at hand?'

'Maybe I don't know enough to judge,' Annie said, 'but I've met both of you, and I'd say Lisa is by far the brightest. Was it you who planted the idea in her mind that her attacker was dark-skinned?'

'I don't know what you mean.'

'Sure you do. It sounds like the kind of thing you would say. The kind of thing you wrote about in that article they wouldn't publish in the school magazine.'

'The school's corrupt. They make their money from terrorists paying to have their kids educated here so they can infiltrate us and kill us.'

'Do you really believe that?' Annie asked.

Jason said nothing.

'The matter at hand, Ms Cabbot,' said Ms Lucas. 'No sense going off on ideological tangents.'

'Lisa didn't see her attacker,' Annie said. 'She had no idea what colour he was. He came from behind, knocked her down.'

'She saw his hand.'

'Did she? Or did you convince her that she did? You got her so confused, Jason, that she thought she'd been attacked by a dark-skinned person because *you* believe they're the ones who do all the raping and assaulting in this country, don't you? You see, Lisa never mentioned that he was dark-skinned when we started our investigation, when DC Masterson first questioned her.'

'She was in shock then. Confused.'

'It was *you* who confused her. Your own sister. Just to fit in with your sick beliefs.'

'DI Cabbot, is any of this really relevant?' asked Ms Lucas.

'I'm trying to discover whether this was a hate crime,' Annie said. 'I'd say that's a reasonable line of inquiry, wouldn't you?'

Ms Lucas sighed. 'Very well. Carry on. But you're on a short leash.'

Annie squared her shoulders. 'Were you getting your revenge for what happened to Lisa, Jason? Taking it out on the first dark-skinned person you could find? Did you do it for Lisa? Because she couldn't go to a posh school? Because she got assaulted on her way home from a dance at the local comprehensive? Did you kill Samir for Lisa?'

Jason put his hands over his ears. 'Stop it! I don't want to hear any more. I didn't kill anyone. I want to go home.'

'Look,' said Banks, gently taking over the questioning again. 'I understand, Jason. Honest, I do. You had all this stuff going around in your head about migrant hordes, Lisa had been assaulted, you'd been smoking marijuana, then all of a sudden this young Arab lad just turns up out of the bushes. He was running away from someone. Someone he thought was going to harm him but was simply charged with taking him home. But he ran into you, didn't he? He startled you. That's understandable. And you took out your knife and stabbed him. Why? Did you think he was armed? Did you think he was going to attack the two of you? Big strapping lads. Bigger than him, older than him.'

Jason started shaking his head from side to side and banging his fist on the table. Ms Lucas put her hand on his shoulder to calm him. Banks glanced at Annie. There wasn't much point going on right now, he thought, so he gave her the nod and they left the room.

'I'm not going to lie to you, Chris,' said Banks, 'but Jason is very upset back there. I think he finally realised the enormity of what you've both done, and it's overwhelmed him.'

Chris Myers gave a sly grin. 'Jason's no fool,' he said. 'Besides, we weren't in the park that night, so why would he say we were?'

'I'm not saying he admitted you were. But something about our questions upset him. Where were you that night?'

'What night?'

'Sunday before last.'

'At home studying.'

'You didn't see Jason?'

'We're not inseparable, you know. Yes, he's my mate, yes, I give him a lift to school, but we're not joined at the hip.'

'Would your parents vouch that you were at home that evening around half past ten?'

'I suppose so. If they remember. I was up in my room most of the evening revising, and they were downstairs watching TV, so I didn't see them.'

'It wouldn't have been too hard to nip out without being seen, then, would it?'

'Why would I want to do that?'

'For a smoke.'

'I don't smoke.'

'You know what I mean. And you do have a track record with drugs.'

'Oh, that fucking stupid party again,' said Chris. 'I wish I'd never been there. Do you know, I had no drugs at all that night? I didn't even get high. Nothing. OK, so I had a few cans of beer, and I wasn't old enough to drink. Big fucking deal. Arrest me. I was only there cause there was a girl I fancied. A college girl. It's not as if we're constantly surrounded by totty at school.'

'I think the statute of limitations has run out on your under-age drinking,' Banks said. 'Not to mention lust.'

Even the duty solicitor, Willy Carnwood, managed a smile at that.

'Who had the knife, Chris? Was it you or Jason? He denies it, but then—'

There came a knock on the door, followed by DC Gerry Masterson carrying a file folder. Normally, Banks would have been annoyed at the interruption, but he had asked Gerry to come immediately if anything turned up at the lab. By the expression on her face, something had.

Banks thanked her, noted what had happened for the tape recordings and took the folder. Annie edged closer to read it over his shoulder. Gerry remained in the interview room, standing by the door.

'Hmm,' said Banks. 'This *is* interesting.'

'May I see it?' asked Willy Carnwood.

Banks had hoped he wouldn't ask, but as he had, he knew he would have to pass the file across. But not just yet. 'It's just come in, as you know,' he said. 'I'll need to refer to it during my questioning. Then I'll make sure you get to see it.'

Carnwood nodded. 'OK.'

'Want to know what it says?' Banks asked Chris.

Chris looked nonchalant, bored even. 'I suppose you're going to tell me anyway,' he said with a sneer.

'Yes. I think we might be able to bring these proceedings to a swift conclusion.'

'You mean I can go home?'

'Quite the opposite, I'm afraid.' Banks tapped the sheets in front of him. 'See, the DNA analysis of the traces of blood we found in the park is a match for the samples taken from Samir Boulad's body. It's Samir's blood, Chris. No doubt about that.'

Though Chris now looked a little less nonchalant, he merely shrugged and said, 'So what? Seeing as I've already told you I wasn't there that night, I don't see what it has to do with me. I'm very sorry and all that. It's terrible that such a thing should happen so close—'

'Oh, cut the crap,' said Banks.

Carnwood shot him a reproving glance, but Banks carried on.

'Well, in itself, maybe it doesn't mean too much to you right now that we found traces of Samir's blood in the woods. But our toxicologist also found two different DNA samples in the saliva from the roaches and chewing gum we recovered; your feelings might change when we have samples for comparison from you and Jason.'

'What? No way.'

'Oh, there's a way, all right,' said Banks. 'Ask your solicitor. We'll be taking mouth swabs or plucked hairs while he's present. Or we can get a doctor to come in and take a blood sample, if you give your written consent. Believe me, we've plenty of grounds for arrest or a court order. Your choice. Anyway, the best is yet to come.'

Banks let the silence stretch and watched Chris chew his lower lip.

'Our technicians haven't finished the analysis and comparisons yet, but they also found traces of blood in the boot of your car. It's being analysed further as we speak. Now what are the odds against us finding it's a match for Samir's, too?'

Chris swallowed and Banks guessed from his expression that he was doing a lot of quick thinking and re-evaluating his position. He hardly seemed aware of the duty solicitor's presence. Finally, he rested his palms on the desk and said, 'OK, I'll make a statement. But it wasn't me who stabbed him. It was Jason.'

As usual, the 'celebration' of a case solved was a sweet and sour affair, taking into account the sense of achievement in uncovering a killer, and the awareness of how many lives the revelation would ruin in addition to the killer's and his family's.

But alcohol helped blur the lines, and in its glow, tears soon turned to euphoria, and the mingled feelings of sorrow and regret had morphed into black humour by the time the third pint came along. It helped that they'd had another, albeit vicarious, success that afternoon: a man caught for a sexual assault in Hull had admitted to also assaulting Lisa Bartlett in Eastvale. A white man.

It also helped that Cyril, the landlord of the Queen's Arms, was playing one of his most upbeat playlists. Even Ray would have appreciated the inclusion of 'Lady Rachel' by Kevin Ayers among the more standard sixties' fare of The Who, Kinks, Byrds and Stones. Banks slugged back some beer. The Beatles' 'And Your Bird Can Sing' came up next, two minutes of pure joy.

Sausage rolls and pasties appeared on their tables, courtesy of Cyril. It was a quiet night, and he clearly appreciated the business a solved case had brought him. Annie was there, deep in conversation with Stefan Nowak, whom Banks knew she fancied. Gerry chatted away with a very pregnant Winsome, demurely sipping orange juice, her husband Terry beside her. Jazz Singh and Vic Manson had got stuck with AC Gervaise – ACC McLaughlin had sent his congratulations, and regrets – and Banks felt outside it all, watching over them like a founding father. One thing was certain, he was the oldest in the group, though Vic couldn't be too far behind.

The door opened and Joanna MacDonald walked in, a breath of fresh air. She smiled all around and made a beeline for Banks. He had invited her, but he hadn't expected her to come.

'All by yourself?' she said, sitting down beside him.

'So it would appear. Drink?'

'I'll have a G&T, please.'

Banks went to the bar and got her one, along with another pint of Timothy Taylor's for himself. The cobbled market square was darkening fast outside, and one or two people still sat drinking and smoking at the tables Cyril had put out. The Beatles finished, and a more subdued Françoise Hardy came on singing 'All Over the World' in English. How Banks had lusted after her when he was a teenager. It wasn't merely her beauty or her voice, but the whole 'Frenchness' of it all; her world was exotic, foreign, intoxicating; it reeked of Gauloises and Calvados. Her French version of Leonard Cohen's 'Suzanne' sounded particularly sexy.

Banks carried the drinks back to the table. Joanna took a dainty sip and said, 'I've heard the edited highlights, but maybe you'd like to tell me the full story?'

'It seems ages since we sat last here and you told me about Blaydon,' Banks said.

'I gather he didn't do it?'

'No. Not to worry, though. He's done plenty, and he certainly had a hand in it. We'll be paying him another visit before too long.'

'So what happened?'

'You were spot on about the county lines connection. They were using a house on the Hollyfield Estate. It belonged to an old sixties junkie called Howard Stokes, who let them use it as a dealing centre in exchange for heroin. The whole estate has been condemned to make way for a new development – one of Blaydon's projects – which I understand isn't progressing too well.'

'Why not?'

Banks shrugged. 'The economy. Austerity. Whatever. It seems people aren't in a mood for new shopping centres, and his home-building plans didn't quite match up with the affordable social housing ideas the government has in mind, so there go the grants. It's on hold, and the investors are getting antsy. Including your Leka Gashi.'

'So Gashi *is* involved?'

'About as deep as you can get. He's known Blaydon for years, from the Corfu days, and he may even have helped him get rid of his partner Norman Peel, all those years ago. Though we'll never prove that. But Gashi and his heavies took over the county line from a dealer called Lenny G, who was a pussycat by comparison. He turned up gutted in the Leeds-Liverpool Canal a few weeks ago.'

'Charming. What's Blaydon's part in all this?'

'I was just coming to that. He's not directly involved, as far as we know, but he's business partners with Gashi and does him little favours now and then. Like you said, Blaydon likes to think he's playing with the big boys. I think Gashi probably treats him like a gofer, but it gives him the criminal's credibility he seems to crave. That and the drugs and girls it gives him access to. He's quite famous for his parties. I walked in on one a few days ago.'

Joanna raised an eyebrow. 'And?'

'It was a sort of aftermath, really, but quite interesting. The morning after. A few people sleeping, one or two lounging about in the pool, a couple of naked girls, three people having sex in one of the bedrooms.'

'You sound envious.'

'Not at all. Especially as the girls were young enough to be his granddaughters. Besides, once you've talked to Zelda, you can never be sure that someone like that doesn't come from a similar background of trafficking and slavery and sexual abuse.'

'But Blaydon didn't kill the Syrian boy?'

'Samir. No. That was a different thing altogether. A different set of unfortunate circumstances. Coincidences, if you like. Of course, the culprits denied it at first, but we got it out of them. We found both their fingerprints matched some on the wheelie bin Samir was dumped in. First Chris Myers, the one who didn't actually stab Samir, cracked and told us his mate Jason Bartlett did it. Then when we confronted Bartlett with the DNA evidence and his friend's statement, he broke down and confessed. All above board. Solicitors present, and all. And both are eighteen, so they'll be facing adult court and adult prison time.'

'That's sad.'

'It is. It's a great waste. But it's not half as fucking sad as what happened to Samir. Pardon my French.'

Joanna smiled and patted his arm. 'You're forgiven.'

'It seems Bartlett had taken to carrying a knife ever since his sister was attacked and sexually assaulted on her way home from a school dance over a month ago. Just a kitchen knife with a four-inch blade, but it was long enough and sharp enough to kill Samir. He says he threw it in the river later. There's not much chance of our finding it. According to his head teacher, Jason Bartlett has got some rather nasty racist views. I read an article he wanted to publish in the school magazine, saw the websites he visits, and it's true. The usual diatribe against immigrants, especially Muslims and everyone with a darker skin colour than himself. We also found some nasty white supremacy sites bookmarked in his Internet browsing history. Anyway, it seemed he somehow half-convinced his sister that she'd been attacked by a dark-skinned man, even though she maintained at first, and later on, that she hadn't seen her attacker, not even his hand.'

'So he was already wound up and jumpy about immigrants?'

'Yes. Just when you start to think that this generation has got beyond the racism of your own, someone like Bartlett comes along.'

'It'll always be around. You know that. What happened on the night of the murder?'

'Two worlds collided. It was Samir's first time in Eastvale as a line manager for Gashi. The poor kid had been through hell.

I'm not saying he didn't know he was doing wrong, but these people groomed him and exploited him. So he came up here on the bus with a backpack full of heroin and crack cocaine and headed straight for Stokes's house. Unfortunately, when he got there, Stokes was dead from an overdose. We think it was either accidental or self-administered, and we may never know which. Anyway, Samir freaked and rang Gashi, who happened to be down in London on business at the time. Gashi phoned Blaydon, who was dining nearby at Le Coq d'Or, and asked him for a favour.'

'Lucky him,' said Joanna. 'It's a really great restaurant.'

'You've eaten there?'

'Yes. Why not?'

'The price, for a start.'

'Let's just say I had a generous boyfriend.'

'Had?'

She thumped him playfully and picked up her glass. 'Get back to your story. Blaydon was having dinner at Le Coq d'Or.'

'With the Kerrigans, who are in cahoots with him on the Elmet Centre development, as you know. Anyway, Gashi asked Blaydon to drive to Eastvale – he didn't know he was already there – and pick up Samir, who was still upset at finding Stokes dead, and drive him back to Leeds. Blaydon was having too much fun eating his snails and frog's legs, so he dispatched his driver, Frankie Wallace, to go pick up Samir.'

'You know, you're showing your ignorance as well as your prejudice when it comes to French food. It's a racial stereotype. They don't have—'

'Frog's legs or snails at Le Coq d'Or. I know. Marcel McGuigan told me. It was just a figure of speech.'

'You *talked* to Marcel McGuigan?'

'Had to do. He was Blaydon's alibi.'

'But he's . . . I mean, he's a foodie GOD. Have you any idea what he can do with sweetbreads?'

'I don't, actually. I'm not that much into puddings. But I know about McGuigan. Michelin stars and all that. He's really quite a nice bloke. No pretensions, down to earth. By the way, he offered me a free dinner any time I want. With a guest of my choice.'

Joanna narrowed her eyes. 'That's playing dirty. If you think . . .'

'I told him no, I couldn't possibly. It might be misconstrued.'

'You're right, I suppose.'

Banks smiled. 'I could always say I've changed my mind . . .'

'Don't hold your breath. Back to the night of the murder.'

Banks drank some more beer and went on. Françoise Hardy gave way to the late great Scott Walker singing 'Joanna'.

Joanna MacDonald's ears perked up on hearing her name. One or two people who knew who she was were looking towards her with silly grins on their faces. 'Did you do that to embarrass me?' she whispered at Banks.

'Me? I have no control over Cyril's playlists,' Banks said. 'Don't you know the song?'

'No.'

'It's Scott Walker.'

'Just go on with your story.'

'Right. Frankie entered through the back door,' Banks went on. 'He's an ex-boxer and can look like a terrifying figure with all his scar tissue and so on, especially to a young lad, I should imagine. Anyway, Samir got scared and ran off through the front door and turned right, towards the park at the bottom of Elmet Hill. That was the last we could find out about his movements until we interviewed Chris Myers and Jason Bartlett. It turns out they're the best of friends, and they both enjoy the occasional joint, so they'd got in the habit of heading down to the park after dark and smoking up in the bushes. There was never anyone around in the park at that time, they said, and they were pretty well hidden from the main path and Cardigan Drive. After that, it all happened so fast, Chris Myers told us. Samir came bursting from the trees and startled them. Without thinking, Jason just reacted, got out his knife and lunged. He might have thought Samir was carrying a weapon, but there's no evidence of that, despite what he says. He was stoned, too, so his senses were befuddled. And it was dark. He saw a dark-skinned guy, and with all that was going around in his head at the time, he just lashed out. Sadly, he did it with a very sharp knife and managed to puncture Samir's aorta.'

'Christ,' said Joanna. 'What a story. I suppose they panicked then?'

'That's right. They couldn't revive Samir, and after a while they figured out he was dead. They couldn't very well leave him there, either. Much too close to home. It was Chris's idea, apparently, to move him, so he got his car and parked it in a lay-by on Cardigan Drive right next to the bushes. They got Samir in the boot without anyone seeing and thought it would be best to dump him on the East Side Estate, where they thought the police would expect to find someone like him.'

'A drug dealer? Did they know him? Did they buy drugs from him?'

'No. They didn't know what he was doing in Eastvale. The county lines operation didn't deal in marijuana. Not enough profit in it, I suppose. The line dealt more addictive products – coke, crack, heroin. And Samir had just arrived in Eastvale that evening to take Greg Janson's place. They didn't know him from Adam. Chris Myers told us eventually that they bought the pot from a bloke in a pub near the college.' Banks shrugged. 'Maybe that's true. Anyway, I suppose it's lucky for us that they forgot about the roaches and possible blood stains in their panic. But then there was no reason they would expect us to search the park if Samir's body was found on the East Side Estate. And we didn't. Not for quite a while. We were lucky the traces were still there. They had no idea of Samir's connection with Hollyfield, that it would eventually come out and lead us to the park. They had no idea where or what he was running from. We wouldn't have had, either, if Frankie Wallace hadn't told us he saw Samir running in that direction.'

'Why did he tell you?'

'Working for Blaydon and Gashi was getting a bit too rich for Frankie's blood. He seemed pretty disgusted by the way things were going. He's not a hardened criminal, really, just an old-fashioned minder. I'm not saying he wouldn't buy something he knew fell off the back of a lorry, maybe even threaten someone who caused a problem, but I think he's the sort of bloke with his own moral code, his own boundaries. The heavy drugs and the underage girls and the violence for its own sake just weren't his scene. At the bottom of it all, he's quite a moralist, is our Frankie. Must be that old Scottish Presbyterian influence.'

'Lucky for you.'

'Yes. It was Frankie who put me on to Jason and Chris. Or at least the idea that Samir might have been killed in the park by someone up to no good, someone who had nothing to do with the county lines. Then we found out about Jason's racism, the drug use, then the forensic evidence in the park. I pushed Jason hard and set Gerry to keep an eye on his movements after I left. Naturally, he phoned his pal and they had a confab. That was when we decided to haul them in. The rest was pretty easy.'

'What are you two up to?' It was Annie, suddenly standing by the table.

'Bring us a couple more drinks and I'll tell you,' said Banks.

'Righty-ho.' Annie wandered off to the bar, not entirely steady on her feet. Luckily, they were all taking taxis home tonight.

'About what I said earlier,' Banks said while Annie waited at the bar. 'You know, about the restaurant and all.'

'Yes.'

She clearly wasn't going to help him. Banks felt his tongue growing too big for his mouth. Annie was paying for the drinks now. 'Well, I mean, would you?'

'Would I what?'

'Like to have dinner with me at Le Coq d'Or.'

'I'd love to,' said Joanna.

'You would? I mean, I don't think I can honestly take a free meal there, but if I start saving up now, I might be able to make a reservation before Christmas.'

16

There were no cars parked outside Connor Clive Blaydon's villa when Banks and Gerry turned up there after the DNA tests had come up positive and Jason Bartlett had been charged with the murder of Samir Boulad. Annie was still working with the CPS on preparing the case for prosecution, along with that of Chris Myers as accessory. Gerry was quite happy to get out of the squad room for a road trip. Banks wondered how Blaydon managed without Frankie Wallace to drive him around. Maybe he'd hired a new chauffeur.

The judge had refused to grant a search warrant for Blaydon's property on the scant evidence the police had presented, dismissing it as hearsay and circumstantial. Banks suspected there was more to it than that – perhaps the occasional golf game, tips on the property market – but he held his tongue. Even without a search warrant, they had one or two things they wanted to discuss in more detail with Blaydon.

They wouldn't have expected to find any incriminating evidence at his house, anyway. Blaydon would be a bigger fool than Banks thought he was if he hadn't quickly got rid of Samir's backpack and jacket after Frankie had handed them over. Gashi would have wanted his drugs back, of course, and Blaydon would probably have burned the jacket. At best they might find a few grams of white powder left over from a party, but that was a charge a man like Blaydon could beat in his sleep with the lawyers he could afford.

The fountain seemed to have dried up, or someone had turned it off at the mains. A dead bird floated among fallen leaves in the brackish water that remained. It had been windy and raining just that morning, but now nothing stirred in the humid air. The topiaries looked frightening and made Banks think of Stephen King's Overlook Hotel in *The Shining*, where the trimmed shapes came to life. Banks felt a trickle of sweat down his back as he walked to the front door and rang the bell. Nobody answered. As far as he could tell, all was silent inside. He touched the door and was surprised when it swung slowly open on its hinges. He glanced at Gerry, went into the hallway and called out Blaydon's name. Nobody answered. Not even Roberts, the butler. His voice echoed in the cavern-ous space.

They crossed the entrance hall, footsteps echoing, and checked the office. Empty. The window was open a few inches, so Blaydon surely couldn't be very far away. Thinking that maybe on a day like today he might be lounging by the pool with his headphones on, or taking a dip to cool himself off, they followed the maze of the corridors to the glassed-in pool area. Banks wasn't sure at what point he noticed that the chlo-rine smell was mixed with something less easily defined, sweet yet metallic. Gerry was the first to mention it. 'What's that funny smell?'

When they got to the pool, Banks walked through the doorway.

Blaydon was in the water, all right. At least, Banks assumed it was Blaydon. It was hard to tell as the water was tinged red and whatever floated there lay face down, naked, with his arms stretched out at the sides like a cross. Underneath him spread what looked like a tangle of tentacles, as if they belonged to an octopus or a giant squid. A Hockney swimming pool painted by Francis Bacon.

Banks had just realised that the tentacles were Blaydon's intestines when he remembered Gerry, and turned to stop her before she got too close. But he was too late. A swarm of flies that had somehow got in rose from the body at the sound of her footsteps echoing on the tiles. Gerry froze in the doorway, turned white and doubled over, vomiting against the wall.

'I'm all right, guv,' she protested, waving Banks away, obviously embarrassed, when he tried to comfort her. 'It's just the shock, that's all. And that smell.'

'You're sure?'

She nodded. 'Maybe a glass of water.'

There was a wet bar beside the pool. Banks poured some tap water into a glass. Gerry drank it and took out a handkerchief to wipe her lips. 'That's better.'

'Look.' Banks pointed across the pool.

They hadn't noticed in the initial shock of seeing Blaydon's floating body, but the butler Roberts lay slumped against the Plexiglas, down which ran a long, ugly smear of red. Roberts hadn't been disfigured, by the looks of him, simply shot or stabbed. Whatever had happened, he was every bit as dead as his boss.

Banks reached for his mobile.

'Christ, what an abattoir,' said Gerry. 'What could he have done to deserve this?'

Banks glanced at her. 'Deserve? Nothing, I should imagine. With people like Gashi's lot, the punishment is usually way out of proportion to any presumed sin.'

'But he was in with them.'

'To a point,' Banks said. 'Remember, I always said Blaydon was trying to play with the big boys. Out of his league. I even warned him about it the first time we met.'

'He obviously didn't listen.'

'No. It doesn't matter what he did, why they did it. For once motive isn't really an issue. Maybe they thought he'd ripped them off? I'm sure he lost their laundered money on investments in the Elmet Centre development. Maybe they thought he'd stolen drugs from them, too, or was a police informer? Whatever it was, they clearly thought he had crossed or betrayed them in some way, and they wanted to make a point.'

'They've certainly done that.'

Banks remembered acting like an old mate the last time he had seen Blaydon alive, patting him on the shoulder while the man in the suit and sunglasses was watching them from across the hall. Had his been the touch of Judas, the mark of death? Had they made the assumption that Blaydon was a police informer? Was he partly responsible for what had happened here?

But Banks brushed such wild and pointless thoughts aside. Blaydon had enjoyed flirting with the dark side, and it had swallowed him whole. Simple as that. Maybe they would catch the men who had done this, and maybe they wouldn't. If the killers had any sense, they would be back in Albania by now.

'Come on.' Banks took Gerry gently by the arm and led her back outside, into the fresh air. She still seemed to be walking in a daze, and he wished he had a hip flask of whisky or brandy or something to put more of a spring in her step. There was sure to be some in the house, but it was best not to disturb anything more than he had done already.

They sat in silence on the parapet of the still fountain; only the birds singing in the trees that ringed the estate made any sounds. Banks phoned in for the full treatment – CSIs, uniformed officers, police surgeon, photographer, the lot – and before long he could hear the sounds of the emergency vehicles, distant at first, then getting louder and louder as they approached.

*   *   *

Raymond's flight was late, and it had started to rain again by the time Zelda had negotiated their way out of Newcastle Airport. Leeds and Bradford would have been marginally closer, but the connection time with the flight from LA didn't work out. So Newcastle it was.

They were soon heading south on the A1, past the Metro Centre, over the Tyne with its famous bridges and the Sage on its south bank in Gateshead. Then on past Team Valley and the Angel of the North, which Raymond said he had always thought looked like a rusty Spitfire standing on its tail.

But Raymond was tired after his long journey, and after a while of excited chat and numerous mentions of how glad he was to be back with Zelda, he drifted off to sleep in the passenger seat and Zelda concentrated on the road through the hypnotic rhythm of the windscreen wipers.

The rain was coming down quite heavily by the time they got back to the cottage above Lyndgarth, but inside it was still cosy and dry. While Raymond unpacked, Zelda put the kettle on and made a pot of tea, chatting about her time in London – the Picasso exhibition she had never seen, the theatre she had never attended, the book shopping she had never done. In his turn, Raymond told her about the parties and the meetings with fellow artists and gallery owners in New York and Los Angeles, and gave her as a present a tiny sketch by a famous artist he knew she admired.

Zelda made Raymond a bacon buttie – his favourite snack, and something he hadn't been able to find in America. After that, they sat and sipped tea and talked until Raymond could no longer keep his eyes open.

While he slept, Zelda sat at the kitchen window with her laptop, half watching the rain running down the glass and distorting the rough moorland landscape beyond. She had certainly felt the isolation and wildness of the moors over the few days she had been alone there, after returning from Banks's cottage. But she had adapted, got used to it again, and she thought she could be happy there.

As she flipped through her usual news sources, she came across a breaking story on Sky News headed POLICE FIND BODY OF MISSING WOMAN. It didn't go into great detail but noted that the Metropolitan police had fished from the Thames the body of a woman called Faye Butler, who had been reported missing by her flatmate two days after failing to return home from her job at Foyles Books. The article didn't say how she had died, but it made reference to multiple injuries and suggested that foul play was suspected.

Zelda felt her blood freeze in her veins. *Faye Butler.* She remembered talking to Faye, remembered her pixie-ish features, her excitement at believing she was talking to the NCA. They must have got to her very quickly, no doubt with Keane's help. He knew where she worked.

The images whirled through Zelda's mind – Petar Tadić and his thugs finding Goran's body and removing it, following the trail of the mysterious woman Goran had met in the hotel bar, trying to work out where the connection lay, who had got to Goran and why, suspecting everyone close to them who was not one of them. Somehow or other – perhaps through Keane – the trail had led to Faye, an outsider who had hung out with them, and they had wanted to know who she had talked to and what she had told them. Perhaps Faye had simply ignored her advice and told them about the woman who had come to the store asking about her ex-boyfriend, or perhaps they had tortured her to get the information. They enjoyed inflicting pain. Maybe the interrogation had excited them, maybe they thought she knew more than she was telling. Whatever the reason, they really went to work on her, torturing her, no doubt, until she ended up dead.

But how much had Faye been able to tell them, and how much had they been able to work out from what she had said? Had they put two and two together?

Goran Tadić hadn't recognised Zelda, she was certain of that, but it didn't mean his brother wouldn't, no matter how much she thought her appearance had changed. Most likely Petar and his cronies would have gained access to the hotel's security cameras and captured her image from there. One thing was for certain: no matter how they might do it, if they found out who she was, they weren't going to go to the police. Perhaps they didn't know where Zelda lived yet, but they would find out. It was only a matter of how long it would take them. How could she stay here and put the man she loved in danger? But how could she just leave him? Should she put her trust in Alan Banks and tell him everything she knew? She might end up in jail, but at least she would still be alive and Raymond would be safe. But would he be? She remembered what had happened to Emile in Paris. When people like the Tadićs took their revenge, they took it on what you loved most.

Raymond stumbled down from the bedroom rubbing his eyes and asking what time it was. Zelda threw her arms around his neck, told him how much she loved him and how glad she was that he was back home, then she buried her head in the soft curve between his neck and shoulder and started to cry.